PENGUIN CLASSICS

EARLY WRITINGS

EZRA POUND, poet, essayist, editor, translator, anthologist and literary provocateur, was one of the major modernists of the twentieth century. Born in Hailey, Idaho, on October 30, 1885, he attended the University of Pennsylvania and Hamilton College, then briefly taught at Wabash College in Crawfordsville, Indiana, before heading to Europe in 1908 and settling for a time in Venice, where he published his first book, *A Lume Spento*. He then moved to London, where he continued to write and met such authors as Yeats, Henry James, Wyndham Lewis, Ford Madox Ford, and T. S. Eliot. In late 1920 he and his wife, Dorothy—they had married in 1914—moved to Paris, but not before he guided movements like Imagism and Vorticism to prominence and aided writers like H.D. and Joyce in getting their early works published.

In Paris, Pound met the American violinist Olga Rudge, who would become his companion for almost fifty years, and continued to work on his long poem, *The Cantos,* which he had begun in 1917. He also edited Eliot's *The Waste Land* and became friendly with Picabia, Brancusi, Duchamp, Cocteau, and Ernest Hemingway, while working on an opera, *Le Testament,* based on the work of François Villon. In 1923 he visited Rimini and became absorbed by the life of Sigismundo Malatesta and his Tempio, which would prompt the Malatesta Cantos, numbers VIII–XI of his long work. He continued to publish criticism and visit Italy, where he and Dorothy, and then Olga, moved in 1924, settling in Rapallo and Venice. At the same time, prose works like the *ABC of Economics* (1933) and *Jefferson and/or Mussolini* (1935), became increasingly economic and social in outlook.

Pound remained in Italy the rest of his life, except for two trips to the United States: the first, in 1939, was an aborted attempt to visit President Roosevelt and several congressmen to prevent U.S. involvement in World War II; the second, in 1945, occurred after his arrest for treason at the end of the war following his anti-American broadcasts on Italian radio. Declared to be mentally unfit to stand trial, Pound was committed to St. Elizabeths mental hospital in Washington, D.C., where he remained from 1946 to 1958, during which time he continued to write. In 1949, he won the prestigious Bollingen Prize for *The Pisan Cantos*, which he began while at a U.S. Army detention camp in Pisa, Italy. Following his release from St. Elizabeths, Pound returned to Italy, where he wrote sporadically. He died in Venice on November 1, 1972.

IRA B. NADEL, educated at Rutgers and Cornell universities, is professor of English and Distinguished University Scholar at the University of British Columbia in Vancouver. He is also a Fellow of the Royal Society of Canada. His books include *Biography: Fiction, Fact and Form; Joyce and the Jews; Various Positions: A Life of Leonard Cohen; Double Act: A Life of Tom Stoppard;* and *Ezra Pound: A Literary Life.* He has also edited *The Letters of Ezra Pound to Alice Corbin Henderson* and the *Cambridge Companion to Ezra Pound.*

EZRA POUND

Early Writings
Poems and Prose

Edited with an Introduction and Notes by
IRA B. NADEL

PENGUIN BOOKS

PENGUIN BOOKS
Published by the Penguin Group
Penguin Group (USA) Inc., 375 Hudson Street, New York, New York 10014, U.S.A.
Penguin Group (Canada), 10 Alcorn Avenue, Toronto, Ontario, Canada M4V 3B2
(a division of Pearson Penguin Canada Inc.)
Penguin Books Ltd, 80 Strand, London WC2R 0RL, England
Penguin Ireland, 25 St Stephen's Green, Dublin 2, Ireland (a division of Penguin Books Ltd)
Penguin Group (Australia), 250 Camberwell Road, Camberwell,
Victoria 3124, Australia (a division of Pearson Australia Group Pty Ltd)
Penguin Books India Pvt Ltd, 11 Community Centre, Panchsheel Park, New Delhi—110 017, India
Penguin Group (NZ), cnr Airborne and Rosedale Roads, Albany, Auckland, 1310
New Zealand (a division of Pearson New Zealand Ltd)
Penguin Books (South Africa) (Pty) Ltd, 24 Sturdee Avenue, Rosebank, Johannesburg 2196, South Africa

Penguin Books Ltd, Registered Offices:
80 Strand, London WC2R 0RL, England

First published in Penguin Books 2005

3   5   7   9   10   8   6   4   2

Introduction and notes copyright © Ira B. Nadel, 2005
All rights reserved

LIBRARY OF CONGRESS CATALOGING-IN-PUBLICATION DATA
Pound, Ezra, 1885–1972.
[Selections. 2005]
Early writings / edited with an introduction and notes by Ira B. Nadel.
p.   cm.
Includes index.
ISBN 0-14-218013-0
I. Nadel, Ira Bruce   II. Title.
PS3531.O82A6 2005
818'.5208—dc22   2004058722

Printed in the United States of America
Set in Sabon

Contents

Introduction

T. S. Eliot called Ezra Pound *"il miglior fabbro,"* "the better craftsman." James Joyce declared he was "a miracle of ebulliency, gusto and help." W. B. Yeats recalled that to "talk over a poem with him" was "like getting you to put a sentence into dialect. All becomes clear and natural." Wyndham Lewis summed him up as the "demon pantechnicon driver, busy with removal of the old world into new quarters." The supercharged Ezra Pound seemed to be everywhere at once in the literary world of the early twentieth century, cajoling, hectoring, provoking, and refashioning literature whether in London, Paris, New York, or Rapallo. He met Henry James and corresponded with Hardy. He redirected the poetry of Yeats, discovered Robert Frost, and promoted H.D. His admirers were right: Pound was the quintessential modernist, the figure who overturned poetic meter, literary style, and the state of the long poem. Only his experimentation with new forms and determination to "make it new" exceeded his boldness in editing *The Waste Land,* overseeing publication of *Ulysses,* and creating new movements like Imagism. As he wrote in a note to his early poem "Histrion," "I do not teach—I awake."

Pound's multiple importance might be condensed to a single conviction: poetry shapes the world. Like Shelley, who believed that poets are "the unacknowledged legislators of the world,"

Pound knew that poetry informed the moral and aesthetic values of a culture: "Poetry is a sort of inspired mathematics which gives us equations . . . for the human soul," he proclaimed. Literature, he announced in the *ABC of Reading,* is "news that stays news" because it galvanizes readers—especially if it follows his precept to "use no superfluous word." "Cut direct," he ordered when discussing style. Pound, in other words, was a literary activist who insisted that ideas be put into action.

Some of Pound's best and most challenging work is his earliest. Rewriting the dramatic monologue, the Provençal lyric, or the pentameter line meant the discovery of personae, Imagism, and a new form of dramatic expression that his earliest poetry embodied. "To break the pentameter, that was the first heave," Pound wrote in *The Pisan Cantos* (Canto LXXXI), recalling his first encounter with late-nineteenth-century poetry but, more important, suggesting the aggressive and challenging approach he took to the task of poetic composition. Self-possessed and assured in his early work, he could fashion a narrative out of "a shifting change, / A broken bundle of mirrors," as he writes in his remarkable reworking of Provençal traditions, "Near Perigord," a poem that combines Dante, Provençal, and modernist form.

Pound contested traditional if not accepted conventions of poetic writing, replacing Swinburne with Arnaut Daniel, late Victorian elaboration with Imagism. The elegance and precision of the Chinese written character, where the ideogram replaced expansive metaphors, became his new focus. From 1908, when his first book, *A Lume Spento,* appeared, through 1923, when he was well under way with his lifetime's preoccupation, *The Cantos* (by 1923 there were 8; the final number, some only fragments, would be 117), Pound tested, revised, rejected, and recovered forms of poetic expression that became a new direction for poetry for a host of contemporaries, including H.D., T. S. Eliot, William Carlos Williams, Louis Zukofsky, and Basil Bunting.

Pound began to remake his language on or about 1910: "I was obfuscated by the Victorian language . . . I hadn't in 1910 made a language . . . to think in" (*LE,* 193–94). His poetic as well as cultural education had been alternately stultifying and

INTRODUCTION xi

liberating. "It takes six or eight years to get educated in one's art, and another ten to get rid of that education," he declared (*LE*, 194). In criticizing his own Rossetti-influenced efforts to translate Guido Cavalcanti, for example, Pound explained that his mistake was "in taking an English sonnet as the equivalent for a sonnet in Italian" (*LE*, 194). They are not the same, and when he realized this it freed him to explore, expand, discover, and construct his version of these works.

The anti-Romantic essays of T. E. Hulme, the English philosopher, provided Pound with an early direction: "beauty may be in small dry things . . . the great aim is accurate, precise and definite description," wrote Hulme.* By 1912, Pound would express similar ideas in a set of rules:

1. Direct treatment of the "thing," whether subjective or objective.
2. To use absolutely no word that does not contribute to the presentation.
3. As regarding rhythm: to compose in the sequence of the musical phrase, not in sequence of a metronome (*LE*, 3).

His own poetry quickly demonstrated this approach, Pound's energetic and aggressive attitude, evident from his earliest work. In his account of the sculptor Gaudier-Brzeska, Pound wrote, "the image is the poet's pigment" (*GB*, 86).

Pound's prose is often a key to his poetry. *The Spirit of Romance* (1910), originally written as a set of lectures on Romance literature given in London in the fall of 1909/1910 and then printed by J. M. Dent, records his absorption with Italian poets and Provençal troubadours. It also contains one of his most important early statements about poetry, defining it as "a sort of inspired mathematics, which gives us equations, not for abstract figures . . . but equations for the human emotions" (*SR*, 14). The work also reflects Pound's focus on the particular and the need for the definite, whether in terminology or imagery. His

*T. E. Hulme, "Romanticism and Classicism," *Speculations,* ed. Herbert Read (London: K. Paul, Trench, Trubner & Co., 1924) 126–27, 131–32.

early aesthetic also favors restraint, "which drives the master to-ward intensity" (*SR*, 18). Arnaut Daniel, Dante, and Cino emerge as heroes. And he cites Dante's praise of Daniel in Canto 26 of *Purgatorio,* adopting the phrase *il miglior fabbro* as a chapter ti-tle in *The Spirit of Romance.* Eliot would use the phrase as part of the dedication to *The Waste Land,* which reads, "For Ezra Pound / il miglior fabbro" (*SR*, 33).

The poetry of Provence becomes Pound's ideal, what he calls the "poetry of democratic aristocracy," drawing its audience through lyricism and drama (*SR*, 39). Its basis in song, expressed through the troubadour's voice, was another foundational idea for Pound, who used the concept of *melopoeia* or song as a key to his own sense of sound, meter, and rhythm: "troubadour poetry was . . . made to sing; the words are but half the art," he believed (*SR*, 53). This ideal sustained Pound's image of the poet and his relation to this culture throughout his writing. To be both poet and warrior, which the Provençal writer Bertran de Born embod-ied, became a further ideal for Pound.

The Spirit of Romance is the sourcebook for understanding Pound's early poetry through its references, history, and detail—as well as its aesthetic. Throughout the account of *El Cid,* Dante, and the troubadours, Pound makes his conception of the artist clear, explaining that "an art is vital only so long as it is interpre-tative, so long . . . as it manifest something which the artist per-ceives at greater intensity and more intimately, than his public" (*SR*, 87). Science, particularly physics, comes to Pound's aid in explaining the evolution of literary culture and how the condi-tions of Provence provided the necessary restraint and tension to produce great writing: "electric current gives light where it meets resistance" (*SR*, 93–94, 97). And as Pound moves slowly from Provence to Italy, he sharpens his distinctions. The poetry of Provence had been "a cult of the emotions," but the poetry of thirteenth- and fourteenth-century Italy is the "cult of harmonies of the mind," an "objective imagination" that appeals by its "re-fined exactness" (*SR*, 116; Pound would call the Renaissance "the cult of culture" [*SR*, 223]).

Pound believed that the Italian *dolce stil novo* poetry of the late thirteenth century—the period of Dante, Cavalcanti, Cino da Pistoia—was the direct descendant of Provençal verse (Makin, 79). Shakespeare's language is "beautifully suggestive," but Dante's is "more beautifully definite"; Shakespeare is a forest, Dante a cathedral (*SR*, 158, 159). Geographically, Pound moves from Provence to Tuscany and then England. Paris and the work of Villon (François Montcorbier) is, however, another stop. Villon's persistent gaze at what is before him, even when it is himself, expressed through a voice of mockery, suffering, and fact, appealed to Pound, who refers to Villon as "the only poet without illusions" and who never lies to himself (*SR*, 169). Dante, writes Pound, is many men; Villon is always himself (*SR*, 177). Arnaut Daniel, Bertran de Born, Dante, Villon—these are the poets who shaped Pound's early ideas and technique.

Rossetti, Browning, and even Swinburne, as well as the Anglo-Saxon poets, were the first in the English tradition to challenge Pound, who alternately found their work admirable and execrable. But he vigorously reacted against "the crust of dead English, the sediment present in my own available vocabulary" (*LE*, 193), determined to renew the language of poetry. Whitman, Noh drama, and Chinese poetry, which he encountered through the work of Ernest Fenollosa, helped him to further his new direction, which in 1912 he labeled "Imagism." Pound defined this as the drive toward precision in contrast to abstraction, replacing Victorian generalities with the clarity found in Japanese haiku, Noh theater, and ancient Greek lyrics. In "A Few Don'ts by an Imagist" (1913), he presented the new aesthetic, defining an image as the presentation of "an intellectual and emotional complex in an instant of time" treated according to certain rules, starting with "direct treatment of the 'thing,' whether subjective or objective." Use "no word that does not contribute to the presentation," he admonished writers (*LE*, 3–4). His anthology, *Des Imagistes* (1914), with work by H.D., Aldington, Williams, Joyce, and himself, exhibited these principles at work.

Succeeding Imagism was Vorticism, a system of energies responding to modern dynamism and technology, which Wyndham Lewis's journal *BLAST* (1914–15) represented. The image is now understood not as an idea but as "a radiant node or cluster . . . a VORTEX from which, and through which, and into which, ideas are constantly rushing" (*GB*, 92). But this, too, was soon revised: Noh theater's "Unity of Image" replaced energy as the intensification of a single image became Pound's concern. But soon even this approach would be too limited, because as Pound embarked on *The Cantos,* he needed a way for the image to arrest the tension of competing materials, while at the same time functioning as an element of reference and allusion. By 1918, between the composition of *Homage to Sextus Propertius* and *Hugh Selwyn Mauberley,* Pound confidently predicted that the poetry of the next decade will "move against poppy-cock, it will be harder and saner . . . we will have fewer painted adjectives impeding the shock and stroke of it" (*LE,* 12). Pound's "Sestina: Altaforte," "The Coming of War: Actæon," and "Near Perigord" had already validated these ideas.

   Homage to Sextus Propertius is the first of Pound's major sequence poems, anticipating *Mauberley* and then *The Cantos.* Based on a series of poems from the four extant books of the Roman elegist Sextus Aurelius Propertius, the work, finished in 1917 but not published until 1919, created controversy because it was a liberal if not free-form "translation," a work that adapted the original to contemporary language rather than imitate the original through a literal translation. This upset classicists, but not readers. Pound defended his work, claiming his goal was "to bring a dead man to life, to present a living figure" (*SL,* 149). T. S. Eliot in his introduction to *Selected Poems* (1928) explained that "it is not a translation, it is a paraphrase, or still more truly . . . a *persona*" (*SPo,* 19).

   What made Propertius central to Pound's reading and study of poetry was the Roman poet's irony. In Propertius, Pound identified *logopoeia,* what he defined as "the dance of the intellect among words" (*LE,* 25). This attitude, he explained, "does not translate; though the attitude of mind it expresses may pass through a paraphrase. Or one might say, you can *not* translate it 'locally'" (*LE,* 25). For Pound and his later translations, tone and color and the state of mind of the poet, not exact expression, are central (*SL,* 231). Pound also argues in his poem that Propertius had been misread by the Victorians, who emphasized the sentimentality of the Roman poet. Pound's *Propertius* criticizes these misreadings as he underscores the ironic play of the Roman's poetry. Jules Laforgue rather than Pater is the proper model, Pound argues, and in response to a remark by Thomas Hardy that the poem should be retitled "Propertius Soliloquizes," Pound explains that "what I do is borrow a term—aesthetic—a term of aesthetic *attitude* from a French musician, Debussy," and develop it rather than concentrate on the subject matter of Propertius (Davie, 49).

Propertius becomes a mask for Pound, a hallmark of his early poetry and the last of the major single *personae* in Pound's work. In selecting and arranging the elegies of Propertius, Pound builds up a complex if unorthodox portrait of the Roman that both interprets the historical original *and* reflects the occupations of the modern translator. The recurrent themes of love, war, death, and poetry are of the present as well as the past. The poem might furthermore be thought of as Pound's elegy to the Edwardian-Georgian reading public, which he could take for granted in the pre–World War I environment but not after. That readership became a casualty of the conflict suggested in *Propertius* but detailed in *Mauberley*.

Hugh Selwyn Mauberley is Pound's most important early poem, refining his sense of sequence and structure. Anticipating the form of *The Cantos* and yet summarizing the issues and outline of works like *Sextus Propertius*, especially in its social criticism, direct voice, and fragmented narrative, *Mauberley* presents, in tone and direction, the format and style of Pound's later development. Essentially the retelling of the poet Mauberley's disaffection with London and its culture, in response to the calamity caused by World War I, the poem also alludes to such influences as Henry James and Théophile Gautier. In James, Pound admired the depiction of atmosphere and impressions; in Gautier, a certain "hardness," which he prophesized in 1917, celebrating verse that was "austere, direct, free from emotional slither" (*LE,* 12). The final poem in the Mauberley sequence, "Medallion," thought to be by Mauberley himself, exhibits the hardness Pound admired in Gautier's *Émaux et Camées* (1852).

Mauberley is a suite of eighteen poems in two parts, the first running from "Ode" to "Envoi (1919)." The second begins with

the title "Mauberley (1920)," from section I to "Medallion." On
the title page of the poem in *Personae* (1926), Pound included a
footnote, since deleted: "The sequence is so distinctly a farewell
to London that the reader who chooses to regard this as an exclusively American edition may as well omit it and turn at once
to *[Homage to Sextus Propertius]*." The epigraph from the
Roman poet Nemesianus, "the heat calls us into the shade," and
the subtitle "Life and Contacts" were omitted in *Selected Poems*
(1949) but reintroduced in a revised version appearing in *Dip-
tych Rome-London* (1958), although the subtitle is reversed
to read "Contacts and Life," which Pound told his publisher,
James Laughlin, was "the actual order of the subject matter"
(Ruthven, 127).

Early readers of the poem had difficulty distinguishing between Pound and the persona of Mauberley. Were they the same
or not? Pound argued they were different, but readers persisted
in linking the two. Another issue was the construction of the
work: were the sections linked or simply arbitrarily joined together? Answers can be found through identifying Pound's
sources, largely French. Indeed, Pound models his work on the
rhythms of Gautier and Bion, poets he had recently reread for
his long article "A Study in French Poets," published in the *Little Review* (February 1918). Pound essentially creates in the person of Mauberley, who appears only in the latter half of the poem
and in contrast to Pound, "a mask of the contemporary aesthete
to show what the minor artist could expect from the England of
the day" (Espey, 14). The poet's place in society is the focus.

Beginning with an ironic "Ode" on Pound himself, the poet
then shifts to his own age, exposing what in society prevents the
artist from fully realizing his own potential because of commer-
cialization and money, which has substituted for aesthetics.
Democracy has also turned toward self-corruption (II, III). Sections IV and V are the climax of Pound's denunciation, underscored by World War I and the sacrifice of the young dying for a
diseased tradition. He then examines the sources of this degener-
ation, locating it in the overpowering of Pre-Raphaelite aesthetics
by the official morality of Gladstone and Ruskin (see the "Yeux

Glauques" and "Siena Mi Fe'" sections). A list of Pound's, and possibly Mauberley's, contacts follows ("Brennbaum," "Mr. Nixon"), including an educated woman who inherits sterile traditions she does not understand (XI). Pound then examines himself in relation to the fashionable circles of literary London and realizes he is unacceptable (XII) and bows out with a love lyric, "Envoi (1919)," which contradicts the surface judgments of the critics in the opening "Ode."

Mauberley emerges as an individual in the second half of the poem, entitled "Mauberley (1920)," where each of the sections opens with an apparent parallel drawn from the first section, although it develops its thematic opposite. Mauberley, however, is inadequate, displaying his limits as an artist (I), realizing that although life may offer him something through active passion, he hesitates and is unable to conform to the age (II, and "The Age Demanded" section). These acknowledgments lead to subjective reveries that engulf him as he drifts to his death (IV), leaving his only work—"Medallion"—behind, an ironic reworking of the "Envoi" that concluded part one of the poem and marked the disappearance of Pound to Paris. But the restatements of phrases in the "Mauberley" section of the poem from part one are thematic variants rather than direct extensions, balancing and ordering what had formerly been seen as disconnected fragments. Even typography contrasts the two parts of the larger work: Pound uses Greek in the first part for his Greek quotations and tags; in the second ("Mauberley (1920)"), he transliterates the Greek into Roman letters.

Complex but revealing, emphasizing the disparity between surface and foundation, between idea and action, *Mauberley* contains various links with *The Cantos*, including the theme of the poet as Odysseus (*Mauberley* and *The Cantos* each opens with this), which functions in both works as a unifying narrative thread (see Cantos I, XX, and XLVII). The abrupt breaking off of the twelfth poem in *Mauberley*, and the coda following the asterisks, anticipate the technical surface of *The Cantos*, where such typographical disruptions culminate in the introduction of Chinese ideographs (Cantos LII–LXXI et al.) and even a musical score (Canto LXXV). *Mauberley* also introduces a series of figures who will reappear in *The Cantos,* from Homer, Dante, and Browning to Pindar, Catullus, and Sappho, as well as Henry James, Pisanello and Edward FitzGerald, translator of *The Rubaiyat.* War, inimical to both poems, expands to a shared indictment of England.

Pound did not forget *Mauberley:* imprisoned by the U.S. Army at the Disciplinary Training Center in Pisa in 1945, he recalled in detail the period the poem evoked when he composed *The Pisan Cantos,* directly quoting from the earlier work. *Mauberley* encompasses many of Pound's early enthusiasms—Browning, Swinburne, the Pre-Raphaelites, *The Rubaiyat*—as well as his classical interests, but it also looks forward to the range and breadth of *The Cantos.* With *Propertius, Mauberley* justifies the artist in times unsympathetic to his art, while *The Cantos,* even the early ones, demonstrate his necessary place in the modern age.

"You will have to go a long way round if you want to avoid them," Basil Bunting wrote in his poem "On the Fly-leaf of Pound's Cantos," addressing them like the Alps. But for many readers, *The Cantos* still remain a mountainous poem, filled with crevices, steep ascents, and glorious views, despite Pound's admonition that "there is no mystery about the Cantos, they are the tale of the tribe—give Rudyard [Kipling] credit for his use of the phrase" (*GK,* 194). Pound first thought of his epic, "a poem including history," as early as 1904 or 1905, but did not begin drafting cantos until 1915 (*ABC,* 46). "Three Cantos of a Poem of Some Length," the early cantos, first appeared in *Poetry* magazine in 1917, but almost immediately after their publication, Pound began to revise them, asking Eliot for editorial advice. Eliot told him to eliminate redundancies and explanatory passages and remove personal pronouns to "impersonalize" the text, making its transitions more elliptical. Pound followed this form of revision throughout the composition of the entire poem, preferring to call several of the later volumes "drafts," as in *A Draft of XVI Cantos for the Beginning of A Poem of Some Length* (1925) or *A Draft of XXX Cantos* (1930).

No section of the work experienced as much revision, however, as "Three Cantos." In fact, a portion of Canto III would form the opening of Canto I, while the later Canto VIII would become a large portion of Canto II. Pound was finding his way. More specifically, in 1923, Pound took part of Canto III, his translation of the *nekuia* passage from *The Odyssey* (Book IX, "The Book of the Dead"), and made it the opening of a revised Canto I and redistributed other passages to provide a more dramatic, *in medias res* beginning. But "Three Cantos," and Cantos IV through VIII, record the poet's original conception and impetus for the poem, which he acknowledged to be digressive and abbreviated:

> the first 11 Cantos are preparation of the palette. I *have* to get down all the colours or elements I want for the poem. Some perhaps too enigmatically and abbreviatedly. I hope to bring them into some sort of design and architecture later (*SL,* 180).

Beginning with Browning's *Sordello,* "Three Cantos"—the so-called Ur-cantos—develop a centralizing consciousness (later to be replaced with a fragmented perception expressed through juxtaposition) by using the poem to establish a dialogue with Browning in Pound's search for form, complaining that Browning had

> Worked out new form, the meditative,
> Semi-dramatic, semi-epic story,
> And we will say: What's left for me to do?
> Whom shall I conjure up; who's my Sordello [?]
>   ("Three Cantos," I)

The answer, of course, is plenty, and Pound proceeds in the "Three Cantos" to build a poetic world around the myth of Odysseus, because no historical literary figure or model could satisfy his demands. He would label this process of image making the Greek *phantastikon,* which he describes at the close of Canto I:

>   And I shall claim;
> Confuse my own phantastikon,
> Or say the filmy shell that circumscribes me
> Contains the actual sun;
>   confuse the thing I see
> With the actual gods behind me?
>   Are they gods behind me?

But historical figures remain subject to the imaginative meta-
morphoses of the poet's *phantastikon,* merging and emerging
with the archetype of a mythical hero free from historical re-
construction: for Pound, this is Odysseus. In the first of "Three
Cantos," he also establishes his style: "set out your matter / As I
do, in straight simple phrases." How to make the long poem
both an epic and modern is the challenge Pound sets for himself. "Three Cantos" is his first answer. Experiment characterizes all of these early efforts plus his realization that the heroes
of the past will not do—or must be reappraised and re-presented
to suit the modern situation.

More specifically, the later half of "Three Cantos, I" introduces motifs developed not only by the "Three Cantos" as
a whole but later Cantos as well (Bush, 117, 135–41).
"Three Cantos, II" begins with a half-regretful soliloquy,
"Leave Casella," abandoning lyric poetry for the epic. The
narrative technique shifts as the persona of the narrator recedes
from the center into a less prominent speaking voice. No
monologue but a series of unrelated vignettes emerges; the
narrator discourses with images of various joyless ghosts, each
presenting a form of spiritual blindness. The theme is "drear
waste" and shows Pound's technique of layering the vital past
and the empty present into an extended sequence. At play are
the techniques of Imagism.

A progression of historical images illustrating the fading
power of the gods ends the Canto; worship disappears as Western culture ages and becomes more commercial. "Three Cantos, III" moves more securely to Homer and Odysseus, recalling
Pound's copy of Andreas Divus's Latin translation of Homer,

which would become the opening of the revised Canto I, Pound offering his own "rough meaning" in English of Divus's Latin.

Cantos IV through VIII push the poem further, moving into the world of ragged textual surfaces and disjointed history but taking Pound closer to an emerging conception of the entire work. Canto IV, published in October 1919, was the first he regarded as capable of standing in the finished sequence, although he revised it slightly. "Three Cantos" orients the reader in psychological space; Canto IV in a flatter, historical space. Events, literary allusions, and the poet coexist now on the same plane. Pieces of text abut one another without an established context set by a single narrator or consciousness. Now the Orient, not Browning, organizes the poem. Japanese Noh drama provides the schema, a kind of theater without drama, using only a change of mask to mark a shift in dialogue. Scenery is minimal; the action is verbal; the language incisive. The drama *Takasago,* read by Pound while composing Canto IV, is central in conception and form for the new confidence and direction represented by this Canto (Albright, 65–67).

Cantos IV and V still celebrate the glamour of troubadour adultery, with short segments spliced together to reveal common themes. Peire de Maensac, a troubadour described in Canto V, may be a *dreitz hom* (good man), but he is still devious as he makes off with Tierci's wife. But Canto V is also a departure, as Pound introduces a secondary intelligence, in this case Benedetto Varchi, a historian who considers whether the murder of Alessandro de' Medici in 1557 by his cousin was petty revenge or a noble act to save Florence from tyranny. Pound enters history in this Canto, although it is uncertain, insecure, and baffling. Contrasting with the identifiable myths of Canto IV are the "facts" of Canto V, which are unreliable. Canto V also elaborates voices other than those of the poets. History itself begins to speak in the poem. Canto VI, for example, is the voice of the troubadour Bernart de Ventadour telling how his music seduced the wife of his patron, Eblis III. The voices of old men who mutter rather than speak fill Canto VII: "Dry casques of departed locusts/speaking a shell of speech" (VII).

Between 1920 and 1921, Pound wrote no Cantos, concentrating instead on *Mauberley*. He also wrote an opera, *Le Testament,* devising his own music for texts by François Villon; he also edited *The Waste Land.* These experiences changed the shape of *The Cantos.* The "impersonations"—the voices Pound employs in Cantos V through VIII—marking his search through history and myth to locate an authentic voice diminish, although in Canto VIII, published in *The Dial* in May 1922, he still maintains strong narrative control. Retelling moments from mythical history, he dramatizes as he juxtaposes, drawing on Anglo-Saxon constructions as much as Dante. But classical writers set the diction, the source texts and incidents in the Canto. Homer and Dante, in fact, become the two hovering figures not only in Canto VIII, (which would be radically revised in 1923–1925 to become Canto II), but also throughout the remainder of the entire poem. Suggesting the competition between two worlds, that of poet and audience and the classical and the modern, is the line "Ear, ear for the sea-surge, murmur of old men's voices," describing Homer's skill and yet neglect. In Acoetus's narration of the adventures of Dionysus, Pound brings a liveliness and drama to the poem not present in the earlier quest to create a new *Sordello.* The dialogue of Canto VIII is never between two poets (Pound and Browning) but between the dramatized lives of figures like Acoetus and Dionysus. Pound recognized this new energy and placed the Canto second in his revised structure, beginning the new version with an admission and a challenge— "Hang it all, Robert Browning,/ there can be but the one 'Sordello'"—and then leaping to the So-shu, seal, and Picasso passage of the original Canto VIII, reworking material from approximately line 15 onward. As the poetic source of the new Canto II, Canto VIII has a crucial place in the evolution of the completed poem.

Pound's early prose similarly redefined his relation with tradition at the same time he formulated a new aesthetic. "What I Feel About Walt Whitman" (1909) is an early attempt to clarify his connection to an American literary past, extended by "The Wisdom of Poetry" (1912), a statement of the value of poetry as an act of liberation achieved through language. He amplifies this through a series of essays on select influences on his work, notably "Psychology and Troubadours" (1912) and "Troubadours—Their Sorts and Conditions" (1913). His essays "Imagisme" (1912) and "The Serious Artist" (1913) clarify his poetics at the same time he glances back in "How I Began" (1913). But Pound always manages to look forward when he looks back, as in "The Tradition" (1914), which focuses on Greece and Provence, and "A Retrospect" (1918), a collection of earlier pieces on Imagism and artistic commitment. "The Prose Tradition in Verse" (1914) strikes a new note as he begins with Yeats and then moves to the value of Hueffer's (later Ford Madox Ford) poetry, not because he has a lyrical gift but because "of his insistence upon clarity and precision, upon the prose tradition; in brief, upon efficient writing—even in verse."

"Vorticism" (1914) and "Chinese Poetry" (1918) are further important topics in Pound's essays; so is the startling work of James Joyce. Two essays on Joyce, in fact, appear here, one dealing with the publication of *A Portrait of the Artist as a Young Man* (1917), the other with *Ulysses* (1922). Both were texts that Pound felt radically revised the novel as it was then understood.

Perhaps the most significant prose work Pound published up to 1923 was "The Chinese Written Character as a Medium for Poetry." In early October 1913, Ernest Fenollosa's widow met the energetic young Pound, who was striding through literary London with his bold ideas and new forms. Mary Fenollosa hoped to appoint Pound her late husband's literary executor. Pound, not an Orientalist but a poet, impressed Mrs. Fenollosa, whose husband went to Japan in 1878 after graduating from Harvard, continuing his studies at Cambridge University, and spending a year at the Boston Museum of Fine Arts. He first taught at the Imperial University in Tokyo, where he began an intensive study of Japanese art. After eight years, Fenollosa helped found the Tokyo Fine Arts Academy and the Imperial Museum, acting as its director in 1888. He also prepared the first inventory of Japan's national treasures. He returned to Boston in 1890 to become curator of Oriental art at the Boston Museum of Fine Arts, but scandal over his divorce and immediate

remarriage to the writer Mary McNeill Scott in 1895 forced his
resignation. Two years later, he returned to Japan but in 1900
made his way back to America and then on to London, where he
died in 1908. Mrs. Fenollosa liked Pound; she appointed him
Fenollosa's literary executor, and passed on to him sixteen or so
notebooks from her husband that concentrated on three subjects: Japanese drama, Chinese verse, and the Chinese writing
system.

While in Japan, Fenollosa undertook the intensive study of
Chinese poetry, especially the work of Li Po (Rihaku, in Japanese). The last topic Fenollosa studied before leaving Japan was
the Chinese writing system, preparing an essay on the written
character of Chinese literature. The work, which Pound edited
and would publish in 1919, strongly influenced Pound's ideas of
poetry and the Orient. Fenollosa believed that Chinese characters are actually representations of ideas (ideograms), which
present concepts in visual forms. This paralleled Pound's work
at the time on Imagism, in which he was seeking a visually focused poetry. In a later work, *ABC of Reading* (1934), Pound
elaborates these concepts, claiming that Fenollosa's essay is
"the first definite assertion of the applicability of scientific
method to literary criticism" (*ABC*, 18).

Pound declares that Fenollosa "was perhaps too far ahead of
his time to be easily comprehended" (*ABC*, 19). In contrast to
European thought, which defines by abstraction, Chinese
thought, as stated by Fenollosa, defines in terms of science, of exactitude through a language based on sight, not sound (*ABC*,
20). The ideogram is not a "written sign recalling a sound" but
"the picture of the thing, . . . it *means* the thing or the actions or
situation, or quality germane to the several things that it pictures"
(*ABC*, 21). To define "red," for example, the Chinese writer puts
together the abbreviated pictures of a rose, iron rust, cherry, and
flamingo. Essentially, Fenollosa for Pound "was telling how and
why a language written in this way simply HAD TO STAY PO-
ETIC" (*ABC*, 22).

In Fenollosa, Pound found confirmation of his commitment
to "the efficiency of verbal manifestation": "a general statement," he announces, is "valuable only in REFERENCE to the

known objects or facts" that the ideogram represents (*ABC*, 27, 26). Practically, this meant the use of transitive verbs and avoidance of "is." English, Fenollosa writes, has a "lazy satisfaction with nouns and adjectives." Pound, however, did not know the sound of Chinese and faced the dilemma of translating Chinese concept figurations with Japanese sound values (Fenollosa's preferred medium). Only when he received R. H. Mathews's Chinese-English dictionary years later, which organized characters by their sounds rather than by their radicals, would Pound begin to understand the phonetic structure of the language. However, the aesthetic value of the ideogram as understood in Fenollosa's essay was incalculable for Pound's developing aesthetic.

Pound's early writings in poetry and prose reveal the direction of his later work. His ideas about language, history, reading, and influence are apparent, whether in the experimental *Homage to Sextus Propertius, Hugh Selwyn Mauberley,* or "Three Cantos," or in essays like "Imagism" or "The Serious Artist." Pound's work up to 1923, when he confidently asserts in "Criticism in General" three broad divisions for poetry: *melopoeia*—when words are charged with musical properties; *phanopoeia*—"a casting of images upon the visual imagination"; and *logopoeia*—"the dance of the intellect upon words," charts his later work. Earlier, in 1915, Pound told Harriet Monroe, editor of *Poetry* magazine, that in good writing "there must be no clichés, set phrases, stereotyped journalese. The only escape from such is by precision, a result of concentrated attention to what is writing . . . objectivity and again objectivity" (*SL*, 49). As his writing up to 1923 evolves, he achieves this goal.

Pound and his wife, Dorothy, spent from January through April 1923 in Italy, anticipating their future residence there (1924–1945; 1958–1972). The period also initiated new work on *The Cantos* as Pound explored the life of Sigismundo Malatesta, the fifteenth-century *condottiere* and art patron of Rimini. In 1923, he also continued to develop his opera on Villon, now with the assistance of the composer George Antheil; reworked the opening of *The Cantos* (making part of Canto III the new beginning of Canto I); published an autobiographical volume, *Indiscretions*; and saw three of the Malatesta Cantos in print in Eliot's *Criterion*. But none of these developments could have occurred without the writing and ideas formulated between 1908 and 1923.

In the material that follows, footnotes are by Pound, endnotes are by the editor. Because the texts for Pound's essays follow those of their first publication, the punctuation reflects differing British and American practices.

Abbreviations

ABC—ABC of Reading. New York: New Directions, 1960.

Albright—Daniel Albright, "Early Cantos I–XLI," *The Cambridge Companion to Ezra Pound*. Ed. Ira B. Nadel. Cambridge: Cambridge University Press, 1999.

Cantos—The Cantos of Ezra Pound. 13th printing. New York: New Directions, 1995.

CEP—Collected Early Poems. Ed. Michael John King. New York: New Directions, 1976.

CSP—Collected Shorter Poems. London: Faber and Faber, 1968.

Davie—Donald Davie. *Pound*. London: Fontana, 1975.

GB—Gaudier-Brzeska: A Memoir. New York: New Directions, 1970.

GK—Guide to Kulchur. New York: New Directions, 1970.

LE—Literary Essays. Ed. T. S. Eliot. New York: New Directions, 1968.

Makin—Peter Makin, *Provence and Pound*. Berkeley: University of California Press, 1978.

PER—Personae: The Shorter Poems of Ezra Pound. Revised edition. Ed. Lea Baechler and A. Walton Litz. New York: New Directions, 1990.

SL—Selected Letters of Ezra Pound, 1907–1941. Ed. D. D. Paige. New York: New Directions, 1971.

SP—Selected Prose, 1909–1965. Ed. William Cookson. London: Faber and Faber, 1973.
SPo—Selected Poems of Ezra Pound. Ed. T. S. Eliot. London: Faber and Faber, 1928.
SR—The Spirit of Romance. New York: New Directions, 1968.

Suggestions for Further Reading

BIOGRAPHY

Brooker, Peter. *Bohemia in London: The Social Scene of Early Modernism*. London: Palgrave/Macmillan, 2004. Pound, Lewis, Eliot, and Ford engage in poetry, ideas, and gossip.

Carpenter, Humphrey. *A Serious Character: The Life of Ezra Pound*. London: Faber and Faber, 1988. A massive account of his life.

Hutchins, Patricia. *Ezra Pound's Kensington: An Exploration, 1885–1913*. Chicago: Henry Regnery Company, 1965. A glimpse at Pound's Kensington period.

Nadel, Ira B. *Ezra Pound: A Literary Life*. London: Palgrave/Macmillan, 2004. A concise life emphasizing his literary development and current scholarship.

Pound, Ezra. *Indiscretions*. Paris: Three Mountains Press, 1923. Reprinted in Pound, *Pavannes and Divigations*. New York: New Directions, 1958. Pound's autobiographical essay.

———. *Selected Letters of Ezra Pound, 1907–1941*. Ed. D. D. Paige. New York: New Directions, 1971. Crucial reading recording Pound's emerging aesthetic, politics, and opinions.

———. *Ezra Pound and Dorothy Shakespear: Their Letters, 1909–1914*. Ed. Omar Pound and A. Walton Litz. New York: New Directions, 1984. An important record of their early relationship.

———. *A Walking Tour in Southern France*. Ed. Richard Sieburth. New York: New Directions, 1992. Pound's 1912 trip through southern France, drawn from his notebooks.

Stock, Noel. *The Life of Ezra Pound*. New York: Pantheon, 1970. An early life of the poet.

CRITICISM AND POETRY

Bornstein, George, ed. *Pound Among the Poets*. Chicago: University of Chicago Press, 1985.
Bush, Ronald. *The Genesis of Ezra Pound's Cantos*. Princeton: Princeton University Press, 1976.
Espey, John J. *Ezra Pound's Mauberley: A Study in Composition*. London: Faber and Faber, 1955.
Gallup, Donald. *Ezra Pound, A Bibliography*. Charlottesville: University Press of Virginia, 1983. The standard bibliography.
Grieve, Thomas F. *Ezra Pound's Early Poetry and Poetics*. Columbia: University of Missouri Press, 1997.
Homberger, Eric, ed. *Ezra Pound: The Critical Heritage*. London: Routledge and Kegan Paul, 1972. Important collection of criticism and commentary from 1904 to 1970.
Kenner, Hugh. *The Poetry of Ezra Pound*. 1951. Reprint, Lincoln: University of Nebraska Press, 1985.
———. *The Pound Era*. Berkeley: University of California Press, 1971.
Pound, Ezra. *ABC of Reading*. 1934. Reprint, New York: New Directions, 1960.
———. *Literary Essays*. Ed. T. S. Eliot. 1954. Reprint, New York: New Directions, 1968.
———. *Guide to Kulchur*. 1938. Reprint, New York: New Directions, 1970.
———. *The Spirit of Romance*. 1910. Reprint, New York: New Directions, 1968.
———. *Personae: The Shorter Poems of Ezra Pound*. Revised edition, ed. Lea Baechler and A. Walton Litz. New York: New Directions, 1990.
———. *Poems and Translations*. Ed. Richard Sieburth. New York: Library of America, 2003. A comprehensive anthology, excluding *The Cantos*.
Ruthven, K. K. *A Guide to Ezra Pound's Personae (1926)*. Berkeley: University of California Press, 1969.
Sullivan, J. P., ed. *Ezra Pound: A Critical Anthology*. Harmondsworth: Penguin, 1970. Criticism by and about Pound.
Witemeyer, Hugh. *The Poetry of Ezra Pound: Forms and Renewal, 1908–1920*. Berkeley: University of California Press, 1969.

Brief Chronology

1885 Ezra Loomis Pound born on October 30 in Hailey, Idaho, to Homer Pound and Isabel Weston Pound. Pound's grandfather was a congressman from Wisconsin whose connections obtained an appointment for his son, Homer, in the Idaho Territories as registrar of the Government Land Office.

1887 The Pounds leave Hailey for New York City, where they live with Uncle Ezra and Aunt Frank Weston.

1889–1897 Homer Pound becomes assistant assayer at the United States Mint in Philadelphia, where he will work until he retires in 1928. Family settles first in Jenkintown and then moves to the adjacent suburb of Wyncote. The young Ezra, nicknamed "Ra" (pronounced "Ray"), publishes his first poem in 1896, a limerick on the defeat of William Jennings Bryan in the presidential election. Poem appears in the *Jenkintown Times-Chronicle*. After several years in public school, enters Cheltenham Military Academy in 1897, where he learns Latin, fencing, tennis, and chess.

1898 First grand tour of Europe with his mother and her aunt Frank. Visits England, Germany, France, Switzerland, and Italy.

1901 Enters the University of Pennsylvania at age fifteen. Meets William Brooke Smith, a young artist, and Hilda Doolittle (later known as the Imagist poet H.D.).

1902 In the summer travels again to Europe with his parents and Aunt Frank. Also visits Gibraltar and Morocco. On return to Penn, meets William Carlos Williams, a medical student two years older than himself. However, Pound's broader reading makes him Williams's poetic mentor.

1903 Poor grades necessitate Pound's transfer to Hamilton College, in Clinton, New York, where he studies Romance languages and Anglo-Saxon.

1905 Graduates from Hamilton College with his bachelor's degree and publishes a translation from Provençal in the *Hamilton Literary Magazine*. Reads Dante and considers writing a modern epic based on *The Divine Comedy*. Begins graduate study at University of Pennsylvania; sees a great deal of Hilda Doolittle, for whom he forms an anthology of his early poems that he calls "Hilda's Book."

1906–1907. Receives M.A. degree in Romance languages and a fellowship for summer doctoral work in Spain on the plays of Lope de Vega. Sails to Gibraltar and visits Madrid, Burgos, Paris, and London. He returns to the University of Pennsylvania in the fall but fails a literary criticism course and becomes disillusioned with his professors. Learns in 1907 that his fellowship will not be renewed. Accepts job in Crawfordsville, Indiana, at Wabash College, where he teaches Spanish and French.

1908 Accused of harboring an actress in his rooms overnight by his landladies, he is dismissed from Wabash. Spurned in love by both Mary Moore of Trenton, New Jersey, and Hilda Doolittle. Father agrees to underwrite a trip to Europe in pursuit of Pound's becoming a poet. Sails in March and ends up in Venice, publishing *A Lume Spento* at his own expense. Moves to London in mid-August and begins to meet literary figures through publisher Elkin Mathews. Publishes *A Quinzaine for This Yule*.

1909 Delivers six lectures on literature of southern Europe, which he will revise and later publish as *The Spirit of Romance*. Meets Olivia Shakespear and her daughter Dorothy. A romance with Dorothy follows, leading to their marriage in 1914. Through May Sinclair meets Ford Madox Hueffer, who prints "Sestina: Altaforte" in his *English Review*. Mathews publishes *Personae* in April. Attends meetings of the Poets' Club and that of the Secessionist Club founded by T. E. Hulme and F. S. Flint. Meets Wyndham Lewis, D. H. Lawrence, and Yeats.

1910 Completes second set of lectures on medieval literature, to be published with the first as *The Spirit of Romance*. Romantically linked with a series of women. William Carlos Williams visits. Leaves for Paris in March and, through the pianist Walter Morse Rummel, meets Margaret Cravens, who becomes his patron. Travels to Sirmione on Lago di Garda, where he is joined by Olivia and Dorothy Shakespear. Works on a translation of Guido Cavalcanti. In June, returns to United States, dividing his time between Philadelphia and New York, seeking either to start a business or an academic career. *Provença*, an American edition of his poems, appears in November. Meets Yeats's father, then living and painting in New York; he, in turn, puts Pound in contact with New York lawyer and patron John Quinn. Renews contact with Hilda Doolittle, who is unaware of Pound's involvement with Dorothy Shakespear. Doolittle considers herself Pound's fiancée.

1911 Returns to London in February but immediately heads to Paris, where he works on a translation of the troubadour poet Arnaut Daniel and collaborates with Rummel on musical settings of troubadour poetry. Mathews brings out *Canzoni*. Translates "The Seafarer" from Anglo-Saxon while at Sirmione in July. Travels to Germany to meet Hueffer, who dismisses Pound's archaic diction and urges him to concentrate on contemporary language. In London, meets A. R. Orage, editor of *The New Age*, where he will begin to publish. Friendship with Yeats becomes closer. Hilda Doolittle arrives to learn that Pound intends to marry Dorothy Shakespear.

1912 Meets Henry James through Hueffer. *Cavalcanti* appears in May, *Ripostes* in October. Introduces Richard Aldington to Hilda Doolittle and they are soon a couple. To Paris in the spring, where he works on Provençal manuscripts. A walking tour in southern France through troubadour country is cut short by learning of Margaret Cravens's suicide in Paris. Returns to London in August and by the fall begins to promote his new school, Imagism. Contacted in August by Harriet Monroe, about to launch a new magazine in Chicago, *Poetry*. Agrees to become their foreign correspondent. Submits work by Yeats, Aldington, himself, and Doolittle, whom he renames "H. D., Imagiste."

1913 Meets Robert Frost; arranges for publication of William Carlos Williams's *The Tempers* by Elkin Mathews; publishes his manifesto on Imagism in *Poetry* (March 1913); "In a Station of a Metro" appears in the April issue; travels to France; becomes literary editor of *The Egoist*. Meets young French sculptor Henri Gaudier-Brzeska; completes *Lustra*, although it won't be published until 1916. Spends the first of three winters with Yeats at Stone Cottage in Sussex; meets Mary Fenollosa, widow of Ernest Fenollosa. Learns of Joyce.

1914 Arranges for serial publication of *A Portrait of the Artist as a Young Man* in *The Egoist*. His anthology *Des Imagistes* appears in New York. Marries Dorothy Shakespear on April 20. Volume 1 of *BLAST*, edited by Pound and Lewis, appears in July, proclaiming the birth of Vorticism. In September the *Fortnightly Review* publishes Pound's essay, "Vorticism." Introduced by Conrad Aiken to T. S. Eliot and enthusiastically recommends publication of "Prufrock" in *Poetry*.

1915 Publishes "Exile's Letter," first of the poems drawn from Fenollosa's notes. *Cathay* appears in April. Gaudier-Brzeska killed in June in France. *BLAST* number 2 appears. Edits and publishes *Catholic Anthology* with work by Eliot, Yeats, Sandburg. Begins work on a "longish new poem," which will become *The Cantos*.

1916 *Gaudier-Brzeska: A Memoir* appears, as well as *Lustra* and *Certain Noble Plays of Japan* from the Fenollosa manuscripts.

1917 *'Noh' or Accomplishment,* an expanded version of *Certain Noble Plays of Japan* with Fenollosa's essay on Japanese theater, published. Egoist Press, at Pound's urging, brings out Joyce's *Portrait* after rejection by several publishers. Becomes foreign editor of New York–based *Little Review*. "Three Cantos" appears in *Poetry*. T. E. Hulme killed at the Front.

Eliot's anonymous pamphlet *Ezra Pound: His Metric and Poetry* appears in New York. Has affair with Iseult MacBride, daughter of Yeats's great love, Maud Gonne. Pound is best man at Yeats's wedding to Dorothy Shakespear's friend Georgiana Hyde-Lees. Writes art criticism as B. H. Dias and music criticism as William Atheling for *The New Age*.

1918 Prose collection *Pavannes and Divisions*, which also includes translations and several poems, published. Meets Major C. H. Douglas, whose Social Credit approach to economics will have a lasting effect on Pound.

1919 Truncated version of *Homage to Sextus Propertius* appears in *Poetry*, resulting in a censorious letter from a classicist in the following issue. Pound severs association with *Poetry*. Spends April through September in France with Dorothy; goes on a walking tour with Eliot through the Dordogne. *Quia Pauper Amavi* published by Egoist Press with the original *Three Cantos* and full *Sextus Propertius*. Writes Cantos V, VI, VII.

1920 Hired as foreign correspondent for New York magazine *The Dial*. *Instigations*, containing "Chinese Written Character as a Medium for Poetry" appears in April. Ovid Press publishes *Homage to Sextus Propertius*. Meets Joyce for the first time at Sirmione in June; helps him settle in Paris in July.

1921 Settles in Paris in April. Meets Picabia, Cocteau, and Brancusi. John Quinn visits Pound and Joyce. Begins composing opera *Le Testament* with the help of Agnes Bedford. Publishes Cantos V, VI, VII in *The Dial*. Eliot passes through and shows Pound early version of what would be *The Waste Land*. Meets Hemingway, who has just moved to Paris.

1922 Eliot in January gives Pound a revised draft of *The Waste Land*. Within three weeks, Pound returns the manuscript with extensive comments and suggested changes. Canto VIII appears in *The Dial*, as well as a review of *Ulysses*, which is published in February. Travels extensively in Italy, discovering the life and work of Sigismundo Malatesta, *condottiere* of Rimini. In Paris, completes rough drafts of Cantos IX–XI. Meets American violinist Olga Rudge and begins lifelong romance.

1923 January through April in Italy. The autobiographical

Indiscretions appears in March. Publishes three Malatesta Cantos in *The Criterion* in July. Completely revises opening section of *The Cantos*.

1925 Eliot rededicates *The Waste Land* to Pound, calling him *il miglior fabbro*, "the better craftsman." *A Draft of XVI Cantos* appears, published by Three Mountains Press, Paris, with ornamental initials printed in red designed by Henry Strater. Settles in Rapallo in a seaside apartment with Dorothy. In July, Olga Rudge gives birth to Pound's daughter, Mary.

1926 Pound's opera *Le Testament*, scored for medieval instruments, performed in Paris. In September, Dorothy gives birth to a son, conceived during a December 1925 trip to Egypt. Publication of *Personae*, selections from his early work, appears late in the year.

1927–1929 Pound edits and publishes four issues of his own magazine, *The Exile*. In February 1927, Olga Rudge performs for Mussolini at his residence. Pound awarded the Dial Prize for 1928 of $2000, which he invests, offering interest to others such as Ford. *A Draft of the Cantos 17–27*, with initials by Gladys Hynes, appears in London, published by John Rodker in 1928. Eliot introduces and edits Pound's *Selected Poems*.

1929 Homer and Isabel Pound retire to Rapallo. Olga moves to Venice, settling in a small house on the Calle Querini.

1930 Two hundred copies of *A Draft of XXX Cantos* appear in Paris, published by Nancy Cunard at her Hours Press. *Imaginary Letters* also published. Begins to contribute literary and other commentary in Italian to *L'Indice*.

1931 *How to Read* published as a pamphlet in London. BBC broadcast of *Le Testament*.

1933 Private audience with Mussolini, who praises *A Draft of XXX Cantos*. Faber and Faber in London publishes *ABC of Economics* as well as *Active Anthology*.

1934 *ABC of Reading*, plus *Make It New*, a collection of his literary criticism, appear. In New York, *Eleven New Cantos XXXI-XLI* published by Farrar and Rinehart. James Laughlin spends several months with Pound in Rapallo at what he calls the "Ezuversity." Laughlin will return to America and begin New Directions press in 1936 at Pound's urging.

1937 *Polite Essays* published by Faber and Faber. Also *The Fifth Decad of Cantos, XLII–LI* (London: Faber and Faber; New York: Farrar and Rinehart).

1938 *Guide to Kulchur* appears in July. Elected to the National Institute of Arts and Letters. Travels to London for funeral of Olivia Shakespear. Meets Yeats for the last time, his son Omar for the first.

1939 Returns to the United States after twenty-eight years. Visits congressmen and senators. Spends time in New York meeting H. L. Mencken, Marianne Moore. Receives honorary degree from Hamilton College, his alma mater. Returns to Italy in late June and begins friendship with philosopher George Santayana in Venice.

1940 *Cantos LII–LXXI* published by Faber and Faber in London and New Directions in Norfolk, Connecticut, with some lines in Canto LII blacked out because of anti-Semitic statements. Writes scripts critical of the United States for Rome Radio, read in English by others. *A Selection of Poems* (London: Faber and Faber), including two Cantos from *A Draft of XXX Cantos* and one from *The Fifth Decad of Cantos*, published.

1941–1945 Pound begins regular shortwave radio broadcasts for Rome Radio in January 1941, beamed to the United States. Will continue with vituperative broadcasts (120 in all) until the fall of the Fascist government in July 1943. German fortifications in Rapallo force Pound and Dorothy to move in with Olga in Sant' Ambrogio, above the city. Begins to compose Cantos LXXII and LXXIII in Italian, supportive of the Italian war effort. Pound arrested by Italian partisans on May 3, 1945, and, after some initial confusion, sent to U.S. Army prison camp in Pisa; spends three weeks in solitary confinement in an exposed steel cage. After breakdown, transferred to medical tent, where he begins to compose what would be *The Pisan Cantos* (LXXIV–LXXXIV). Flown to Washington on November 17 and arraigned; assessed as mentally unfit to stand trial. Transferred to St. Elizabeths hospital, a federal asylum where he would remain until 1958.

1948 *The Cantos* published (New York: New Directions). All the Cantos completed to date appear, including *The Pisan Cantos,* which are published in a separate volume the same month (July). The Faber and Faber edition would be delayed almost a full year while British editors expurgated sections they feared might cause libel actions.

1949 Awarded the Bollingen Prize for Poetry for *The Pisan Cantos,* published the previous year. Controversy follows and Congress reacts by preventing the Library of Congress from awarding any more literary prizes.

1951–1958 Translations, anthologies and more Cantos prepared. Publication of *Literary Essays,* edited by T. S. Eliot, in 1954. *Section: Rock-Drill: 85–95 de los cantares* appears in 1955, published first in Italy by Vanni Scheiwiller's All'Insegna del Pesce d'Oro. On May 7, 1958, the seventy-two-year-old Pound released from St. Elizabeths; visits William Carlos Williams before returning to Italy on July 9 with Dorothy and a young admirer, Marcella Spann.

1959 *Thrones: 96–100 de los cantares,* written at St. Elizabeths, published by All'Insegna del Pesce d'Oro in Milan. Composes some of the Cantos to appear later in *Drafts and Fragments.*

1962 Wins Harriet Monroe Memorial Prize offered by *Poetry* magazine. Acknowledging the award, he replies that he is content to be remembered as a "minor satirist who contributed something to a refinement of language."

1964 Anthology *Confucius to Cummings* appears, edited with Marcella Spann.

1967 Publication of *Selected Cantos* and *Pound/Joyce* letters. Pirated edition of *Cantos 110–116* appears in New York.

1969 *Drafts and Fragments of Cantos CX–CXVII* published by New Directions. Visits United States for exhibit of *The Waste Land* manuscript at the New York Public Library. Returns to Hamilton College, where James Laughlin is awarded an honorary degree.

1972 Dies on November 1. Buried in Venice on the island cemetery of San Michele.

POEMS

POEMS

TO THE
RAPHAELITE LATINISTS

By Weston Llewmys

YE fellowship that sing the woods and spring,
   Poets of joy that sing the day's delight,
   Poets of youth that 'neath the aisles of night
Your flowers and sighs against the lintels fling;

Who rose and myrtle in your garlands bring
   To marble altars, though their gods took flight
   Long ere your dream-shot eyes drank summer light
And wine of old time myth and vintaging,

Take of our praise one cup, though thin the wine
   That Bacchus may not bless nor Pan outpour:
Though reed pipe and the lyre be names upon
The wind, and moon-lit dreams be quite out-gone
   From ways we tread, one cup to names ye bore,
One wreath from ashes of your songs we twine!

CINO

Italian Campagna 1309, the open road

Bah! I have sung women in three cities,
But it is all the same;
And I will sing of the sun.

Lips, words, and you snare them,
Dreams, words, and they are as jewels,
Strange spells of old deity,
Ravens, nights, allurement:
And they are not;
Having become the souls of song.

Eyes, dreams, lips, and the night goes.
Being upon the road once more,
They are not.
Forgetful in their towers of our tuneing
Once for Wind-runeing[1]
They dream us-toward and
Sighing, say, "Would Cino,
Passionate Cino, of the wrinkling eyes,
Gay Cino, of quick laughter,
Cino, of the dare, the jibe,
Frail Cino, strongest of his tribe

That tramp old ways beneath the sun-light,
Would Cino of the Luth[2] were here!"

Once, twice, a year—
Vaguely thus word they:
   "Cino?" "Oh, eh, Cino Polnesi
   The singer is't you mean?"
   "Ah yes, passed once our way,
   A saucy fellow, but . . .
   (Oh they are all one these vagabonds),
   Peste![3] 'tis his own songs?
   Or some other's that he sings?
   But *you*, My Lord, how with your city?"

But you "My Lord," God's pity!
And all I knew were out, My Lord, you
Were Lack-land Cino, e'en as I am,
O Sinistro.[4]

I have sung women in three cities.
But it is all one.
I will sing of the sun.
. . . eh? . . . they mostly had grey eyes,
But it is all one, I will sing of the sun.

   " 'Pollo Phoibee,[5] old tin pan, you
   Glory to Zeus' aegis-day,[6]
   Shield o' steel-blue, th' heaven o'er us
   Hath for boss[7] thy lustre gay!

   'Pollo Phoibee, to our way-fare
   Make thy laugh our wander-lied;
   Bid thy 'fulgence bear away care.
   Cloud and rain-tears pass they fleet!

   Seeking e'er the new-laid rast-way[8]
   To the gardens of the sun.

I have sung women in three cities
But it is all one.

I will sing of the white birds
In the blue waters of heaven,
The clouds that are spray to its sea.

NA AUDIART

Que be-m vols mal[1]

Note: Anyone who has read anything of the troubadours knows well the tale of Bertran of Born and My Lady Maent of Montagnac, and knows also the song he made when she would none of him, the song wherein he, seeking to find or make her equal, begs of each preëminent lady of Langue d'Oc some trait or some fair semblance: thus of Cembelins her "esgart amoros" to wit, her love-lit glance, of Aelis her speech free-running, of the Vicomtess of Chalais her throat and her two hands, at Roacoart of Anhes her hair golden as Iseult's; and even in this fashion of Lady Audiart "although she would that ill come unto him" he sought and praised the lineaments of the torse. And all this to make "Una dompna soiseubuda" a borrowed lady or as the Italians translated it "Una donna ideale."[2]

Though thou well dost wish me ill
                    Audiart, Audiart,
Where thy bodice laces start
As ivy fingers clutching through
Its crevices,
                    Audiart, Audiart,
Stately, tall and lovely tender
Who shall render
                    Audiart, Audiart,
Praises meet unto thy fashion?
Here a word kiss!
                    Pass I on

Unto Lady "Miels-de-Ben,"[3]
Having praised thy girdle's scope
How the stays ply back from it;
I breathe no hope
That thou shouldst . . .
                                   Nay no whit
Bespeak thyself for anything.
Just a word in thy praise, girl,
Just for the swirl
Thy satins make upon the stair,
'Cause never a flaw was there
Where thy torse and limbs are met
Though thou hate me, read it set
In rose and gold.[4]
Or when the minstrel, tale half told,
Shall burst to lilting at the phrase
                         "Audiart, Audiart" . . .
Bertrans, master of his lays,[5]
Bertrans of Aultaforte[6] thy praise
Sets forth, and though thou hate me well,
Yea though thou wish me ill,
                         Audiart, Audiart.
Thy loveliness is here writ till,
                         Audiart,
Oh, till thou come again.*
And being bent and wrinkled, in a form
That hath no perfect limning,[7] when the warm
Youth dew is cold
Upon thy hands, and thy old soul
Scorning a new, wry'd[8] casement,
Churlish at seemed misplacement,
Finds the earth as bitter
As now seems it sweet,
Being so young and fair
As then only in dreams,
Being then young and wry'd,

                    *Reincarnate.

Broken of ancient pride,
Thou shalt then soften,
Knowing, I know not how,
Thou wert once she

                              Audiart, Audiart
For whose fairness one forgave
                              Audiart,
Audiart
          Que be-m vols mal.

VILLONAUD FOR
THIS YULE

Towards the Noel that morte saison
(*Christ make the shepherds' homage dear!*)
Then when the grey wolves everychone
Drink of the winds their chill small-beer
And lap o' the snows food's gueredon[1]
Then makyth my heart his yule-tide cheer
(Skoal! with the dregs if the clear be gone!)
Wining the ghosts of yester-year.

Ask ye what ghosts I dream upon?
(*What of the magians' scented gear?*)
The ghosts of dead loves everyone
That make the stark winds reek with fear
Lest love return with the foison[2] sun
And slay the memories that me cheer
(Such as I drink to mine fashion)
Wining the ghosts of yester-year.

Where are the joys my heart had won?
(*Saturn and Mars to Zeus drawn near!*)*

Signum Nativitatis.

Where are the lips mine lay upon,
Aye! where are the glances feat[3] and clear
That bade my heart his valour don?
I skoal to the eyes as grey-blown mere
(Who knows whose was that paragon?)
Wining the ghosts of yester-year.

Prince: ask me not what I have done
Nor what God hath that can me cheer
But ye ask first where the winds are gone
Wining the ghosts of yester-year.

HISTRION

No man hath dared to write this thing as yet,
And yet I know, how that the souls of all men great
At times pass through us,
And we are melted into them, and are not
Save reflexions of their souls.
Thus am I Dante for a space and am
One François Villon, ballad-lord and thief
Or am such holy ones I may not write,
Lest blasphemy be writ against my name;
This for an instant and the flame is gone.

'Tis as in midmost us there glows a sphere
Translucent, molten gold, that is the "I"
And into this some form projects itself:
Christus, or John, or eke the Florentine;[1]
And as the clear space is not if a form's
Imposed thereon,
So cease we from all being for the time,
And these, the Masters of the Soul, live on.

IN DURANCE

(1907)

I am homesick after mine own kind,
Oh I know that there are folk about me, friendly faces,
But I am homesick after mine own kind.

"These sell our pictures"! Oh well,
They reach me not, touch me some edge or that,
But reach me not and all my life's become
One flame, that reaches not beyond
My heart's own hearth,
Or hides among the ashes there for thee.
"Thee"? Oh, "Thee" is who cometh first
Out of mine own soul-kin,
For I am homesick after mine own kind
And ordinary people touch me not.
                                    And I am homesick
After mine own kind that know, and feel
And have some breath for beauty and the arts.

Aye, I am wistful for my kin of the spirit
And have none about me save in the shadows
When come *they*, surging of power, "DAEMON,"
"Quasi KALOUN." S.T. says Beauty is most that, a
     "calling to the soul."

Well then, so call they, the swirlers out of the mist of my soul,
They that come mewards, bearing old magic.

But for all that, I am homesick after mine own kind
And would meet kindred even as I am,
Flesh-shrouded bearing the secret.
"All they that with strange sadness"
Have the earth in mockery, and are kind to all,
My fellows, aye I know the glory
Of th' unbounded ones, but ye, that hide
As I hide most the while
And burst forth to the windows only whiles or whiles
For love, or hope, or beauty or for power,
Then smoulder, with the lids half closed
And are untouched by echoes of the world.

Oh ye, my fellows: with the seas between us some be,
Purple and sapphire for the silver shafts
Of sun and spray all shattered at the bows;
And some the hills hold off,
The little hills to east of us, though here we
Have damp and plain to be our shutting in.

And yet my soul sings "Up!" and we are one.
Yea thou, and Thou, and THOU, and all my kin
To whom my breast and arms are ever warm,
For that I love ye as the wind the trees
That holds their blossoms and their leaves in cure
And calls the utmost singing from the boughs
That 'thout him, save the aspen, were as dumb
Still shade, and bade no whisper speak the birds of how
"Beyond, beyond, beyond, there lies . . ."

REVOLT

Against the Crepuscular Spirit in Modern Poetry

I would shake off the lethargy of this our time,
   and give
For shadows—shapes of power
For dreams—men.

"It is better to dream than do"?
                        Aye! and, No!

Aye! if we dream great deeds, strong men,
Hearts hot, thoughts mighty.

No! if we dream pale flowers,
Slow-moving pageantry of hours that languidly
Drop as o'er-ripened fruit from sallow trees.
If so we live and die not life but dreams,
Great God, grant life in dreams,
Not dalliance, but life!

Let us be men that dream,
Not cowards, dabblers, waiters
For dead Time to reawaken and grant balm
For ills unnamed.

Great God, if we be damn'd to be not men but only dreams,
Then let us be such dreams the world shall tremble at
And know we be its rulers though but dreams!
Then let us be such shadows as the world shall tremble at
And know we be its masters though but shadow!

Great God, if men are grown but pale sick phantoms
That must live only in these mists and tempered lights
And tremble for dim hours that knock o'er loud
Or tread too violent in passing them;

Great God, if these thy sons are grown such thin ephemera,
I bid thee grapple chaos and beget
Some new titanic spawn to pile the hills and stir
This earth again.

SESTINA: ALTAFORTE

LOQUITUR[1]: *En*[2] Bertrans de Born.

Dante[3] Alighieri put this man in hell for that he was a
stirrer up of strife.
Eccovi![4]
Judge ye!
Have I dug him up again?

The scene is at his castle, Altaforte. "Papiols" is his jongleur.[5]
"The Leopard," the *device* of Richard Cœur de Lion.

I

Damn it all! all this our South stinks peace.
You whoreson dog, Papiols, come! Let's to music!
I have no life save when the swords clash.
But ah! when I see the standards gold, vair, purple, opposing
And the broad fields beneath them turn crimson,
Then howl I my heart nigh mad with rejoicing.

II

In hot summer have I great rejoicing
When the tempests kill the earth's foul peace,
And the lightnings from black heav'n flash crimson,
And the fierce thunders roar me their music
And the winds shriek through the clouds mad, opposing,
And through all the riven skies God's swords clash.

III

Hell grant soon we hear again the swords clash!
And the shrill neighs of destriers[6] in battle rejoicing,

Spiked breast to spiked breast opposing!
Better one hour's stour than a year's peace
With fat boards, bawds, wine and frail music!
Bah! there's no wine like the blood's crimson!

IV

And I love to see the sun rise blood-crimson.
And I watch his spears through the dark clash
And it fills all my heart with rejoicing
And pries wide my mouth with fast music
When I see him so scorn and defy peace,
His lone might 'gainst all darkness opposing.

V

The man who fears war and squats opposing
My words for stour, hath no blood of crimson
But is fit only to rot in womanish peace
Far from where worth's won and the swords clash
For the death of such sluts I go rejoicing;
Yea, I fill all the air with my music.

VI

Papiols, Papiols, to the music!
There's no sound like to swords swords opposing,
No cry like the battle's rejoicing
When our elbows and swords drip the crimson
And our charges 'gainst "The Leopard's" rush clash.
May God damn for ever all who cry "Peace!"

VII

And let the music of the swords make them crimson!
Hell grant soon we hear again the swords clash!
Hell blot black for alway the thought "Peace"!

PIERE VIDAL OLD

It is of Piere Vidal, the fool *par excellence* of all Provence, of whom the tale tells how he ran mad, as a wolf, because of his love for Loba of Penautier, and how men hunted him with dogs through the mountains of Cabaret and brought him for dead to the dwelling of this Loba (she-wolf) of Penautier, and how she and her Lord had him healed and made welcome, and he stayed some time at that court. He speaks:

When I but think upon the great dead days
And turn my mind upon that splendid madness,
Lo! I do curse my strength
And blame the sun his gladness;
For that the one is dead
And the red sun mocks my sadness.

Behold me, Vidal, that was fool of fools!
Swift as the king wolf was I and as strong
When tall stags fled me through the alder brakes,
And every jongleur knew me in his song,
And the hounds fled and the deer fled
And none fled over-long.

Even the grey pack knew me and knew fear.
God! how the swiftest hind's blood spurted hot
Over the sharpened teeth and purpling lips!
Hot was that hind's blood yet it scorched me not
As did first scorn, then lips of the Penautier!
Aye ye are fools, if ye think time can blot

From Piere Vidal's remembrance that blue night.
God! but the purple of the sky was deep!

Clear, deep, translucent, so the stars me seemed
Set deep in crystal; and because my sleep
—Rare visitor—came not,—the Saints I guerdon[1]
For that restlessness—Piere set to keep

One more fool's vigil with the hollyhocks.
Swift came the Loba, as a branch that's caught,
Torn, green and silent in the swollen Rhone,
Green was her mantle, close, and wrought
Of some thin silk stuff that's scarce stuff at all,
But like a mist wherethrough her white form fought,

And conquered! Ah God! conquered!
Silent my mate came as the night was still.
Speech? Words? Faugh! Who talks of words and love?!
Hot is such love and silent,
Silent as fate is, and as strong until
It faints in taking and in giving all.

Stark, keen, triumphant, till it plays at death.
God! she was white then, splendid as some tomb
High wrought of marble, and the panting breath
Ceased utterly. Well, then I waited, drew,
Half-sheathed, then naked from its saffron sheath
Drew full this dagger that doth tremble here.

Just then she woke and mocked the less keen blade.
Ah God, the Loba! and my only mate!
Was there such flesh made ever and unmade!
God curse the years that turn such women grey!
Behold here Vidal, that was hunted, flayed,
Shamed and yet bowed not and that won at last.

And yet I curse the sun for his red gladness,
I that have known strath, garth, brake, dale,
And every run-away of the wood through that great madness,
Behold me shrivelled as an old oak's trunk
And made men's mock'ry in my rotten sadness!

No man hath heard the glory of my days:
No man hath dared and won his dare as I:
One night, one body and one welding flame!
What do ye own, ye niggards! that can buy
Such glory of the earth? Or who will win
Such battle-guerdon with his "prowesse high"?

O Age gone lax! O stunted followers,
That mask at passions and desire desires,
Behold me shrivelled, and your mock of mocks;
And yet I mock you by the mighty fires
That burnt me to this ash.
. . . .
Ah! Cabaret! Ah Cabaret, thy hills again!
. . . .
Take your hands off me! . . .   [*Sniffing the air.*
                        Ha! this scent is hot!

BALLAD OF THE
GOODLY FERE

Simon Zelotes[1] speaketh it somewhile after the Crucifixion
Fere = Mate, Companion.

Ha' we lost the goodliest fere o' all
For the priests and the gallows tree?
Aye lover he was of brawny men,
O' ships and the open sea.

When they came wi' a host to take Our Man
His smile was good to see,
"First let these go!" quo' our Goodly Fere,
"Or I'll see ye damned," says he.

Aye he sent us out through the crossed high spears
And the scorn of his laugh rang free,
"Why took ye not me when I walked about
Alone in the town?" says he.

Oh we drunk his "Hale" in the good red wine
When we last made company,
No capon priest was the Goodly Fere
But a man o' men was he.

I ha' seen him drive a hundred men
Wi' a bundle o' cords swung free,

That they took the high and holy house
For their pawn and treasury.

They'll no' get him a' in a book I think
Though they write it cunningly;
No mouse of the scrolls was the Goodly Fere
But aye loved the open sea.

If they think they ha' snared our Goodly Fere
They are fools to the last degree.
"I'll go to the feast," quo' our Goodly Fere,
"Though I go to the gallows tree."

"Ye ha' seen me heal the lame and blind,
And wake the dead," says he,
"Ye shall see one thing to master all:
'Tis how a brave man dies on the tree."

A son of God was the Goodly Fere
That bade us his brothers be.
I ha' seen him cow a thousand men.
I have seen him upon the tree.

He cried no cry when they drave the nails
And the blood gushed hot and free,
The hounds of the crimson sky gave tongue
But never a cry cried he.

I ha' seen him cow a thousand men
On the hills o' Galilee,
They whined as he walked out calm between,
Wi' his eyes like the grey o' the sea.

Like the sea that brooks no voyaging
With the winds unleashed and free,
Like the sea that he cowed at Genseret
Wi' twey words spoke' suddenly.

A master of men was the Goodly Fere,
A mate of the wind and sea,
If they think they ha' slain our Goodly Fere
They are fools eternally.

I ha' seen him eat o' the honey-comb
Sin' they nailed him to the tree.

"BLANDULA, TENULLA, VAGULA"

What hast thou, O my soul, with paradise?
Will we not rather, when our freedom's won,
Get us to some clear place wherein the sun
Lets drift in on us through the olive leaves
A liquid glory? If at Sirmio,[1]
My soul, I meet thee, when this life's outrun,
Will we not find some headland consecrated
By aery apostles of terrene delight,
Will not our cult be founded on the waves,
Clear sapphire, cobalt, cyanine,
On triune[2] azures, the impalpable
Mirrors unstill of the eternal change?

Soul, if She meet us there, will any rumour
Of havens more high and courts desirable
Lure us beyond the cloudy peak of Riva?[3]

UND DRANG

Nay, dwells he in cloudy rumour alone?
Binyon[1]

I

I am worn faint,
The winds of good and evil
Blind me with dust
And burn me with the cold,
There is no comfort being over-man;
Yet are we come more near
The great oblivions and the labouring night,
Inchoate truth and the sepulchral forces.

II

Confusion, clamour, 'mid the many voices
Is there a meaning, a significance?
That life apart from all life gives and takes,
This life, apart from all life's bitter and life's sweet,
Is good.
                    Ye see me and ye say: exceeding sweet
Life's gifts, his youth, his art,
And his too soon acclaim.

I also knew exceeding bitterness,
Saw good things altered and old friends fare forth,
And what I loved in me hath died too soon,
Yea I have seen the "gray above the green";
Gay have I lived in life;
                                        Though life hath lain
Strange hands upon me and hath torn my sides,

Yet I believe.

. . . .

Life is most cruel where she is most wise.

III

The will to live goes from me.
                              I have lain
Dull and out-worn
                      with some strange, subtle sickness.
Who shall say
That love is not the very root of this,
O thou afar?

Yet she was near me,
                    that eternal deep.
O it is passing strange that love
Can blow two ways across one soul.

. . . .

And I was Aengus[2] for a thousand years,
And she, the ever-living, moved with me
And strove amid the waves, and
                          would not go.

IV

ELEGIA
"Far buon tempo e trionfare"

"I have put my days and dreams out of mind"[3]
For all their hurry and their weary fret
Availed me little. But another kind
Of leaf that's fast in some more sombre wind,
Is man on life, and all our tenuous courses
Wind and unwind as vainly.

. . . . . .

I have lived long, and died,

Yea I have been dead, right often,
And have seen one thing:
The sun, while he is high, doth light our wrong
And none can break the darkness with a song.

To-day's the cup. To-morrow is not ours:
Nay, by our strongest bands we bind her not,
Nor all our fears and our anxieties
Turn her one leaf or hold her scimitar.

The deed blots out the thought
And many thoughts, the vision;
And right's a compass with as many poles
As there are points in her circumference,
'Tis vain to seek to steer all courses even,
And all things save sheer right are vain enough.
The blade were vain to grow save toward the sun,
And vain th' attempt to hold her green forever.

All things in season and no thing o'er long!
Love and desire and gain and good forgetting,
Thou canst not stay the wheel, hold none too long!

V

How our modernity,
Nerve-wracked and broken, turns
Against time's way and all the way of things,
Crying with weak and egoistic cries!
                    .   .   .   .   .

All things are given over,
Only the restless will
Surges amid the stars
Seeking new moods of life,
New permutations.
                    .   .   .   .   .

See, and the very sense of what we know

Dodges and hides as in a sombre curtain
Bright threads leap forth, and hide, and leave no pattern.

VI

I thought I had put Love by for a time
And I was glad, for to me his fair face
Is like Pain's face.
                    A little light,
The lowered curtain and the theatre!
And o'er the frail talk of the inter-act
Something that broke the jest! A little light,
The gold, and half the profile!
                                The whole face
Was nothing like you, yet that image cut
Sheer through the moment.

VI*b*

I have gone seeking for you in the twilight,
Here in the flurry of Fifth Avenue,
Here where they pass between their teas and teas.
Is it such madness? though you could not be
Ever in all that crowd, no gown
Of all their subtle sorts could be your gown.

Yet I am fed with faces, is there one
That even in the half-light mindeth me.

VII

THE HOUSE OF SPLENDOUR

'Tis Evanoe's,
A house not made with hands,
But out somewhere beyond the worldly ways

Her gold is spread, above, around, inwoven,
Strange ways and walls are fashioned out of it.

And I have seen my Lady in the sun,
Her hair was spread about, a sheaf of wings,
And red the sunlight was, behind it all.

And I have seen her there within her house,
With six great sapphires hung along the wall,
Low, panel-shaped, a-level with her knees,
And all her robe was woven of pale gold.

There are there many rooms and all of gold,
Of woven walls deep patterned, of email,
Of beaten work; and through the claret stone,
Set to some weaving, comes the aureate light.

Here am I come perforce my love of her,
Behold mine adoration
Maketh me clear, and there are powers in this
Which, played on by the virtues of her soul,
Break down the four-square walls of standing time.

VIII

THE FLAME

'Tis not a game that plays at mates and mating,
Provençe knew;
'Tis not a game of barter, lands and houses,
Provençe knew.
We who are wise beyond your dream of wisdom,
Drink our immortal moments; we "pass through."
We have gone forth beyond your bonds and borders,
Provençe knew;
And all the tales they ever writ of Oisin[4]
Say but this:

That man doth pass the net of days and hours.
Where time is shrivelled down to time's seed corn
We of the Ever-living, in that light
Meet through our veils and whisper, and of love.

O smoke and shadow of a darkling world,
Barters of passion, and that tenderness
That's but a sort of cunning! O my Love,
These, and the rest, and all the rest we knew.

'Tis not a game that plays at mates and mating,
'Tis not a game of barter, lands and houses,
'Tis not "of days and nights" and troubling years,
Of cheeks grown sunken and glad hair gone gray;
There *is* the subtler music, the clear light
Where time burns back about th' eternal embers.
We are not shut from all the thousand heavens:
Lo, there are many gods whom we have seen,
Folk of unearthly fashion, places splendid,
Bulwarks of beryl[5] and of chrysoprase.[6]

Sapphire Benacus,[7] in thy mists and thee
Nature herself's turned metaphysical,
Who can look on that blue and not believe?

Thou hooded opal, thou eternal pearl,
O thou dark secret with a shimmering floor,
Through all thy various mood I know thee mine;

If I have merged my soul, or utterly
Am solved and bound in, through aught here on earth,
There canst thou find me, O thou anxious thou,
Who call'st about my gates for some lost me;
I say my soul flowed back, became translucent.
Search not my lips, O Love, let go my hands,
This thing that moves as man is no more mortal.
If thou hast seen my shade sans character,

If thou hast seen that mirror of all moments,
That glass to all things that o'ershadow it,
Call not that mirror me, for I have slipped
Your grasp, I have eluded.

IX

(HORAE BEATAE INSCRIPTIO)[8]

How will this beauty, when I am far hence,
Sweep back upon me and engulf my mind!

How will these hours, when we twain are gray,
Turned in their sapphire tide, come flooding o'er us!

X

(THE ALTAR)

Let us build here an exquisite friendship,
The flame, the autumn, and the green rose of love
Fought out their strife here, 'tis a place of wonder;
Where these have been, meet 'tis, the ground is holy.

XI

(AU SALON)

Her grave, sweet haughtiness
Pleaseth me, and in like wise
Her quiet ironies.
Others are beautiful, none more, some less.

I suppose, when poetry comes down to facts,
When our souls are returned to the gods
                    and the spheres they belong in,
Here in the every-day where our acts
Rise up and judge us;

I suppose there are a few dozen verities
That no shift of mood can shake from us:
One place where we'd rather have tea
(Thus far hath modernity brought us)
"Tea" (Damn you)
                                    Have tea, damn the Caesars,
Talk of the latest success, give wing to some scandal,
Garble a name we detest, and for prejudice?
Set loose the whole consummate pack
                        to bay like Sir Roger de Coverley's.[9]

This our reward for our works,
                        sic crescit gloria mundi:[10]
Some circle of not more than three
                        that we prefer to play up to,

Some few whom we'd rather please
        than hear the whole aegrum vulgus[11]
Splitting its beery jowl
        a-meaowling our praises.

Some certain peculiar things,
        cari laresque, penates,[12]
Some certain accustomed forms,
        the absolute unimportant.

XII

(AU JARDIN)

O you away high there,
                        you that lean
From amber lattices upon the cobalt night,
I am below amid the pine trees,
Amid the little pine trees, hear me!

"The jester walked in the garden."
                        Did he so?

34 EZRA POUND

Well, there's no use your loving me
That way, Lady;
For I've nothing but songs to give you.
I am set wide upon the world's ways
To say that life is, some way, a gay thing,
But you never string two days upon one wire
But there'll come sorrow of it.

                      And I loved a love once,
Over beyond the moon there,
                  I loved a love once,
And, may be, more times,

But she danced like a pink moth in the shrubbery.

Oh, I know you women from the "other folk,"
And it'll all come right,
O' Sundays.

"The jester walked in the garden."
                      Did he so?

REDONDILLAS, OR SOMETHING OF THAT SORT

I sing the gaudy to-day and cosmopolite civilization
Of my hatred of crudities, of my weariness of banalities,
I sing of the ways that I love, of Beauty and delicate savours.

No man may pass beyond
    the nets of good and evil
For joy's in deepest hell
    and in high heaven,
About the very ports
    are subtle devils.

I would sing of exquisite sights,
    of the murmur of Garda:[1]
I would sing of the amber lights,
    or of how Desenzano[2]
Lies like a topaz chain
    upon the throat of the waters.

I sing of natural forces
    I sing of refinements
I would write of the various moods
    of nuances, of subtleties.

I would sing of the hatred of dullness,
    of the search for sensation.

I would sing the American people,
    God send them some civilization;
I would sing of the nations of Europe,
    God grant them some method of cleansing
The fetid extent of their evils.
    I would sing of my love "To-morrow,"
But Yeats has written an essay,
    Why should I stop to repeat it?
I don't like this hobbledy metre
    but find it easy to write in,
I would sing to the tune of *"Mi Platz"*[3]
    were it not for the trouble of riming,
Besides, not six men believe me
    when I sing in a beautiful measure.

I demonstrate the breadth of my vision.
    I am bored of this talk of the tariff,
I too have heard of T. Roosevelt.
    I have met with the "Common Man,"
I admit that he usually bores me,
    He is usually stupid or smug.
I praise God for a few royal fellows
    like Plarr[4] and Fred Vance and Whiteside,
I grant them fullest indulgence
    each one for his own special queerness.

I believe in some lasting sap
    at work in the trunk of things;
I believe in a love of deeds,
    in a healthy desire for action;
I believe in double-edged thought
    in careless destruction.

I believe in some parts of Nietzsche,[5]
    I prefer to read him in sections;

In my heart of hearts I suspect him
      of being the one modern christian;
Take notice I never have read him
      except in English selections.
I am sick of the toothless decay
      of God's word as they usually preach it;
I am sick of bad blasphemous verse
      that they sell with their carols and hymn tunes.

I would sing of the soft air
      and delight that I have in fine buildings,
Pray that God better my voice
      before you are forced to attend me.
I would turn from superficial things
      for a time, into the quiet
I would draw your minds to learn
      of sorrow in quiet,
To watch for signs and strange portents.
      . . . . . .

Delicate beauty on some sad, dull face
Not very evil, but just damned, through weakness,
Drawn down against hell's lips by some soft sense;
When you shall find such a face
      how far will your thought's lead fathom?
Oh, it's easy enough to say
      'tis this, that and the other,
But when some truth is worn smooth
      how many men really do think it?
We speak to a surfeited age,
      Grant us keen weapons for speaking.

Certain things really do matter:
      Love, and the comfort of friendship.
After we are burnt clear,
      or even deadened with knowledge;
After we have gone the whole gamut,
      exhausted our human emotions,

Still is there something greater,
            some power, some recognition,
Some bond beyond the ordinary bonds
            of passion and sentiment
And the analyzed method of novels,
            some saner and truer course
That pays us for foregoing blindness.

Whenever we dare, the angels crowd about us.
There is no end to the follies
            sprung from the full fount of weakness;
There is great virtue in strength
            even in passive resistance.
God grant us an open mind
            and the poise and balance to use it.
They tell me to "Mirror my age,"
            God pity the age if I do do it,
Perhaps I myself would prefer
            to sing of the dead and the buried:
At times I am wrapped in my dream
            of my mistress "To-morrow"
We ever live in the now
            it is better to live in than sing of.

Yet I sing of the diverse moods
            of effete modern civilization.
I sing of delicate hues
            and variations of pattern;
I sing of risorgimenti,[6]
            of old things found that were hidden,
I sing of the senses developed,
            I reach towards perceptions scarce heeded.
If you ask me to write world prescriptions
            I write so that any can read it:
A little less Paul Verlaine,[7]
            A good sound stave of Spinoza,
A little less of our nerves
            A little more will toward vision.

I sing of the fish and the sauce,
    I sing of the *rôti de dindon*;[8]
I sing of delectable things that
    I scarcely ever can pay for.
I love the subtle accord
    of rimes wound over and over;
I sing of the special case,
    The truth is the individual.

Tamlin[9] is the truest of ballads,
    There is more in heaven and earth
Than the priest and the scientists think of.
    The core in the heart of man
Is tougher than any "system."
    I sing devils, thrones and dominions
At work in the air round about us,
    Of powers ready to enter
And thrust our own being from us.
    I sing of the swift delight
Of the clear thrust and riposte in fencing,
    I sing of the fine overcoming,
I sing of the wide comprehension.
    I toast myself against the glow of life
I had a trace of mind, perhaps some heart
    Nature I loved, in her selected moods,
And art,
    perhaps a little more than need be.

I have no objection to wealth,
    the trouble is the acquisition,
It would be rather a horrible sell
    to work like a dog and not get it.
Arma, virumque cano, qui primus, etcetera, ab oris,[10]
Even this hobbledy-hoy
    is not my own private invention.
We are the heirs of the past,
    it is asinine not to admit it.

O Virgil, from your green elysium
          see how that dactyl stubs his weary toes.

I too have been to the play-house,
          often bored with vapid inventions;
I too have taken delight
          in the maze of the Russian dancers.
I am that terrible thing,
          the product of American culture,
Or rather that product improved
          by considerable care and attention.
I am really quite modern, you know,
          despite my affecting the ancients.
I sing of the pleasure of teas
          when one finds someone brilliant to talk to.
I know this age and its works
          with some sort of moderate intelligence,
It does nothing so novel or strange
          except in the realm of mechanics.
Why should I cough my head off
          with that old gag of "Nascitur ordo"?[11]
(The above is not strictly the truth
          I've just heard of a German named Ehrlich.[12]
Medical science is jolted,
          we'll have to call back Fracastori
To pen a new end for "De Morbo.")[13]
          But setting science aside
To return to me and my status;
          I'm not specifically local,
I'm more or less Europe itself,
          More or less Strauss and De Bussy.
I even admire and am
          Klimt and that horrible Zwintscher.
Shall I write it: *Admiror, sum ergo?*[14]
          Deeds are not always first proof,
Write it thus: By their Gods ye shall know them.
The chief god in hell is convention,
          'got by that sturdy sire Stupidity

Upon pale Fear, in some most proper way.
   Where people worship a sham
There is hardly room for a devil.
   You'll find some such thing in Hen. Ibsen.
I'm sorry Dame Fashion has left him
  and prefers to imbibe him diluted
In . . . Why name our whole tribe of playwrights?
   Mistrust the good of an age
That swallows a whole code of ethics.
   Schopenhauer's[15] a gloomy decadent
Somewhat chewed by the worms of his wisdom.
   Our mud was excreted of mind,
That mudless the mind should be clearer.
   Behold how I chivvy Lucretius,[16]
Behold how I dabble in cosmos.
   Behold how I copy my age,
Dismissing great men with a quibble.
   I know not much save myself,
I know myself pretty completely.
   I prefer most white wine to red,
Bar only some lordly Burgundy.
   We all of us make mistakes,
Give us reasonable time to retrieve them.
   The future will probably meet
With people who know more than we do.
   There's no particular end
To this sort of a statement of being,
   no formal envoi or tornata[17]
But perhaps a sort of a bow.
   The musician returns to the dominant.
Behold then the the that I am;
   Behold me sententious, *dégagé,*
Behold me my saeculum in parvo,[18]
   Bergson's objective fact,
London's last foible in poets.
   I love all delicate sounds,
The purple fragrance of incense;
   I love the flaked fire of sunlight

Where it glints like red rain on the water;
            I love the quaint patterns inwoven
In Mozart, Steibelt,[19] Scarlatti,
            I love their quavers and closes,
The passionate moods of singing.

TO WHISTLER,
AMERICAN

On the loan exhibit of his paintings
at the Tate Gallery.

You also, our first great,
Had tried all ways;
Tested and pried and worked in many fashions,
And this much gives me heart to play the game.

Here is a part that's slight, and part gone wrong,
And much of little moment, and some few
Perfect as Dürer!

"In the Studio" and these two portraits,* if I had my choice!
And then these sketches in the mood of Greece?

You had your searches, your uncertainties,
And this is good to know—for us, I mean,
Who bear the brunt of our America
And try to wrench her impulse into art.

You were not always sure, not always set
To hiding night or tuning "symphonies";

*"Brown and Gold—de Race."
"Grenat et Or—Le Petit Cardinal."

Had not one style from birth, but tried and pried
And stretched and tampered with the media.

You and Abe Lincoln from that mass of dolts
Show us there's chance at least of winning through.

PORTRAIT D'UNE FEMME

Your mind and you are our Sargasso Sea,[1]
London has swept about you this score years
And bright ships left you this or that in fee:
Ideas, old gossip, oddments of all things,
Strange spars of knowledge and dimmed wares of price.
Great minds have sought you—lacking someone else.
You have been second always. Tragical?
No. You preferred it to the usual thing:
One dull man, dulling and uxorious,
One average mind—with one thought less, each year.
Oh, you are patient, I have seen you sit
Hours, where something might have floated up.
And now you pay one. Yes, you richly pay.
You are a person of some interest, one comes to you
And takes strange gain away:
Trophies fished up; some curious suggestion;
Fact that leads nowhere; and a tale or two,
Pregnant with mandrakes, or with something else
That might prove useful and yet never proves,
That never fits a corner or shows use,
Or finds its hour upon the loom of days:
The tarnished, gaudy, wonderful old work;

Idols and ambergris and rare inlays,
These are your riches, your great store; and yet
For all this sea-hoard of deciduous things,
Strange woods half sodden, and new brighter stuff:
In the slow float of differing light and deep,
No! there is nothing! In the whole and all,
Nothing that's quite your own.
                         Yet this is you.

N.Y.

My City, my beloved, my white! Ah, slender,
Listen! Listen to me, and I will breathe into thee a soul.
Delicately upon the reed, attend me!

Now do I know that I am mad,
For here are a million people surly with traffic;
This is no maid.
Neither could I play upon any reed if I had one.

My City, my beloved,
Thou art a maid with no breasts,
Thou art slender as a silver reed.
Listen to me, attend me!
And I will breathe into thee a soul,
And thou shalt live for ever.

THE SEAFARER

From the Anglo-Saxon

May I for my own self song's truth reckon,
Journey's jargon, how I in harsh days
Hardship endured oft.
Bitter breast-cares have I abided,
Known on my keel many a care's hold,
And dire sea-surge, and there I oft spent
Narrow nightwatch nigh the ship's head
While she tossed close to cliffs. Coldly afflicted,
My feet were by frost benumbed.
Chill its chains are; chafing sighs
Hew my heart round and hunger begot
Mere-weary mood. Lest man know not
That he on dry land loveliest liveth,
List how I, care-wretched, on ice-cold sea,
Weathered the winter, wretched outcast
Deprived of my kinsmen;
Hung with hard ice-flakes, where hail-scur flew,
There I heard naught save the harsh sea
And ice-cold wave, at whiles the swan cries,
Did for my games the gannet's clamour,
Sea-fowls' loudness was for me laughter,
The mews' singing all my mead-drink.

Storms, on the stone-cliffs beaten, fell on the stern
In icy feathers; full oft the eagle screamed
With spray on his pinion.
                            Not any protector
May make merry man faring needy.
This he little believes, who aye in winsome life
Abides 'mid burghers some heavy business,
Wealthy and wine-flushed, how I weary oft
Must bide above brine.
Neareth nightshade, snoweth from north,
Frost froze the land, hail fell on earth then,
Corn of the coldest. Nathless there knocketh now
The heart's thought that I on high streams
The salt-wavy tumult traverse alone.
Moaneth alway my mind's lust
That I fare forth, that I afar hence
Seek out a foreign fastness.
For this there's no mood-lofty man over earth's midst,
Not though he be given his good, but will have in his youth
    greed;
Nor his deed to the daring, nor his king to the faithful
But shall have his sorrow for sea-fare
Whatever his lord will.
He hath not heart for harping, nor in ring-having
Nor winsomeness to wife, nor world's delight
Nor any whit else save the wave's slash,
Yet longing comes upon him to fare forth on the water.
Bosque taketh blossom, cometh beauty of berries,
Fields to fairness, land fares brisker,
All this admonisheth man eager of mood,
The heart turns to travel so that he then thinks
On flood-ways to be far departing.
Cuckoo calleth with gloomy crying,
He singeth summerward, bodeth sorrow,
The bitter heart's blood. Burgher knows not—
He the prosperous man—what some perform
Where wandering them widest draweth.

So that but now my heart burst from my breastlock,
My mood 'mid the mere-flood,
Over the whale's acre, would wander wide.
On earth's shelter cometh oft to me,
Eager and ready, the crying lone-flyer,
Whets for the whale-path the heart irresistibly,
O'er tracks of ocean; seeing that anyhow
My lord deems to me this dead life
On loan and on land, I believe not
That any earth-weal eternal standeth
Save there be somewhat calamitous
That, ere a man's tide go, turn it to twain.
Disease or oldness or sword-hate
Beats out the breath from doom-gripped body.
And for this, every earl whatever, for those speaking after—
Laud of the living, boasteth some last word,
That he will work ere he pass onward,
Frame on the fair earth 'gainst foes his malice,
Daring ado, . . .
So that all men shall honour him after
And his laud beyond them remain 'mid the English,
Aye, for ever, a lasting life's-blast,
Delight 'mid the doughty.
                                  Days little durable,
And all arrogance of earthen riches,
There come now no kings nor Cæsars
Nor gold-giving lords like those gone.
Howe'er in mirth most magnified,
Whoe'er lived in life most lordliest,
Drear all this excellence, delights undurable!
Waneth the watch, but the world holdeth.
Tomb hideth trouble. The blade is layed low.
Earthly glory ageth and seareth.
No man at all going the earth's gait,
But age fares against him, his face paleth,
Grey-haired he groaneth, knows gone companions,
Lordly men, are to earth o'ergiven,
Nor may he then the flesh-cover, whose life ceaseth,

Nor eat the sweet nor feel the sorry,
Nor stir hand nor think in mid heart,
And though he strew the grave with gold,
His born brothers, their buried bodies
Be an unlikely treasure hoard.

THE RETURN

See, they return; ah, see the tentative
   Movements, and the slow feet,
   The trouble in the pace and the uncertain
   Wavering!

See, they return, one, and by one,
With fear, as half-awakened;
As if the snow should hesitate
And murmur in the wind,
                  and half turn back;
These were the "Wing'd-with-Awe,"
                  Inviolable.

Gods of the wingèd shoe!
With them the silver hounds,
                  sniffing the trace of air!

Haie! Haie!
      These were the swift to harry;
These the keen-scented;
These were the souls of blood.

Slow on the leash,
                  pallid the leash-men!

FRATRES MINORES

With minds still hovering above their testicles
Certain poets here and in France
Still sigh over established and natural fact
Long since fully discussed by Ovid.
They howl. They complain in delicate and exhausted metres
That the twitching of three abdominal nerves
Is incapable of producing a lasting Nirvana.

THE COMPLETE POETICAL WORKS OF T. E. HULME

First published at the end of *Ripostes* 1912

Prefatory Note: In publishing his *Complete Poetical Works* at thirty,* Mr Hulme has set an enviable example to many of his contemporaries who have had less to say.

They are reprinted here for good fellowship; for good custom, a custom out of Tuscany and of Provence; and thirdly, for convenience, seeing their smallness of bulk; and for good memory, seeing that they recall certain evenings and meetings of two years gone, dull enough at the time, but rather pleasant to look back upon.

As for the "School of Images," which may or may not have existed, its principles were not so interesting as those of the "inherent dynamists" or of *Les Unanimistes,* yet they were probably sounder than those of a certain French school which attempted to dispense with verbs altogether; or of the Impressionists who brought forth:

"Pink pigs blossoming upon the hillside";

or of the Post-Impressionists who beseech their ladies to let down slate-blue hair over their raspberry-coloured flanks.

Ardoise rimed richly—ah, richly and rarely rimed!— with *framboise.*

As for the future, *Les Imagistes,* the descendants of the forgotten school of 1909, have that in their keeping.

*Mr Pound has grossly exaggerated my age.—T.E.H.

I refrain from publishing my proposed *Historical Memoir* of their forerunners, because Mr Hulme has threatened to print the original propaganda.

E. P.

AUTUMN

A touch of cold in the Autumn night—
I walked abroad,
And saw the ruddy moon lean over a hedge
Like a red-faced farmer.
I did not stop to speak, but nodded,
And round about were the wistful stars
With white faces like town children.

MANA ABODA

Beauty is the marking-time, the stationary vibration, the feigned ecstasy of an arrested impulse unable to reach its natural end.

Mana Aboda, whose bent form
The sky in archèd circle is,
Seems ever for an unknown grief to mourn.
Yet on a day I heard her cry:
"I weary of the roses and the singing poets—
Josephs all, not tall enough to try."

ABOVE THE DOCK

Above the quiet dock in mid night,
Tangled in the tall mast's corded height,
Hangs the moon. What seemed so far away
Is but a child's balloon, forgotten after play.

THE EMBANKMENT

(The fantasia of a fallen gentleman on a cold, bitter night.)

Once, in finesse of fiddles found I ecstasy,
In the flash of gold heels on the hard pavement.
Now see I
That warmth's the very stuff of poesy.
Oh, God, make small
The old star-eaten blanket of the sky,
That I may fold it round me and in comfort lie.

CONVERSION

Lighthearted I walked into the valley wood
In the time of hyacinths,
Till beauty like a scented cloth
Cast over, stifled me. I was bound
Motionless and faint of breath
By loveliness that is her own eunuch.

Now pass I to the final river
Ignominiously, in a sack, without sound,
As any peeping Turk to the Bosphorus.

SALUTATION THE THIRD

Let us deride the smugness of "The Times":
GUFFAW!
        So much for the gagged reviewers,
It will pay them when the worms are wriggling in their vitals;
These are they who objected to newness,
Here are their tomb-stones.
        They supported the gag and the ring:
A little BLACK BOX contains them.
        So shall you be also,
You slut-bellied obstructionist,
You sworn foe to free speech and good letters,
You fungus, you continuous gangrene.

Come, let us on with the new deal,
        Let us be done with pandars and jobbery,
Let us spit upon those who pat the big-bellies for profit,
Let us go out in the air a bit.

Or perhaps I *will* die at thirty?
Perhaps you will have the pleasure of defiling my pauper's
      grave;
I wish you joy, I proffer you all my assistance.

It has been your habit for long
          to do away with good writers,
You either drive them mad, or else you blink at their suicides,
Or else you condone their drugs,
          and talk of insanity and genius,
But I will not go mad to please you,
          I will not flatter you with an early death,
Oh, no, I will stick it out,
          Feel your hates wriggling about my feet
As a pleasant tickle,
          to be observed with derision,
Though many move with suspicion,
          Afraid to say that they hate you;
The taste of my boot?
          Here is the taste of my boot,
Caress it,
          lick off the blacking.

SONG OF THE
BOWMEN OF SHU

Here we are, picking the first fern-shoots[1]
And saying: When shall we get back to our country?
Here we are because we have the Ken-nin[2] for our foemen,
We have no comfort because of these Mongols.
We grub the soft fern-shoots,
When anyone says "Return," the others are full of sorrow.[3]
Sorrowful minds, sorrow is strong, we are hungry and thirsty.
Our defence is not yet made sure, no one can let his friend
     return.
We grub the old fern-stalks.
We say: Will we be let to go back in October?
There is no ease in royal affairs, we have no comfort.
Our sorrow is bitter, but we would not return to our country.
What flower has come into blossom?
Whose chariot? The General's.
Horses, his horses even, are tired. They were strong.
We have no rest, three battles a month.
By heaven, his horses are tired.
The generals are on them, the soldiers are by them.
The horses are well trained, the generals have ivory arrows and
     quivers ornamented with fish-skin.
The enemy is swift, we must be careful.

When we set out, the willows were drooping with spring,
We come back in the snow,
We go slowly, we are hungry and thirsty,
Our mind is full of sorrow, who will know of our grief?

By Bunno,[4] *reputedly 1100 B.C.*

THE RIVER SONG

This boat is of shato-wood,[1] and its gunwales are cut magnolia,
Musicians with jewelled flutes and with pipes of gold
Fill full the sides in rows, and our wine
Is rich for a thousand cups.
We carry singing girls, drift with the drifting water,
Yet Sennin[2] needs
A yellow stork for a charger, and all our seamen
Would follow the white gulls or ride them.
Kutsu's[3] prose song
Hangs with the sun and moon.

King So's[4] terraced palace
             is now but barren hill,
But I draw pen on this barge
Causing the five peaks to tremble,
And I have joy in these words
             like the joy of blue islands.
(If glory could last forever
Then the waters of Han[5] would flow northward.)
            • • •

And I have moped[6] in the Emperor's garden, awaiting an
    order-to-write!
I looked at the dragon-pond, with its willow-coloured water

Just reflecting the sky's tinge,
And heard the five-score nightingales aimlessly singing.

The eastern wind brings the green colour into the island
    grasses at Yei-shu,
The purple house and the crimson are full of Spring softness.
South of the pond the willow-tips are half-blue and bluer,
Their cords tangle in mist, against the brocade-like palace.
Vine-strings a hundred feet long hang down from carved
    railings,
And high over the willows, the fine birds sing to each other,
    and listen,
Crying—"Kwan, Kuan,"[7] for the early wind, and the feel of it.
The wind bundles itself into a bluish cloud and wanders off.
Over a thousand gates, over a thousand doors are the sounds of
    spring singing,
And the Emperor is at Ko.[8]
Five clouds hang aloft, bright on the purple sky,
The imperial guards come forth from the golden house with
    their armour a-gleaming.
The Emperor in his jewelled car goes out to inspect his flowers,
He goes out to Hori, to look at the wing-flapping storks,
He returns by way of Sei rock, to hear the new nightingales,
For the gardens at Jo-run[9] are full of new nightingales,
Their sound is mixed in this flute,
Their voice is in the twelve pipes here.

By Rihaku, 8th century A.D.

THE RIVER-MERCHANT'S
WIFE: A LETTER

While my hair was still cut straight across my forehead
I played about the front gate, pulling flowers.
You came by on bamboo stilts, playing horse,
You walked about my seat, playing with blue plums.
And we went on living in the village of Chokan:
Two small people, without dislike or suspicion.

At fourteen I married My Lord you.
I never laughed, being bashful.
Lowering my head, I looked at the wall.
Called to, a thousand times, I never looked back.

At fifteen I stopped scowling,
I desired my dust to be mingled with yours
Forever and forever and forever.
Why should I climb the look out?

At sixteen you departed,
You went into far Ku-to-yen,[1] by the river of swirling eddies,
And you have been gone five months.
The monkeys make sorrowful noise overhead.
You dragged your feet when you went out.
By the gate now, the moss is grown, the different mosses,

Too deep to clear them away!
The leaves fall early this autumn, in wind.
The paired butterflies are already yellow with August
Over the grass in the West garden;
They hurt me. I grow older.
If you are coming down through the narrows of the river
    Kiang,[2]
Please let me know beforehand,
And I will come out to meet you
                As far as Cho-fu-Sa.[3]

By Rihaku

EXILE'S LETTER

To So-Kin of Rakuyo, ancient friend, Chancellor of Gen.
Now I remember that you built me a special tavern
By the south side of the bridge at Ten-Shin.
With yellow gold and white jewels, we paid for songs and
　　　　laughter
And we were drunk for month on month, forgetting the kings
　　　　and princes.
Intelligent men came drifting in from the sea and from the
　　　　west border,
And with them, and with you especially
There was nothing at cross purpose,
And they made nothing of sea-crossing or of mountain-
　　　　crossing,
If only they could be of that fellowship,
And we all spoke out our hearts and minds, and without
　　　　regret.
And then I was sent off to South Wei,
　　　　　　smothered in laurel groves,
And you to the north of Raku-hoku,
Till we had nothing but thoughts and memories in common.
And then, when separation had come to its worst,
We met, and travelled in Sen-Go,

Through all the thirty-six folds of the turning and twisting
     waters,
Into a valley of the thousand bright flowers,
That was the first valley;
And into ten thousand valleys full of voices and pine-winds.
And with silver harness and reins of gold,
Out came the East of Kan foreman and his company.
And there came also the "True man" of Shi-yo to meet me,
Playing on a jewelled mouth-organ.
In the storied houses of San-Ko they gave us more Sennin music,
Many instruments, like the sound of young phœnix broods.
The foreman of Kan Chu, drunk, danced
                    because his long sleeves wouldn't keep still
With that music playing,
And I, wrapped in brocade, went to sleep with my head on his
     lap,
And my spirit so high it was all over the heavens,
And before the end of the day we were scattered like stars, or
     rain.
I had to be off to So, far away over the waters,
You back to your river-bridge.

And your father, who was brave as a leopard,
Was governor in Hei Shu, and put down the barbarian rabble.
And one May he had you send for me,
                    despite the long distance.
And what with broken wheels and so on, I won't say it wasn't
     hard going,
Over roads twisted like sheep's guts.
And I was still going, late in the year,
                    in the cutting wind from the North,
And thinking how little you cared for the cost,
                    and you caring enough to pay it.
And what a reception:
Red jade cups, food well set on a blue jewelled table,
And I was drunk, and had no thought of returning.
And you would walk out with me to the western corner of the
     castle,

To the dynastic temple, with water about it clear as blue jade,
With boats floating, and the sound of mouth-organs and drums,
With ripples like dragon-scales, going grass green on the water,
Pleasure lasting, with courtezans, going and coming without
    hindrance,
With the willow flakes falling like snow,
And the vermilioned girls getting drunk about sunset,
And the water, a hundred feet deep, reflecting green eyebrows
—Eyebrows painted green are a fine sight in young moonlight,
Gracefully painted—
And the girls singing back at each other,
Dancing in transparent brocade,
And the wind lifting the song, and interrupting it,
Tossing it up under the clouds.
        And all this comes to an end.
        And is not again to be met with.
I went up to the court for examination,
Tried Layu's luck, offered the Choyo song,
And got no promotion,
        and went back to the East Mountains
        White-headed.
And once again, later, we met at the South bridge-head.
And then the crowd broke up, you went north to San palace,
And if you ask how I regret that parting:
It is like the flowers falling at Spring's end
        Confused, whirled in a tangle.
What is the use of talking, and there is no end of talking,
There is no end of things in the heart.
I call in the boy,
Have him sit on his knees here
        To seal this,
And send it a thousand miles, thinking.

    By Rihaku

TENZONE[1]

Will people accept them?
    (i.e. these songs).
As a timorous wench from a centaur[2]
    (or a centurion),
Already they flee, howling in terror.

Will they be touched with the verisimilitudes?
    Their virgin stupidity is untemptable.
I beg you, my friendly critics,
Do not set about to procure me an audience.

I mate with my free kind upon the crags;
    the hidden recesses
Have heard the echo of my heels,
    in the cool light,
    in the darkness.

THE GARDEN

En robe de parade.[1]
—Samain

Like a skein of loose silk blown against a wall
She walks by the railing of a path in Kensington Gardens,
And she is dying piece-meal
       of a sort of emotional anæmia.

And round about there is a rabble
Of the filthy, sturdy, unkillable infants of the very poor.
They shall inherit the earth.

In her is the end of breeding.
Her boredom is exquisite and excessive.
She would like some one to speak to her,
And is almost afraid that I
       will commit that indiscretion.

1915: FEBRUARY

The smeared, leather-coated, leather-greaved engineer
Walks in front of his traction-engine
Like some figure out of the sagas,
Like Grettir[1] or like Skarpheddin,[2]
With a sort of majestical swagger.
And his machine lumbers after him
Like some mythological beast,
Like Grendel[3] bewitched and in chains,
But his ill luck will make me no sagas,
Nor will you crack the riddle of his skull,
O you over-educated, over-refined literati!
Nor yet you, store-bred realists,
You multipliers of novels!
He goes, and I go.
He stays and I stay.
He is mankind and I am the arts.
We are outlaws.
This war is not our war,
Neither side is on our side:
A vicious mediaevalism,
A belly-fat commerce,
Neither is on our side:
Whores, apes, rhetoricians,

Flagellants! in a year
Black as the *dies irae*.[4]
We have about us only the unseen country road,
The unseen twigs, breaking their tips with blossom.

COMMISSION

Go, my songs, to the lonely and the unsatisfied,
Go also to the nerve-wracked, go to the enslaved-by-
    convention,
Bear to them my contempt for their oppressors.
Go as a great wave of cool water,
Bear my contempt of oppressors.

Speak against unconscious oppression,
Speak against the tyranny of the unimaginative,
Speak against bonds.
Go to the bourgeoise who is dying of her ennuis,
Go to the women in suburbs.
Go to the hideously wedded,
Go to them whose failure is concealed,
Go to the unluckily mated,
Go to the bought wife,
Go to the woman entailed.

Go to those who have delicate lust,
Go to those whose delicate desires are thwarted,
Go like a blight upon the dulness of the world;
Go with your edge against this,

COMMISSION 73

Strengthen the subtle cords,
Bring confidence upon the algæ and the tentacles of the soul.

Go in a friendly manner,
Go with an open speech.
Be eager to find new evils and new good,
Be against all forms of oppression.
Go to those who are thickened with middle age,
To those who have lost their interest.

Go to the adolescent who are smothered in family—
Oh how hideous it is
To see three generations of one house gathered together!
It is like an old tree with shoots,
And with some branches rotted and falling.

Go out and defy opinion,
Go against this vegetable bondage of the blood.
Be against all sorts of mortmain.

A PACT

I make a pact with you, Walt Whitman—[1]
I have detested you long enough.
I come to you as a grown child
Who has had a pig-headed father;
I am old enough now to make friends.
It was you that broke the new wood,
Now is a time for carving.
We have one sap and one root—
Let there be commerce between us.

FURTHER INSTRUCTIONS

Come, my songs, let us express our baser passions,
Let us express our envy of the man with a steady job and no
    worry about the future.
You are very idle, my songs.
I fear you will come to a bad end.
You stand about in the streets,
You loiter at the corners and bus-stops,
You do next to nothing at all.

You do not even express our inner nobilities,
You will come to a very bad end.

And I?
I have gone half cracked,
I have talked to you so much that
                    I almost see you about me,
Insolent little beasts, shameless, devoid of clothing!

But you, newest song of the lot,
You are not old enough to have done much mischief,
I will get you a green coat out of China
With dragons worked upon it,

I will get you the scarlet silk trousers
From the statue of the infant Christ in Santa Maria Novella,[1]
Lest they say we are lacking in taste,
Or that there is no caste in this family.

A SONG OF THE DEGREES[1]

I

Rest me with Chinese colours,
For I think the glass is evil.

II

The wind moves above the wheat—
With a silver crashing,
A thin war of metal.

I have known the golden disc,
I have seen it melting above me.
I have known the stone-bright place,
        The hall of clear colours.

III

O glass subtly evil, O confusion of colours!
O light bound and bent in, O soul of the captive,

Why am I warned? Why am I sent away?
Why is your glitter full of curious mistrust?
O glass subtle and cunning, O powdery gold!
O filaments of amber, two-faced iridescence!

ITÉ[1]

Go, my songs, seek your praise from the young and from the
    intolerant,
Move among the lovers of perfection alone.
Seek ever to stand in the hard Sophoclean light[2]
And take your wounds from it gladly.

LIU CH'E[1]

The rustling of the silk is discontinued,
Dust drifts over the court-yard,
There is no sound of foot-fall, and the leaves
Scurry into heaps and lie still,
And she the rejoicer of the heart is beneath them:

A wet leaf that clings to the threshold.

THE COMING OF WAR: ACTÆON

An image of Lethe,[1]
    and the fields
Full of faint light
    but golden,
Gray cliffs,
    and beneath them
A sea
Harsher than granite,
    unstill, never ceasing;
High forms
    with the movement of gods,
Perilous aspect;
    And one said:
"This is Actæon."
    Actæon of golden greaves![2]
Over fair meadows,
Over the cool face of that field,
Unstill, ever moving
Hosts of an ancient people,
The silent cortège.

IN A STATION OF
THE METRO

The apparition   of these faces   in the crowd   :
Petals   on a wet, black   bough   .

[first version, *Poetry,* 1913]

IN A STATION OF
THE METRO

The apparition of these faces in the crowd;
Petals on a wet, black bough.

[*Lustra,* 1916]

THE ENCOUNTER

All the while they were talking the new morality
Her eyes explored me.
And when I arose to go
Her fingers were like the tissue
Of a Japanese paper napkin.

L'ART, 1910

Green arsenic smeared on an egg-white cloth,
Crushed strawberries! Come, let us feast our eyes.

ANCIENT MUSIC

Winter is icummen in,
Lhude sing Goddamm,
Raineth drop and staineth slop,
And how the wind doth ramm!
                Sing: Goddamm.
Skiddeth bus and sloppeth us,
An ague hath my ham.
Freezeth river, turneth liver,
              Damn you, sing: Goddamm.
Goddamm, Goddamm, 'tis why I am, Goddamm,
                So 'gainst the winter's balm.
Sing goddamm, damm, sing Goddamm,
Sing goddamm, sing goddamm, DAMM.

Note:—This is not folk music, but Dr. Ker writes that the tune is to be found under the Latin words of a very ancient canon.

PROVINCIA DESERTA

At Rochecoart,
Where the hills part
              in three ways,
And three valleys, full of winding roads,
Fork out to south and north,
There is a place of trees . . . gray with lichen.
I have walked there
              thinking of old days.
At Chalais
              is a pleached arbour;
Old pensioners and old protected women
Have the right there—
              it is charity.
I have crept over old rafters,
              peering down
Over the Dronne,
              over a stream full of lilies.
Eastward the road lies,
              Aubeterre is eastward,
With a garrulous old man at the inn.
I know the roads in that place:
Mareuil to the north-east,
              La Tour,

There are three keeps near Mareuil,
And an old woman,
                    glad to hear Arnaut,
Glad to lend one dry clothing.

I have walked
                    into Perigord,
I have seen the torch-flames, high-leaping,
Painting the front of that church;
Heard, under the dark, whirling laughter.
I have looked back over the stream
                    and seen the high building,
Seen the long minarets, the white shafts.
I have gone in Ribeyrac
                    and in Sarlat,
I have climbed rickety stairs, heard talk of Croy,
Walked over En Bertran's old layout,
Have seen Narbonne, and Cahors and Chalus,
Have seen Excideuil, carefully fashioned.

I have said:
                    "Here such a one walked.
Here Cœur-de-Lion was slain.
                    Here was good singing.
Here one man hastened his step.
                    Here one lay panting."
I have looked south from Hautefort,
                    thinking of Montaignac, southward.
I have lain in Rocafixada,
                    level with sunset,
Have seen the copper come down
                    tingeing the mountains,
I have seen the fields, pale, clear as an emerald,
Sharp peaks, high spurs, distant castles.
I have said: "The old roads have lain here.
Men have gone by such and such valleys
Where the great halls were closer together."
I have seen Foix on its rock, seen Toulouse, and
                    Arles greatly altered,

I have seen the ruined "Dorata."
         I have said:
"Riquier! Guido."
             I have thought of the second Troy,
Some little prized place in Auvergnat:
Two men tossing a coin, one keeping a castle,
One set on the highway to sing.
           He sang a woman.
Auvergne rose to the song;
           The Dauphin backed him.
"The castle to Austors!"
          "Pieire kept the singing—
A fair man and a pleasant."
         He won the lady,
Stole her away for himself, kept her against armed
           force:
So ends that story.
That age is gone;
Pieire de Maensac is gone.
I have walked over these roads;
I have thought of them living.

VILLANELLE:
THE PSYCHOLOGICAL
HOUR

I had over-prepared the event,
      that much was ominous.
With middle-ageing care
      I had laid out just the right books.
I had almost turned down the pages.

     Beauty is so rare a thing.
     So few drink of my fountain.

So much barren regret,
So many hours wasted!
And now I watch, from the window,
      the rain, the wandering busses.

"Their little cosmos is shaken"—
      the air is alive with that fact.
In their parts of the city
      they are played on by diverse forces.
How do I know?
      Oh, I know well enough.
For them there is something afoot.
      As for me;
I had over-prepared the event—

Beauty is so rare a thing
So few drink of my fountain.

Two friends: a breath of the forest . . .
Friends? Are people less friends
       because one has just, at last, found them?
Twice they promised to come.

    "Between the night and morning?"

Beauty would drink of my mind.
Youth would awhile forget
       my youth is gone from me.

II

("Speak up! You have danced so stiffly?
    Someone admired your works,
    And said so frankly.

    "Did you talk like a fool,
    The first night?
    The second evening?"

"*But* they promised again:
       'To-morrow at tea-time'.")

III

Now the third day is here—
       no word from either;
No word from her nor him,
Only another man's note:
       "Dear Pound, I am leaving England."

NEAR PERIGORD

A Perigord, pres del muralh
Tan que i puosch' om gitar ab malh.[1]

You'd have men's hearts up from the dust
And tell their secrets, Messire Cino,[2]
Right enough? Then read between the lines of Uc St. Circ,[3]
Solve me the riddle, for you know the tale.

Bertrans, En[4] Bertrans, left a fine canzone:[5]
"Maent,[6] I love you, you have turned me out.
The voice at Montfort,[7] Lady Agnes' hair,
Bel Miral's[8] stature, the viscountess' throat,
Set all together, are not worthy of you. . . ."
And all the while you sing out that canzone,
Think you that Maent lived at Montagnac,
One at Chalais, another at Malemort
Hard over Brive—for every lady a castle,
Each place strong.

　　　　　　Oh, *is* it easy enough?
Tairiran[9] held hall in Montagnac,
His brother-in-law was all there was of power
In Perigord, and this good union
Gobbled all the land, and held it later for some hundred years.
And our En Bertrans was in Altafort,[10]
Hub of the wheel, the stirrer-up of strife,

As caught by Dante[11] in the last wallow of hell—
The headless trunk "that made its head a lamp,"
For separation wrought out separation,
And he who set the strife between brother and brother
And had his way with the old English king,
Viced in such torture for the "counterpass."[12]

How would you live, with neighbours set about you—
Poictiers and Brive, untaken Rochecouart,
Spread like the finger-tips of one frail hand;
And you on that great mountain of a palm—
Not a neat ledge, not Foix[13] between its streams,
But one huge back half-covered up with pine,
Worked for and snatched from the string-purse of Born—
The four round towers, four brothers—mostly fools:
What could he do but play the desperate chess,
And stir old grudges?
                    "Pawn your castles, lords!
Let the Jews pay."
                    And the great scene—
(That, maybe, never happened!)
                    Beaten at last,
Before the hard old king:
                    "Your son, ah, since he died
My wit and worth are cobwebs brushed aside
In the full flare of grief. Do what you will."

    Take the whole man, and ravel out the story.
He loved this lady in castle Montagnac?
The castle flanked him—he had need of it.
You read to-day, how long the overlords of Perigord,
The Talleyrands, have held the place; it was no transient
    fiction.
And Maent failed him? Or saw through the scheme?

    And all his net-like thought of new alliance?
Chalais is high, a-level with the poplars.
Its lowest stones just meet the valley tips

NEAR PERIGORD   93

Where the low Dronne is filled with water-lilies.
And Rochecouart can match it, stronger yet,
The very spur's end, built on sheerest cliff,
And Malemort keeps its close hold on Brive,
While Born, his own close purse, his rabbit warren,
His subterranean chamber with a dozen doors,
A-bristle with antennæ to feel roads,
To sniff the traffic into Perigord.
And that hard phalanx, that unbroken line,
The ten good miles from there to Maent's castle,
All of his flank—how could he do without her?
And all the road to Cahors, to Toulouse?
What would he do without her?

    "Papiol,
Go forthright singing—Anhes, Cembelins.
There is a throat; ah, there are two white hands;
There is a trellis full of early roses,
And all my heart is bound about with love.
Where am I come with compound flatteries—
What doors are open to fine compliment?"
And every one half jealous of Maent?
He wrote the catch to pit their jealousies
Against her; give her pride in them?

Take his own speech, make what you will of it—
And still the knot, the first knot, of Maent?

   Is it a love poem? Did he sing of war?
Is it an intrigue to run subtly out,
Born of a jongleur's tongue, freely to pass
Up and about and in and out the land,
Mark him a craftsman and a strategist?
(St. Leider had done as much at Polhonac,
Singing a different stave, as closely hidden.)
Oh, there is precedent, legal tradition,
To sing one thing when your song means another,
"Et albirar ab lor bordon—"[14]
Foix' count knew that. What is Sir Bertrans' singing?

Maent, Maent, and yet again Maent,
Or war and broken heaumes[15] and politics?

II

      End fact. Try fiction. Let us say we see
En Bertrans, a tower-room at Hautefort,
Sunset, the ribbon-like road lies, in red cross-light,
Southward toward Montagnac, and he bends at a table
Scribbling, swearing between his teeth; by his left hand
Lie little strips of parchment covered over,
Scratched and erased with *al* and *ochaisos.*
Testing his list of rhymes, a lean man? Bilious?
With a red straggling beard?
And the green cat's-eye lifts toward Montagnac.

      Or take his "magnet" singer setting out,
Dodging his way past Aubeterre,[16] singing at Chalais
      In the vaulted hall,
Or, by a lichened tree at Rochecouart
Aimlessly watching a hawk above the valleys,
Waiting his turn in the mid-summer evening,
Thinking of Aelis, whom he loved heart and soul . . .
To find her half alone, Montfort away,
And a brown, placid, hated woman visiting her,
Spoiling his visit, with a year before the next one.
Little enough?
Or carry him forward. "Go through all the courts,
My Magnet," Bertrans had said.

      We came to Ventadour[17]
In the mid love court, he sings out the canzon,
No one hears save Arrimon Luc D'Esparo—
No one hears aught save the gracious sound of compliments.
Sir Arrimon counts on his fingers, Montfort,
Rochecouart, Chalais, the rest, the tactic,

Malemort, guesses beneath, sends word to Cœur-de-Lion:
The compact, de Born smoked out, trees felled
About his castle, cattle driven out!
Or no one sees it, and En Bertrans prospered?

    And ten years after, or twenty, as you will,
Arnaut and Richard lodge beneath Chalus:
The dull round towers encroaching on the field,
The tents tight drawn, horses at tether
Further and out of reach, the purple night,
The crackling of small fires, the bannerets,
The lazy leopards on the largest banner,
Stray gleams on hanging mail, an armourer's torch-flare
Melting on steel.

    And in the quietest space
They probe old scandals, say de Born is dead;
And we've the gossip (skipped six hundred years).
Richard shall die to-morrow—leave him there
Talking of *trobar clus* with Daniel.[18]
And the "best craftsman" sings out his friend's song,
Envies its vigour . . . and deplores the technique,
Dispraises his own skill?—That's as you will.
And they discuss the dead man,
Plantagenet puts the riddle: "Did he love her?"
And Arnaut parries: "Did he love your sister?
True, he has praised her, but in some opinion
He wrote that praise only to show he had
The favour of your party; had been well received."

"You knew the man."
    "*You* knew the man.
I am an artist, you have tried both métiers."
"You were born near him."
    "Do we know our friends?"
"Say that he saw the castles, say that he loved Maent!"
"Say that he loved her, does it solve the riddle?"
    End the discussion, Richard goes out next day

And gets a quarrel-bolt shot through his vizard,
Pardons the bowman, dies,[19]

          Ends our discussion. Arnaut ends
"In sacred odour"—(that's apocryphal!)
And we can leave the talk till Dante writes:
Surely I saw, and still before my eyes
Goes on that headless trunk, that bears for light
Its own head swinging, gripped by the dead hair,
And like a swinging lamp that says, "Ah me!
I severed men, my head and heart
Ye see here severed, my life's counterpart."[20]

Or take En Bertrans?

III

Ed eran due in uno, ed uno in due;
Inferno, XXVIII, *125*[21]

Bewildering spring, and by the Auvezere[22]
Poppies and day's eyes[23] in the green émail[24]
Rose over us; and we knew all that stream,
And our two horses had traced out the valleys;
Knew the low flooded lands squared out with poplars,
In the young days when the deep sky befriended.
          And great wings beat above us in the twilight,
And the great wheels in heaven
Bore us together . . . surging . . . and apart . . .
Believing we should meet with lips and hands,

   High, high and sure . . . and then the counter-thrust:
'Why do you love me? Will you always love me?
But I am like the grass, I can not love you.'
Or, 'Love, and I love and love you,
And hate your mind, not *you*, your soul, your hands.'

So to this last estrangement, Tairiran!

There shut up in his castle, Tairiran's,
She who had nor ears nor tongue save in her hands,
Gone—ah, gone—untouched, unreachable!
She who could never live save through one person,
She who could never speak save to one person,
And all the rest of her a shifting change,
A broken bundle of mirrors . . . !

L'HOMME MOYEN
SENSUEL*

"I hate a dumpy woman"
—George Gordon, Lord Byron.[1]

'Tis of my country that I would endite,
In hope to set some misconceptions right.
My country? I love it well, and those good fellows
Who, since their wit's unknown, escape the gallows.
But you stuffed coats who're neither tepid nor distinctly
    boreal,
Pimping, conceited, placid, editorial,
Could I but speak as 'twere in the "Restoration"
I would articulate your perdamnation.
This year perforce I must with circumspection—
For Mencken states somewhere, in this connection:

*(*Note*: It is through no fault of my own that this diversion was not given to
the reader two years ago; but the commercial said it would not add to their
transcendent popularity, and the vers-libre fanatics pointed out that I had used
a form of terminal consonance no longer permitted, and my admirers (j'en ai),
ever nobly desirous of erecting me into a sort of national institution, declared
the work "unworthy" of my mordant and serious genius. So a couple of the old
gentlemen are dead in the interim, and, alas, two of the great men mentioned in
passing, and the reader will have to accept the opusculus for what it is, some
rhymes written in 1915. I would give them now with dedication "To the
Anonymous Compatriot Who Produced the Poem 'Fanny,' Somewhere About
1820," if this form of centennial homage be permitted me. It was no small
thing to have written, in America, at that distant date, a poem of over forty
pages which one can still read without labour. *E. P.*)

"It is a moral nation we infest."
Despite such reins and checks I'll do my best,
An art! You all respect the arts, from that infant tick
Who's now the editor of *The Atlantic*,[2]
From Comstock's self,[3] down to the meanest resident,
Till up again, right up, we reach the president,
Who shows his taste in his ambassadors:
A novelist, a publisher, to pay old scores,
A novelist, a publisher and a preacher,[4]
That's sent to Holland, a most particular feature,
Henry Van Dyke, who thinks to charm the Muse you pack
    her in
A sort of stinking deliquescent saccharine.
The constitution of our land, O Socrates,
Was made to incubate such mediocrities,
These and a taste in books that's grown perennial
And antedates the Philadelphia centennial.
Still I'd respect you more if you could bury
Mabie, and Lyman Abbot and George Woodberry,[5]
For minds so wholly founded upon quotations
Are not the best of pulse for infant nations.
Dulness herself, that abject spirit, chortles
To see your forty self-baptized immortals,
And holds her sides where swelling laughter cracks 'em
Before the "Ars Poetica" of Hiram Maxim.[6]
All one can say of this refining medium
Is "Zut! Cinque lettres!" a banished gallic idiom,
Their doddering ignorance is waxed so notable
'Tis time that it was capped with something quotable.

Here Radway grew, the fruit of pantosocracy,[7]
The very fairest flower of their gynocracy.
Radway? My hero, for it will be more inspiring
If I set forth a bawdy plot like Byron
Than if I treat the nation as a whole.
Radway grew up. These forces shaped his soul;
These, and yet God, and Dr. Parkhurst's[8] god, the N.Y.
    Journal

(Which pays him more per week than The Supernal).
These and another godlet of that day, your day
(You feed a hen on grease, perhaps she'll lay
The sterile egg that is still eatable:
"Prolific Noyes"[9] with output undefeatable).
From these he (Radway) learnt, from provosts and from
    editors unyielding
And innocent of Stendhal, Flaubert, Maupassant and Fielding.
They set their mind (it's still in that condition)—
May we repeat; the Centennial Exposition
At Philadelphia, 1876?
What it knew then, it knows, and there it sticks.
And yet another, a "charming man," "sweet nature," but was
    Gilder,
De mortuis verum,[10] truly the master builder?

From these he learnt. Poe, Whitman, Whistler, men, their
    recognition
Was got abroad, what better luck do you wish 'em,
When writing well has not yet been forgiven
In Boston, to Henry James, the greatest whom we've seen
    living.
And timorous love of the innocuous
Brought from Gt. Britain and dumped down a'top of us,
Till you may take your choice: to feel the edge of satire or
Read Bennett or some other flaccid flatterer.

Despite it all, despite your Red Bloods, febrile concupiscence
Whose blubbering yowls you take for passion's essence;
Despite it all, your compound predilection
For ignorance, its growth and its protection
(Vide the tariff), I will hang simple facts
Upon a tale, to combat other tracts,
"Message to Garcia," Mosher's propagandas[11]
That are the nation's botts, collicks and glanders.
Or from the feats of Sumner cull it? Think,
Could Freud or Jung unfathom such a sink?

My hero, Radway, I have named, in truth,
Some forces among those which "formed" his youth:
These heavy weights, these dodgers and these preachers,
Crusaders, lecturers and secret lechers,
Who wrought about his "soul" their stale infection.
These are the high-brows, add to this collection
The social itch, the almost, all but, not quite, fascinating,
Piquante, delicious, luscious, captivating:
Puffed satin, and silk stockings, where the knee
Clings to the skirt in strict (vide: "*Vogue*") propriety.
Three thousand chorus girls and all unkissed,
O state sans song, sans home-grown wine, sans realist!
"Tell me not in mournful wish-wash
Life's a sort of sugared dish-wash!"
Radway had read the various evening papers
And yearned to imitate the Waldorf capers
As held before him in that unsullied mirror
The daily press, and monthlies nine cents dearer.
They held the very marrow of the ideals
That fed his spirit; were his mental meals.
Also, he'd read of christian virtues in
That canting rag called *Everybody's Magazine,*
And heard a clergy that tries on more wheezes
Than e'er were heard of by Our Lord Ch . . . . J . . . .
So he "faced life" with rather mixed intentions,
He had attended country Christian Endeavour Conventions,
Where one gets more chances
Than Spanish ladies had in old romances.
(Let him rebuke who ne'er has known the pure Platonic
        grapple,
Or hugged two girls at once behind a chapel.)
Such practices diluted rural boredom
Though some approved of them, and some deplored 'em.
Such was he when he got his mother's letter
And would not think a thing that could upset her. . . .
Yet saw an "ad." "To-night, THE HUDSON SAIL,
With forty queens, and music to regale
The select company: beauties you all would know

By name, if named." So it was phrased, or rather somewhat so
I have mislaid the "ad.," but note the touch,
Note, reader, note the sentimental touch:
His mother's birthday gift. (How pitiful
That only sentimental stuff will sell!)

Yet Radway went. A circumspectious prig!
And then that woman like a guinea-pig
Accosted, that's the word, accosted him,
Thereon the amorous calor slightly frosted him.
(I burn, I freeze, I sweat, said the fair Greek,
I speak in contradictions, so to speak.)

I've told his training, he was never bashful,
And his pockets by ma's aid, that night with cash full,
The invitation had no need of fine aesthetic,
Nor did disgust prove such a strong emetic
That we, with Masefield's vein, in the next sentence
Record "Odd's blood! Ouch! Ouch!" a prayer, his swift
    repentance.

No, no, they danced. The music grew much louder
As he inhaled the still fumes of rice-powder.
Then there came other nights, came slow but certain
And were such nights that we should "draw the curtain"
In writing fiction on uncertain chances
Of publication; "Circumstances,"
As the editor of *The Century* says in print,
"Compel a certain silence and restraint."
Still we will bring our "fiction as near to fact" as
The Sunday school brings virtues into practice.

Soon our hero could manage once a week,
Not that his pay had risen, and no leak
Was found in his employer's cash. He learned the lay of
    cheaper places,
And then Radway began to go the paces:
A rosy path, a sort of vernal ingress,

And Truth should here be careful of her thin dress—
Though males of seventy, who fear truths naked harm us,
Must think Truth looks as they do in wool pyjamas.
(My country, I've said your morals and your thoughts are
    stale ones,
But surely the worst of your old-women are the male ones.)

Why paint these days? An insurance inspector
For fires and odd risks, could in this sector
Furnish more data for a compilation
Than I can from this distant land and station,
Unless perhaps I should have recourse to
One of those firm-faced inspecting women, who
Find pretty Irish girls, in Chinese laundries,
Upstairs, the third floor up, and have such quandaries
As to how and why and whereby they got in
And for what earthly reason they remain. . . .
Alas, eheu, one question that sorely vexes
The serious social folk is "just what sex is."
Though it will, of course, pass off with social science
In which their mentors place such wide reliance.
De Gourmont[12] says that fifty grunts are all that will be
    prized.
Of language, by men wholly socialized,
With signs as many, that shall represent 'em
When thoroughly socialized printers want to print 'em.
"As free of mobs as kings"? I'd have men free of that invidious,
Lurking, serpentine, amphibious and insidious
Power that compels 'em
To be so much alike that every dog that smells 'em,
Thinks one identity is
Smeared o'er the lot in equal quantities.
Still we look toward the day when man, with unction,
Will long only to be a *social function,*
And even Zeus' wild lightning fear to strike
Lest it should fail to treat all men alike.
And I can hear an old man saying: "Oh, the rub!
I see them sitting in the Harvard Club,

And rate 'em up at just so much per head,
Know what they think, and just what books they've read,
Till I have viewed straw hats and their habitual clothing
All the same style, same cut, with perfect loathing."

So Radway walked, quite like the other men,
Out into the crepuscular half-light, now and then;
Saw what the city offered, cast an eye
Upon Manhattan's gorgeous panoply,
The flood of limbs upon Eighth Avenue
To beat Prague, Budapesht, Vienna or Moscow,*
Such animal invigorating carriage
As nothing can restrain or much disparage. . . .
Still he was not given up to brute enjoyment,
An anxious sentiment was his employment,
For memory of the first warm night still cast a haze o'er
The mind of Radway, whene'er he found a pair of purple
    stays or
Some other quaint reminder of the occasion
That first made him believe in immoral suasion.
A temperate man, a thin potationist, each day
A silent hunter off the Great White Way,
He read *The Century* and thought it nice
To be not too well known in haunts of vice—
The prominent haunts, where one might recognize him,
And in his daily walks duly capsize him.
Thus he eschewed the bright red-walled cafés and
Was never one of whom one speaks as "brazen'd."

Some men will live as prudes in their own village
And make the tour abroad for their wild tillage—
I knew a tourist agent, one whose art is
To run such tours. He calls 'em. . . . house parties.
But Radway was a patriot whose venality
Was purer in its love of one locality,
A home-industrious worker to perfection,

*Pronounce like respectable Russians: *"Mussqu."*

A senatorial jobber for protection,
Especially on books, lest knowledge break in
Upon the national brains and set 'em achin'.
('Tis an anomaly in our large land of freedom,
You can not get cheap books, even if you need 'em).
Radway was ignorant as an editor,
And, heavenly, holy gods! I can't say more,
Though I know one, a very base detractor,
Who has the phrase "As ignorant as an actor."

But turn to Radway: the first night on the river,
Running so close to "hell" it sends a shiver
Down Rodyheaver's[13] prophylactic spine,
Let me return to this bold theme of mine,
Of Radway. O clap hand ye moralists!
And meditate upon the Lord's conquests.
When last I met him, he was a pillar in
An organization for the suppression of sin. . . .
Not that he'd changed his tastes, nor yet his habits,
(Such changes don't occur in men, or rabbits).
Not that he was a saint, nor was top-loftical
In spiritual aspirations, but he found it profitable,
For as Ben Franklin said, with such urbanity:
"Nothing will pay thee, friend, like Christianity."
And in our day thus saith the Evangelist:
"Tent preachin' is the kind that pays the best."

'Twas as a business asset *pure an' simple*
That Radway joined the Baptist Broadway Temple.

I find no moral for a peroration,
He is the prototype of half the nation.

HOMAGE TO SEXTUS PROPERTIUS

Orfeo
"Quia pauper amavi."

I

Shades of Callimachus, Coan ghosts of Philetas[1]
It is in your grove I would walk,
I who come first from the clear font
Bringing the Grecian orgies into Italy,
                              and the dance into Italy.
Who hath taught you so subtle a measure,
                    in what hall have you heard it;
What foot beat out your time-bar,
              what water has mellowed your whistles?

Out-weariers of Apollo will, as we know, continue their
    Martian generalities,
  We have kept our erasers in order.[2]
A new-fangled chariot follows the flower-hung horses;
A young Muse with young loves clustered about her
                    ascends with me into the æther, . . .
And there is no high-road to the Muses.

Annalists will continue to record Roman reputations,
Celebrities from the Trans-Caucasus will belaud Roman
    celebrities

And expound the distentions of Empire,
But for something to read in normal circumstances?
For a few pages brought down from the forked hill unsullied?
I ask a wreath which will not crush my head.
                          And there is no hurry about it;
I shall have, doubtless, a boom after my funeral,
Seeing that long standing increases all things
                                    regardless of quality.
And who would have known the towers
                    pulled down by a deal-wood horse;
Or of Achilles withstaying waters by Simois[3]
Or of Hector[4] spattering wheel-rims,
Or of Polydmantus, by Scamander, or Helenus and
      Deiphoibos?[5]
Their door-yards would scarcely know them, or Paris.[6]
Small talk O Ilion, and O Troad[7]
                          twice taken by Oetian gods,[8]
If Homer had not stated your case!

And I also among the later nephews of this city
                    shall have my dog's day,
With no stone upon my contemptible sepulchre;
My vote coming from the temple of Phoebus in Lycia,[9] at Patara,
And in the meantime my songs will travel,
And the devirginated young ladies[10] will enjoy them
            when they have got over the strangeness,
For Orpheus tamed the wild beasts—
                    and held up the Threician river;
And Cithaeron shook up the rocks[11] by Thebes
      and danced them into a bulwark at his pleasure,
And you, O Polyphemus?[12] Did harsh Galatea almost
Turn to your dripping horses, because of a tune, under Aetna?
We must look into the matter.
Bacchus and Apollo in favour of it,
There will be a crowd of young women doing homage to my
      palaver,
Though my house is not propped up by Taenarian columns[13]
      from Laconia (associated with Neptune and Cerberus),

Though it is not stretched upon gilded beams:
My orchards do not lie level and wide
               as the forests of Phaeacia,
               the luxurious and Ionian,
Nor are my caverns stuffed stiff with a Marcian vintage,[14]
My cellar does not date from Numa Pompilius,[15]
Nor bristle with wine jars,
Nor is it equipped with a frigidaire patent;
Yet the companions of the Muses
        will keep their collective nose in my books,
And weary with historical data, they will turn to my
    dance tune.

Happy who are mentioned in my pamphlets,
    the songs shall be a fine tomb-stone over their beauty.
        But against this?
Neither expensive pyramids scraping the stars in their route,
Nor houses modelled upon that of Jove in East Elis,[16]
Nor the monumental effigies of Mausolus,
             are a complete elucidation of death.

Flame burns, rain sinks into the cracks
And they all go to rack ruin beneath the thud of the years.
Stands genius a deathless adornment,
    a name not to be worn out with the years.

II

I had been seen in the shade, recumbent on cushioned
    Helicon,[17]
The water dripping from Bellerophon's horse,[18]
Alba, your kings, and the realm your folk
           have constructed with such industry
Shall be yawned out on my lyre—with such industry.
My little mouth shall gobble in such great fountains,
"Wherefrom father Ennius,[19] sitting before I came, hath
    drunk."

I had rehearsed the Curian brothers, and made remarks on
    the Horatian javelin[20]
(Near Q. H. Flaccus'[21] book-stall).
"Of" royal Aemilia, drawn on the memorial raft,
"Of" the victorious delay of Fabius, and the left-handed
                              battle at Cannae,[22]
Of lares fleeing the "Roman seat" . . .
                    I had sung of all these
And of Hannibal,
                and of Jove protected by geese.
And Phoebus looking upon me from the Castalian tree,
Said then "You idiot! What are you doing with that water:
Who has ordered a book about heroes?
                You need, Propertius, not think
About acquiring that sort of a reputation.
      Soft fields must be worn by small wheels,
Your pamphlets will be thrown, thrown often into a chair
Where a girl waits alone for her lover;
      Why wrench your page out of its course?
No keel will sink with your genius
      Let another oar churn the water,
Another wheel, the arena; mid-crowd is as bad as mid-sea."
He had spoken, and pointed me a place with his plectrum:

      Orgies of vintages, an earthen image of Silenus
Strengthened with rushes, Tegaean Pan,[23]
The small birds of the Cytherean mother,[24]
      their Punic faces dyed in the Gorgon's lake;[25]
Nine girls, from as many countrysides
      bearing her offerings in their unhardened hands,

Such my cohort and setting. And she bound ivy to his thyrsos;[26]
Fitted song to the strings;
                Roses twined in her hands.
And one among them looked at me with face offended,
Calliope:[27]
      "Content ever to move with white swans!
Nor will the noise of high horses lead you ever to battle;

Nor will the public criers ever have your name
                              in their classic horns,
Nor Mars shout you in the wood at Aeonia,
                Nor where Rome ruins German riches,
Nor where the Rhine flows with barbarous blood,
                and flood carries wounded Suevi.[28]
Obviously crowned lovers at unknown doors,
Night dogs, the marks of a drunken scurry,
These are your images, and from you the sorcerizing of
   shut-in young ladies,
The wounding of austere men by chicane."
        Thus Mistress Calliope,
        Dabbling her hands in the fount, thus she
Stiffened our face with the backwash of Philetas the Coan.

III

Midnight, and a letter comes to me from our mistress:
     Telling me to come to Tibur:
                              At once!!
"Bright tips reach up from twin towers,
Anienan spring water falls into flat-spread pools."

What *is* to be done about it?
     Shall I entrust myself to entangled shadows,
Where bold hands may do violence to my person?

Yet if I postpone my obedience
                because of this respectable terror,
I shall be prey to lamentations worse than a nocturnal
   assailant.
And I shall be in the wrong,
                and it will last a twelve month,
For her hands have no kindness me-ward,

Nor is there anyone to whom lovers are not sacred at midnight
     And in the Via Sciro.

If any man would be a lover
                    he may walk on the Scythian coast,
No barbarism would go to the extent of doing him harm,
The moon will carry his candle,
                    the stars will point out the stumbles,
Cupid will carry lighted torches before him
                    and keep mad dogs off his ankles.
Thus all roads are perfectly safe
                            and at any hour;
Who so indecorous as to shed the pure gore of a suitor?!
        Cypris[29] is his cicerone.
What if undertakers follow my track,
                    such a death is worth dying.
She would bring frankincense and wreaths to my tomb,
        She would sit like an ornament on my pyre.

Gods' aid, let not my bones lie in a public location
With crowds too assiduous in their crossing of it;
For thus are tombs of lovers most desecrated.

May a woody and sequestered place cover me with its foliage
Or may I inter beneath the hummock
                    of some as yet uncatalogued sand;
At any rate I shall not have my epitaph in a high road.

IV

Difference of Opinion With Lygdamus[30]

Tell me the truths which you hear of our constant young lady,
        Lygdamus,
And may the bought yoke of a mistress lie with
                    equitable weight on your shoulders;
For I am swelled up with inane pleasurabilities
                    and deceived by your reference
To things which you think I would like to believe.

No messenger should come wholly empty,
                and a slave should fear plausibilities;
Much conversation is as good as having a home.
Out with it, tell it to me, all of it, from the beginning,
I guzzle with outstretched ears.
Thus? She wept into uncombed hair,
                                        And you saw it.
Vast waters flowed from her eyes?
                        You, you Lygdamus
Saw her stretched on her bed,—
                        it was no glimpse in a mirror;
No gawds on her snowy hands, no orfevrerie,[31]
Sad garment draped on her slender arms.
Her escritoires lay shut by the bed-feet.
Sadness hung over the house, and the desolated female
    attendants
Were desolated because she had told them her dreams.

She was veiled in the midst of that place,
Damp woolly handkerchiefs were stuffed into her undryable
    eyes,
And a querulous noise responded to our solicitous reprobations.
For which things you will get a reward from me,
                    Lygdamus?
To say many things is equal to having a home.
And the other woman "has not enticed me
                            by her pretty manners,
She has caught me with herbaceous poison,
            she twiddles the spiked wheel of a rhombus,
She stews puffed frogs, snake's bones, the moulted feathers of
    screech owls,

She binds me with ravvles of shrouds.
                Black spiders spin in her bed!
Let her lovers snore at her in the morning!
                May the gout cramp up her feet!

Does he like me to sleep here alone,
                    Lygdamus?
Will he say nasty things at my funeral?"

And you expect me to believe this
                    after twelve months of discomfort?

V

I

Now if ever it is time to cleanse Helicon;
                    to lead Emathian horses afield,
And to name over the census of my chiefs in the Roman camp.
If I have not the faculty, "The bare attempt would be
    praiseworthy."
"In things of similar magnitude
                    the mere will to act is sufficient."

The primitive ages sang Venus,
                    the last sings of a tumult,
And I also will sing war when this matter of a girl is exhausted.
I with my beak hauled ashore would proceed in a more stately
    manner,
My Muse is eager to instruct me in a new gamut, or gambetto,
Up, up my soul, from your lowly cantilation,
                    put on a timely vigour.

Oh august Pierides![32] Now for a large-mouthed product.
Thus:
"The Euphrates denies its protection to the Parthian and
                    apologizes for Crassus,"
And "It is, I think, India which now gives necks to your
    triumph,"
And so forth, Augustus. "Virgin Arabia shakes in her inmost
    dwelling."

If any land shrink into a distant seacoast,
    it is a mere postponement of your domination.
And I shall follow the camp, I shall be duly celebrated
        for singing the affairs of your cavalry.
May the fates watch over my day.

2

Yet you ask on what account I write so many love-lyrics
And whence this soft book comes into my mouth.
Neither Calliope nor Apollo sung these things into my ear,
    My genius is no more than a girl.

If she with ivory fingers drive a tune through the lyre,
    We look at the process.
How easy the moving fingers; if hair is mussed on her
    forehead,
If she goes in a gleam of Cos, in a slither of dyed stuff,
There is a volume in the matter; if her eyelids sink into sleep,
There are new jobs for the author;
And if she plays with me with her shirt off,
    We shall construct many Iliads.
And whatever she does or says
    We shall spin long yarns out of nothing.

Thus much the fates have allotted me, and if, Maecenas,
I were able to lead heroes into armour, I would not,
Neither would I warble of Titans, nor of Ossa
                                spiked onto Olympus,
Nor of causeways over Pelion,[33]
Nor of Thebes in its ancient respectability,
            nor of Homer's reputation in Pergamus,
Nor of Xerxes' two-barreled kingdom, nor of Remus and his
    royal family,
Nor of dignified Carthaginian characters,
Nor of Welsh mines and the profit Marus had out of them.

I should remember Caesar's affairs . . .

                         for a background,

Although Callimachus did without them,

                   and without Theseus,

Without an inferno, without Achilles attended of gods,

Without Ixion, and without the sons of Menoetius and the Argo

    and without Jove's grave and the Titans.

And my ventricles do not palpitate to Caesarial *ore rotundos*,[34]

Nor to the tune of the Phrygian fathers.[35]

Sailor, of winds; a plowman, concerning his oxen;

Soldier, the enumeration of wounds; the sheepfeeder, of

    ewes;

We, in our narrow bed, turning aside from battles:

Each man where he can, wearing out the day in his manner.

3

It is noble to die of love, and honourable to remain

                       uncuckolded for a season.

And she speaks ill of light women,

               and will not praise Homer

Because Helen's conduct is "unsuitable."

VI

When, when, and whenever death closes our eyelids,

Moving naked over Acheron[36]

Upon the one raft, victor and conquered together,

Marius and Jugurtha together,[37]

               one tangle of shadows.

Caesar plots against India,

Tigris and Euphrates shall, from now on, flow at his bidding,

Tibet shall be full of Roman policemen,

The Parthians shall get used to our statuary
                    and acquire a Roman religion;
One raft on the veiled flood of Acheron,
            Marius and Jugurtha together.

Nor at my funeral either will there be any long trail,
                    bearing ancestral lares and images;
No trumpets filled with my emptiness,
Nor shall it be on an Attalic bed;
            The perfumed cloths shall be absent.
A small plebeian procession.
            Enough, enough and in plenty
There will be three books at my obsequies
Which I take, my not unworthy gift, to Persephone.

You will follow the bare scarified breast
Nor will you be weary of calling my name, nor too weary
            To place the last kiss on my lips
When the Syrian onyx is broken.

                "He who is now vacant dust
                Was once the slave of one passion:"
Give that much inscription
                "Death why tardily come?"

You, sometimes, will lament a lost friend,
            For it is a custom:
This care for past men,

Since Adonis was gored in Idalia, and the Cytherean[38]
Ran crying with out-spread hair,
            In vain, you call back the shade,
In vain, Cynthia. Vain call to unanswering shadow,
            Small talk comes from small bones.

VII

Me happy, night, night full of brightness;
Oh couch made happy by my long delectations;
How many words talked out with abundant candles;
Struggles when the lights were taken away;
Now with bared breasts she wrestled against me,
                    Tunic spread in delay;
And she then opening my eyelids fallen in sleep,
Her lips upon them; and it was her mouth saying:
    Sluggard!

In how many varied embraces, our changing arms,
Her kisses, how many, lingering on my lips.
"Turn not Venus into a blinded motion,
            Eyes are the guides of love,
Paris took Helen naked coming from the bed of Menelaus,
Endymion's[39] naked body, bright bait for Diana,"
            —such at least is the story.

While our fates twine together, sate we our eyes with love;
For long night comes upon you
                and a day when no day returns.
Let the gods lay chains upon us
                so that no day shall unbind them.

Fool who would set a term to love's madness,
For the sun shall drive with black horses,
            earth shall bring wheat from barley,
The flood shall move toward the fountain
            Ere love know moderations,
            The fish shall swim in dry streams.
No, now while it may be, let not the fruit of life cease.

            Dry wreaths drop their petals,
                their stalks are woven in baskets,
            To-day we take the great breath of lovers,
                to-morrow fate shuts us in.

Though you give all your kisses
                        you give but few.

Nor can I shift my pains to other,
            Hers will I be dead,
If she confer such nights upon me,
                        long is my life, long in years,
If she give me many,
            God am I for the time.

VIII

Jove, be merciful to that unfortunate woman
            Or an ornamental death will be held to your debit,
The time is come, the air heaves in torridity,
The dry earth pants against the canicular heat,
But this heat is not the root of the matter:
            She did not respect all the gods;
Such derelictions have destroyed other young ladies aforetime,
And what they swore in the cupboard
                        wind and wave scattered away.

Was Venus exacerbated by the existence of a comparable equal?
            Is the ornamental goddess full of envy?
Have you contempted Juno's Pelasgian temples.[40]
            Have you denied Pallas[41] good eyes?
Or is it my tongue that wrongs you
                        with perpetual ascription of graces?
There comes, it seems, and at any rate
            through perils, (so many) and of a vexed life,
The gentler hour of an ultimate day.

Io mooed the first years with averted head,
            And now drinks Nile water like a god,
Ino in her young days fled pellmell out of Thebes,
            Andromeda was offered to a sea-serpent
                        and respectably married to Perseus,

Callisto,[42] disguised as a bear,
        wandered through the Arcadian prairies
        While a black veil was over her stars,
What if your fates are accelerated,
                your quiet hour put forward,
You may find interment pleasing,

You will say that you succumbed to a danger identical,
        charmingly identical, with Semele's,[43]
And believe it, and she also will believe it,
          being expert from experience,
And amid all the gloried and storied beauties of Maeonia[44]
There shall be none in a better seat, not
            one denying your prestige,

Now you may bear fate's stroke unperturbed,
Or Jove, harsh as he is, may turn aside your ultimate day.
Old lecher, let not Juno get wind of the matter,
Or perhaps Juno herself will go under,
          If the young lady is taken?

There will be, in any case, a stir on Olympus.

IX

I

The twisted rhombs[45] ceased their clamour of accompaniment;
The scorched laurel lay in the fire-dust;
The moon still declined to descend out of heaven,

But the black ominous owl hoot was audible.

And one raft bears our fates
        on the veiled lake toward Avernus[46]
Sails spread on cerulean waters, I would shed tears
    for two;

I shall live, if she continue in life,
       If she dies, I shall go with her.
Great Zeus, save the woman,
         or she will sit before your feet in a veil,
         and tell out the long list of her troubles.

2

Persephone and Dis, Dis, have mercy upon her,[47]
There are enough women in hell,
               quite enough beautiful women,
Iope, and Tyro, and Pasiphae, and the formal girls of Achaia,
And out of Troad, and from the Campania,[48]
Death has his tooth in the lot,
           Avernus lusts for the lot of them,
Beauty is not eternal, no man has perennial fortune,
Slow foot, or swift foot, death delays but for a season.

3

My light, light of my eyes,
          you are escaped from great peril,
Go back to Great Dian's dances bearing suitable gifts,
Pay up your vow of night watches
             to Dian goddess of virgins,
And unto me also pay debt:
The ten nights of your company you have
              promised me.

X

Light, light of my eyes, at an exceeding late hour I was
    wandering,
And intoxicated,
            and no servant was leading me,
And a minute crowd of small boys came from opposite,
            I do not know what boys,
And I am afraid of numerical estimate,

And some of them shook little torches,
                    and others held onto arrows,
And the rest laid their chains upon me,
                    and they were naked, the lot of them,
And one of the lot was given to lust.

"That incensed female has consigned him to our pleasure."
So spoke. And the noose was over my neck.
And another said "Get him plumb in the middle!
                    Shove along there, shove along!"
And another broke in upon this:
                    "He thinks that we are not gods."
"And she has been waiting for the scoundrel,
                    and in a new Sidonian night cap,[49]
And with more than Arabian odours,
                    God knows where he has been.
She could scarcely keep her eyes open
                    enter that much for his bail.
                        Get along now!"

We were coming near to the house,
                    and they gave another yank to my cloak,
And it was morning, and I wanted to see if she was alone, and
      resting,
And Cynthia was alone in her bed.
                            I was stupefied.
I had never seen her looking so beautiful,
          No, not when she was tunick'd in purple.

Such aspect was presented to me, me recently emerged from
      my visions,
You will observe that pure form has its value.

"You are a very early inspector of mistresses.
Do you think I have adopted your habits?"
          There were upon the bed no signs of a voluptuous
                encounter,
          No signs of a second incumbent.

She continued:

> "No incubus has crushed his body against me,
> Though spirits are celebrated for adultery.
> And I am going to the temple of Vesta . . ."

                                    and so on.

Since that day I have had no pleasant nights.

XI

1

The harsh acts of your levity!
                    Many and many.
I am hung here, a scare-crow for lovers.

2

Escape! There is, O Idiot, no escape,
      Flee if you like into Tanais,
                    desire will follow you thither,
Though you heave into the air upon the gilded Pegasean back,
Though you had the feathery sandals of Perseus[50]
To lift you up through split air,
The high tracks of Hermes would not afford you shelter.

Amor stands upon you, Love drives upon lovers,
                    a heavy mass on free necks.

It is our eyes you flee, not the city,
You do nothing, you plot inane schemes against me,
Languidly you stretch out the snare
                    with which I am already familiar,

And yet again, and newly rumour strikes on my ears.

Rumours of you throughout the city,
                    and no good rumour among them.

"You should not believe hostile tongues.
                    Beauty is slander's cock-shy.
All lovely women have known this."
                    "Your glory is not outblotted by venom,
Phoebus our witness, your hands are unspotted."
A foreign lover brought down Helen's kingdom
                    and she was led back, living, home;
The Cytherean brought low by Mars' lechery[51]
                    reigns in respectable heavens, . . .

Oh, oh, and enough of this,
                    by dew-spread caverns,
The Muses clinging to the mossy ridges;
                    to the ledge of the rocks:
Zeus' clever rapes, in the old days,
                    combusted Semele's, of Io strayed.
Oh how the bird flew from Trojan rafters,
Ida[52] has lain with a shepherd, she has slept between sheep.

                    Even there, no escape
Not the Hyrcanian seaboard, not in seeking the shore of Eos.[53]

All things are forgiven for one night of your games. . . .
Though you walk in the Via Sacra,[54] with a peacock's tail for
    a fan.

XII

Who, who will be the next man to entrust his girl to a friend?
Love interferes with fidelities;
The gods have brought shame on their relatives;
Each man wants the pomegranate for himself;
Amiable and harmonious people are pushed incontinent into
    duels,
A Trojan and adulterous person came to Menelaus under the
    rites of hospitium,

And there was a case in Colchis,[55] Jason and that woman in
    Colchis;
And besides, Lynceus,[56]

                 you were drunk.

Could you endure such promiscuity?
             She was not renowned for fidelity;
But to jab a knife in my vitals, to have passed on a swig of
    poison,
Preferable, my dear boy, my dear Lynceus,
Comrade, comrade of my life, of my purse, of my person;
But in one bed, in one bed alone, my dear Lynceus,
         I deprecate your attendance;
I would ask a like boon of Jove.

And you write of Achelöus, who contended with Hercules,
You write of Adrastus' horses and the funeral rites of Achenor,
And you will not leave off imitating Aeschylus.
        Though you make a hash of Antimachus,[57]
You think you are going to do Homer.
        And still a girl scorns the gods,
Of all these young women
     not one has enquired the cause of the world,
Nor the modus of lunar eclipses
       Nor whether there be any patch left of us
After we cross the infernal ripples,
      nor if the thunder fall from predestination;
Nor anything else of importance.

Upon the Actian marshes[58] Virgil is Phoebus' chief of police,
        He can tabulate Caesar's great ships.
He thrills to Ilian arms,
        He shakes the Trojan weapons of Aeneas,
And casts stores on Lavinian beaches.[59]
Make way, ye Roman authors,
           clear the street, O ye Greeks,
For a much larger Iliad is in the course of construction

(and to Imperial order)
Clear the streets, O ye Greeks!

And you also follow him "neath Phrygian pine shade:"
        Thyrsis and Daphnis[60] upon whittled reeds,
And how ten sins can corrupt young maidens;
        Kids for a bribe and pressed udders,
Happy selling poor loves for cheap apples.

Tityrus[61] might have sung the same vixen;
        Corydon tempted Alexis,
Head farmers do likewise, and lying weary amid their oats
They get praise from tolerant Hamadryads,[62]
Go on, to Ascraeus'[63] prescription, the ancient,
                        respected, Wordsworthian:
"A flat field for rushes, grapes grow on the slope."

And behold me, small fortune left in my house.
Me, who had no general for a grandfather!
I shall triumph among young ladies of indeterminate character,
My talent acclaimed in their banquets,
        I shall be honoured with yesterday's wreaths.
And the god strikes to the marrow.

        Like a trained and performing tortoise,
I would make verse in your fashion, if she should command it,
With her husband asking a remission of sentence,
        And even this infamy would not attract
                numerous readers
Were there an erudite or violent passion,
For the nobleness of the populace brooks nothing below its
    own altitude.
One must have resonance, resonance and sonority . . . like a
    goose.

Varro sang Jason's expedition,
        Varro, of his great passion Leucadia,[64]

There is song in the parchment; Catullus the highly
    indecorous,
Of Lesbia, known above Helen;
And in the dyed pages of Calvus,
        Calvus mourning Quintilia,[65]
And but now Gallus had sung of Lycoris.[66]
        Fair, fairest Lycoris—
The waters of Styx poured over the wound:
And now Propertius of Cynthia, taking his stand among these.

HUGH SELWYN MAUBERLEY

(Contacts and Life)

"Vocal æstus in umbram"[1]
—Nemesianus, Ec. IV.

E. P. ODE POUR L'ELECTION DE SON SEPULCHRE[2]

For three years, out of key with his time,
He strove to resuscitate the dead art
Of poetry; to maintain "the sublime"
In the old sense. Wrong from the start—

No, hardly, but seeing he had been born
In a half savage country, out of date;
Bent resolutely on wringing lilies from the acorn;
Capaneus;[3] trout for factitious bait;

῎Ιδμεν γάρ τοι πάνθ᾽, δ᾽σ᾽ ἐνὶ Τροίη[4]
Caught in the unstopped ear;
Giving the rocks small lee-way
The chopped seas held him, therefore, that year.

His true Penelope was Flaubert,
He fished by obstinate isles;
Observed the elegance of Circe's hair
Rather than the mottoes on sun-dials.

Unaffected by "the march of events,"
He passed from men's memory in *l'an trentuniesme*
De son eage;[5] the case presents
No adjunct to the Muses' diadem.

II

The age demanded an image
Of its accelerated grimace,
Something for the modern stage,
Not, at any rate, an Attic grace;[6]

Not, not certainly, the obscure reveries
Of the inward gaze;
Better mendacities
Than the classics in paraphrase!

The "age demanded" chiefly a mould in plaster,
Made with no loss of time,
A prose kinema, not, not assuredly, alabaster
Or the "sculpture" of rhyme.

III

The tea-rose tea-gown, etc.
Supplants the mousseline of Cos,
The pianola "replaces"
Sappho's barbitos.[7]

Christ follows Dionysus,
Phallic and ambrosial
Made way for macerations;
Caliban casts out Ariel.

All things are a flowing,
Sage Heracleitus says;

But a tawdry cheapness
Shall outlast our days.

Even the Christian beauty
Defects—after Samothrace;[8]
We see τὸ καλόν[9]
Decreed in the market place.

Faun's flesh is not to us,
Nor the saint's vision.
We have the press for wafer;
Franchise for circumcision.

All men, in law, are equals.
Free of Pisistratus,[10]
We choose a knave or an eunuch
To rule over us.

O bright Apollo,
τίν' ἄνδρα, τίν' ἥρωα, τίνα θεὸν,[11]
What god, man, or hero
Shall I place a tin wreath upon!

IV

These fought in any case,
and some believing,
          pro domo,[12] in any case ...

Some quick to arm,
some for adventure,
some from fear of weakness,
some from fear of censure,
some for love of slaughter, in imagination,
learning later ...
some in fear, learning love of slaughter;

Died some, pro patria,
            non "dulce" non "et decor" . . . [13]
walked eye-deep in hell
believing in old men's lies, then unbelieving
came home, home to a lie,
home to many deceits,
home to old lies and new infamy;
usury[14] age-old and age-thick
and liars in public places.

Daring as never before, wastage as never before.
Young blood and high blood,
fair cheeks, and fine bodies;

fortitude as never before

frankness as never before,
disillusions as never told in the old days,
hysterias, trench confessions,
laughter out of dead bellies.

V

There died a myriad,
And of the best, among them,
For an old bitch gone in the teeth,
For a botched civilization,

Charm, smiling at the good mouth,
Quick eyes gone under earth's lid,

For two gross of broken statues,
For a few thousand battered books.

YEUX GLAUQUES[15]

Gladstone was still respected,
When John Ruskin produced
"Kings' Treasures";[16] Swinburne
And Rossetti still abused.

Fœtid Buchanan lifted up his voice
When that faun's head of hers
Became a pastime for
Painters and adulterers.

The Burne-Jones cartons
Have preserved her eyes;
Still, at the Tate, they teach
Cophetua[17] to rhapsodize;

Thin like brook-water,
With a vacant gaze.
The English Rubaiyat was still-born
In those days.

The thin, clear gaze, the same
Still darts out faun-like from the half-ruin'd face,
Questing and passive. . . .
"Ah, poor Jenny's case" . . .

Bewildered that a world
Shows no surprise
At her last maquero's[18]
Adulteries.

"SIENA MI FE'; DISFECEMI MAREMMA"[19]

Among the pickled fœtuses and bottled bones,
Engaged in perfecting the catalogue,

I found the last scion of the
Senatorial families of Strasbourg, Monsieur Verog.[20]

For two hours he talked of Gallifet;[21]
Of Dowson; of the Rhymers' Club;[22]
Told me how Johnson (Lionel) died
By falling from a high stool in a pub . . .

But showed no trace of alcohol
At the autopsy, privately performed—
Tissue preserved—the pure mind
Arose toward Newman as the whiskey warmed.

Dowson found harlots cheaper than hotels;
Headlam for uplift; Image impartially imbued[23]
With raptures for Bacchus, Terpsichore[24] and the Church.
So spoke the author of "The Dorian Mood,"

M. Verog, out of step with the decade,
Detached from his contemporaries,
Neglected by the young,
Because of these reveries.

BRENNBAUM[25]

The sky-like limpid eyes,
The circular infant's face,
The stiffness from spats to collar
Never relaxing into grace;

The heavy memories of Horeb, Sinai[26] and the forty years,
Showed only when the daylight fell
Level across the face
Of Brennbaum "The Impeccable."

MR. NIXON[27]

In the cream gilded cabin of his steam yacht
Mr. Nixon advised me kindly, to advance with fewer
Dangers of delay. "Consider
         Carefully the reviewer.

I was as poor as you are;
When I began I got, of course,
Advance on royalties, fifty at first," said Mr. Nixon,
"Follow me, and take a column,
Even if you have to work free.

Butter reviewers. From fifty to three hundred
I rose in eighteen months;
The hardest nut I had to crack
Was Dr. Dundas.

I never mentioned a man but with the view
Of selling my own works.
The tip's a good one, as for literature
It gives no man a sinecure.

And no one knows, at sight, a masterpiece.
And give up verse, my boy,
There's nothing in it."
                    .   .   .   .   .
Likewise a friend of Blougram's[28] once advised me:
Don't kick against the pricks,
Accept opinion. The "Nineties" tried your game
And died, there's nothing in it.

X

Beneath the sagging roof
The stylist has taken shelter,

Unpaid, uncelebrated,
At last from the world's welter

Nature receives him;
With a placid and uneducated mistress
He exercises his talents
And the soil meets his distress.

The haven from sophistications and contentions
Leaks through its thatch;
He offers succulent cooking;
The door has a creaking latch.

XI

"Conservatrix of Milésien"[29]
Habits of mind and feeling,
Possibly. But in Ealing
With the most bank-clerkly of Englishmen?

No, "Milesian" is an exaggeration.
No instinct has survived in her
Older than those her grandmother
Told her would fit her station.

XII

"Daphne with her thighs in bark
Stretches toward me her leafy hands,"—
Subjectively. In the stuffed-satin drawing-room
I await The Lady Valentine's commands,

Knowing my coat has never been
Of precisely the fashion
To stimulate, in her,
A durable passion;

Doubtful, somewhat, of the value
Of well-gowned approbation
Of literary effort,
But never of The Lady Valentine's vocation:

Poetry, her border of ideas,
The edge, uncertain, but a means of blending
With other strata
Where the lower and higher have ending;

A hook to catch the Lady Jane's attention,
A modulation toward the theatre,
Also, in the case of revolution,
A possible friend and comforter.
        . . . . . .
Conduct, on the other hand, the soul
"Which the highest cultures have nourished"
To Fleet St. where
Dr. Johnson flourished;

Beside this thoroughfare
The sale of half-hose has
Long since superseded the cultivation
Of Pierian roses.[30]

ENVOI (1919)

Go, dumb-born book,
Tell her that sang me once that song of Lawes:[31]
Hadst thou but song
As thou hast subjects known,
Then were there cause in thee that should condone
Even my faults that heavy upon me lie,
And build her glories their longevity.

Tell her that sheds
Such treasure in the air,

Recking naught else but that her graces give
Life to the moment,
I would bid them live
As roses might, in magic amber laid,
Red overwrought with orange and all made
One substance and one colour
Braving time.

Tell her that goes
With song upon her lips
But sings not out the song, nor knows
The maker of it, some other mouth,
May be as fair as hers,
Might, in new ages, gain her worshippers,
When our two dusts with Waller's shall be laid,
Siftings on siftings in oblivion,
Till change hath broken down
All things save Beauty alone.

MAUBERLEY
1920

"Vacuos exercet in aera morsus."[32]

I

Turned from the "eau-forte
Par Jacquemart"[33]
To the strait head
Of Messalina:[34]

"His true Penelope
Was Flaubert,"
And his tool
The engraver's.

Firmness,
Not the full smile,
His art, but an art
In profile;

Colourless
Pier Francesca,
Pisanello lacking the skill
To forge Achaia.[35]

II

"Qu'est ce qu'ils savent de l'amour, et qu'est ce qu'ils peuvent comprendre?
S'ils ne comprennent pas la poésie, s'ils ne sentent pas la musique, qu'est ce qu'ils peuvent comprendre de cette passion en comparaison avec laquelle la rose est grossière et le parfum des violettes un tonnerre?"

—Caid Ali[36]

For three years, diabolus in the scale,[37]
He drank ambrosia,
All passes, ANANGKE prevails,[38]
Came end, at last, to that Arcadia.

He had moved amid her phantasmagoria,
Amid her galaxies,
NUKTOS AGALMA[39]

        · · · · ·

Drifted . . . drifted precipitate,
Asking time to be rid of . . .
Of his bewilderment; to designate
His new found orchid. . . .

To be certain . . . certain . . .
(Amid ærial flowers) . . . time for arrangements—

Drifted on
To the final estrangement;

Unable in the supervening blankness
To sift TO AGATHON[40] from the chaff
Until he found his sieve . . .
Ultimately, his seismograph:

Given that is his "fundamental passion,"
This urge to convey the relation
Of eye-lid and cheek-bone
By verbal manifestation;

To present the series
Of curious heads in medallion—

He had passed, inconscient, full gaze,
The wide-banded irides[41]
And botticellian sprays implied
In their diastasis;[42]

Which anæsthesis,[43] noted a year late,
And weighed, revealed his great affect,
(Orchid), mandate
Of Eros, a retrospect.

      .   .   .   .   .

Mouths biting empty air,
The still stone dogs,
Caught in metamorphosis, were
Left him as epilogues.

"THE AGE DEMANDED"

Vide Poem II.

For this agility chance found
Him of all men, unfit

As the red-beaked steeds of
The Cytheræan[44] for a chain bit.

The glow of porcelain
Brought no reforming sense
To his perception
Of the social inconsequence.

Thus, if her colour
Came against his gaze,
Tempered as if
It were through a perfect glaze

He made no immediate application
Of this to relation of the state
To the individual, the month was more temperate
Because this beauty had been.

> The coral isle, the lion-coloured sand
> Burst in upon the porcelain revery:
> Impetuous troubling
> Of his imagery.

Mildness, amid the neo-Nietzschean clatter,
His sense of graduations,
Quite out of place amid
Resistance to current exacerbations,

Invitation, mere invitation to perceptivity
Gradually led him to the isolation
Which these presents place
Under a more tolerant, perhaps, examination.

By constant elimination
The manifest universe
Yielded an armour
Against utter consternation,

A Minoan undulation,
Seen, we admit, amid ambrosial circumstances
Strengthened him against
The discouraging doctrine of chances,

And his desire for survival,
Faint in the most strenuous moods,
Became an Olympian *apathein*[45]
In the presence of selected perceptions.

A pale gold, in the aforesaid pattern,
The unexpected palms
Destroying, certainly, the artist's urge,
Left him delighted with the imaginary
Audition of the phantasmal sea-surge,

Incapable of the least utterance or composition,
Emendation, conservation of the "better tradition,"
Refinement of medium, elimination of superfluities,
August attraction or concentration.

Nothing, in brief, but maudlin confession,
Irresponse to human aggression,
Amid the precipitation, down-float
Of insubstantial manna,
Lifting the faint susurrus[46]
Of his subjective hosannah.

Ultimate affronts to
Human redundancies;

Non-esteem of self-styled "his betters"
Leading, as he well knew,
To his final
Exclusion from the world of letters.

IV

Scattered Moluccas[47]
Not knowing, day to day,
The first day's end, in the next noon;
The placid water
Unbroken by the Simoon;[48]

Thick foliage
Placid beneath warm suns,
Tawn fore-shores
Washed in the cobalt of oblivions;

Or through dawn-mist
The grey and rose
Of the juridical
Flamingoes;

A consciousness disjunct,
Being but this overblotted
Series
Of intermittences;

Coracle[49] of Pacific voyages,
The unforecasted beach;
Then on an oar
Read this:

"I was
And I no more exist;
Here drifted
An hedonist."

MEDALLION

Luini[50] in porcelain!
The grand piano

Utters a profane
Protest with her clear soprano.

The sleek head emerges
From the gold-yellow frock
As Anadyomene[51] in the opening
Pages of Reinach.[52]

Honey-red, closing the face-oval,
A basket-work of braids which seem as if they were
Spun in King Minos' hall
From metal, or intractable amber;

The face-oval beneath the glaze,
Bright in its suave bounding-line, as,
Beneath half-watt rays,
The eyes turn topaz.

THE CANTOS
(1917–1922)

THREE CANTOS OF A
POEM OF SOME LENGTH

I

Hang it all, there can be but one *Sordello!*[1]
But say I want to, say I take your whole bag of tricks,
Let in your quirks and tweeks, and say the thing's an art-form,
Your *Sordello,* and that the modern world
Needs such a rag-bag to stuff all its thought in;
Say that I dump my catch, shiny and silvery
As fresh sardines flapping and slipping on the marginal cobbles?
(I stand before the booth, the speech; but the truth
Is inside this discourse—this booth is full of the marrow of
    wisdom.)
Give up th' intaglio method.[2]

                        Tower by tower
Red-brown the rounded bases, and the plan
Follows the builder's whim. Beaucaire's[3] slim gray
Leaps from the stubby base of Altaforte—[4]
Mohammed's windows, for the Alcazar[5]
Has such a garden, split by a tame small stream.
The moat is ten yards wide, the inner courtyard
Half a-swim with mire.
Trunk hose?

              There are not. The rough men swarm out

In robes that are half Roman, half like the Knave of Hearts;
And I discern your story:
                        Peire Cardinal
Was half forerunner of Dante.[6] Arnaut's[7] that trick
Of the unfinished address,
And half your dates are out, you mix your eras;
For that great font[8] Sordello sat beside—
'Tis an immortal passage, but the font?—
Is some two centuries outside the picture.
Does it matter?
                        Not in the least. Ghosts move about me
Patched with histories. You had your business:
To set out so much thought, so much emotion;
To paint, more real than any dead Sordello,
The half or third of your intensest life
And call that third *Sordello;*
And you'll say, "No, not your life,
He never showed himself."
Is't worth the evasion, what were the use
Of setting figures up and breathing life upon them,
Were 't not *our* life, your life, my life, extended?
I walk Verona. (I am here in England.)
I see Can Grande.[9] (Can see whom you will.)
                        You had one whole man?
And I have many fragments, less worth? Less worth?
Ah, had you quite my age, quite such a beastly and
        cantankerous age?
You had some basis, had some set belief.
Am I let preach? Has it a place in music?

                        I walk the airy street,
See the small cobbles flare with the poppy spoil.
'Tis your "great day," the Corpus Domini,
And all my chosen and peninsular village
Has made one glorious blaze of all its lanes—
Oh, before I was up—with poppy flowers.
Mid-June: some old god eats the smoke, 'tis not the
        saints;

And up and out to the half-ruined chapel—
Not the old place at the height of the rocks,
But that splay, barn-like church the Renaissance
Had never quite got into trim again.
As well begin here. Began our Catullus:
"Home to sweet rest, and to the waves' deep laughter,"
The laugh they wake amid the border rushes.
This is our home, the trees are full of laughter,
And the storms laugh loud, breaking the riven waves
On "north-most rocks"; and here the sunlight
Glints on the shaken waters, and the rain
Comes forth with delicate tread, walking from Isola Garda—
                    Lo soleils plovil,[10]
As Arnaut had it in th' inextricable song.
The very sun rains and a spatter of fire
Darts from the "Lydian" ripples; "locus undae," as Catullus,
        "Lydiae,"[11]
And the place is full of spirits.
Not lemures,[12] not dark and shadowy ghosts,
But the ancient living, wood-white,
Smooth as the inner bark, and firm of aspect,
And all agleam with colors—no, not agleam,
But colored like the lake and like the olive leaves,
Glaukopos,[13] clothed like the poppies, wearing golden greaves,
Light on the air.
Are they Etruscan gods?
The air is solid sunlight, apricus,[14]
Sun-fed we dwell there (we in England now);
It's your way of talk, we can be where we will be,
Sirmio serves my will better than your Asolo[15]
Which I have never seen.
                    Your "palace step"?
My stone seat was the Dogana's curb,[16]
And there were not "those girls," there was one flare, one face.
'Twas all I ever saw, but it was real. . . .
And I can no more say what shape it was . . .
But she was young, too young.
                    True, it was Venice,

And at Florian's[17] and under the north arcade
I have seen other faces, and had my rolls for breakfast, for that
      matter;
So, for what it's worth, I have the background.
                              And you had a background,
Watched "the soul," Sordello's soul,
And saw it lap up life, and swell and burst—
"Into the empyrean?"
So you worked out new form, the meditative,
Semi-dramatic, semi-epic story,
And we will say: What's left for me to do?
Whom shall I conjure up; who's my Sordello,
My pre-Daun Chaucer,[18] pre-Boccacio,
                              As you have done pre-Dante?
Whom shall I hang my shimmering garment on;
Who wear my feathery mantle, *hagoromo;*[19]
Whom set to dazzle the serious future ages?
Not Arnaut, not De Born, not Uc St. Circ[20] who has writ out
      the stories.
Or shall I do your trick, the showman's booth, Bob Browning,
Turned at my will into the Agora,
Or into the old theatre at Arles,
And set the lot, my visions, to confounding
The wits that have survived your damn'd *Sordello?*
(Or sulk and leave the word to novelists?)
What a hodge-podge you have made there!—
Zanze and *swanzig,* of all opprobrious rhymes!
And you turn off whenever it suits your fancy,
Now at Verona, now with the early Christians,
Or now a-gabbling of the "Tyrrhene whelk."
"The lyre should animate but not mislead the pen"—
That's Wordsworth, Mr. Browning. (What a phrase!—
That lyre, that pen, that bleating sheep, Will Wordsworth!)
That should have taught you avoid speech figurative
                              And set out your matter
As I do, in straight simple phrases:
                              Gods float in the azure air,
Bright gods, and Tuscan, back before dew was shed,

It is a world like Puvis'?[21]
                            Never so pale, my friend,
'Tis the first light—not half light—Panisks[22]
And oak-girls and the Maenads[23]
Have all the wood. Our olive Sirmio
Lies in its burnished mirror, and the Mounts Balde and Riva
Are alive with song, and all the leaves are full of voices.
"Non è fuggito."
                      "It is not gone." Metastasio
Is right—we have that world about us,
And the clouds bow above the lake, and there are folk upon
    them
Going their windy ways, moving by Riva,
By the western shore, far as Lonato,
And the water is full of silvery almond-white swimmers,
The silvery water glazes the up-turned nipple.

How shall we start hence, how begin the progress?
Pace naif Ficinus,[24] say when Hotep-Hotep
Was a king in Egypt—
   When Atlas sat down with his astrolabe,
     He, brother to Prometheus, physicist—
                 Say it was Moses' birth-year?
Exult with Shang[25] in squatness? The sea-monster
Bulges the squarish bronzes.
(Confucius later taught the world good manners,
Started with himself, built out perfection.)
                With Egypt!
Daub out in blue of scarabs, and with that greeny turquoise?
Or with China, *O Virgilio mio,* and gray gradual steps
Lead up beneath flat sprays of heavy cedars,
Temple of teak wood, and the gilt-brown arches
Triple in tier, banners woven by wall,
Fine screens depicted, sea waves curled high,
Small boats with gods upon them,
Bright flame above the river! Kwannon[26]
Footing a boat that's but one lotus petal,
With some proud four-spread genius

Leading along, one hand upraised for gladness,
Saying, "Tis she, his friend, the mighty goddess! Paean!
Sing hymns ye reeds,
        and all ye roots and herons and swans be glad,
Ye gardens of the nymphs put forth your flowers."
What have I of this life,
        Or even of Guido?[27]
        Sweet lie!—Was I there truly?
Did I know Or San Michele?[28]
        Let's believe it.
Believe the tomb he leapt[29] was Julia Laeta's?
Friend, I do not even—when he led that street charge—
I do not even know which sword he'd with him.
Sweet lie, "I lived!" Sweet lie, "I lived beside him."
And now it's all but truth and memory,
Dimmed only by the attritions of long time.
"But we forget not."
                        No, take it all for lies.
I have but smelt this life, a whiff of it—
The box of scented wood
Recalls cathedrals. And shall I claim;
Confuse my own phantastikon,[30]
Or say the filmy shell that circumscribes me
Contains the actual sun;
                        confuse the thing I see
With actual gods behind me?
                        Are they gods behind me?
How many worlds we have! If Botticelli
Brings her ashore on that great cockle-shell—
His Venus (Simonetta?),
And Spring and Aufidus[31] fill all the air
With their clear-outlined blossoms?
World enough. Behold, I say, she comes
"Apparelled like the spring, Graces her subjects,"
(That's from *Pericles*).
Oh, we have worlds enough, and brave *décors*,
And from these like we guess a soul for man
And build him full of aery populations.

Mantegna[32] a sterner line, and the new world about us:
Barred lights, great flares, new form, Picasso or Lewis.
If for a year man write to paint, and not to music—
O Casella![33]

II

        Leave Casella.[1]
Send out your thought upon the Mantuan palace—[2]
Drear waste, great halls,
Silk tatters still in the frame, Gonzaga's splendor
Alight with phantoms! What have we of them,
Or much or little?
Where do we come upon the ancient people?
"All that I know is that a certain star"—
All that I know of one, Joios, Tolosan,[3]
Is that in middle May, going along
A scarce discerned path, turning aside,
In level poplar lands, he found a flower, and wept.
"Y *a la primera flor*," he wrote,
"*Qu'ieu trobei, tornei em plor*."[4]
There's the one stave, and all the rest forgotten.
I've lost the copy I had of it in Paris,
Out of the blue and gilded manuscript
Decked out with Couci's rabbits,
And the pictures, twined with the capitals,
Purporting to be Arnaut's and the authors.
Joios we have. By such a margent stream,
He strayed in the field, wept for a flare of color,
When Coeur de Lion was before Chalus.[5]
Or there's En Arnaut's score of songs, two tunes;
The rose-leaf casts her dew on the ringing glass,
Dolmetsch[6] will build our age in witching music.
Viols da Gamba, tabors, tympanons:

        "Yin-yo laps in the reeds, my guest departs,
The maple leaves blot up their shadows,

The sky is full of autumn,
We drink our parting in saki.
Out of the night comes troubling lute music,
And we cry out, asking the singer's name,
And get this answer:
                      'Many a one
Brought me rich presents; my hair was full of jade,
And my slashed skirts, drenched in expensive dyes,
Were dipped in crimson, sprinkled with rare wines.
I was well taught my arts at Ga-ma-rio,
And then one year I faded out and married.'
The lute-bowl hid her face.
                      We heard her weeping."[7]

Society, her sparrows, Venus' sparrows, and Catullus
Hung on the phrase (played with it as Mallarmé
Played for a fan, *"Rêveuse pour que je plonge,"*);[8]
Wrote out his crib from Sappho:
"God's peer that man is in my sight—
Yea, and the very gods are under him,
Who sits opposite thee, facing thee, near thee,
Gazing his fill and hearing thee,
And thou smilest. Woe to me, with
Quenched senses, for when I look upon thee, Lesbia,
There is nothing above me
And my tongue is heavy, and along my veins
Runs the slow fire, and resonant
Thunders surge in behind my ears,
And the night is thrust down upon me."

That was the way of love, *flamma dimanat.*[9]
And in a year, "I love her as a father";
And scarce a year, "Your words are written in water";
And in ten moons, *"Caelius, Lesbia illa—*
That Lesbia, Caelius, our Lesbia, that Lesbia
Whom Catullus once loved more
Than his own soul and all his friends,
Is now the drab of every lousy Roman."

So much for him who puts his trust in woman.
So the murk opens.
                         Dordoigne! When I was there,
There came a centaur, spying the land,
And there were nymphs behind him.
Or going on the road by Salisbury
Procession on procession—
For that road was full of peoples,
Ancient in various days, long years between them.
Ply over ply of life still wraps the earth here.
Catch at Dordoigne.
                  Viscount St. Antoni
In the warm damp of spring,
Feeling the night air full of subtle hands,
Plucks at a viol, singing:
                    "As the rose—
Si com, si com"—they all begin *"si com."*
"For as the rose in trellis
Winds in and through and over,
So is your beauty in my heart, that is bound through and over.
So lay Queen Venus in her house of glass,
The pool of worth thou art,
                         Flood-land of pleasure."
   But the Viscount Pena
Went making war into an hostile country
Where he was wounded:
"The news held him dead."
St. Antoni in favor, and the lady
Ready to hold his hands—
This last report upset the whole convention.
She rushes off to church, sets up a gross of candles,
Pays masses for the soul of Viscount Pena.

   Thus St. Circ has the story:
"That sire Raimon Jordans, of land near Caortz,
Lord of St. Antoni, loved this Viscountess of Pena[10]
'Gentle' and 'highly prized.'
And he was good at arms and *bos trobaire*,[11]

And they were taken with love beyond all measure,"
And then her husband was reported dead,
"And at this news she had great grief and sorrow,"
And gave the church such wax for his recovery,
That he recovered, and
"At this news she had great grief and teen,"
And fell to moping, dismissed St. Antoni;
"Thus was there more than one in deep distress."

    So ends that novel. And the blue Dordoigne
Stretches between white cliffs,
Pale as the background of a Leonardo.
"As rose in trellis, that is bound over and over,"
A wasted song?

                    No Elis, Lady of Montfort,
Wife of William à Gordon, heard of the song,
Sent him her mild advances.
                  Gordon? Or Gourdon[12]
Juts into the sky
                  Like a thin spire,
Blue night's pulled down around it
Like tent flaps, or sails close hauled. When I was there,
La noche de San Juan, a score of players
Were walking about the streets in masquerade,
With pikes and paper helmets, and the booths,
Were scattered align, the rag ends of the fair.
False arms! True arms? You think a tale of lances . . .
A flood of people storming about Spain!
                My cid rode up to Burgos,[13]
Up to the studded gate between two towers,
Beat with his lance butt.
                A girl child of nine,
Comes to a little shrine-like platform in the wall,
Lisps out the words, a-whisper, the King's writ:
"Let no man speak to Diaz or give him help or food
On pain of death, his eyes torn out,
His heart upon a pike, his goods sequestered."

He from Bivar, cleaned out,
From empty perches of dispersed hawks,
From empty presses,
Came riding with his company up the great hill—
"Afe Minaya!"—[14]

          to Burgos in the spring,
And thence to fighting, to down-throw of Moors,
And to Valencia rode he, by the beard!—
Muy velida.[15]

          Of onrush of lances,
Of splintered staves, riven and broken casques,
Dismantled castles, of painted shields split up,
Blazons hacked off, piled men and bloody rivers;
Then "sombre light upon reflecting armor"
And portents in the wind, when De las Nieblas
Set out to sea-fight,
"Y dar neuva lumbre las armas y hierros."[16]
Full many a fathomed sea-change in the eyes
That sought with him the salt sea victories.
Another gate?

          And Kumasaka's ghost[17] come back to tell
The honor of the youth who'd slain him.
Another gate.

          The kernelled walls of Toro, las almenas;[18]
Afield, a king come in an unjust cause.
Atween the chinks aloft flashes the armored figure,
Muy linda, a woman, Helen, a star,
Lights the king's features . . .

          "No use, my liege—
She is your highness' sister," breaks in Ancures;
"Mal fuego s'enciende!"[19]
Such are the gestes of war "told over and over."
And Ignez?

          Was a queen's tire-woman,
Court sinecure, the court of Portugal;
And the young prince loved her—Pedro,
Later called the cruel. And other courtiers were jealous.
Two of them stabbed her with the king's connivance,

And he, the prince, kept quiet a space of years—
                    Uncommon the quiet.
And he came to reign, and had his will upon the dagger-
    players,
And held his court, a wedding ceremonial—
He and her dug-up corpse in cerements
Crowned with the crown and splendor of Portugal.
A quiet evening and a decorous procession;
Who winked at murder kisses the dead hand,
Does leal homage,
"Que depois de ser morta foy Rainha."[20]
Dig up Camoens,[21] hear out his resonant bombast:
                    "That among the flowers,
As once was Proserpine,
Gatheredst thy soul's light fruit and every blindness,
Thy Enna the flary mead-land of Mondego,
Long art thou sung by maidens in Mondego."
What have we now of her, his *"linda Ignez"*?
Houtmans in jail for debt in Lisbon—how long after?—
Contrives a company, the Dutch eat Portugal,
Follow her ship's tracks, Roemer Vischer's daughters,
Talking some Greek, dally with glass engraving;
Vondel, the Eglantine, Dutch Renaissance[22]—
The old tale out of fashion, daggers gone;
And Gaby wears Braganza[23] on her throat—
Commuted, say, another public pearl
Tied to a public gullet. Ah, *mon rêve,*
It happened; and now go think—
Another crown, thrown to another dancer, brings you to
    modern times?

   I knew a man,[24] but where 'twas is no matter:
Born on a farm, he hankered after painting;
His father kept him at work;
No luck—he married and got four sons;
Three died, the fourth he sent to Paris—
Ten years of Julian's and the ateliers,
Ten years of life, his pictures in the salons,

Name coming in the press.
                    And when I knew him,
Back once again, in middle Indiana,
Acting as usher in the theatre,
Painting the local drug-shop and soda bars,
The local doctor's fancy for the mantel-piece;
Sheep—jabbing the wool upon their flea-bit backs—
The local doctor's ewe-ish pastoral;
Adoring Puvis, giving his family back
What they had spent for him, talking Italian cities,
Local excellence at Perugia,
                    dreaming his renaissance,
Take my Sordello!

III

Another's a half-cracked fellow—John Heydon,[1]
Worker of miracles, dealer in levitation,
In thoughts upon pure form, in alchemy,
Seer of pretty visions ("servant of God and secretary of
    nature");
Full of a plaintive charm, like Botticelli's,
With half-transparent forms, lacking the vigor of gods.
Thus Heydon, in a trance, at Bulverton,
Had such a sight:
Decked all in green, with sleeves of yellow silk
Slit to the elbow, slashed with various purples.
Her eyes were green as glass, her foot was leaf-like.
She was adorned with choicest emeralds,
And promised him the way of holy wisdom.
"Pretty green bank," began the half-lost poem.
Take the old way, say I met John Heydon,
Sought out the place,
Lay on the bank, was "plungèd deep in swevyn;"
And saw the company—Layamon, Chaucer—
Pass each in his appropriate robes;
Conversed with each, observed the varying fashion.

And then comes Heydon.
                    "I have seen John Heydon."
Let us hear John Heydon!
                    "*Omniformis*
Omnis intellectus est"[2]—thus he begins, by spouting half of
    Psellus.[3]
(Then comes a note, my assiduous commentator:
Not Psellus *De Daemonibus*, but Porphyry's *Chances*,
In the thirteenth chapter, that "every intellect is omniform.")
Magnifico Lorenzo used the dodge,
Says that he met Ficino[4]
In some Wordsworthian, false-pastoral manner,
And that they walked along, stopped at a wellhead,
And heard deep platitudes about contentment
From some old codger with an endless beard.
"A daemon is not a particular intellect,
But is a substance differed from intellect,"
Breaks in Ficino,
"Placed in the latitude or locus of souls"—
That's out of Proclus, take your pick of them.
Valla,[5] more earth and sounder rhetoric—
Prefacing praise to his Pope Nicholas:
"A man of parts, skilled in the subtlest sciences;
A patron of the arts, of poetry; and of a fine discernment."
Then comes a catalogue, his jewels of conversation.
No, you've not read your *Elegantiae*—
A dull book?—shook the church.
The prefaces, cut clear and hard:
"Know then the Roman speech, a sacrament,"
Spread for the nations, eucharist of wisdom,
Bread of the liberal arts.
                    Ha! Sir Blancatz,[6]
Sordello would have your heart to give to all the princes;
Valla, the heart of Rome,
Sustaining speech, set out before the people.
"*Nec bonus Christianus ac bonus*[7]
                    Tullianus."

Marius, Du Bellay, wept for the buildings,
Baldassar Castiglione saw Raphael
"Lead back the soul into its dead, waste dwelling,"
Corpore laniato,[8] and Lorenzo Valla,
"Broken in middle life? bent to submission?—
Took a fat living from the Papacy"
(That's in Villari,[9] but Burckhardt's statement is different)—
"More than the Roman city, the Roman speech"
(Holds fast its part among the ever-living).
"Not by the eagles only was Rome measured."
"Wherever the Roman speech was, there was Rome,"
Wherever the speech crept, there was mastery
Spoke with the law's voice while your Greek logicians . . .
More Greeks than one! Doughty's "divine Homeros"
Came before sophistry. Justinopolitan
Uncatalogued Andreas Divus,[10]
Gave him in Latin, 1538 in my edition, the rest uncertain,
Caught up his cadence, word and syllable:
"Down to the ships we went, set mast and sail,
Black keel and beasts for bloody sacrifice,
Weeping we went."[11]
I've strained my ear for *-ensa, -ombra,* and *-ensa*
And cracked my wit on delicate canzoni—
                    Here's but rough meaning:
"And then went down to the ship, set keel to breakers,
Forth on the godly sea;
We set up mast and sail on the swarthy ship,
Sheep bore we aboard her, and our bodies also
Heavy with weeping. And winds from sternward
Bore us out onward with bellying canvas—
Circe's this craft, the trim-coifed goddess.
Then sat we amidships, wind jamming the tiller.
Thus with stretched sail
                    We went over sea till day's end:
Sun to his slumber, shadows o'er all the ocean.
Came we then to the bounds of deepest water,
To the Kimmerian lands and peopled cities

Covered with close-webbed mist, unpiercèd ever
With glitter of sun-rays,
Nor with stars stretched, nor looking back from heaven,
Swartest night stretched over wretched men there.
Thither we in that ship, unladed sheep there,
The ocean flowing backward, came we through to the place
Aforesaid by Circe.
Here did they rites, Perimedes and Eurylochus,
And drawing sword from my hip
I dug the ell-square pitkin,[12] poured we libations unto each the
    dead,
First mead and then sweet wine,
Water mixed with white flour.
Then prayed I many a prayer to the sickly death's-heads
As set in Ithaca, sterile bulls of the best,
For sacrifice, heaping the pyre with goods.
Sheep, to Tiresias only,
Black, and a bell sheep;
Dark blood flowed in the fosse.
Souls out of Erebus, cadaverous dead
Of brides, of youths, and of many passing old,
Virgins tender, souls stained with recent tears,
Many men mauled with bronze lance-heads,
Battle spoil, bearing yet dreary arms:
These many crowded about me,
With shouting, pallor upon me, cried to my men for more
    beasts;
Slaughtered the herds—sheep slain of bronze,
Poured ointment, cried to the gods,
To Pluto the strong, and praised Proserpine.
Unsheathed the narrow steel,
I sat to keep off the impetuous, impotent dead
Till I should hear Tiresias.
But first Elpenor came, our friend Elpenor,
Unburied, cast on the wide earth—
Limbs that we left in the house of Circe,
Unwept, unwrapped in sepulchre, since toils urged other,

Pitiful spirit—and I cried in hurried speech:
'Elpenor, how art thou come to this dark coast?
Cam'st thou afoot, outstripping seamen?' And he in heavy
     speech:
'Ill fate and abundant wine! I slept in Circe's ingle,[13]
Going down the long ladder unguarded, I fell against the
     buttress,
Shattered the nape-nerve, the soul sought Avernus.
But thou, O King, I bid remember me, unwept, unburied!
Heap up mine arms, be tomb by the sea-board, and inscribed,
A man of no fortune and with a name to come;
And set my oar up, that I swung 'mid fellows.'
Came then another ghost, whom I beat off, Anticlea,
And then Tiresias, Theban,
Holding his golden wand, knew me and spoke first:
'Man of ill hour, why come a second time,
Leaving the sunlight, facing the sunless dead and this joyless
     region?
Stand from the fosse, move back, leave me my bloody bever,
And I will speak you true speeches.'
                                   And I stepped back,
Sheathing the yellow sword. Dark blood he drank then
And spoke: 'Lustrous Odysseus, shalt
Return through spiteful Neptune, over dark seas,
Lose all companions.' Foretold me the ways and the signs.
Came then Anticlea, to whom I answered:
'Fate drives me on through these deeps; I sought Tiresias.'
I told her news of Troy, and thrice her shadow
                     Faded in my embrace.
Then had I news of many faded women—
Tyro, Alemena, Chloris—
Heard out their tales by that dark fosse, and sailed
By sirens and thence outward and away,
And unto Circe buried Elpenor's corpse."

Lie quiet, Divus.
               In Officina Wechli, Paris,

M. D. three X's, Eight, with Aldus on the Frogs,
And a certain Cretan's
                    Hymni Deorum:
(The thin clear Tuscan stuff
    Gives way before the florid mellow phrase.)
Take we the Goddess, Venus:
                                    Venerandam,
Aurean coronam habentem, pulchram,
Cypri munimenta sortita est,[14] maritime,
Light on the foam, breathed on by zephyrs,
And air-tending hours. Mirthful, *orichalci,*[15] with golden
Girdles and breast bands.
                              Thou with dark eye-lids,
Bearing the golden bough of Argicida.[16]

  [*Poetry, 1917*]

THE FOURTH CANTO

Palace in smoky light,
Troy but a heap of smouldering boundary-stones,
ANAXIFORMINGES! Aurunculeia![1]
Hear me. Cadmus of Golden Prows;[2]
The silver mirrors catch the bright stones and flare,
Dawn, to our waking, drifts in the green cool light;
Dew-haze blurrs, in the grass, pale ankles moving.
Beat, beat, whirr, thud, in the soft turf under the apple trees,
Choros nympharum, goat-foot with the pale foot alternate;
Crescent of blue-shot waters, green-gold in the shallows
A black cock crows in the sea-foam;

And by the curved carved foot of the couch,
                    claw-foot and lion head, an old man seated
Speaking in the low drone: . . .
                                                        "Ityn!
"Et ter flebiliter. Ityn, Ityn![3]
"And she went toward the window and cast her down,
                    "All the while, the while, swallows crying:
"Ityn!
                    " "It is Cabestan's[4] heart in the dish."
                    " "It is Cabestan's heart in the dish?
                    " "No other taste shall change this."

And she went toward the window,

                         the slim white stone bar

Making a double arch;
Firm even fingers held to the firm pale stone;
Swung for a moment,

                    and the wind out of Rhodez[5]

Caught in the full of her sleeve.

                  . . . the swallows crying:

Ityn! Ityn!"

              Actaeon. . . .[6]

                     And a valley,
The valley is thick with leaves, with leaves, the trees,
The sunlight glitters, glitters a-top,
Like a fish-scale roof,

      Like the church-roof in Poictiers
If it were gold.

                       Beneath it, beneath it
Not a ray, not a slivver, not a spare disk of sunlight
Flaking the black, soft water;
Bathing the body of nymphs, of nymphs, and Diana,
Nymphs, white-gathered about her, and the air, air,
Shaking, air alight with the goddess

                  fanning their hair in the dark,
Lifting, lifting and waffing:
Ivory dipping in silver,

             Shadow'd, o'ershadow'd
Ivory dipping in silver,
Not a splotch, not a lost shatter of sunlight.
Then Actaeon: Vidal,
Vidal.[7] It is old Vidal speaking,

                stumbling along in the wood
Not a patch, not a lost shimmer of sunlight,

                the pale hair of the goddess,
The dogs leap on Actaeon,

      "Hither, hither, Actaeon,"
Spotted stag of the wood;
Gold, gold, a sheaf of hair,

        Thick like a wheat swath,

Blaze, blaze in the sun,
        The dogs leap on Actaeon.

Stumbling, stumbling along in the wood,
Muttering, muttering Ovid:
        "Pergusa . . . pool . . pool . . . Gargaphia
'Pool, pool of Salmacis.[8]
          The empty armour shakes as the cygnet moves,
Thus the light rains, thus pours, *e lo soleils plovil*,[9]
The liquid, and rushing crystal
                   whirls up the bright brown sand.
Ply over ply,[10] thin glitter of water;
Brook film bearing white petals
   ("The pines of Takasago[11] grow with pines of Ise"[12])
        "Behold the Tree of the Visages."
The forked tips flaming as if with lotus,
        Ply over ply
The shallow eddying fluid
              beneath the knees of the gods.
Torches melt in the glare
        Set flame of the corner cook-stall,
Blue agate casing the sky, a sputter of resin;
The saffron sandal petals the tender foot, Hymenaeus!
        Io Hymen, Io Hymenaee![13] Aurunculeia[14]
The scarlet flower is cast on the blanch-white stone,
Amaracus, Hill of Urania's Son.
        Meanwhile So-Gioku:[15]
"This wind, sire, is the king's wind,
        this wind is wind of the palace
Shaking imperial water-jets."
        And Ran-Ti, opening his collar:
"This wind roars in the earth's bag,
               it lays the water with rushes;
"No wind is the king's wind.
        Let every cow keep her calf."
"This wind is held in gauze curtains. . . . ."
        No wind is the king's . . ."

'The camel drivers sit in the turn of the stairs
        look down to Ecbatan[16] of plotted streets,
"Danae! Danae!"[17]
          What wind is the king's?
Smoke hangs on the stream,
The peach-trees shed bright leaves in the water,
Sound drifts in the evening haze,
        The barge scrapes at the ford.
Gilt rafters above black water;
                     three steps in an open field
Gray stone-posts leading nowhither.
The Spanish poppies swim in an air of glass.
Père Henri Jacques[18] still seeks the sennin on Rokku.[19]
              Polhonac,[20]
As Gyges[21] on Thracian platter, set the feast;
Cabestan, Terreus.
        It is Cabestan's heart in the dish.
Vidal, tracked out with dogs . . for glamour of Loba;
Upon the gilded tower in Ecbatan
        Lay the god's bride, lay ever
Waiting the golden rain.
        Et saave!
But to-day, Garonne[22] is thick like paint, beyond Dorada,
The worm of the Procession bores in the soup of the crowd,
The blue thin voices against the crash of the crowd
        Et "Salve regina."[23]
In trellises
  Wound over with small flowers, beyond Adige[24]
In the but half-used room, thin film of images,
        (by Stefano)[25]
Age of unbodied gods, the vitreous fragile images
Thin as the locust's wing
Haunting the mind . . as of Guido . . .
Thin as the locust's wing. The Centaur's heel
Plants in the earth-loam.

THE FIFTH CANTO

Great bulk, huge mass, thesaurus;
Ecbatan,[1] the clock ticks and fades out;
The bride awaiting the god's touch; Ecbatan,
City of patterned streets; again the vision:
Down in the viae stradae, toga'd the crowd, and arm'd,
Rushing on populous business, and from parapets
Looked down—at North
Was Egypt, and the celestial Nile, blue-deep
                    cutting low barren land,
Old men and camels working the water-wheels;
                    Measureless seas and stars,
Iamblichus'[2] light, the souls ascending,
Sparks like a partridge covey,
                    Like the "ciocco,"[3] brand struck in the game.
"Et omniformis":[4]
                    Air, fire, the pale soft light.
Topaz, I manage, and three sorts of blue;
                    but on the barb of time.
The fire? always, and the vision always,
Ear dull, perhaps, with the vision, flitting
And fading at will. Weaving with points of gold,
Gold-yellow, saffron . . .
                    The roman shoe, Aurunculeia's,

And come shuffling feet, and cries "Da nuces!⁵
"Nuces!" praise and Hymenaeus "brings the girl to her man."
Titter of sound about me, always,
                              and from "Hesperus . . ."
Hush of the older song: "Fades light from seacrest,
"And in Lydia walks with pair'd women
"Peerless among the pairs, and that once in Sardis
"In satieties . . .
                    "Fades the light from the sea, and many things
"Are set abroad and brought to mind of thee,"
And the vinestocks lie untended, new leaves come to the
        shoots,
North wind nips on the bough, and seas in heart
Toss up chill crests,
                    And the vine stocks lie untended
And many things are set abroad and brought to mind
Of thee, Atthis,⁶ unfruitful.
                    The talks ran long in the night.
And from Mauleon,⁷ fresh with a new earned grade,
In maze of approaching rain-steps, Poicebot—⁸
The air was full of women.
                              And Savairic Mauleon
Gave him his land and knight's fee, and he wed the woman.
Came lust of travel on him, of *romerya;*⁹
And out of England a knight with slow-lifting eyelids
*Lei fassar furar a del,*¹⁰ put glamour upon her . . .
And left her an eight months gone.
                    "Came lust of woman upon him,"
Poicebot, now on North road from Spain
(Sea-change, a grey in the water)
                    And in small house by town's edge
Found a woman, changed and familiar face;
Hard night, and parting at morning.

And Pieire won the singing, Pieire de Maensac,¹¹
Song or land on the throw, and was *dreitz hom*¹²
And had De Tierci's wife and with the war they made:
                    Troy in Auvergnat

While Menelaus piled up the church at port
He kept Tyndarida. Dauphin stood with de Maensac.

John Borgia[13] is bathed at last.
                    (Clock-tick pierces the vision)
Tiber, dark with the cloak, wet cat gleaming in patches.
Click of the hooves, through garbage,
Clutching the greasy stone. "And the cloak floated"
Slander is up betimes.
                            But Varchi[14] of Florence,
Steeped in a different year, and pondering Brutus,
Then
            "SIGA MAL AUTHIS DEUTERON![15]
"Dog-eye!!" (to Alessandro)
                "Whether for Love of Florence," Varchi leaves it,
Saying, "I saw the man, came up with him at Venice,
"I, one wanting the facts,
"And no mean labour.
                            "Or for a privy spite?"
            Good Varchi leaves it,
But: "I saw the man. *Se pia?*
"*O impia?*[16] For Lorenzaccio[17] had thought of stroke in the
        open
"But uncertain (for the Duke went never unguarded) . . .
"And would have thrown him from wall
"Yet feared this might not end him," or lest Alessandro
Know not by whom death came,
                            O si credesse[18]
"If when the foot slipped, when death came upon him,
"Lest cousin Duke Alessandro think he'd fallen alone
"No friend to aid him in falling."
                        Caina attende.[19]
As beneath my feet a lake, was ice in seeming.
And all of this, runs Varchi, dreamed out beforehand
In Perugia, caught in the star-maze by Del Carmine,
Cast on a natal paper, set with an exegesis, told,
All told to Alessandro, told thrice over,
Who held his death for a doom.

In abuleia.
                                        But Don Lorenzino
"Whether for love of Florence . . . but
            "O si morisse, credesse caduto da se."

                                    SIGA, SIGA![20]
The wet cloak floats on the surface,
Schiavoni, caught on the wood-barge,
Gives out the afterbirth, Giovanni Borgia,[21]
Trails out no more at nights, where Barabello[22]
Prods the Pope's elephant, and gets no crown, where
        Mozarello
Takes the Calabrian roadway, and for ending
Is smothered beneath a mule,
                                        a poet's ending,[23]
Down a stale well-hole, oh a poet's ending. "Sanazarro[24]
"Alone out of all the court was faithful to him"
For the gossip of Naples' trouble drifts to North,
Fracastor (lightning was midwife) Cotta, and Ser D'Alviano,
Al poco giorno ed al gran cerchio d'ombra,[25]
Talk the talks out with Navighero,[26]
Burner of yearly Martials,
                    (The slavelet is mourned in vain)
And the next comer
                    says "were nine wounds,
"Four men, white horse with a double rider,"
The hooves clink and slick on the cobbles . . .
Schiavoni . . . the cloak floats on the water,
"Sink the thing," splash wakes Schiavoni;
Tiber catching the nap, the moonlit velvet,
A wet cat gleaming in patches.
                                        "Se pia," Varchi,
"O empia, ma risoluto
"E terribile deliberazione"[27]
                    Both sayings run in the wind,
Ma si morisse![28]

THE SIXTH CANTO

"The tale of thy deeds, Odysseus!" and Tolosan
Ground rents, sold by Guillaume,[1] ninth duke of Aquitaine;
Till Louis is wed with Eleanor; the wheel . . .
("Conrad, the wheel turns and in the end turns ill")
And Acre and boy's love . . . for her uncle was
Commandant at Acre, she was pleased with him;
And Louis, French King,[2] was jealous of days unshared
This pair had had together in years gone;
And he drives on for Zion, as "God wills"
To find, in six weeks time, the Queen's scarf is
Twisted atop the casque of Saladin.
"For Sandbrueil's ransom." But the pouch-mouths add,
"She went out hunting, there, the tuft-top palms
"Give spot of shade, she rode back rather late,
"Late, latish, yet perhaps it was not too late."
Then France again, and to be rid of her
And brush his antlers; Aquitaine, Poictiers!
Buckle off the lot! And Adelaide Castilla wears the crown.
Eleanor down water-butt, dethroned, debased, unqueen'd.
                    Unqueen'd for five rare months,
And frazzle-top, the sand-red face, the pitching gait,
Harry Plantagent, the sputter in place of speech,
But King about to be, King Louis, takes a queen.

"E quand lo reis Louis lo entendit
                    mout er faschée[3]
And yet Gisors,[4] in six years thence,
Was Marguerite's. And Harry *joven*
In pledge for all his life and life of all his heirs
Shall have Gisors and Vexis[5] and Neauphal, Neufchastel;
But if no issue, Gisors shall revert
And Vexis and Neufchastel and Neauphal to the French
     crown.
A song: *Si tuit li dol el plor el marrimen*
Del mon[6] were set together they would seem but light
Against the death of the young English King,
Harry the Young is dead and all men mourn,
Mourn all good courtiers, fighters, cantadors.
And still Old Harry keeps grip on Gisors
And Neufchastel and Neauphal and Vexis;
And two years war, and never two years go by
                    but come new forays, and "The wheel
"Turns, Conrad, turns, and in the end toward ill."
And Richard and Alix[7] span the gap, Gisors,
And Eleanor and Richard face the King,
For the fourth family time Plantagenet
Faces his dam and whelps, . . . and holds Gisors,
Now Alix' dowry, against Philippe-Auguste
(Louis' by Adelaide, wood-lost, then crowned at
     Etampe)
And never two years sans war.
                              And Zion still
Bleating away to Eastward, the lost lamb,
Damned city (was only Frederic knew
The true worth, and patched with Malek Kamel[8]
The sane and sensible peace to bait the world
And set all camps disgruntled with all leaders.
"Damn'd atheists!" alike Mahomet growls,
And Christ grutches more sullen for Sicilian sense
Than does Mahound on Malek.)
                              The bright coat
Is more to the era, and in Messina's beach-way

Des Barres and Richard split the reed-lances
And the coat is torn.

        (Moving in heavy air: Henry and Saladin.[9]
The serpent coils in the crowd.)
The letters run: Tancred[10] to Richard:

        That the French King is
        More against thee, than is his will to me
        Good and in faith; and moves against your safety.

Richard to Tancred:

        That our pact stands firm,
        And, for these slanders, that I think you lie.

Proofs, and in writing:

        And if Bourgogne say they were not
        Deliver'd by hand and his,
        Let him move sword against me and my word.

Richard to Philip: silence, with a tone.
Richard to Flanders: the subjoined and precedent.
Philip a silence; and then, "Lies and turned lies
"For that he will fail Alix
"Affianced, and Sister to Ourself."
Richard: "My Father's bed-piece! A Plantagenet
"Mewls on the covers, with a nose like his already."
Then:

        In the Name
        Of Father and of Son Triune and Indivisible
        Philip of France by Goddes Grace
        To all men presents that our noble brother
        Richard of England engaged by our mutual oath

           (a sacred covenant applicable to both)

Need *not* wed Alix[11] but whomso he choose
We cede him Gisors, Neauphal and Vexis
And to the heirs male of his house
Cahors and Querci Richard's The abbeys ours
Of Figeac and Souillac   And St Gilles left still in peace

Alix returns to France.

Made in Messina in
The year 1190 of the Incarnation of the Word.

Reed lances broken, a cloak torn by Des Barres
Do turn King Richard from the holy wars.
                    And "God aid Conrad
"For man's aid comes slow," Aye tarries upon the road,
En Bertrans cantat.
                    And before all this
By Correze, Malemort[12]
A young man walks, at church with galleried porch
By river-marsh, a sad man, pacing
Come from Ventadorn; and Eleanor turning on thirty years,
Domna jauzionda,[13] and then Bernart saying:
                    "My Lady of Ventadorn
"Is shut by Eblis in,[14] and will not hawk nor hunt
"Nor get her free in the air,
                    nor watch fish rise to bait
"Nor the glare-wing'd flies alight in the creek's edge
"Save in my absence, Madame.
                    '*Que la lauzeta mover,*'
"Send word, I ask you, to Eblis,
                    you have seen that maker
"And finder of songs, so far afield as this
"That he may free her,
                    who sheds such light in the air."

THE SEVENTH CANTO

Eleanor (she spoiled in a British climate)
'Ελανδρος and 'Ελέπτολις,[1] and poor old Homer blind,
                        blind as a bat,
Ear, ear for the sea-surge; rattle of old men's voices.
And then the phantom Rome, marble narrow for seats
                "Si pulvis nullus erit"[2]
The chatter above the circus, "Nullum tamen excute."
Then file and candles, e li mestiers ecoutes;[3]
Scene for the battle only, but still scene,
Pennons and standards y cavals armatz,[4]
Not mere succession of strokes, sightless narration,
And Dante's "ciocco,"[5] brand struck in the game.
Un peu moisi, plancher plus bas que le jardin.

"Contre le lambris, fauteuil de paille,
"Un vieux piano, et sous le baromètre . . .[6]

The old men's voices, beneath the columns of false marble,
And the walls tinted discreet, the modish, darkish green-blue,
Discreeter gilding, and the pannelled wood
Not present, but suggested, for the leasehold is
Touched with an imprecision . . . about three squares;

The house a shade too solid, and the art
A shade off action, paintings a shade too thick.

And the great domed head, *con gli occhi onesti e tardi*[7]
Moves before me, phantom with weighted motion,
Grave incessu, drinking the tone of things,
And the old voice lifts itself
                              weaving an endless sentence.
We also made ghostly visits, and the stair
That knew us, found us again on the turn of it,
Knocking at empty rooms, seeking for buried beauty;
And the sun-tanned, gracious and well-formed fingers
Lift no latch of bent bronze, no Empire handle
Twists for the knocker's fall; no voice to answer.
A strange concierge, in place of the gouty-footed.

Skeptic against all this one seeks the living,
Stubborn against the fact. The wilted flowers
Brushed out a seven year since, of no effect.
Damn the partition! Paper, dark brown and stretched,
Flimsy and damned partition.
                              Ione, dead the long year,[8]
My lintel, and Liu Ch'e's lintel.[9]
Time blacked out with the rubber.
                      The Elysée[10] carries a name on
And the bus behind me gives me a date for peg;
Low ceiling and the Erard[11] and the silver,
These are in "time." Four chairs, the bow-front dresser,
The pannier of the desk, cloth top sunk in.
                      "Beer-bottle on the statue's pediment!
"That, Fritz, is the era, to-day against the past,
"Contemporary." And the passion endures.
Against their action, aromas. Rooms, against chronicles.
Smaragdos, chrysolitos; De Gama[12] wore striped pants in
   Africa
And "Mountains of the sea gave birth to troops";

Le vieux commode en acajou:[13]
                    beer-bottles of various strata,
But is she as dead as Tyro? In seven years?
                    Ἐλέναυς, ἔλανδρος, ἐλέπτολις[14]
The sea runs in the beach-groove, shaking the floated pebbles,
Eleanor!
              The scarlet curtain throws a less scarlet shadow;
Lamplight at Buovilla, e quel remir,[15]
                                And all that day
Nicea[16] moved before me
And the cold gray air troubled her not
For all her naked beauty, bit not the tropic skin,
And the long slender feet lit on the curb's marge
And her moving height went before me,
                          We alone having being.
And all that day, another day:
              Thin husks I had known as men,
Dry casques of departed locusts
                          speaking a shell of speech . . .
Propped between chairs and table . . .
Words like the locust-shells, moved by no inner being;
              A dryness calling for death;

Another day, between walls of a sham Mycenian,
"Toc"[17] sphinxes, sham-Memphis columns,
And beneath the jazz a cortex, a stiffness or stillness,
              The older shell, varnished to lemon colour,
Brown-yellow wood, and the no colour plaster,
Dry professorial talk . . .
                    now stilling the ill beat music,
House expulsed by this house, but not extinguished.
              Square even shoulders and the satin skin,
Gone cheeks of the dancing woman,
              Still the old dead dry talk, gassed out—
It is ten years gone, makes stiff about her a glass,
A petrifaction of air.
              The old room of the tawdry class asserts itself;

The young men, never!
                    Only the husk of talk.

O voi che siete in piccioletta barca,[18]
Dido choked up with sobs for her Sicheus[19]
Lies heavy in my arms, dead weight
                    Drowning, with tears, new Eros,

And the life goes on, mooning upon bare hills;
Flame leaps from the hand, the rain is listless,
Yet drinks the thirst from our lips,
                    solid as echo,
Passion to breed a form in shimmer of rain-blur;
    But Eros drowned, drowned, heavy—half dead with tears
                    For dead Sicheus.
    Life to make mock of motion:
For the husks, before me, move,
                    The words rattle: shells given out by shells.
The live man, out of lands and prisons,
                    shakes the dry pods.
Probes for old wills and friendships, and the big locust-casques
Bend to the tawdry table,

Lift up their spoons to mouths, put forks in cutlets,
And make sound like the sound of voices.
                    Lorenzaccio[20]
Being more live than they, more full of flames and voices.
Ma si morisse![21]
                    Credesse caduto da se, ma si morisse.
And the tall indifference moves,
                    a more living shell,
Drift in the air of fate, dry phantom, but intact.
O Alessandro, chief and thrice warned, watcher,
                    Eternal watcher of things,
Of things, of men, of passions.
                    Eyes floating in dry, dark air,
E biondo,[22] with glass-grey iris, with an even side-fall of hair
The stiff, still features.

EIGHTH CANTO

Dido choked up with tears for dead Sichaeus;[1]
And the weeping Muse, weeping, widowed, and willing,
The weeping Muse
                    Mourns Homer,
Mourns the days of long song,
Mourns for the breath of the singers,
Winds stretching out, seas pulling to eastward,
Heaving breath of the oarsmen,
                    triremes[2] under Cyprus,
The long course of the seas,
The words woven in wind-wrack,
                    salt spray over voices.
Tyro[3] to shoreward lies lithe with Neptunus
And the glass-clear wave arches over them;
Seal sports in the spray-whited circles of cliff-wash,
Sleek head, daughter of Lir,[4]
                    eyes of Picasso
Under black fur-hood, lithe daughter of Ocean;
And the wave runs in the beach-groove:
Eleanor, ἐλέναυς and ἐλέπτολις,[5]
                    and poor old Homer blind, blind, as a bat,
Ear, ear for the sea-surge, murmur of old men's voices:
"Let her go back to the ships,

Back among Grecian faces,
                lest evil come on our own,
Evil and further evil, and a curse cursed on our children.
Moves, yes she moves like a goddess
And has the face of a god
                and the voice of Schoeney's daughters,[6]
And doom goes with her in walking,
Let her go back to the ships,
                back among Grecian voices."
And by the beach-run, Tyro,
        Twisted arms of the sea-god,
Lithe sinews of water, gripping her, cross-hold,
And the blue-gray glass of the wave tents them,
Glare azure of water,
                cord-welter, close cover.

Quiet sun-tawny sand-stretch,
The gulls broad out their wings,
                nipping between the splay feathers;
Snipe come for their bath,
                bend out their wing-joints,
Spread wet wings to the sun-film,

And by Scios,
                to left of the Naxos[7] passage,
Naviform rock overgrown
                algae cling to its edge,
There is a wine-red glow in the shallows,
                a tin flash in the sun-dazzle.

The ship landed in Scios,
                men wanting spring-water,
And by the rock-pool a young boy[8] loggy with vine-must,
        "To Naxos? yes, we'll take yuh to Naxos,
Cum' along lad."
                "Not that way!"
"Aye, that way is Naxos."

And I said: "It's a straight ship."
And an ex-convict out of Italy
                    knocked me into the fore-stays,
(He was wanted for manslaughter in Tuscany)
                    And the whole twenty against me,
Mad for a little slave money.
                    And they took her out of Scios
And off her course . . .
                    And the boy came to again with the racket,
And looked out over the bows,
                    and to eastward, and to the Naxos passage.

God-sleight then, god-sleight:
                    Ship stock fast in sea-swirl,
Ivy upon the oars, King Pentheus,[9]
                         grapes with no seed but sea-foam,
Ivy in scupper-hole
Aye, I, Acoetes,[10] stood there,
                    and the god stood by me,
Water cutting under the keel,

Sea-break from stern forrards,
                    wake running off from the bow,
And where was gunwale, there now was vine-trunk,
And tenthril where cordage had been,
                    grape-leaves on the rowlocks
Heavy vine on the oarshafts,
And, out of nothing, a breathing,
                    hot breath on my ankles,
Beasts like shadows in glass,
                    a furred tail upon nothingness.
Lynx-purr, and heathery smell of beasts,
                    where tar smell had been,
Sniff and pad-foot of beasts,
                    eye-glitter out of black air,
The sky overshot, dry, with no tempest,
Sniff and pad-foot of beasts,
                    fur brushing my knee-skin,

Rustle of airy sheaths,
          dry forms in the *aether*,

And the ship like a keel in ship-yard,
          slung like an ox in smith's sling,
Ribs stuck fast in the ways,
          grape-cluster over pin-rack,
                   Void air taking pelt,
Lifeless air become sinewed,
          feline leisure of panthers,
Leopards sniffing the grape shoots by scupper-hole,
Crouched panthers by fore-hatch,
And the sea blue-deep about us,
          green-ruddy in shadows,

And Lyaeus:[11]
          "From now, Acoetes, my altars,
  Fearing no bondage,
          fearing no cat of the wood,
  Safe with my lynxes,
          feeding grapes to my leopards,
Olibanum[12] is my incense,
          the vines grow in my homage."

The back-swell now smooth in the rudder-chains,
Black snout of a porpoise
          where Lycabs[13] had been,
Fish-scales on the oarsmen.
          And I worship.

I have seen what I have seen.
          When they brought the boy I said:
"He has a god in him,
          though I do not know which god,"
And they kicked me into the fore-stays,
And I was frightened,
          but I am not afraid any longer,

I have seen what I have seen:
        Medon's face like the face of a dory,[14]
Arms shrunk into fins.
            And you, Pentheus,
Had as well listen to Tiresias,[15] and to Cadmus,[16]
          or your luck will go out of you.
Fish-scales over groin muscles,
          lynx-purr amid sea . . .

And of a later year,
          pale in the wine-red algae,
If you will lean over the rock,
          the coral face under wave-tinge,
Rose-paleness under water-shift,
          Ileuthyeria fair Dafne[17] of sea-bords,
The swimmer's arms turned to branches,
Who will say in what year,
          fleeing what band of tritons,
The smooth brows, seen, and half seen,
          now ivory stillness.

And So-shu[18] churned in the sea, So-shu also,
          using the long moon for a churn-stick . . .
Lithe turning of water,
          sinews of Poseidon,
Black-azure and hyaline,
          glass wave over Tyro,
Close cover,
      unstillness,
          bright welter of wave-cords,
Then quiet water,
          quiet in the buff sands,
Sea-fowl stretching wing-joints,
          splashing in rock-hollows and sand-hollows
In the wave-runs by the half-dune;
Glass-glint of wave in the tide-rips against sunlight,
          pallor of Hesperus,[19]

Grey peak of the wave,
               wave, colour of grape's pulp,
Olive grey in the near,
               far, smoke-grey of the rock-slide.
Salmon-pink wings of the fish-hawk
               cast grey shadows in water,
The tower like a one-eyed great goose
               cranes up out of the olive-grove,

And we have heard the fauns chiding Proteus[20]
               in the smell of hay under the olive-trees.
And the frogs singing against the fauns
                          in the half-light.

PROSE

FROST

WHAT I FEEL ABOUT
WALT WHITMAN

From this side of the Atlantic I am for the first time able to read
Whitman, and from the vantage of my education and—if it
be permitted a man of my scant years—my world citizenship: I
see him America's poet. The only Poet before the artists of the
Carmen-Hovey period,[1] or better, the only one of the conven-
tionally recognised 'American Poets' who is worth reading.

He *is* America. His crudity is an exceeding great stench, but
it *is* America. He is the hollow place in the rock that echoes
with his time. He *does* 'chant the crucial stage' and he is the
'voice triumphant'. He is disgusting. He is an exceedingly nau-
seating pill, but he accomplishes his mission.

Entirely free from the renaissance humanist ideal of the complete man or from the Greek idealism, he is content to be what
he is, and he is his time and his people. He is a genius because he
has vision of what he is and of his function. He knows that he is
a beginning and not a classically finished work.

I honour him for he prophesied me while I can only recognise
him as a forebear of whom I ought to be proud.

In America there is much for the healing of the nations, but
woe unto him of the cultured palate who attempts the dose.

As for Whitman, I read him (in many parts) with acute
pain, but when I write of certain things I find myself using his

rhythms. The expression of certain things related to cosmic consciousness seems tainted with this maramis.

I am (in common with every educated man) an heir of the ages and I demand my birth-right. Yet if Whitman represented his time in language acceptable to one accustomed to my standard of intellectual-artistic living he would belie his time and nation. And yet I am but one of his 'ages and ages' encrustations' or to be exact an encrustation of the next age. The vital part of my message, taken from the sap and fibre of America, is the same as his.

Mentally I am a Walt Whitman who has learned to wear a collar and a dress shirt (although at times inimical to both). Personally I might be very glad to conceal my relationship to my spiritual father and brag about my more congenial ancestry— Dante, Shakespeare, Theocritus, Villon, but the descent is a bit difficult to establish. And, to be frank, Whitman is to my fatherland (*Patriam quam odi et amo*[2] for no uncertain reasons) what Dante is to Italy and I at my best can only be a strife for a renaissance in America of all the lost or temporarily mislaid beauty, truth, valour, glory of Greece, Italy, England and all the rest of it.

And yet if a man has written lines like Whitman's to the *Sunset Breeze* one has to love him. I think we have not yet paid enough attention to the deliberate artistry of the man, not in details but in the large.

I am immortal even as he is, yet with a lesser vitality as I am the more in love with beauty (If I really do love it more than he did). Like Dante he wrote in the 'vulgar tongue', in a new metric. The first great man to write in the language of his people.

Et ego Petrarca in lingua vetera scribo, and in a tongue my people understood not.

It seems to me I should like to drive Whitman into the old world. I sledge, he drill—and to scourge America with all the old beauty. (For Beauty *is* an accusation) and with a thousand thongs from Homer to Yeats, from Theocritus to Marcel Schwob.[3] This desire is because I am young and impatient, were I old and wise I should content myself in seeing and saying that these things will come. But now, since I am by no means sure it would be true prophecy, I am fain set my own hand to the labour.

It is a great thing, reading a man to know, not 'His Tricks are not as yet my Tricks, but I can easily make them mine' but 'His message is my message. We will see that men hear it.'

THE WISDOM OF POETRY

A book which was causing some clatter about a year ago, and which has been mercifully forgotten, a book displaying considerable vigorous, inaccurate thought, fathomless ignorance, and no taste whatever, claimed, among other things less probable, that it presented the first 'scientific and satisfactory definition of poetry'. The definition ran as follows: 'Poetry is the expression of insensuous thought in sensuous terms by means of artistic trope, and the dignification of thought by analogically articulated imagery.' The word 'artistic' remains undefined and we have, therefore, one unknown thing defined in terms of another unknown thing of similar nature; a mode of definition neither 'scientific' nor 'satisfactory'—even though one should agree with the dogma of trope.

There follows this 'more extended definition': 'Poetry is the expression of imaginative thought by means only of the essentials to thought, conserving energy for thought perception—to which end all animate, inanimate and intangible things may assume the properties and attributes of tangible, living, thinking and speaking things, possessing the power of becoming what they seem, or of transfiguration into what they suggest.'

This is applicable in part to the equations of analytics, *in toto* to painting, sculpture and certain other arts; for it is nonsense to consider words as the only 'essentials to thought'; some people think in terms of objects themselves, some in pictures, diagrams, or in musical sounds, and perception by symbolic vision is swifter and more complex than that by ratiocination.

Throughout the volume our scientist shows himself incapable of distinguishing between poetry and a sort of florid rhetorical bombast, but the definitions quoted do not suffice to prove his ignorance of his subject. They betray rather his confused mode of thought and his nescience of the very nature of definition. I shall assume that any definition to be 'scientific' or 'satisfactory' should have at least four parts; it should define with regard to: purpose or function; to relation; to substance; to properties.

Poetry, as regards its function or purpose, has the common purpose of the arts, which purpose Dante most clearly indicates in the line where he speaks of:

> That melody which most doth draw
> The soul unto itself.

Borrowing a terminology from Spinoza, we might say: The function of an art is to free the intellect from the tyranny of the affects, or, leaning on terms, neither technical nor metaphysical: the function of an art is to strengthen the perceptive faculties and free them from encumbrance, such encumbrances, for instance, as set moods, set ideas, conventions; from the results of experience which is common but unnecessary, experience induced by the stupidity of the experiencer and not by inevitable laws of nature. Thus Greek sculpture freed men's minds from the habit of considering the human body merely with regard to its imperfections. The Japanese grotesque frees the mind from the conception of things merely as they *have been* seen. With the art of Beardsley,[1] we enter the realm of pure intellect; the beauty of the work is wholly independent of the appearance of the things portrayed. With Rembrandt we are brought to consider the exact nature of things seen, to consider the individual face, not the conventional or type face which we may have learned to expect on canvas.

Poetry is identical with the other arts in this main purpose, that is, of liberation; it differs from them in its media, to wit, words as distinct from pigment, pure sound, clay and the like. It shares its media with music in so far as words are composed of inarticulate sounds.

Our scientist reaching toward a truth speaks of 'the essentials to thought'; these are not poetry, but a constituent substance of poetry.

The Art of Poetry consists in combining these 'essential to thought', these dynamic particles, *si licet,* this radium, with that melody of words which shall most draw the emotions of the hearer toward accord with their import, and with that 'form' which shall most delight the intellect.

By 'melody' I mean variation of sound quality, mingling with a variation of stress. By 'form' I mean the arrangement of the verse [*sic*], into ballades, canzoni, and the like symmetrical forms, or into blank verse or into free verse, where presumably, the nature of the thing expressed or of the person supposed to be expressing it, is antagonistic to external symmetry. Form may delight by its symmetry or by its aptness.

The methods of this fusing, tempering and shaping concern the artist; the results alone are of import to the public.

Poets in former ages were of certain uses to the community; i.e., as historians, genealogists, religious functionaries. In Provence the *gai savoir* was both theatre and opera. The troubadour and jongleur[2] were author, dramatist, composer, actor and popular tenor. In Tuscany the canzone and the sonnet held somewhat the place of the essay and the short story. Elizabethan drama appeared at a time when it was a society fad to speak beautifully. Has the poet, apart from these obsolete and accidental uses, any permanent function in society? I attempt the following scientific answers:

Thought is perhaps important to the race, and language, the medium of thought's preservation, is constantly wearing out. It has been the function of poets to new-mint the speech, to supply the vigorous terms for prose. Thus Tacitus is full of Vergilian half lines; and poets may be 'kept on' as conservators of the public speech, or prose, perhaps, becoming more and more an art, may become, or may have become already, self-sustaining.

As the poet was, in ages of faith, the founder and emendor of all religions, so, in ages of doubt, is he the final agnostic; that which the philosopher presents as truth, the poet presents as that which appears as truth to a certain sort of mind under certain conditions.

'To thine own self be true. . . .' were nothing were it not spoken by Polonius, who has never called his soul his own.

The poet is consistently agnostic in this; that he does not postulate his ignorance as a positive thing. Thus his observations rest as the enduring data of philosophy. He grinds an axe for no dogma. Now that mechanical science has realised his ancient dreams of flight and sejunct communication, he is the advance guard of the psychologist on the watch for new emotions, new vibrations sensible to faculties as yet ill understood. As Dante writes of the sunlight coming through the clouds from a hidden source and illuminating part of a field, long before the painters had depicted such effects of light and shade, so are later watchers on the alert for colour perceptions of a subtler sort, neither affirming them to be 'astral' or 'spiritual' nor denying the formulae of theosophy. The traditional methods are not antiquated, nor are poets necessarily the atavisms which they seem. Thus poets may be retained as friends of this religion of doubt, but the poet's true and lasting relation to literature and life is that of the abstract mathematician to science and life. As the little world of abstract mathematicians is set a-quiver by some young Frenchman's deductions on the functions of imaginary values—worthless to applied science of the day—so is the smaller world of serious poets set a-quiver by some new subtlety of cadence. Why?

A certain man named Plarr[3] and another man whose name I have forgotten, some years since, developed the functions of a certain obscure sort of equation, for no cause save their own pleasure in the work. The applied science of their day had no use for the deductions, a few sheets of paper covered with arbitrary symbols—without which we should have no wireless telegraph.

What the analytical geometer does for space and form, the poet does for the states of consciousness. Let us therefore consider the nature of the formulae of analytics.

By the signs $a^2 + b^2 = c^2$, I imply the circle. By $(a-r)^2 + (b-r)^2 = (c-r)^2$, I imply the circle and its mode of birth. I am led from the consideration of the particular circles formed by my ink-well and my table-rim, to the contemplation of the circle absolute, its law; the circle free in all space, unbounded, loosed from the accidents of time and place. Is the formula nothing, or is it cabala and the sign of unintelligible magic? The engineer, understanding and translating to the many, builds for the uninitiated bridges and devices. He speaks their language. For the initiated the signs are a door into eternity and into the boundless ether.

As the abstract mathematician is to science so is the poet to the world's consciousness. Neither has direct contact with the many, neither of them is superhuman or arrives at his utility through occult and inexplicable ways. Both are scientifically demonstrable.

PSYCHOLOGY AND
TROUBADOURS

A DIVAGATION[1] FROM QUESTIONS OF TECHNIQUE

Behind the narratives is a comparatively simple state of "romanticism," behind the canzos, the "love code."

One or two theories as to its inner significance may in some way promote an understanding of the period.

The "chivalric love," was, as I understand it, an art, that is to say, a religion. The writers of "trobar clus"[2] did not seek obscurity for the sake of obscurity.

An art is vital only so long as it is interpretative, so long, that is, as it manifests something which the artist perceives at greater intensity, and more intimately, than his public. If he be the seeing man among the sightless, they will attend him only so long as his statements seem, or are proven, true. If he forsake this honor of interpreting, if he speak for the pleasure of hearing his own voice, they may listen for a while to the babble and to the sound of the painted words, but there comes, after a little, a murmur, a slight stirring, and then that condition which we see about us, disapproved as the "divorce of art and life."

The interpretive function is the highest honor of the arts, and because it is so we find that a sort of hyper-scientific precision is the touchstone and assay of the artist's power, of his honor, his authenticity. Constantly he must distinguish between the shades and the degrees of the ineffable.

If we apply this test, first, as to the interpretive intention on the part of the artist, second, as to the exactness of presentation, we shall find that the *Divina Commedia* is a single elaborated metaphor of life; it is an accumulation of fine discriminations arranged in orderly sequence. It makes no difference *in kind* whether the artist treat of heaven and hell, of paradise upon earth and of the elysian enamelled fields beneath it, or of Love appearing in an ash-grey vision, or of the seemingly slight matter of birds and branches . . . through one and the other of all these, there is to the artist a like honorable opportunity for precision, for that precision through which alone can any of these matters take on their immortality.

"Magna pars mei," says Horace, speaking of his own futurity, "that in me which is greatest shall escape dissolution": The *accurate* artist seems to leave not only his greater self, but beside it, upon the films of his art, some living print of the circumvolving man, his taste, his temper and his foible—of the things about which he felt it never worth his while to bother other people by speaking, the things he forgot for some major interest; of these, and of another class of things, things that his audience would have taken for granted; or thirdly, of things about which he had, for some reason or other, a reticence. We find these not so much in the words—which anyone may read—but in the subtle joints of the craft, in the crannies perceptible only to the craftsman.

Such is the record left us by a man whom Dante found "best verse-wright in the fostering tongue," the *lingua materna*, Provençal Langue d'Oc; and in that affectionate epithet, *materna,* we have a slight evidence of the regard in which this forgotten speech was held by the Tuscan poets, both for its sound and for its matter.

We find this poetry divided into two schools; the first school complained about the obscurities of the second—we have them always with us. They claimed, or rather jeered in Provence, remonstrated in Tuscany, wrangle today, and will wrangle

tomorrow—and not without some show of reason—that poetry, especially lyric poetry, must be simple; that you must get
the meaning while the man sings it. This school had, and has always, the popular ear. The other school culminated in Dante
Alighieri. There is, of course, ample room for both schools. The
ballad-concert ideal is correct, in its own way. A song is a thing
to sing. If you approach the canzoni of the second school with
this bias you will be disappointed, *not* because their sound or
form is not as lyric as that of the canzoni of the first school, but
because they are not always intelligible at first hearing. They
are good art as the high mass is good art. The first songs are apt
to weary you after you know them; they are especially tiresome
if one tries to read them *after* one has read fifty others of more
or less the same sort.

The second sort of canzone is a ritual. It must be conceived
and approached as ritual. It has its purpose and its effect. These
are different from those of simple song. They are perhaps subtler. They make their revelations to those who are already expert.

Apart from Arnaut's[3] aesthetic merits, his position in the history of poetry, etc., his music, the fineness of his observation
and of his perceptive senses, there is a problem of meaning.

The crux of the matter might seem to rest on a very narrow
base; it might seem to be a matter of taste or of opinion, of
scarcely more than a personal predilection to ascribe or not to
ascribe to one passage in the canzon "Doutz brais e critz," a visionary significance, where, in the third stanza, he speaks of a
castle, a dream-castle, or otherwise—as you like—and says of
the "lady":

> She made me a shield, extending over me her fair mantle of
> indigo, so that the slanderers might not see this.

This may be merely a conceit, a light and pleasant phrase; if
we found it in Herrick or Decker,[4] or some minor Elizabethan,
we might well consider it so, and pass without further ado. If
one consider it as historical, the protection offered the secret

might seem inadequate. I have, however, no quarrel with those who care to interpret the passage in either of these more obvious and, to me, less satisfactory ways.

We must, however, take into our account a number of related things; consider, in following the clue of a visionary interpretation, whether it will throw light upon events and problems other than our own, and weigh the chances in favor of, or against, this interpretation. Allow for climate, consider the restless sensitive temper of our jongleur, and the quality of the minds which appreciated him. Consider what poetry was to become, within less than a century, at the hands of Guinicelli,[5] or of "il nostro Guido" in such a poem as the *ballata*, ending: "Vedrai la sua virtù nel ciel salita,"* and consider the whole temper of Dante's verse. In none of these things singly is there any specific *proof*. Consider the history of the time, the Albigensian Crusade, nominally against a sect tinged with Manichean heresy, and remember how Provençal song is never wholly disjunct from pagan rites of May Day. Provence was less disturbed than the rest of Europe by invasion from the North in the darker ages; if paganism survived anywhere it would have been, unofficially, in the Langue d'Oc. That the spirit was, in Provence, Hellenic is seen readily enough by anyone who will compare the *Greek Anthology* with the work of the troubadours. They have, in some way, lost the names of the gods and remembered the names of lovers. Ovid and *The Eclogues* of Virgil would seem to have been their chief documents.

The question: Did this "close ring," this aristocracy of emotion, evolve, out of its half memories of Hellenistic mysteries, a cult—a cult stricter, or more subtle, than that of the celibate ascetics, a cult for the purgation of the soul by a refinement of, and lordship over, the senses? Consider in such passages in Arnaut as, "E quel remir contral lums de la lampa," whether a sheer love of beauty and a delight in the perception of it have

---

*In this *ballata*, Guido speaks of seeing issue from his lady's lips a subtle body, from that a subtler body, from that a star, from that a voice, proclaiming the ascent of the virtu. For effect upon the air, upon the soul, etc., the "lady in Tuscan poetry has assumed all the properties of the Alchemist's stone.

not replaced all heavier emotion, whether or no the thing has not become a function of the intellect.*

Some mystic or other speaks of the intellect as standing in the same relation to the soul as do the senses to the mind; and beyond a certain border, surely we come to this place where the ecstasy is not a whirl or a madness of the senses, but a glow arising from the exact nature of the perception. We find a similar thought in Spinoza where he says that "the intellectual love of a thing consists in the understanding of its perfections," and adds "all creatures whatsoever desire this love."

If a certain number of people in Provence developed their own unofficial mysticism, basing it for the most part on their own experience, if the servants of Amor saw visions quite as well as the servants of the Roman ecclesiastical hierarchy, if they were, moreover, troubled with no "dark night of the soul," and the kindred incommodities of ascetic yoga, this may well have caused some scandal and jealousy to the orthodox. If we find a similar mode of thought in both devotions, we find a like similarity in the secular and sacred music. "Alba" was probably sung to "Hallelujah's" melody. Many of the troubadours, in fact nearly all who knew letters or music, had been taught in the monasteries (St. Martial, St. Leonard and the other abbeys of Limoges). Visions and the doctrines of the early Fathers could not have been utterly strange to them. The rise of Mariolatry, its pagan lineage, the romance of it, find modes of expression which verge over-easily into the speech and casuistry of Our Lady of Cyprus, as we may see in Arnaut, as we see so splendidly in Guido's "Una figura della donna miae." And there is the consummation of it all in Dante's glorification of Beatrice. There is the inexplicable address to the lady in the masculine.

---

*Let me admit at once that a recent lecture by Mr. Mead on Simon Magus has opened my mind to a number of new possibilities. There would seem to be in the legend of Simon Magus and Helen of Tyre a clearer prototype of "chivalric love" than in anything hereinafter discussed. I recognize that all this matter of mine may have to be reconstructed or at least re-oriented about that tradition. Such rearrangement would not, however, enable us to dispense with a discussion of the parallels here collected, nor would it materially affect the manner in which they are treated. (1916.)

There is the final evolution of Amor by Guido and Dante, a new and paganish god, neither Erôs nor an angel of the Talmud.

I believe in a sort of permanent basis in humanity, that is to say, I believe that Greek myth arose when someone having passed through delightful psychic experience tried to communicate it to others and found it necessary to screen himself from persecution. Speaking aesthetically, the myths are explications of mood: you may stop there, or you may probe deeper. Certain it is that these myths are only intelligible in a vivid and glittering sense to those people to whom they occur. I know, I mean, one man who understands Persephone and Demeter, and one who understands the Laurel, and another who has, I should say, met Artemis. These things are for them *real*.

Let us consider the body as pure mechanism. Our kinship to the ox we have constantly thrust upon us; but beneath this is our kinship to the vital universe, to the tree and the living rock, and, because this is less obvious—and possibly more interesting—we forget it.

We have about us the universe of fluid force, and below us the germinal universe of wood alive, of stone alive. Man is—the sensitive physical part of him—a mechanism, for the purpose of our further discussion a mechanism rather like an electric appliance, switches, wires, etc. Chemically speaking, he is *ut credo*, a few buckets of water, tied up in a complicated sort of fig-leaf. As to his consciousness, the consciousness of some seems to rest, or to have its center more properly, in what the Greek psychologists called the *phantastikon*. Their minds are, that is, circumvolved about them like soap-bubbles reflecting sundry patches of the macrocosmos. And with certain others their consciousness is "germinal." Their thoughts are in them as the thought of the tree is in the seed, or in the grass, or the grain, or the blossom. And these minds are the more poetic, and they affect mind about them, and transmute it as the seed the earth. And this latter sort of mind is close on the vital universe; and the strength of the Greek beauty rests in this, that it is ever at the interpretation of this vital universe, by its signs of gods and godly attendants and oreads.

In the Trecento[6] the Tuscans are busy with their *phantastikon*. In Provence we may find preparation for this, or we may find faint *reliqua* of the other consciousness; though one misses the pantheon. Line after line of Arnaut will repeat from Sappho, but the whole seems curiously barren if we turn suddenly from the Greek to it.

After the Trecento we get Humanism,* and as the art is carried northward we have Chaucer and Shakespeare, (Jacquespère). Man is concerned with man and forgets the whole and the flowing. And we have in sequence, first the age of drama, and then the age of prose. At any rate, when we do get into contemplation of the flowing we find sex, or some correspondance to it, "positive and negative," "North and South," "sun and moon," or whatever terms of whatever cult or science you prefer to substitute.

For the particular parallel I wish to indicate, our handiest illustrations are drawn from physics: 1st, the common electric machine, the glass disc and rotary brushes; 2nd, the wireless telegraph receiver. In the first we generate a current, or if you like, split up a static condition of things and produce a tension. This is focussed on two brass knobs or "poles." These are first in contact, and after the current is generated we can gradually widen the distance between them, and a spark will leap across it, the wider the stronger, until with the ordinary sized laboratory appliance it will leap over or around a large obstacle or pierce a heavy book cover. In the telegraph we have a charged surface—produced in a cognate manner—attracting to it, or registering movements in the invisible aether.

Substituting in these equations a more complex mechanism and a possibly subtler form of energy is, or should be, simple enough. I have no dogma, but the figures may serve as an assistance to thought.

It is an ancient hypothesis that the little cosmos "corresponds" to the greater, that man has in him both "sun" and "moon." From this I should say that there are at least two paths—I do not

*The Italian, not the recent American brand.

say that they lead to the same place—the one ascetic, the other for want of a better term "chivalric." In the first the monk or whoever he may be, develops, at infinite trouble and expense, the secondary pole within himself, produces his charged surface which registers the beauties, celestial or otherwise, by "contemplation." In the second, which I must say seems more in accord with "mens sana in corpore sano" the charged surface is produced between the predominant natural poles of two human mechanisms.

Sex is, that is to say, of a double function and purpose, reproductive and educational; or, as we see in the realm of fluid force, one sort of vibration produces at different intensities, heat and light. No scientist would be so stupid as to affirm that heat produced light, and it is into a similar sort of false ratiocination that those writers fall who find the source of illumination, or of religious experience, centred solely in the philo-progenitive instinct.

The problem, in so far as it concerns Provence, is simply this: Did this "chivalric love," this exotic, take on mediumistic properties? Stimulated by the color or quality of emotion did that "color" take on forms interpretive of the divine order? Did it lead to an "exteriorization of the sensibility," and interpretation of the cosmos by feeling?

For our basis in nature we rest on the indisputable and very scientific fact that there are in the "normal course of things" certain times, a certain sort of moment more than another when a man feels his immortality upon him. As for the effect of this phenomenon in Provence, before coming to any judgment upon it we should consider carefully the history of the various cults or religions of orgy and of ecstasy, from the simpler Bacchanalia to the more complicated rites of Isis or Dionysus— sudden rise and equally sudden decline. The corruptions of their priesthoods follow, probably, the admission thereto of one neophyte who was not properly "sacerdos."

There are, as we see, only two kinds of religion. There is the Mosaic or Roman or British Empire type, where someone, having to keep a troublesome rabble in order, invents and scares them with a disagreeable bogie, which he calls god.

Christianity and all other forms of ecstatic religion, on the other hand, are not in inception dogma or propaganda of something called the *one truth* or the *universal truth;* they *seem* little concerned with ethics; their general object appears to be to stimulate a sort of confidence in the life-force. Their teaching is variously and constantly a sort of working hypothesis acceptable to people of a certain range of temperament—a "regola" which suits a particular constitution of nerves and intellect, and in accord with which the people of this temperament can live at greatest peace with "the order," with man and nature. The old cults were sane in their careful inquisition or novitiate, which served to determine whether the candidates were or were not of such temper and composition.

One must consider that the types which joined these cults survived, in Provence, and survive, today—priests, maenads and the rest—though there is in our society no provision for them.

I have no particular conclusion to impose upon the reader; for a due consideration of Provençal poetry in "trobar clus," I can only suggest the evidence and lines of inquiry. The Pauline position on wedlock is of importance—I do not mean its general and inimical disapproval, but its more specific utterances. Whatever one may think of the pagan survivals in Mariolatry or of the cult of virginity, it is certain that nothing exists without due cause or causes. The language of the Christian mystics concerning the "bride" and the rest of it; the ancient ideas of union with the god, or with Queen Isis—all these, as "atmospheric influences," must be weighed; together with the testimony of the arts, and their progression of content.

In Catullus' superb epithalamium "Collis O Heliconii," we find the affair is strictly on one plane; the bride is what she is in Morocco today, and the function is "normal" and eugenic. It is the sacrificial concept. Yet Catullus, recording his own emotion, could say: "More as a father than a lover." Propertius writes: "Ingenium nobis ipsa puella fecit."

Christianity had, one might say, brought in the mystic note; but this would be much too sweeping. Anatole France, in his commentary on Horace's "Tu ne quaesaris," has told us a good deal about the various Oriental cults thronging the Eternal City. At Marseille the Greek settlement was very ancient. How much of the Roman tone, or the Oriental mode, went out from Rome to the Roman country houses which were the last hold of culture, we can hardly say; and from the end of the Sixth Century until the beginning of the Twelfth there is supposed to be little available evidence. At least we are a fair distance from Catullus when we come to Peire Vidal's: "Good Lady, I think I see God when I gaze on your delicate body."

You may take this if you like *cum grano*. Vidal was confessedly erratic. Still it is an obvious change from the manner of the Roman classics, and it cannot be regarded as a particularly pious or Christian expression. If this state of mind was fostered by the writings of the early Christian Fathers, we must regard their influence as purely indirect and unintentional.

Richard St. Victor has left us one very beautiful passage on the splendors of paradise.

They are ineffable and innumerable and no man having beheld them can fittingly narrate them or even remember them exactly. Nevertheless by naming over all the most beautiful things we know we may draw back upon the mind some vestige of the heavenly splendor.

I suggest that the troubadour, either more indolent or more logical, progresses from correlating all these details for purpose of comparison, and lumps the matter. The Lady contains the catalogue, is more complete. She serves as a sort of *mantram*.

"The lover stands ever in unintermittent imagination of his lady (co-amantis)." This is clause 30 of a chivalric code in Latin, purporting to have been brought to the court of Arthur. This code is not, I should say, the code of the "trobar clus," not the esoteric rule, but such part of it as has been more generally propagated for the pleasure of Eleanor of Poictiers or Marie de Champagne.

Yet there is, in what I have called the "natural course of events," the exalted moment, the vision unsought, or at least the vision gained without machination.

Though the servants of Amor went pale and wept and suffered heat and cold, they came on nothing so apparently morbid as the "dark night." The electric current gives light where it meets resistance. I suggest that the living conditions of Provence gave the necessary restraint, produced the tension sufficient for the results, a tension unattainable under, let us say, the living conditions of imperial Rome.

So far as "morals" go, or at least a moral code in the modern sense, which might interfere in art, Arnaut can no more be accused of having one than can Ovid.* Yet the attitude of the Latin *doctor amoris* and that of the *gran maestro de amor* are notably different, as for instance on such a matter as delay. Ovid takes no account of the psychic function.

It is perhaps as far a cry from a belief in higher affection to a mediumistic function or cult of Amor, as is the latter from Ovid. One must consider the temper of the time, and some of the most interesting evidence as to this temper has been gathered by Remy de Gourmont,[7] in *Le Latin Mystique*, from which:

> Qui pascis inter lilia
> Septus choreis virginum.
> Quocumque pergis virgines
> Sequntur, atque laudibus
> Post te canentes cursitant,
> Hymnosque dulces personant[†]

> Who feedest 'mid the lilies,
> Ringed with dancing virgins
> Where'er Thou runnest, maidens
> Follow, and with praises
> Run behind Thee singing,
> Carolling their hymns.

Or:

> Nard of Columba flourisheth;
> The little gardens flame with privet;
> Stay the glad maid with flowers,
> Encompass her with apple boughs.[‡]

---

*Ovid, outside his poetry, perhaps, superficially had one.
†From *Hymns to Christ*.
‡From *Ode on St. Colum*.

As for the personae of the Christian cult they are indeed treated as pagan gods—Apollo with his chorus of Muses, Adonis, the yearly slain, "victima paschalis,"* yet in the "sequaire" of Godeschalk, a monk in the Eleventh Century, we see a new refinement, an enrichment, I think, of paganism. The god has at last succeeded in becoming human, and it is not the beauty of the god but the personality which is the goal of the love and the invocation.

> The Pharisee murmurs when the woman weeps, conscious of guilt.
> Sinner, he despises a fellow-in-sin. Thou, unacquainted with sin, hast regard for the penitent, cleansest the soiled one, loved her to make her most fair.
> She embraces the feet of the master, washes them with tears, dries them with her hair; washing and drying them she anointed them with unguent, covered them with kisses.
> These are the feasts which please thee, O Wisdom of the Father!
> Born of the Virgin, who disdained not the touch of a sinner.
> Chaste virgins, they immaculately offer unto the Lord the sacrifice of their pure bodies, choosing Christ for their deathless bridegroom.
> O happy bridals, whereto there are no stains, no heavy dolors of childbirth, no rival mistress to be feared, no nurse molestful!
> Their couches, kept for Christ alone, are walled about by angels of the guard, who, with drawn swords, ward off the unclean lest any paramour defile them.
> Therein Christ sleepeth with them: happy is this sleep, sweet the rest there, wherein true maid is fondled in the embraces of her heavenly spouse.
> Adorned are they with fine linen, and with a robe of purple; their left hands hold lilies, their right hands roses.
> On these the lamb feedeth, and with these is he refreshed; these flowers are his chosen food.

*There is a magnificent thesis to be written on the role of Fortune, coming down through the Middle Ages, from pagan mythology, via Seneca, into Guido and Dante.

He leapeth, and boundeth and gamboleth among them.

With them doth he rest through the noon-heat.

It is upon their bosoms that he sleepeth at mid-day, placing his head between their virgin breasts.

Virgin Himself, born of a virgin mother, virginal retreats above all he seeketh and loveth.

Quiet is his sleep upon their bosoms, that no spot by any chance should soil His snowy fleece.

Give ear unto this canticle, most noble company of virgin devotees, that by it our devotion may with greater zeal prepare a temple for the Lord.

With such language in the cloisters, would it be surprising that the rebels from it, the clerks who did not take orders, should have transferred something of the manner, and something of the spirit, to the beauty of life as they found it, that souls who belonged, not in heaven but, by reason of their refinement, somewhat above the mortal turmoil, should have chosen some middle way, something short of grasping at the union with the absolute, nor yet that their cult should have been extra-marital? Arnaut was taught in cloister, Dante praises certain "prose di romanzi"[8] and no one can say precisely whether or no they were such *prose* for music as the Latin sequence I have just quoted. Yet one would be rash to affirm that the "passada folor"[9] which he laments* at almost the summit of the purifying hill, and just below the earthly paradise, was anything more than such deflection.

CHRONOLOGICAL CHART

Scotus Eriugina, died 877		Arab philosophers Alkindi, died 870 Comment on Aristotle Avicenna, born 980
Guillaume de Poitiers 1071–1127		
	1170 ... 1228	
circa 1190	Vogelweide	Averroes, died 1198
Bertrans de Born	Hauenstaufen	
Plantagenets	Curious lack of persona-	German translations of

Purgatorio, Canto 26.

Arnaut Daniel	lity in Sicilian poetry.	Ovid & The Song of
Philippe August	Falcon Book.	Songs.
		Albert von Halberstadt.
	Sordello	
Guillaume Figueira	Eccelin	Aristotle translated
Albigeois infamy	Charles of Anjou	into Latin & forbidden.
	1200–1269	
		Albertus Magnus
		1193–1280
	1250	Fat-headed Aquinas
	Death of Frederic of	1227–1274
	Sicily	
	Birth of Guido	
	Cavalcanti	Grosseteste

The period might be made more transparent by a more thorough table of dates; affiliations of troubadours and dynasties; of books available or newly active at a given time.

IMAGISME*

Some curiosity has been aroused concerning *Imagisme*, and as I was unable to find anything definite about it in print, I sought out an *imagiste*, with intent to discover whether the group itself knew anything about the "movement." I gleaned these facts.

The *imagistes* admitted that they were contemporaries of the Post Impressionists and the Futurists; but they had nothing in common with these schools. They had not published a manifesto. They were not a revolutionary school; their only endeavor was to write in accordance with the best tradition, as they found it in the best writers of all time,—in Sappho, Catullus, Villon. They seemed to be absolutely intolerant of all poetry that was not written in such endeavor, ignorance of the best tradition forming no excuse. They had a few rules, drawn up for their own satisfaction only, and they had not published them. They were:

1. Direct treatment of the "thing," whether subjective or objective.

*Editor's Note—In response to many requests for information regarding *Imagism* and the *Imagistes,* we publish this note by Mr. Flint, supplementing it with further exemplification by Mr. Pound. It will be seen from these that *Imagism* is not necessarily associated with Hellenic subjects, or with *vers libre* as a prescribed form.

2. To use absolutely no word that did not contribute to the presentation.
3. As regarding rhythm: to compose in sequence of the musical phrase, not in sequence of a metronome.

By these standards they judged all poetry, and found most of it wanting. They held also a certain 'Doctrine of the Image,' which they had not committed to writing; they said that it did not concern the public, and would provoke useless discussion.

The devices whereby they persuaded approaching poetasters to attend their instruction were:

1. They showed him his own thought already splendidly expressed in some classic (and the school musters altogether a most formidable erudition).
2. They re-wrote his verses before his eyes, using about ten words to his fifty.

Even their opponents admit of them—ruefully—"At least they do keep bad poets from writing!"

I found among them an earnestness that is amazing to one accustomed to the usual London air of poetic dilettantism. They consider that Art is all science, all religion, philosophy and metaphysic. It is true that *snobisme* may be urged against them; but it is at least *snobisme* in its most dynamic form, with a great deal of sound sense and energy behind it; and they are stricter with themselves than with any outsider.

F. S. Flint

HOW I BEGAN

If the verb is put in the past tense there is very little to be said about this matter.

The artist is always beginning. Any work of art which is not a beginning, an invention, a discovery, is of little worth. The very name Troubadour means a "finder," one who discovers.

So far as the public is concerned my "career" has been of the simplest; during the first five years of it I had exactly one brief poem accepted by one American magazine, although I had during that time submitted "La Fraisne" and various other poems now held as a part of my best work. Net result of my activities in cash, five dollars which works out to about 4s. 3d. per year.

Mr. Elkin Mathews was the first publisher to whom I submitted my work in London. He printed my first three volumes, "Personae," "Exultations," and "Canzoni," at his own expense. So far as I can remember our only discussion of business was as follows:—

Mr. E. M.: "Ah, eh, do you care to contribute to the costs of publishing?"

Mr. E. P.: "I've got a shilling in my clothes, if that's any use to you."

Mr. E. M.: "Oh well, I rather want to publish 'em anyhow."

I have not yet received a brass farthing from these books, nor do I think that Mr. Mathews has up to date a clear balance against his expenses. One's name is known, in so far as it is known at all widely, through hearsay and reviews and through a wholesale quotation.

My books have made me friends. I came to London with £3 knowing no one.

I had been hungry all my life for "interesting people." I wanted to meet certain men whose work I admired. I have done this. I have had good talk in plenty.

I have paid a certain price, I have endured a certain amount of inconvenience, enough to put an edge on my enjoyment. I believe I have had more solid pleasure in life than any fellow of my years whom I have ever met.

I have "known many men's manners and seen many cities."

Besides knowing living artists I have come in touch with the tradition of the dead. I have had in this the same sort of pleasure that a schoolboy has in hearing of the star plays of former athletes. I have renewed my boyhood. I have repeated the sort of thrill that I used to have in hearing of the deeds of T. Truxton Hare;[1] the sort that future Freshmen will have in hearing how "Mike" Bennet stopped Weeks. I have relished this or that about "old Browning," or Shelley sliding down his front banisters "with almost incredible rapidity."

There is more, however, in this sort of Apostolic Succession than a ludicrous anecdote, for people whose minds have been enriched by contact with men of genius retain the effects of it.

I have enjoyed meeting Victorians and Pre-Raphaelites and men of the nineties through their friends. I have seen Keats' proof sheets, I have had personal tradition of his time at secondhand. This, perhaps, means little to a Londoner, but it is good fun if you have grown up regarding such things as about as distant as Ghengis Khan or the days of Lope de Vega.

If by the question "How I began?" you mean "How did I learn my trade?" it is much too long to answer, and the details would be too technical.

I knew at fifteen pretty much what I wanted to do. I believed that the "Impulse" is with the gods; that technique is a man's own responsibility. A man either is or is not a great poet, that is not within his control, it is the lightning from heaven, the "fire of the gods," or whatever you choose to call it.

His recording instrument is in his own charge. It is his own fault if he does not become a good artist—even a flawless artist.

I resolved that at thirty I would know more about poetry than any man living, that I would know the dynamic content from the shell, that I would know what was accounted poetry everywhere, what part of poetry was "indestructible," what part could *not be lost* by translation, and—scarcely less important what effects were obtainable in *one* language only and were utterly incapable of being translated.

In this search I learned more or less of nine foreign languages, I read Oriental stuff in translations, I fought every University regulation and every professor who tried to make me learn anything except this, or who bothered me with "requirements for degrees."

Of course, no amount of scholarship will help a man to write poetry; it may even be regarded as a great burden and hindrance, but it does help him to destroy a certain percentage of his failures. It keeps him discontented with mediocrity.

I have written a deal about technique for I detest a botch in a poem or in a donkey engine. I detest people who are content with botches. I detest a satisfaction with second-rateness.

As touching the Impulse, that is another affair. You may even call it "Inspiration." I do not mind the term, although it is in great disfavour with those who never experience the light of it.

The Impulse is a very different thing from the *furor scribendi,* which is a sort of emotional excitement due, I think, to weakness, and often preceding or accompanying early work. It means that the subject has you, not you the subject. There is no formula for the Impulse. Each poem must be a new and strange adventure if it is worth recording at all.

I know that for days the "Night Litany" seemed a thing so little my own that I could not bring myself to sign it. In the case of the "Goodly Fare" [*sic*][2] I was not excited until some hours after I had written it. I had been the evening before in the "Turkish Coffee" café in Soho. I had been made very angry by a certain sort of cheap irreverence which was new to me. I had

lain awake most of the night. I got up rather late in the morning and started for the Museum with the first four lines in my
head. I wrote the rest of the poem at a sitting, on the left side
of the reading-room, with scarcely any erasures. I lunched at
the Vienna Café, and later in the afternoon, being unable to
study, I peddled the poem about Fleet Street, for I began to realise that for the first time in my life I had written something
that "everyone could understand," and I wanted it to go to the
people.

The poem was not accepted. I think the "Evening Standard"
was the only office where it was even considered. Mr. Ford Madox Hueffer first printed the poem in his review some three
months afterwards.

My other "vigorous" poem, the "Alta forte" was also written
in the British Museum reading-room. I had had De Born on my
mind. I had found him untranslatable. Then it occurred to me
that I might present him in this manner. I wanted the curious
involution and recurrence of the Sestina. I knew more or less of
the arrangement. I wrote the first strophe and then went to the
Museum to make sure of the right order of permutations, for I
was then living in Langham Street, next to the "pub," and had
hardly any books with me. I did the rest of the poem at a sitting. Technically it is one of my best, though a poem on such a
theme could never be very important.

I waited three years to find the words for "Piccadilly"; it is
eight lines long, and they tell me now it is "sentiment." For well
over a year I have been trying to make a poem of a very beautiful thing that befell me in the Paris Underground. I got out of a
train at, I think, La Concorde and in the jostle I saw a beautiful
face, and then, turning suddenly, another and another, and then
a beautiful child's face, and then another beautiful face. All that
day I tried to find words for what this made me feel. That night
as I went home along the rue Raynouard I was still trying. I
could get nothing but spots of colour. I remember thinking that
if I had been a painter I might have started a wholly new school
of painting. I tried to write the poem weeks afterwards in Italy,
but found it useless. Then only the other night, wondering how
I should tell the adventure, it struck me that in Japan, where a

work of art is not estimated by its acreage and where sixteen syllables are counted enough for a poem if you arrange and punctuate them properly, one might make a very little poem which would be translated about as follows:—

"The apparition of these faces in the crowd :
Petals on a wet, black bough."

And there, or in some other very old, very quiet civilisation, some one else might understand the significance.

TROUBADOURS—
THEIR SORTS AND
CONDITIONS

The argument whether or no the troubadours are a subject worthy of study is an old and respectable one. If Guillaume, Count of Peiteus, grandfather of King Richard Cœur de Leon, had not been a man of many energies, there might have been little food for this discussion. He was, as the old book says of him, 'of the greatest counts in the world, and he had his way with women.' He made songs for either them or himself or for his more ribald companions. They say that his wife was Countess of Dia, 'fair lady and righteous', who fell in love with Raimbaut d'Aurenga and made him many a song. Count Guillaume brought composition in verse into court fashions, and gave it a social prestige which it held till the crusade of 1208 against the Albigenses. The mirth of Provençal song is at times anything but sunburnt, and the mood is often anything but idle. De Born advises the barons to pawn their castles before making war, thus if they won they could redeem them, if they lost the loss fell on the holder of the mortgage.

The forms of this poetry are highly artificial, and as artifice they have still for the serious craftsman an interest, less indeed than they had for Dante, but by no means inconsiderable. No student of the period can doubt that the involved forms, and the veiled meanings in the 'trobar clus', grew out of living conditions, and that these songs played a very real part in love intrigue and in the intrigue preceding warfare. The time had no press and no theatre. If you wish to make love to women in public, and out loud, you must resort to subterfuge; and Guillaume St Leider even went so far as to get the husband of his lady to do the seductive singing.

If a man of our time be so crotchety as to wish emotional, as well as intellectual, acquaintance with an age so out of fashion as the twelfth century, he may try in several ways to attain it. He may read the songs themselves from the old books—from the illuminated vellum—and he will learn what the troubadours meant to the folk of the century just after their own. He will learn a little about their costume from the illuminated capitals. Or he may try listening to the words with the music, for, thanks to Jean Beck and others,* it is now possible to hear the old tunes. They are perhaps a little Oriental in feeling, and it is likely that the spirit of Sufism is not wholly absent from their content. Or, again, a man may walk[1] the hill roads and river roads from Limoges and Charente to Dordogne and Narbonne and learn a little, or more than a little, of what the country meant to the wandering singers, he may learn, or think he learns, why so many canzos open with speech of the weather; or why such a man made war on such and such castles. Or he may learn the outlines of these events from the 'razos', or prose paragraphs of introduction, which are sometimes called 'lives of the troubadours'. And, if he have mind for these latter, he will find in the Bibliothèque Nationale at Paris the manuscript of Miquel de la Tour,[2] written perhaps in the author's own handwriting; at least we read 'I Miquel de la Tour, scryven, do ye to wit'.

Miquel gives us to know that such and such ladies were courted with greater or less good fortune by such and such minstrels of various degree, for one man was a poor vavassour, and another was King Amfos of Aragon; and another, Vidal, was son of a furrier, and sang better than any man in the world; and

*Walter Morse Rummel's *Neuf Chansons de Troubadours,* pub. Augener, Ltd., etc; also the settings by Aubry.

Raimon de Miraval was a poor knight that had but part of a castle; and Uc Brunecs was a clerk and he had an understanding with a *borgesa* who had no mind to love him or to keep him, and who became mistress to the Count of Rodez. 'Voila l'estat divers d'entre eulx.'

The monk, Gaubertz de Poicebot, 'was a man of birth; he was of the bishopric of Limozin, son of the castellan of Poicebot. And he was made monk when he was a child in a monastery, which is called Sain Leonart. And he knew well letters, and well to sing and well *trobar*.* And for desire of woman he went forth from the monastery. And he came thence to the man to whom came all who for courtesy wished honour and good deeds—to Sir Savaric de Mauleon—and this man gave him the harness of a joglar and a horse and clothing; and then he went through the courts and composed and made good canzos. And he set his heart upon a donzella gentle and fair and made his songs of her, and she did not wish to love him unless he should get himself made a knight and take her to wife. And he told En Savaric how the girl had refused him, wherefore En Savaric made him a knight and gave him land and the income from it. And he married the girl and held her in great honour. And it happened that he went into Spain, leaving her behind him. And a knight out of England set his mind upon her and did so much and said so much that he led her with him, and he kept her long time his mistress and then let her go to the dogs (malamen anar). And En Gaubertz returned from Spain, and lodged himself one night in the city where she was. And he went out for desire of woman, and he entered the *alberc* of a poor woman; for they told him there was a fine woman within. And he found his wife. And when he saw her, and she him, great was the grief between them and great shame. And he stopped the night with her, and on the morrow he went forth with her to a nunnery where he had her enter. And for this grief he ceased to sing and to compose.' If you are minded, as Browning was in his *One Word More,* you may search out the song that En Gaubertz made, riding down

---

*Poetical composition, literally 'to find'.

the second time from Malleon, flushed with the unexpected knighthood.

> Per amor del belh temps suau
> E quar fin amor men somo.*

'For love of the sweet time and soft' he beseeches this 'lady in whom joy and worth have shut themselves and all good in its completeness' to give him grace and the kisses due to him a year since. And he ends in envoi to Savaric.

> Senher savaric larc e bo
> Vos troba hom tota fazo
> Quel vostre ric fag son prezan
> El dig cortes e benestan.†

La Tour has given us seed of drama in the passage above rendered. He has left us also an epic in his straightforward prose. 'Piere de Maensac was of Alverne (Auvergne) a poor knight, and he had a brother named Austors de Maensac, and they both were troubadours and they both were in concord that one should take the castle and the other the *trobar*.' And presumably they tossed up a *marabotin* or some such obsolete coin, for we read, 'And the castle went to Austors and the poetry to Piere, and he sang of the wife of Bernart de Tierci. So much he sang of her and so much he honoured her that it befell that the lady let herself go gay (*furar a del*). And he took her to the castle of the Dalfin of Auvergne, and the husband, in the manner of the golden Menelaus, demanded her much, with the church to back him and with the great war that they made. But the Dalfin maintained him (Piere) so that he never gave her up. He (Piere) was a straight man (*dreitz om*) and good company, and he made charming songs, tunes and the words, and good coblas of pleasure.' And among them is one beginning

---

*For love of the fair time and soft, / And because fine love calls me to it.
†Milord Savaric, generous / To thy last bond, men find thee thus, / That thy rich acts are food for praise / And courtly are thy words and days.

Longa saison ai estat vas amor
Humils e francs, y ai faich son coman.*

Dante and Browning have created so much interest in Sordello[3] that it may not be amiss to give the brief account of him as
it stands in a manuscript in the Ambrosian library at Milan. 'Lo
Sordels *si fo di Mantovana*. Sordello was of Mantuan territory of
Sirier (this would hardly seem to be Goito), son of a poor cavalier who had name Sier Escort (Browning's El Corte), and he delighted himself in chançons, to learn and to make them. And he
mingled with the good men of the court. And he learned all that
he could and he made coblas and sirventes. And he came thence
to the court of the Count of St Bonifaci, and the Count honoured
him much. And he fell in love with the wife of the Count, in the
form of pleasure (*a forma de solatz*), and she with him. (The
Palma of Browning's poem and the Cunizza of Dante's.) And it
befell that the Count stood ill with her brothers. And thus he estranged himself from her and from Sier Sceillme and Sier Albrics.
Thus her brothers caused her to be stolen from the Count by Sier
Sordello and the latter came to stop with them. And he (Sordello)
stayed a long time with them in great happiness, and then he
went into Proenssa where he received great honours from all the
good men and from the Count and from the Countess who gave
him a good castle and a wife of gentle birth.' (Browning with
perfect right alters this ending to suit his own purpose.)

The luck of the troubadours was as different as their ranks,
and they were drawn from all social orders. We are led far
from polite and polished society when we come to take note
of that Gringoire, Guillem Figiera, 'son of a tailor; and he was
a tailor; and when the French got hold of Toulouse he departed into Lombardy. And he knew well *trobar* and to sing,
and he made himself *joglar* among the townsfolk (*ciutadins*).
He was not a man who knew how to carry himself among the
barons or among the better class, but much he got himself
welcomed among harlots and slatterns and by innkeepers and

---

*For a long time have I stood toward Love / Humble and frank, and have done
his commands.

taverners. And if he saw coming a good man of the court, there where he was, he was sorry and grieved at it, and he nearly split himself to take him down a peg (*et ades percussava de lui abaissar*).'

For one razo that shows an unusual character there are a dozen that say simply that such or such a man was of Manes, or of Cataloigna by Rossilon, or of elsewhere, 'a poor cavalier.'* They made their way by favour at times, or by singing, or by some form of utility. Ademar of Gauvedan 'was of the castle Marvois, son of a poor knight. He was knighted by the lord of Marvois. He was a brave man but could not keep his estate as knight, and he became jongleur and was respected by all the best people. And later he went into orders at Gran Mon'. Elias Cairels 'was of Sarlat; ill he sang, ill he composed, ill he played the fiddle and worse he spoke, but he was good at writing out words and tunes. And he was a long time wandering, and when he quitted it, he returned to Sarlat and died there'. Perdigo was the son of a fisherman and made his fortune by his art. Peirol was a poor knight who was fitted out by the Dalfin of Auvergne and made love to Sail de Claustra; and all we know of Cercamon is that he made *vers* and *pastorelas* in the old way and that 'he went everywhere he could get to'. Pistoleta 'was a singer for Arnaut of Marvoil, and later he took to *trobar* and made songs with pleasing tunes and he was well received by the best people, although a man of little comfort and of poor endowment and of little stamina. And he took a wife at Marseilles and became a merchant and became rich and ceased going about the courts'. Guillems the skinny was a joglar of Manes, and the capital letter shows him throwing 3, 5, and 4, on a red dice board. 'Never had he on harness, and what he gained he lost *malamen,* to the taverns and the women. And he ended in a hospital in Spain.

The razos have in them the seeds of literary criticism. The speech is, however, laconic. Aimar lo Ners was a gentleman. 'He made such songs as he knew how to.' Aimeric de Sarlat, a joglar, became a troubadour, 'and yet he made but one song.' Piere Guillem of Toulouse 'Made good coblas, but he made too many'.

*For example Piere Bermon and Palazol.

Daude of Pradas made canzos 'per sen de trobar', which I think
we may translate 'from a mental grasp of the craft'. 'But they did
not move from love, wherefore they had not favour among folk.
They were not sung.' We find also that the labour and skill were
divided. One man played the viol most excellently, and another
sang, and another spoke his songs to music,* and another,
Jaufre Rudel, Brebezieu's father-in-law, made 'good tunes with
poor words to go with them'.

The troubadour's person comes in for as much free criticism as
his performance. Elias fons Slada was a 'fair man verily, as to feature, a joglar, no good troubadour'.† But Faidit, a joglar of
Uzerche, 'was exceedingly greedy both to drink and to eat, and he
became fat beyond measure. And he took to wife a public woman;
very fair and well taught she was, but she became as big and fat as
he was. And she was from a rich town Alest of the Mark of
Provenca from the seignory of En Bernart d'Andussa.'

One of the noblest figures of the time, if we are to believe the
chronicle, was Savaric de Mauleon, the rich baron of Peiteu,
mentioned above, son of Sir Reios de Malleon; 'lord was he of
Malleon and of Talarnom and of Fontenai, and of castle Aillon
and of Boetand of Benaon and of St Miquel en Letz and of the
isles of Ners and of the isle of Mues and of Nestrine and of
Engollius and of many other good places.' As one may read in the
continuation of this notice and verify from the razos of the other
troubadours, 'he was of the most open-handed men in the world.'
He seems to have left little verse save the tenzon with Faidit.

'Behold divers estate between them all!' Yet, despite the difference in conditions of life between the twelfth century and
our own, these few citations should be enough to prove that the
people were much the same, and if the preceding notes do not
do this, there is one tale left that should succeed.

'The Vicomte of St Antoni was of the bishopric of Caortz
(Cahors), Lord and Vicomte of St Antoni; and he loved a noble
lady who was wife of the seignor of Pena Dalbeges, of a rich

*Richard of Brebezieu (disia sons).
†The 'joglar' was the player and singer, the 'troubadour' the 'finder' or composer of songs and words.

castle and a strong. The lady was gentle and fair and valiant and highly prized and much honoured; and he very valiant and well trained and good at arms and charming, and a good trobaire, and had name Raimons Jordans; and the lady was called the Vicomtesse de Pena; and the love of these two was beyond all measure. And it befell that the Vicount went into a land of his enemies and was grievous wounded, so that report held him for dead. And at the news she in great grief went and gave candles at church for his recovery. And he recovered. And at this news also she had great grief.' And she fell a-moping, and that was the end of the affair with St Antoni, and 'thus was there more than one in deep distress'. 'Wherefore' Elis of Montfort, wife of William à-Gordon, daughter of the Viscount of Trozena, the glass of fashion and the mould of form, the pride of 'youth, beauty, courtesy', and presumably of justice, mercy, long-suffering, and so forth, made him overtures, and successfully. And the rest is a matter much as usual.

If humanity was much the same, it is equally certain that individuals were not any more like one another; and this may be better shown in the uncommunicative *canzoni* than in the razos. Thus we have a pastoral from the sensitive and little known Joios of Tolosa:

Lautrier el dous temps de pascor
En una ribeira,

which runs thus:
'The other day, in the sweet time of Easter, I went across a flat land of rivers hunting for new flowers, walking by the side of the path, and for delight in the greenness of things and because of the complete good faith and love which I bear for her who inspires me, I felt a melting about my heart and at the first flower I found, I burst into tears.

'And I wept until, in a shady place, my eyes fell upon a shepherdess. Fresh was her colour, and she was white as a snowdrift, and she had doves' eyes,' . . .

In very different key we find the sardonic Count of Foix, in a song which begins mildly enough for a spring song:

Mas qui a flor si vol mesclar,

and turns swiftly enough to a livelier measure:

Ben deu gardar lo sieu baston
Car frances sabon grans colps dar
Et albirar ab lor bordon
E nous fizes in carcasses
Ni en genes ni en gascon.
. . . . . .

Let no man lounge amid the flowers
Without a stout club of some kind.
Know ye the French are stiff in stour
And sing not all they have in mind,
So trust ye not in Carcason,
In Genovese, nor in Gascon.

My purpose in all this is to suggest to the casual reader that the Middle Ages did not exist in the tapestry alone, nor in the fourteenth-century romances, but that there was a life like our own, no mere sequence of citherns and citoles, nor a continuous stalking about in sendal and diaspre. Men were pressed for money. There was unspeakable boredom in the castles. The chivalric singing was devised to lighten the boredom; and this very singing became itself in due time, in the manner of all things, an ennui.

There has been so much written about the poetry of the best Provençal period, to wit the end of the twelfth century, that I shall say nothing of it here, but shall confine the latter part of this essay to a mention of three efforts, or three sorts of effort which were made to keep poetry alive after the crusade of 1208.

Any study of European poetry is unsound if it does not commence with a study of that art in Provence. The art of quantitative verse had been lost. This loss was due more to ignorance than to actual changes of language, from Latin, that is, into the younger tongues. It is open to doubt whether the Aeolic singing was ever comprehended fully even in Rome. When men began to write on tablets and ceased singing to the *barbitos*, a loss of some sort was unavoidable. Propertius may be cited as an exception, but Propertius writes only one meter. In any case the classic culture of the Renaissance was grafted on to medieval culture, a process which is excellently illustrated by Andreas Divus Justinopolitanus's[4] translation of the *Odyssey* into Latin. It is true that each century after the Renaissance has tried in its own way to come nearer the classic, but, if we are to understand that part of our civilization which is the art of verse, we must begin at the root, and that root is medieval. The poetic art of Provence paved the way for the poetic art of Tuscany; and to this Dante bears sufficient witness in the *De Vulgari Eloquio*. The heritage of art is one thing to the public and quite another to the succeeding artists. The artist's inheritance from other artists can be little more than certain enthusiasms, which usually spoil his first work; and a definite knowledge of the modes of expression, which knowledge contributes to perfecting his more mature performance. This is a matter of technique.

After the compositions of Vidal, Rudel, Ventadour, of Bornelh and Bertrans de Born and Arnaut Daniel, there seemed little chance of doing distinctive work in the 'canzon de l'amour courtois'. There was no way, or at least there was no man in Provence capable of finding a new way of saying in six closely rhymed strophes that a certain girl, matron or widow was like a certain set of things, and that the troubadour's virtues were like another set, and that all this was very sorrowful or otherwise, and that there was but one obvious remedy. Richard of Brebezieu had done his best for tired ears; he had made similes of beasts and of stars which got him a passing favour. He had compared himself to the fallen elephant and to the self-piercing pelican, and no one could go any further. Novelty is reasonably rare even in modes of decadence and revival. The three devices tried for poetic restoration in the early thirteenth century were the three usual devices. Certain men turned to talking art and aesthetics and attempted to dress up the folk-song. Certain men tried to make verse more engaging by stuffing it with an intellectual and argumentative content. Certain men turned to social

satire. Roughly, we may divide the interesting work of the later
provençal period into these three divisions. As all of these men
had progeny in Tuscany, they are, from the historical point of
view, worth a few moments' attention.

The first school is best represented in the work of Giraut
Riquier of Narbonne. His most notable feat was the revival of
the *Pastorela*. The Pastorela is a poem in which a knight tells of
having met with a shepherdess or some woman of that class,
and of what fortune and conversation befell him. The form had
been used long before by Marcabrun, and is familiar to us in
such poems as Guido Cavalcanti's *In un boschetto trovai pas-
torella,* or in Swinburne's *An Interlude.* Guido, who did all
things well, whenever the fancy took him, has raised this form
to a surpassing excellence in his poem *Era in pensier d'Amor,
quand' io trovai.* Riquier is most amusing in his account of the
inn-mistress at Sant Pos de Tomeiras, but even there he is less
amusing than was Marcabrun when he sang of the shepherdess
in *L'autrier iost' una sebissa.* Riquier has, however, his place in
the apostolic succession; and there is no reason why Cavalcanti
and Riquier should not have met while the former was on his
journey to Campostella, although Riquier may as easily have not
been in Spain at the time. At any rate the Florentine noble would
have heard the *Pastorelas* of Giraut; and this may have set him
to his *ballate,* which seem to date from the time of his meeting
with Mandetta in Toulouse. Or it may have done nothing of the
kind. The only more or less settled fact is that Riquier was then
the best known living troubadour and near the end of his course.

The second, and to us the dullest of the schools, set to explaining the nature of love and its effects. The normal modern
will probably slake all his curiosity for this sort of work in
reading one such poem as the King of Navarre's *De Fine amour
vient science e beautez.* 'Ingenium nobis ipsa puella fecit', as
Propertius put it, or *anglice*:

Knowledge and beauty from true love are wrought,
And likewise love is born from this same pair;
These three are one to whomso hath true thought, etc.

There might be less strain if one sang it. This peculiar variety of flame was carried to the altars of Bologna, whence Guinicello sang:

Al cor gentil ripara sempre amore,
Come l'augello in selva alla verdura

And Cavalcanti wrote: 'A lady asks me, wherefore I wish to speak of an accident* which is often cruel', and Dante, following in his elders' footsteps, the *Convito*.

The third school is the school of satire, and is the only one which gives us a contact with the normal life of the time. There had been Provençal satire before Piere Cardinal; but the sirventes of Sordello and De Born were directed for the most part against persons, while the Canon of Clermont drives rather against conditions. In so far as Dante is critic of morals, Cardinal must be held as his forerunner. Miquel writes of him as follows:

'Piere Cardinal was of Veillac of the city Pui Ma Donna, and he was of honourable lineage, son of a knight and a lady. And when he was little his father put him for canon in the *canonica major* of Puy; and he learnt letters, and he knew well how to read and to sing; and when he was come to man's estate he had high knowledge of the vanity of this world, for he felt himself gay and fair and young. And he made many fair arguments and fair songs. And he made canzos, but he made only a few of these, and sirventes; and he did best in the said sirventes where he set forth many fine arguments and fair examples for those who understand them; for much he rebuked the folly of this world and much he reproved the false clerks, as his sirventes show. And he went through the courts of kings and of noble barons and took with him his joglar who sang the sirventes. And much was he honoured and welcomed by my lord the good king of Aragon and by honourable barons. And I, master Miquel de la Tour, escriuan (scribe), do ye to wit that N. Piere Cardinal when he passed from

* *Accidente,* used as a purely technical term of his scholastic philosophy.

this life was nearly a hundred. And I, the aforesaid Miquel, have written these sirventes in the city of Nemze (Nîmes) and here are written some of his sirventes.'

If the Vicomtesse de Pena reminds us of certain ladies whom we have met, these sirventes of Cardinal may well remind us that thoughtful men have in every age found almost the same set of things or at least the same sort of things to protest against; if it be not a corrupt press or some monopoly, it is always some sort of equivalent, some conspiracy of ignorance and interest. And thus he says, 'Li clerc si fan pastor.' The clerks pretend to be shepherds, but they are wolfish at heart.

If he can find a straight man, it is truly matter for song; and so we hear him say of the Duke of Narbonne, who was apparently, making a fight for honest administration:

> Coms raymon duc de Narbona
> Marques de proensa
> Vostra valors es tan bona
> Que tot lo mon gensa,
> Quar de la mar de bayona
> En tro a valenca
> Agra gent falsae fellona
> Lai ab vil temensa,
> Mas vos tenetz vil lor
> Q'n frances bevedor
> Plus qua perditz austor
> No vos fan temensa.

'Now is come from France what one did not ask for'—he is addressing the man who is standing against the North—

> Count Raymon, Duke of Narbonne,
> Marquis of Provence,
> Your valour is sound enough
> To make up for the cowardice of
> All the rest of the gentry.
> For from the sea at Bayonne,

Even to Valence,
Folk would have given in (sold out),
But you hold them in scorn,
[Or, reading 'l'aur', 'scorn the gold'.]
So that the drunken French
Alarm you no more
Than a partridge frightens a hawk.

Cardinal is not content to spend himself in mere abuse, like the little tailor Figeira, who rhymes Christ's 'mortal pena' with

Car voletz totzjors portar la borsa plena,

which is one way of saying 'Judas!' to the priests. He, Cardinal, sees that the technique of honesty is not always utterly simple.

Li postilh, legat elh cardinal
La cordon tug, y an fag establir
Que qui nos pot de traisson esdir,

which may mean, 'The pope and the legate and the cardinal have twisted such a cord that they have brought things to such a pass that no one can escape committing treachery.' As for the rich:

Li ric home an pietat tan gran
Del autre gen quon ac caym da bel.
Que mais volon tolre q̄ lop no fan
E mais mentir que tozas de bordelh.
· · · · · ·
The rich men have such pity
For other folk—about as much as Cain had for Abel.
For they would like to leave less than the wolves do,
And to lie more than girls in a brothel.

Of the clergy, 'A tantas vey baylia', 'So much the more do I see clerks coming into power that all the world will be theirs, whoever objects. For they'll have it with taking or with giving' (i.e. by granting land, belonging to one man, to someone else who will pay allegiance for it, as in the case of De Montfort), 'or with pardon or with hypocrisy; or by assault or by drinking and eating; or by prayers or by praising the worse; or with God or with devilry.' We find him putting the age-long query about profit in the following:

> He may have enough harness
> And sorrel horses and bays;
> Tower, wall, and palace,
> May he have
> —the rich man denying his God.

The stanza runs very smoothly to the end

> Si mortz no fos
> Elh valgra per un cen

> A hundred men he would be worth
> Were there no death.

The modern Provençal enthusiast in raptures at the idea of chivalric love (a term which he usually misunderstands), and little concerned with the art of verse, has often failed to notice how finely the sound of Cardinal's poems is matched with their meaning. There is a lash and sting in his timbre and in his movement. Yet the old man is not always bitter; or, if he is bitter, it is with the bitterness of a torn heart and not a hard one. It is so we find him in the sirvente beginning:

> As a man weeps for his son or for his father,
> Or for his friend when death has taken him,
> So do I mourn for the living who do their own ill,
> False, disloyal, felon, and full of ill-fare,
> Deceitful, breakers-of-pact,
> Cowards, complainers,
> Highwaymen, thieves-by-stealth, turn-coats,
> Betrayers, and full of treachery,

    Here where the devil reigns
      And teaches them to act thus.

He is almost the only singer of his time to protest against the follies of war. As here:

    Ready for war, as night is to follow the sun,
    Readier for it than is the fool to be cuckold
    When he has first plagued his wife!
    And war is an ill thing to look upon,
    And I know that there is not one man drawn into it
    But his child, or his cousin or someone akin to him
    Prays God that it be given over.

He says plainly, in another place, that the barons make war for their own profit, regardless of the peasants. 'Fai mal senher vas los sieu.' His sobriety is not to be fooled with sentiment either martial or otherwise. There is in him little of the fashion of feminolatry, and the gentle reader in search of trunk-hose and the light guitar had better go elsewhere. As for women: 'L'una fai drut.'

    One turns leman for the sake of great possessions;
    And another because poverty is killing her,
    And one hasn't even a shift of coarse linen;
    And another has two and does likewise.
    And one gets an old man—and she is a young wench,
    And the old woman gives the man an elixir.

As for justice, there is little now: 'If a rich man steal by chicanery, he will have right before Constantine (i.e. by legal circumambience) but the poor thief may go hang.' And after this there is a passage of pity and of irony fine-drawn as much of his work is, for he keeps the very formula that De Born had used in his praise of battle, 'Belh mes quan vey'; and, perhaps, in Sir Bertrans' time even the Provençal wars may have seemed more like a game, and may have appeared to have some element of sport and chance in them. But the twelfth century had gone, and the spirit of the people was weary, and the old canon's passage may well serve as a final epitaph on all that remained of silk thread and *cisclatons,* of viol and *gai saber.*

Never agin shall we see the Easter come in so fairly,
That was wont to come in with pleasure and with song,
No! but we see it arrayed with alarms and excursions,
Arrayed with war and dismay and fear,
Arrayed with troops and with cavalcades,
Oh, yes, it's a fine sight to see holder and shepherd
Going so wretched that they know not where they are

THE SERIOUS ARTIST

I

It is curious that one should be asked to rewrite Sidney's *Defence of Poesy* in the year of grace 1913. During the intervening centuries, and before them, other centres of civilization had decided that good art was a blessing and that bad art was criminal, and they had spent some time and thought in trying to find means whereby to distinguish the true art from the sham. But in England now, in the age of Gosse as in the age of Gosson we are asked if the arts are moral. We are asked to define the relation of the arts to economics, we are asked what position the arts are to hold in the ideal republic. And it is obviously the opinion of many people less objectionable than the Sydney Webbs[1] that the arts had better not exist at all.

I take no great pleasure in writing prose about æasthetic. I think one work of art is worth forty prefaces and as many apologiæ. Nevertheless I have been questioned earnestly and by a person certainly of good will. It is as if one said to me: what is the use of open spaces in this city, what is the use of rose-trees and why do you wish to plant trees and lay out parks and gardens? There are some who do not take delight in these things. The rose springs fairest from some buried Cæsar's throat and the dogwood with its flower of four petals (our dogwood, not

the tree you call by that name) is grown from the heart of Aucassin,[2] or perhaps this is only fancy. Let us pursue the matter in
ethic.

It is obvious that ethics are based on the nature of man, just
as it is obvious that civics are based upon the nature of men
when living together in groups.

It is obvious that the good of the greatest number cannot be
attained until we know in some sort of what that good must
consist. In other words we must know what sort of an animal
man is, before we can contrive his maximum happiness, or before we can decide what percentage of that happiness he can
have without causing too great a percentage of unhappiness to
those about him.

The arts, literature, poesy, are a science, just as chemistry is a
science. Their subject is man, mankind and the individual. The
subject of chemistry is matter considered as to its composition.

The arts give us a great percentage of the lasting and unassailable data regarding the nature of man, of immaterial man,
of man considered as a thinking and sentient creature. They begin where the science of medicine leaves off or rather they over-
lap that science. The borders of the two arts overcross.

From medicine we learn that man thrives best when duly
washed, aired and sunned. From the arts we learn that man is
whimsical, that one man differs from another. That men differ
among themselves as leaves upon trees differ. That they do not
resemble each other as do buttons cut by machine.

From the arts also we learn in what ways man resembles and
in what way he differs from certain other animals. We learn
that certain men are often more akin to certain animals than
they are to other men of different composition. We learn that
all men do not desire the same things and that it would therefore be inequitable to give to all men two acres and a cow.

It would be manifestly inequitable to treat the ostrich and the
polar bear in the same fashion, granted that it is not unjust to
have them pent up where you can treat them at all.

An ethic based on a belief that men are different from what
they are is manifestly stupid. It is stupid to apply such an ethic
as it is to apply laws and morals designed for a nomadic tribe,

or for a tribe in the state of barbarism, to a people crowded into the slums of a modern metropolis. Thus in the tribe it is well to beget children, for the more strong male children you have in the tribe the less likely you are to be bashed on the head by males of the neighbouring tribes, and the more female children the more rapidly the tribe will increase. Conversely it is a crime rather worse than murder to beget children in a slum, to beget children for whom no fitting provision is made, either as touching their physical or economic wellbeing. The increase not only afflicts the child born but the increasing number of the poor keeps down the wage. On this count the bishop of London, as an encourager of this sort of increase, is a criminal of a type rather lower and rather more detestable than the souteneur.

I cite this as one example of inequity persisting because of a continued refusal to consider a code devised for one state of society, in its (the code's) relation to a different state of society. It is as if, in physics or engineering, we refused to consider a force designed to affect one mass, in its relation (i.e. the force's) to another mass wholly differing, or in some notable way differing, from the first mass.

As inequities can exist because of refusals to consider the actualities of a law in relation to a social condition, so can inequities exist through refusal to consider the actualities of the composition of the masses, or of the individuals to which they are applied.

If all men desired above everything else two acres and a cow, obviously the perfect state would be that state which gave to each man two acres and a cow.

If any science save the arts were able more precisely to determine what the individual does not actually desire, then that science would be of more use in providing the data for ethics.

In the like manner, if any sciences save medicine and chemistry were more able to determine what things were compatible with physical wellbeing, then those sciences would be of more value for providing the data of hygiene.

This brings us to the immorality of bad art. Bad art is inaccurate art. It is art that makes false reports. If a scientist falsifies a report either deliberately or through negligence we consider him as either a criminal or a bad scientist according to the enormity of his offence, and he is punished or despised accordingly.

If he falsifies the reports of a maternity hospital in order to retain his position and get profit and advancement from the city board, he may escape detection. If he declines to make such falsification he may lose financial rewards, and in either case his baseness or his pluck may pass unknown and unnoticed save by a very few people. Nevertheless one does not have to argue his case. The layman knows soon enough on hearing it whether the physician is to be blamed or praised.

If an artist falsifies his report as to the nature of man, as to his own nature, as to the nature of his ideal of the perfect, as to the nature of his ideal of this, that or the other, of god, if god exist, of the life force, of the nature of good and evil, if good and evil exist, of the force with which he believes or disbelieves this, that or the other, of the degree in which he suffers or is made glad; if the artist falsifies his reports on these matters or on any other matter in order that he may conform to the taste of his time, to the proprieties of a sovereign, to the conveniences of a preconceived code of ethics, then that artist lies. If he lies out of deliberate will to lie, if he lies out of carelessness, out of laziness, out of cowardice, out of any sort of negligence whatsoever, he nevertheless lies and he should be punished or despised in proportion to the seriousness of his offence. His offence is of the same nature as the physician's and according to his position and the nature of his lie he is responsible for future oppressions and for future misconceptions. Albeit his lies are known to only a few, or his truthtelling to only a few. Albeit he may pass without censure for one and without praise for the other. Albeit he can only be punished on the plane of his crime and by nothing save the contempt of those who know of his crime. Perhaps it is caddishness rather than crime. However there is perhaps nothing worse for a man than to know that he is a cur and to know that someone else, if only one person, knows it.

We distinguish very clearly between the physician who is doing his best for a patient, who is using drugs in which he believes, or who is in a wilderness, let us say, where the patient can get no other medical aid. We distinguish, I say, very clearly between the failure of such a physician, and the act of that physician, who ignorant of the patient's disease, being in reach of more skilful physicians, deliberately denies an ignorance of which he is quite conscious, refuses to consult other physicians, tries to prevent the patient's having access to more skilful physicians, or deliberately tortures the patient for his own ends.

One does not need to read black print to learn this ethical fact about physicians. Yet it takes a deal of talking to convince a layman that bad art is 'immoral'. And that good art however 'immoral' it is, is wholly a thing of virtue. Purely and simply that good art can NOT be immoral. By good art I mean art that bears true witness, I mean the art that is most precise. You can be wholly precise in representing a vagueness. You can be wholly a liar in pretending that the particular vagueness was precise in its outline. If you cannot understand this with regard to poetry, consider the matter in terms of painting.

If you have forgotten my statement that the arts bear witness and define for us the inner nature and conditions of man, consider the Victory of Samothrace and the Taj of Agra.[3] The man who carved the one and the man who designed the other may either or both of them have looked like an ape, or like two apes respectively. They may have looked like other apelike or swine-like men. We have the Victory and the Taj to witness that there was something within them differing from the contents of apes and of the other swinelike men. Thus we learn that humanity is a species or genus of animals capable of a variation that will produce the desire for a Taj or a Victory, and moreover capable of effecting that Taj or Victory in stone. We know from other testimony of the arts and from ourselves that the desire often overshoots the power of efficient presentation; we therefore conclude that other members of the race may have desired to effect a Taj or a Victory. We even suppose that men have desired to effect more beautiful things although few of us are capable of forming any precise mental image of things, in their particular way, more beautiful than this statue or this building. So difficult is this that no one has yet been able to effect a restoration for the missing head of the Victory. At least no one has done so in stone, so far as I know. Doubtless many people

238   EZRA POUND

have stood opposite the statue and made such heads in their imagination.

As there are in medicine the art of diagnosis and the art of cure, so in the arts, so in the particular arts of poetry and of literature, there is the art of diagnosis and there is the art of cure. They call one the cult of ugliness and the other the cult of beauty.

The cult of beauty is the hygiene, it is sun, air and the sea and the rain and the lake bathing. The cult of ugliness, Villon, Baudelaire, Corbière, Beardsley are diagnosis. Flaubert is diagnosis. Satire, if we are to ride this metaphor to staggers, satire is surgery, insertions and amputations.

Beauty in art reminds one what is worth while. I am not now speaking of shams. I mean beauty, not slither, not sentimentalizing about beauty, not telling people that beauty is the proper and respectable thing. I mean beauty. You don't argue about an April wind, you feel bucked up when you meet it. You feel bucked up when you come on a swift moving thought in Plato or on a fine line in a statue.

Even this pother about gods reminds one that something is worth while. Satire reminds one that certain things are not worth while. It draws one to consider time wasted.

The cult of beauty and the delineation of ugliness are not in mutual opposition.

II

I have said that the arts give us our best data for determining what sort of creature man is. As our treatment of man must be determined by our knowledge or conception of what man is, the arts provide data for ethics.

These data are sound and the data of generalizing psychologists and social theoricians are usually unsound, for the serious artist is scientific and the theorist is usually empiric in the medieval fashion. That is to say a good biologist will make a reasonable number of observations of any given phenomenon before he draws a conclusion, thus we read such phrases as 'over 100 cultures from the secretions of the respiratory tracts of over

500 patients and 30 nurses and attendants'. The results of each observation must be precise and no single observation must in itself be taken as determining a general law, although, after experiment, certain observations may be held as typical or normal. The serious artist is scientific in that he presents the image of his desire, of his hate, of his indifference as precisely that, as precisely the image of his own desire, hate or indifference. The more precise his record the more lasting and unassailable his work of art.

The theorist, and we see this constantly illustrated by the English writers on sex, the theorist constantly proceeds as if his own case, his own limits and predilections were the typical case, or even as if it were the universal. He is constantly urging someone else to behave as he, the theorist, would like to behave. Now art never asks anybody to do anything, or to think anything, or to be anything. It exists as the trees exist, you can admire, you can sit in the shade, you can pick bananas, you can cut firewood, you can do as you jolly well please.

Also you are a fool to seek the kind of art you don't like. You are a fool to read classics because you are told to and not because you like them. You are a fool to aspire to good taste if you haven't naturally got it. If there is one place where it is idiotic to sham that place is before a work of art. Also you are a fool not to have an open mind, not to be eager to enjoy something you might enjoy but don't know how to. But it is not the artist's place to ask you to learn, or to defend his particular works of art, or to insist on your reading his books. Any artist who wants your particular admiration is, by just so much, the less artist.

The desire to stand on the stage, the desire of plaudits has nothing to do with serious art. The serious artist may like to stand on the stage, he may, apart from his art, be any kind of imbecile you like, but the two things are not connected, at least they are not concentric. Lots of people who don't even pretend to be artists have the same desire to be slobbered over, by people with less brains than they have.

The serious artist is usually, or is often as far from the ægrum vulgus[4] as is the serious scientist. Nobody has heard of the abstract mathematicians who worked out the determinants that Marconi made use of in his computations for the wireless telegraph. The public, the public so dear to the journalistic heart, is far more concerned with the shareholders in the Marconi company.

The permanent property, the property given to the race at large is precisely these data of the serious scientist and of the serious artist; of the scientist as touching the relations of abstract numbers, of molecular energy, of the composition of matter, etc.; of the serious artist, as touching the nature of man, of individuals.

Men have ceased trying to conquer the world* and to acquire universal knowledge. Men still try to promote the ideal state. No perfect state will be founded on the theory, or on the working hypothesis that all men are alike. No science save the arts will give us the requisite data for learning in what ways men differ.

The very fact that many men hate the arts is of value, for we are enabled by finding out what part of the arts they hate, to learn something of their nature. Usually when men say they hate the arts we find that they merely detest quackery and bad artists.

In the case of a man's hating one art and not the others we may learn that he is of defective hearing or of defective intelligence. Thus an intelligent man may hate music or a good musician may detest very excellent authors.

And all these things are very obvious.

Among thinking and sentient people the bad artist is contemned as we would contemn a negligent physician or a sloppy, inaccurate scientist, and the serious artist is left in peace, or even supported and encouraged. In the fog and the outer darkness no measures are taken to distinguish between the serious and the unserious artist. The unserious artist being the commoner brand and greatly outnumbering the serious variety, and it being to the temporary and apparent advantage of the false artist to gain the rewards proper to the serious artist, it is natural

*Blind Optimism A.D. 1913.

that the unserious artist should do all in his power to obfuscate the lines of demarcation.

Whenever one attempts to demonstrate the difference between serious and unserious work, one is told that 'it is merely a technical discussion'. It has rested at that—in England it has rested at that for more than three hundred years. The people would rather have patent medicines than scientific treatment. They will occasionally be told that art as art is not a violation of God's most holy laws. They will not have a specialist's opinion as to what art is good. They will not consider the 'problem of style'. They want 'The value of art to life' and 'Fundamental issues'.

As touching fundamental issues: The arts give us our data of psychology, of man as to his interiors, as to the ratio of his thought to his emotions, etc., etc., etc.

The touchstone of an art is its precision. This precision is of various and complicated sorts and only the specialist can determine whether certain works of art possess certain sorts of precision. I don't mean to say that any intelligent person cannot have more or less sound judgement as to whether a certain work of art is good or not. An intelligent person can usually tell whether or not a person is in good health. It is none the less true that it takes a skilful physician to make certain diagnoses or to discern the lurking disease beneath the appearance of vigour.

It is no more possible to give in a few pages full instructions for knowing a masterpiece than it would be to give full instructions for all medical diagnosis.

III

EMOTION AND POESY

Obviously, it is not easy to be a great poet. If it were, many more people would have done so. At no period in history has the world been free of people who have mildly desired to be great poets and not a few have endeavoured conscientiously to be such.

I am aware that adjectives of magnitude are held to savour of barbarism. Still there is no shame in desiring to give great gifts and an enlightened criticism does not draw ignominious comparisons between Villon and Dante. The so-called major poets have most of them given their *own* gift but the peculiar term 'major' is rather a gift to them from Chronos. I mean that they have been born upon the stroke of their hour and that it has been given them to heap together and arrange and harmonize the results of many men's labour. This very faculty for amalgamation is a part of their genius and it is, in a way, a sort of modesty, a sort of unselfishness. They have not wished for property.

The men from whom Dante borrowed are remembered as much for the fact that he did borrow as for their own compositions. At the same time he gave of his own, and no mere compiler and classifier of other men's discoveries is given the name of 'major poet' for more than a season.

If Dante had not done a deal more than borrow rhymes from Arnaut Daniel and theology from Aquinas he would not be published by Dent in the year of grace 1913.

We might come to believe that the thing that matters in art is a sort of energy, something more or less like electricity or radioactivity, a force transfusing, welding, and unifying. A force rather like water when it spurts up through very bright sand and sets it in swift motion. You may make what image you like.

I do not know that there is much use in composing an answer to the often asked question: What is the difference between poetry and prose?

I believe that poetry is the more highly energized. But these things are relative. Just as we say that a certain temperature is hot and another cold. In the same way we say that a certain prose passage 'is poetry' meaning to praise it, and that a certain passage of verse is 'only prose' meaning dispraise. And at the same time 'Poetry!!!' is used as a synonym for 'Bosh! Rott!! Rubbish!!!' The thing that counts is 'Good writing'.

And 'Good writing' is perfect control. And it is quite easy to control a thing that has in it no energy—provided that it be not too heavy and that you do not wish to make it move.

And, as all the words that one would use in writing about these things are the vague words of daily speech, it is nearly impossible to write with scientific preciseness about 'prose and verse' unless one writes a complete treatise on the 'art of writing', defining each word as one would define the terms in a treatise on chemistry. And on this account all essays about 'poetry' are usually not only dull but inaccurate and wholly useless. And on like account if you ask a good painter to tell you what he is trying to do to a canvas he will very probably wave his hands helplessly and murmur that 'He—eh—eh—he can't talk about it'. And that if you 'see anything at all, he is quite—eh—more or less—eh—satisfied'.

Nevertheless it has been held for a shameful thing that a man should not be able to give a reason for his acts and words. And if one does not care about being taken for a mystificateur one may as well try to give approximate answers to questions asked in good faith. It might be better to do the thing thoroughly, in a properly accurate treatise, but one has not always two or three spare years at one's disposal, and one is dealing with very subtle and complicated matter, and even so, the very algebra of logic is itself open to debate.

Roughly then, Good writing is writing that is perfectly controlled, the writer says just what he means. He says it with complete clarity and simplicity. He uses the smallest possible number of words. I do not mean that he skimps paper, or that he screws about like Tacitus to get his thought crowded into the least possible space. But, granting that two sentences are at times easier to understand than one sentence containing the double meaning, the author tries to communicate with the reader with the greatest possible despatch, save where for any one of forty reasons he does not wish to do so.

Also there are various kinds of clarity. There is the clarity of the request: Send me four pounds of ten-penny nails. And there is the syntactical simplicity of the request: Buy me the kind of Rembrandt I like. This last is an utter cryptogram. It presupposes a more complex and intimate understanding of the speaker than most of us ever acquire of anyone. It has as many meanings, almost, as there are persons who might speak it. To a stranger it conveys nothing at all.

It is the almost constant labour of the prose artist to translate this latter kind of clarity into the former; to say 'Send me the kind of Rembrandt I like' in the terms of 'Send me four pounds of ten-penny nails'.

The whole thing is an evolution. In the beginning simple words were enough: Food; water; fire. Both prose and poetry are but an extension of language. Man desires to communicate with his fellows. He desires an ever increasingly complicated communication. Gesture serves up to a point. Symbols may serve. When you desire something not present to the eye or when you desire to communicate ideas, you must have recourse to speech. Gradually you wish to communicate something less bare and ambiguous than ideas. You wish to communicate an idea and its modifications, an idea and a crowd of its effects, atmospheres, contradictions. You wish to question whether a certain formula works in every case, or in what per cent of cases, etc., etc., etc., you get the Henry James novel.

You wish to communicate an idea and its concomitant emotions, or an emotion and its concomitant ideas, or a sensation and its derivative emotions, or an impression that is emotive, etc., etc., etc. You begin with the yeowl and the bark, and you develop into the dance and into music, and into music with words, and finally into words with music, and finally into words with a vague adumbration of music, words suggestive of music, words measured, or words in a rhythm that preserves some accurate trait of the emotive impression, or of the sheer character of the fostering or parental emotion.

When this rhythm, or when the vowel and consonantal melody or sequence seems truly to bear the trace of emotion which the poem (for we have come at last to the poem) is intended to communicate, we say that this part of the work is good. And 'this part of the work' is by now 'technique'. That 'dry, dull, pedantic' technique, that all bad artists rail against. It is only a part of technique, it is rhythm, cadence, and the arrangement of sounds.

Also the 'prose', the words and their sense must be such as fit the emotion. Or, from the other side, ideas, or fragments of ideas, the emotion and concomitant emotions of this 'Intellectual and

Emotional Complex' (for we have come to the intellectual and emotional complex) must be in harmony, they must form an organism, they must be an oak sprung from an acorn.

When you have words of a lament set to the rhythm and tempo of *There'll be a Hot Time in the Old Town to-night* you have either an intentional burlesque or you have rotten art. Shelley's *Sensitive Plant* is one of the rottenest poems ever written, at least one of the worst ascribable to a recognized author. It jiggles to the same tune as *A little peach in the orchard grew*. Yet Shelley recovered and wrote the fifth act of the Cenci.

IV

It is occasionally suggested by the wise that poets should acquire the graces of prose. That is an extension of what has been said above anent control. Prose does not need emotion. It may, but it need not, attempt to portray emotion.

Poetry is a centaur. The thinking word-arranging, clarifying faculty must move and leap with the energizing, sentient, musical faculties. It is precisely the difficulty of this amphibious existence that keeps down the census record of good poets. The accomplished prose author will tell you that he 'can only write poetry when he has a bellyache' and thence he will argue that poetry just isn't an art.

I dare say there are very good marksmen who just can't shoot from a horse.

Likewise if a good marksman only mounted a few times he might never acquire any proficiency in shooting from the saddle. Or leaving metaphor, I suppose that what, in the long run, makes the poet is a sort of persistence of the emotional nature, and, joined with this, a peculiar sort of control.

The saying that 'a lyric poet might as well die at thirty' is simply saying that the emotional nature seldom survives this age, or that it becomes, at any rate, subjected and incapable of moving the whole man. Of course this is a generality, and, as such, inaccurate.

It is true that most people poetize more or less, between the ages of seventeen and twenty-three. The emotions are new, and, to their possessor, interesting, and there is not much mind or personality to be moved. As the man, as his mind, becomes a heavier and heavier machine, a constantly more complicated structure, it requires a constantly greater voltage of emotional energy to set it in harmonious motion. It is certain that the emotions increase in vigour as a vigorous man matures. In the case of Guido we have his strongest work at fifty. Most important poetry has been written by men over thirty.

'En l'an trentiesme de mon eage', begins Villon and considering the nature of his life thirty would have seen him more spent than forty years of more orderly living.

Aristotle will tell you that 'The apt use of metaphor, being as it is, the swift perception of relations, is the true hall-mark of genius'. That abundance, that readiness of the figure is indeed one of the surest proofs that the mind is upborne upon the emotional surge.

By 'apt use', I should say it were well to understand, a swiftness, almost a violence, and certainly a vividness. This does not mean elaboration and complication.

There is another poignancy which I do not care to analyse into component parts, if, indeed, such vivisection is possible. It is not the formal phrasing of Flaubert much as such formality is desirable and noble. It is such phrasing as we find in

> Era già l'ora che volge il disio
> Ai naviganti. . . .

Or the opening of the ballata which begins:

> Perch 'io non spero di tornar già mai
> Ballatetta, in Toscana.

Or:

> S'ils n 'ayment fors que pour l'argent,
> On ne les ayme que pour l'heure.

Or, in its context:

The fire that stirs about her, when she stirs,

or, in its so different setting,

> Ne maeg werigmod wryde withstondan
> ne se hreo hyge helpe gefremman:
> forthon domgeorne dreorigne oft
> in hyra breostcofan bindath faeste.

These things have in them that passionate simplicity which is beyond the precisions of the intellect. Truly they are perfect as fine prose is perfect, but they are in some way different from the clear statements of the observer. They are in some way different from that so masterly ending of the Herodias: 'Comme elle était très lourde ils la portaient alternativement' or from the constatation in St. Julian Hospitalier: 'Et l'idée lui vient d'employer son existence au service des autres.'

The prose author has shown the triumph of his intellect and one knows that such triumph is not without its sufferings by the way, but by the verses one is brought upon the passionate moment. This moment has brought with it nothing that violates the prose simplicities. The intellect has not found it but the intellect has been moved.

There is little but folly in seeking the lines of division, yet if the two arts must be divided we may as well use that line as any other. In the verse something has come upon the intelligence. In the prose the intelligence has found a subject for its observations. The poetic fact pre-exists.

In a different way, of course, the subject of the prose pre-exists. Perhaps the difference is undemonstrable, perhaps it is not even communicable to any save those of good will. Yet I think this orderliness in the greatest poetic passages, this quiet statement that partakes of the nature of prose and is yet floated and tossed in the emotional surges, is perhaps as true a test as that mentioned by the Greek theorician.

V

La poésie, avec ses comparaisons obligées, sa mythologie que
ne croit pas le poète, sa dignité de style à la Louis XIV, et
tout l'attirail de ses ornements appelés poétiques, est bien
audessous de la prose dès qu'il s'agit de donner une idée
claire et précise des mouvements du coeur; or, dans ce
genre, on n'émeut que par la clarté.

—*Stendhal*

And that is precisely why one employs oneself in seeking precisely the poetry that shall be without this flummery, this fustian *à la Louis XIV, 'farcie de comme'*. The above critique of
Stendhal's does not apply to the Poema del Cid, nor to the parting of Odysseus and Calypso. In the writers of the duo-cento
and early tre-cento we find a precise psychology, embedded in a
now almost unintelligible jargon, but there nevertheless. If we
cannot get back to these things; if the serious artist cannot attain this precision in verse, then he must either take to prose or
give up his claim to being a serious artist.

It is precisely because of this fustian that the Parnassiads[5] and
epics of the eighteenth century and most of the present-day
works of most of our contemporary versifiers are pests and
abominations.

As the most efficient way to say nothing is to keep quiet, and
as technique consists precisely in doing the thing that one sets
out to do, in the most efficient manner, no man who takes three
pages to say nothing can expect to be seriously considered as a
technician. To take three pages to say nothing is not style, in
the serious sense of that word.

There are several kinds of honest work. There is the thing that
will out. There is the conscientious formulation, a thing of infinitely greater labour, for the first is not labour at all, though the
efficient doing of it may depend on a deal of labour foregoing.

There is the 'labour foregoing', the patient testing of media,
the patient experiment which shall avail perhaps the artist himself, but is as likely to avail some successor.

The first sort of work may be poetry.

The second sort, the conscientious formulation, is more than likely to be prose.

The third sort of work savours of the laboratory, it concerns the specialist, and the dilettante, if that word retains any trace of its finer and original sense. A dilettante proper is a person who takes delight in the art, not a person who tries to interpose his inferior productions between masterwork and the public.

I reject the term connoisseurship, for 'connoisseurship' is so associated in our minds with a desire for acquisition. The person possessed of connoisseurship is so apt to want to buy the rare at one price and sell it at another. I do not believe that a person with this spirit has ever *seen* a work of art. Let me restore the foppish term dilettante, the synonym for folly, to its place near the word *diletto*.

The dilettante has no axe to grind for himself. If he be artist as well, he will be none the less eager to preserve the best precedent work. He will drag out 'sources' that prove him less original than his public would have him.

As for Stendhal's stricture, if we can have a poetry that comes as close as prose, *pour donner une idée claire et précise,* let us have it, *'E di venire a ciò io studio quanto posso . . . che la mia vita per alquanti anni duri.'* . . . And if we cannot attain to such a poetry, noi altri poeti, for God's sake let us shut up. Let us 'Give up, go down', etcetera; let us acknowledge that our art, like the art of dancing in armour, is out of date and out of fashion. Or let us go to our ignominious ends knowing that we have strained at the cords, that we have spent our strength in trying to pave the way for a new sort of poetic art—it is not a new sort but an old sort—but let us know that we have tried to make it more nearly possible for our successors to recapture this art. To write a poetry that can be carried as a communication between intelligent men.

To this end *io studio quanto posso.* I have tried to establish a clear demarcation. I have been challenged on my use of the phrase 'great art' in an earlier article. It is about as useless to search for a definition of 'great art' as it is to search for a scientific definition of life. One knows fairly well what one means.

One means something more or less proportionate to one's experience. One means something quite different at different periods of one's life.

It is for some such reason that all criticism should be professedly personal criticism. In the end the critic can only say 'I like it', or 'I am moved', or something of that sort. When he has shown us himself we are able to understand him.

Thus, in painting, I mean something or other vaguely associated in my mind with work labelled Dürer, and Rembrandt, and Velasquez, etc., and with the painters whom I scarcely know, possibly of T'ang and Sung—though I dare say I've got the wrong labels—and with some Egyptian designs that should probably be thought of as sculpture.

And in poetry I mean something or other associated in my mind with the names of a dozen or more writers.

On closer analysis I find that I mean something like 'maximum efficiency of expression'; I mean that the writer has expressed something interesting in such a way that one cannot re-say it more effectively. I also mean something associated with discovery. The artist must have discovered something—either of life itself or of the means of expression.

Great art must of necessity be a part of good art. I attempted to define good art in an earlier chapter. It must bear true witness. Obviously great art must be an exceptional thing. It cannot be the sort of thing anyone can do after a few hours' practice. It must be the result of some exceptional faculty, strength, or perception. It must almost be that strength of perception working with the connivance of fate, or chance, or whatever you choose to call it.

And who is to judge? The critic, the receiver, however stupid or ignorant, must judge for himself. The only really vicious criticism is the academic criticism of those who make the grand abnegation, who refuse to say what they think, if they do think, and who quote accepted opinion; these men are the vermin, their treachery to the great work of the past is as great as that of the false artist to the present. If they do not care enough for the heritage to have a personal conviction then they have no licence to write.

Every critic should give indication of the sources and limits of his knowledge. The criticism of English poetry by men who knew no language but English, or who knew little but English and school-classics, has been a marasmus.

When we know to what extent each sort of expression has been driven, in, say, half a dozen great literatures, we begin to be able to tell whether a given work has the excess of great art. We would not think of letting a man judge pictures if he knew only English pictures, or music if he knew only English music— or only French or German music for that matter.

The stupid or provincial judgment of art bases itself on the belief that great art must be like the art that it has been reared to respect.

A RETROSPECT*

There has been so much scribbling about a new fashion in poetry, that I may perhaps be pardoned this brief recapitulation and retrospect.

In the spring or early summer of 1912, 'H. D.', Richard Aldington and myself decided that we were agreed upon the three principles following:

1. Direct treatment of the 'thing' whether subjective or objective.
2. To use absolutely no word that does not contribute to the presentation.
3. As regarding rhythm: to compose in the sequence of the musical phrase, not in sequence of a metronome.

Upon many points of taste and of predilection we differed, but agreeing upon these three positions we thought we had as much right to a group name, at least as much right, as a number of French 'schools' proclaimed by Mr Flint[1] in the August number of Harold Monro's magazine[2] for 1911.

---

*A group of early essays and notes which appeared under this title in *Pavannes and Divisions* (1918). 'A Few Dont's' was first printed in *Poetry*, I, 6 (March, 1913).

This school has since been 'joined' or 'followed' by numerous people who, whatever their merits, do not show any signs of agreeing with the second specification. Indeed *vers libre* has become as prolix and as verbose as any of the flaccid varieties that preceded it. It has brought faults of its own. The actual language and phrasing is often as bad as that of our elders without even the excuse that the words are shovelled in to fill a metric pattern or to complete the noise of a rhyme-sound. Whether or no the phrases followed by the followers are musical must be left to the reader's decision. At times I can find a marked metre in 'vers libres', as stale and hackneyed as any pseudo-Swinburnian, at times the writers seem to follow no musical structure whatever. But it is, on the whole, good that the field should be ploughed. Perhaps a few good poems have come from the new method, and if so it is justified.

Criticism is not a circumscription or a set of prohibitions. It provides fixed points of departure. It may startle a dull reader into alertness. That little of it which is good is mostly in stray phrases; or if it be an older artist helping a younger it is in great measure but rules of thumb, cautions gained by experience.

I set together a few phrases on practical working about the time the first remarks on imagisme were published. The first use of the word 'Imagiste' was in my note to T. E. Hulme's five poems, printed at the end of my 'Ripostes' in the autumn of 1912. I reprint my cautions from *Poetry* for March, 1913.

A FEW DON'TS

An 'Image' is that which presents an intellectual and emotional complex in an instant of time. I use the term 'complex' rather in the technical sense employed by the newer psychologists, such as Hart, though we might not agree absolutely in our application.

It is the presentation of such a 'complex' instantaneously which gives that sense of sudden liberation; that sense of freedom from time limits and space limits; that sense of sudden growth, which we experience in the presence of the greatest works of art.

It is better to present one Image in a lifetime than to produce voluminous works.

All this, however, some may consider open to debate. The immediate necessity is to tabulate A LIST OF DON'TS for those beginning to write verses. I can not put all of them into Mosaic negative.

To begin with, consider the three propositions (demanding direct treatment, economy of words, and the sequence of the musical phrase), not as dogma—never consider anything as dogma—but as the result of long contemplation, which, even if it is some one else's contemplation, may be worth consideration.

Pay no attention to the criticism of men who have never themselves written a notable work. Consider the discrepancies between the actual writing of the Greek poets and dramatists, and the theories of the Graeco-Roman grammarians, concocted to explain their metres.

LANGUAGE

Use no superfluous word, no adjective which does not reveal something.

Don't use such an expression as 'dim lands *of peace*'. It dulls the image. It mixes an abstraction with the concrete. It comes from the writer's not realizing that the natural object is always the *adequate* symbol.

Go in fear of abstractions. Do not retell in mediocre verse what has already been done in good prose. Don't think any intelligent person is going to be deceived when you try to shirk all the difficulties of the unspeakably difficult art of good prose by chopping your composition into line lengths.

What the expert is tired of today the public will be tired of tomorrow.

Don't imagine that the art of poetry is any simpler than the art of music, or that you can please the expert before you have spent at least as much effort on the art of verse as the average piano teacher spends on the art of music.

Be influenced by as many great artists as you can, but have

the decency either to acknowledge the debt outright, or to try to conceal it.

Don't allow 'influence' to mean merely that you mop up the particular decorative vocabulary of some one or two poets whom you happen to admire. A Turkish war correspondent was recently caught red-handed babbling in his despatches of 'dove-grey' hills, or else it was 'pearl-pale', I can not remember.

Use either no ornament or good ornament.

RHYTHM AND RHYME

Let the candidate fill his mind with the finest cadences he can discover, preferably in a foreign language,* so that the meaning of the words may be less likely to divert his attention from the movement; e.g. Saxon charms, Hebridean Folk Songs, the verse of Dante, and the lyrics of Shakespeare—if he can dissociate the vocabulary from the cadence. Let him dissect the lyrics of Goethe coldly into their component sound values, syllables long and short, stressed and unstressed, into vowels and consonants.

It is not necessary that a poem should rely on its music, but if it does rely on its music that music must be such as will delight the expert.

Let the neophyte know assonance and alliteration, rhyme immediate and delayed, simple and polyphonic, as a musician would expect to know harmony and counterpoint and all the minutiae of his craft. No time is too great to give to these matters or to any one of them, even if the artist seldom have need of them.

Don't imagine that a thing will 'go' in verse just because it's too dull to go in prose.

Don't be 'viewy'—leave that to the writers of pretty little philosophic essays. Don't be descriptive; remember that the painter can describe a landscape much better than you can, and that he has to know a deal more about it.

When Shakespeare talks of the 'Dawn in russet mantle clad'

*This is for rhythm, his vocabulary must of course be found in his native tongue.

he presents something which the painter does not present. There is in this line of his nothing that one can call description; he presents.

Consider the way of the scientists rather than the way of an advertising agent for a new soap.

The scientist does not expect to be acclaimed as a great scientist until he has *discovered* something. He begins by learning what has been discovered already. He goes from that point onward. He does not bank on being a charming fellow personally. He does not expect his friends to applaud the results of his freshman class work. Freshmen in poetry are unfortunately not confined to a definite and recognizable class room. They are 'all over the shop'. Is it any wonder 'the public is indifferent to poetry?'

Don't chop your stuff into separate *iambs*. Don't make each line stop dead at the end, and then begin every next line with a heave. Let the beginning of the next line catch the rise of the rhythm wave, unless you want a definite longish pause.

In short, behave as a musician, a good musician, when dealing with that phase of your art which has exact parallels in music. The same laws govern, and you are bound by no others.

Naturally, your rhythmic structure should not destroy the shape of your words, or their natural sound, or their meaning. It is improbable that, at the start, you will be able to get a rhythm-structure strong enough to affect them very much, though you may fall a victim to all sorts of false stopping due to line ends and cæsurae.

The Musician can rely on pitch and the volume of the orchestra. You can not. The term harmony is misapplied in poetry; it refers to simultaneous sounds of different pitch. There is, however, in the best verse a sort of residue of sound which remains in the ear of the hearer and acts more or less as an organ-base.

A rhyme must have in it some slight element of surprise if it is to give pleasure; it need not be bizarre or curious, but it must be well used if used at all.

Vide further Vildrac and Duhamel's notes[3] on rhyme in 'Technique Poétique'.

That part of your poetry which strikes upon the imaginative *eye* of the reader will lose nothing by translation into a foreign tongue; that which appeals to the ear can reach only those who take it in the original.

Consider the definiteness of Dante's presentation, as compared with Milton's rhetoric. Read as much of Wordsworth as does not seem too unutterably dull.*

If you want the gist of the matter go to Sappho, Catullus, Villon, Heine when he is in the vein, Gautier when he is not too frigid; or, if you have not the tongues, seek out the leisurely Chaucer. Good prose will do you no harm, and there is good discipline to be had by trying to write it.

Translation is likewise good training, if you find that your original matter 'wobbles' when you try to rewrite it. The meaning of the poem to be translated can not 'wobble'.

If you are using a symmetrical form, don't put in what you want to say and then fill up the remaining vacuums with slush.

Don't mess up the perception of one sense by trying to define it in terms of another. This is usually only the result of being too lazy to find the exact word. To this clause there are possibly exceptions.

The first three simple prescriptions will throw out nine-tenths of all the bad poetry now accepted as standard and classic; and will prevent you from many a crime of production.

'. . . *Mais d'abord il faut être un poète*', as MM. Duhamel and Vildrac have said at the end of their little book, '*Notes sur la Technique Poétique.*'

Since March 1913, Ford Madox Hueffer has pointed out that Wordsworth was so intent on the ordinary or plain word that he never thought of hunting for *le mot juste*.

John Butler Yeats has handled or man-handled Wordsworth and the Victorians, and his criticism, contained in letters to his son, is now printed and available.

*Vide infra.

I do not like writing *about* art, my first, at least I think it was
my first essay on the subject, was a protest against it.

PROLEGOMENA*

Time was when the poet lay in a green field with his head
against a tree and played his diversion on a ha'penny whistle,
and Caesar's predecessors conquered the earth, and the predecessors of golden Crassus embezzled, and fashions had their
say, and let him alone. And presumably he was fairly content in
this circumstance, for I have small doubt that the occasional
passerby, being attracted by curiosity to know why any one
should lie under a tree and blow diversion on a ha'penny whistle, came and conversed with him, and that among these
passers-by there was on occasion a person of charm or a young
lady who had not read *Man and Superman*,[4] and looking back
upon this naïve state of affairs we call it the age of gold.

Metastasio,[5] and he should know if any one, assures us that
this age endures—even though the modern poet is expected to
holloa his verses down a speaking tube to the editors of cheap
magazines—S. S. McClure,[6] or some one of that sort—even
though hordes of authors meet in dreariness and drink healths
to the 'Copyright Bill'; even though these things be, the age of
gold pertains. Imperceivably, if you like, but pertains. You
meet unkempt Amyclas[7] in a Soho restaurant and chant together of dead and forgotten things—it is a manner of speech
among poets to chant of dead, half-forgotten things, there
seems no special harm in it; it has always been done—and it's
rather better to be a clerk in the Post Office than to look after
a lot of stinking, verminous sheep—and at another hour of the
day one substitutes the drawing-room for the restaurant and
tea is probably more palatable than mead and mare's milk, and
little cakes than honey. And in this fashion one survives the
resignation of Mr Balfour, and the iniquities of the American

---

Poetry and Drama (then the *Poetry Review*, edited by Harold Monro), Feb.
1912.

customs-house, *e quel bufera infernal*, the periodical press. And then in the middle of it, there being apparently no other person at once capable and available one is stopped and asked to explain oneself.

I begin on the chord thus querulous, for I would much rather lie on what is left of Catullus' parlour floor[8] and speculate the azure beneath it and the hills off to Salo and Riva with their forgotten gods moving unhindered amongst them, than discuss any processes and theories of art whatsoever. I would rather play tennis. I shall not argue.

CREDO

Rhythm.—I believe in an 'absolute rhythm', a rhythm, that is, in poetry which corresponds exactly to the emotion or shade of emotion to be expressed. A man's rhythm must be interpretative, it will be, therefore, in the end, his own, uncounterfeiting, uncounterfeitable.

Symbols.—I believe that the proper and perfect symbol is the natural object, that if a man use 'symbols' he must so use them that their symbolic function does not obtrude; so that *a* sense, and the poetic quality of the passage, is not lost to those who do not understand the symbol as such, to whom, for instance, a hawk is a hawk.

Technique.—I believe in technique as the test of a man's sincerity; in law when it is ascertainable; in the trampling down of every convention that impedes or obscures the determination of the law, or the precise rendering of the impulse.

Form.—I think there is a 'fluid' as well as a 'solid' content, that some poems may have form as a tree has form, some as water poured into a vase. That most symmetrical forms have certain uses. That a vast number of subjects cannot be precisely, and therefore not properly rendered in symmetrical forms.

'Thinking that alone worthy wherein the whole art is employed'.* I think the artist should master all known forms and

---

*Dante, *De Volgari Eloquio*.

systems of metric, and I have with some persistence set about doing this, searching particularly into those periods wherein the
systems came to birth or attained their maturity. It has been complained, with some justice, that I dump my note-books on the
public. I think that only after a long struggle will poetry attain
such a degree of development, or, if you will, modernity, that it
will vitally concern people who are accustomed, in prose, to
Henry James and Anatole France, in music to Debussy. I am constantly contending that it took two centuries of Provence and one
of Tuscany to develop the media of Dante's masterwork, that it
took the latinists of the Renaissance, and the Pleiade, and his own
age of painted speech to prepare Shakespeare his tools. It is
tremendously important that great poetry be written, it makes no
jot of difference who writes it. The experimental demonstrations
of one man may save the time of many—hence my furore over
Arnaut Daniel—if a man's experiments try out one new rime, or
dispense conclusively with one iota of currently accepted nonsense, he is merely playing fair with his colleagues when he
chalks up his result.

No man ever writes very much poetry that 'matters'. In bulk,
that is, no one produces much that is final, and when a man is
not doing this highest thing, this saying the thing once for all
and perfectly; when he is not matching Ποικιλόθρον', ὀθάνατ'
'ΑφρόδιΤα, or 'Hist—said Kate the Queen', he had much better
be making the sorts of experiment which may be of use to him
in his later work, or to his successors.

'The lyf so short, the craft so long to lerne.' It is a foolish
thing for a man to begin his work on a too narrow foundation,
it is a disgraceful thing for a man's work not to show steady
growth and increasing fineness from first to last.

As for 'adaptations'; one finds that all the old masters of
painting recommend to their pupils that they begin by copying
masterwork, and proceed to their own composition.

As for 'Every man his own poet', the more every man knows
about poetry the better. I believe in every one writing poetry
who wants to; most do. I believe in every man knowing enough
of music to play 'God bless our home' on the harmonium, but I

do not believe in every man giving concerts and printing his sin.

The mastery of any art is the work of a lifetime. I should not discriminate between the 'amateur' and the 'professional'. Or rather I should discriminate quite often in favour of the amateur, but I should discriminate between the amateur and the expert. It is certain that the present chaos will endure until the Art of poetry has been preached down the amateur gullet, until there is such a general understanding of the fact that poetry is an art and not a pastime; such a knowledge of technique; of technique of surface and technique of content, that the amateurs will cease to try to drown out the masters.

If a certain thing was said once for all in Atlantis or Arcadia, in 450 Before Christ or in 1290 after, it is not for us moderns to go saying it over, or to go obscuring the memory of the dead by saying the same thing with less skill and less conviction.

My pawing over the ancients and semi-ancients has been one struggle to find out what has been done, once for all, better than it can ever be done again, and to find out what remains for us to do, and plenty does remain, for if we still feel the same emotions as those which launched the thousand ships, it is quite certain that we come on these feelings differently, through different nuances, by different intellectual gradations. Each age has its own abounding gifts yet only some ages transmute them into matter of duration. No good poetry is ever written in a manner twenty years old, for to write in such a manner shows conclusively that the writer thinks from books, convention and *cliché,* and not from life, yet a man feeling the divorce of life and his art may naturally try to resurrect a forgotten mode if he finds in that mode some leaven, or if he think he sees in it some element lacking in contemporary art which might unite that art again to its sustenance, life.

In the art of Daniel and Cavalcanti, I have seen that precision which I miss in the Victorians, that explicit rendering, be it of external nature, or of emotion. Their testimony is of the eyewitness, their symptoms are first hand.

As for the nineteenth century, with all respect to its achievements, I think we shall look back upon it as a rather blurry, messy sort of a period, a rather sentimentalistic, mannerish sort of a period. I say this without any self-righteousness, with no self-satisfaction.

As for there being a 'movement' or my being of it, the conception of poetry as a 'pure art' in the sense in which I use the term, revived with Swinburne. From the puritanical revolt to Swinburne, poetry had been merely the vehicle—yes, definitely, Arthur Symon's scruples and feelings about the word not withholding—the ox-cart and post-chaise for transmitting thoughts poetic or otherwise. And perhaps the 'great Victorians', though it is doubtful, and assuredly the 'nineties' continued the development of the art, confining their improvements, however, chiefly to sound and to refinements of manner.

Mr Yeats has once and for all stripped English poetry of its perdamnable rhetoric. He has boiled away all that is not poetic—and a good deal that is. He has become a classic in his own lifetime and *nel mezzo del cammin*. He has made our poetic idiom a thing pliable, a speech without inversions.

Robert Bridges, Maurice Hewlett and Frederic Manning are* in their different ways seriously concerned with overhauling the metric, in testing the language and its adaptability to certain modes. Ford Hueffer is making some sort of experiments in modernity. The Provost of Oriel[9] continues his translation of the *Divina Commedia*.

As to Twentieth century poetry, and the poetry which I expect to see written during the next decade or so, it will, I think, move against poppy-cock, it will be harder and saner, it will be what Mr Hewlett calls 'nearer the bone'. It will be as much like granite as it can be, its force will lie in its truth, its interpretative power (of course, poetic force does always rest there); I mean it will not try to seem forcible by rhetorical din, and luxurious riot. We will have fewer painted adjectives impeding the shock and stroke of it. At least for myself, I want it so, austere, direct, free from emotional slither.

What is there now, in 1917, to be added?

*(Dec. 1911)

RE VERS LIBRE

I think the desire for vers libre is due to the sense of quantity re-asserting itself after years of starvation. But I doubt if we can take over, for English, the rules of quantity laid down for Greek and Latin, mostly by Latin grammarians.

I think one should write vers libre only when one 'must', that is to say, only when the 'thing' builds up a rhythm more beautiful than that of set metres, or more real, more a part of the emotion of the 'thing', more germane, intimate, interpretative than the measure of regular accentual verse; a rhythm which discontents one with set iambic or set anapaestic.

Eliot has said the thing very well when he said, 'No *vers* is *libre* for the man who wants to do a good job.'

As a matter of detail, there is vers libre with accent heavily marked as a drum-beat (as par example my 'Dance Figure'), and on the other hand I think I have gone as far as can profitably be gone in the other direction (and perhaps too far). I mean I do not think one can use to any advantage rhythms much more tenuous and imperceptible than some I have used. I think progress lies rather in an attempt to approximate classical quantitative metres (NOT to copy them) than in a carelessness regarding such things.*

I agree with John Yeats[10] on the relation of beauty to certitude. I prefer satire, which is due to emotion, to any sham of emotion.

I have had to write, or at least I have written a good deal about art, sculpture, painting and poetry. I have seen what seemed to me the best of contemporary work reviled and obstructed. Can any one write prose of permanent or durable interest when he is merely saying for one year what nearly every one will say at the end of three or four years? I have been battistrada[11] for a sculptor, a painter, a novelist, several poets. I wrote also of certain French writers in *The New Age* in nineteen twelve or eleven.

*Let me date this statement 20 Aug. 1917.

I would much rather that people would look at Brzeska's sculpture and Lewis's drawings, and that they would read Joyce, Jules Romains, Eliot, than that they should read what I have said of these men, or that I should be asked to republish argumentative essays and reviews.

All that the critic can do for the reader or audience or spectator is to focus his gaze or audition. Rightly or wrongly I think my blasts and essays have done their work, and that more people are now likely to go to the sources than are likely to read this book.

Jammes's 'Existences' in 'La Triomphe de la Vie' is available. So are his early poems. I think we need a convenient anthology rather than descriptive criticism. Carl Sanburg wrote me from Chicago, 'It's hell when poets can't afford to buy each other's books.' Half the people who care, only borrow. In America so few people know each other that the difficulty lies more than half in distribution. Perhaps one should make an anthology: Romains's 'Un Etre en Marche' and 'Prières', Vildrac's 'Visite'. Retrospectively the fine wrought work of Laforgue, the flashes of Rimbaud, the hard-bit lines of Tristan Corbière, Tailhade's sketches in 'Poèmes Aristophanesques', the 'Litanies' of De Gourmont.

It is difficult at all times to write of the fine arts, it is almost impossible unless one can accompany one's prose with many reproductions. Still I would seize this chance or any chance to reaffirm my belief in Wyndham Lewis's genius, both in his drawings and his writings. And I would name an out of the way prose book, the 'Scenes and Portraits' of Frederic Manning, as well as James Joyce's short stories and novel, 'Dubliners' and the now well known 'Portrait of the Artist' as well as Lewis' 'Tarr', if, that is, I may treat my strange reader as if he were a new friend come into the room, intent on ransacking my bookshelf.

ONLY EMOTION ENDURES

'Only emotion endures.' Surely it is better for me to name over the few beautiful poems that still ring in my head than for me to search my flat for back numbers of periodicals and rearrange all that I have said about friendly and hostile writers.

The first twelve lines of Padraic Colum's 'Drover'; his 'O Woman shapely as a swan, on your account I shall not die'; Joyce's 'I hear an army'; the lines of Yeats that ring in my head and in the heads of all young men of my time who care for poetry: Braseal and the Fisherman, 'The fire that stirs about her when she stirs'; the later lines of 'The Scholars', the faces of the Magi; William Carlos Williams's 'Postlude', Aldington's version of 'Atthis', and 'H. D.'s' waves like pine tops, and her verse in 'Des Imagistes' the first anthology; Hueffer's 'How red your lips are' in his translation from Von der Vogelweide, his 'Three Ten', the general effect of his 'On Heaven'; his sense of the prose values or prose qualities in poetry; his ability to write poems that half-chant and are spoiled by a musician's additions; beyond these a poem by Alice Corbin, 'One City Only', and another ending 'But sliding water over a stone'. These things have worn smooth in my head and I am not through with them, nor with Aldington's 'In Via Sestina' nor his other poems in 'Des Imagistes', though people have told me their flaws. It may be that their content is too much embedded in me for me to look back at the words.

I am almost a different person when I come to take up the argument for Eliot's poems.

THE TRADITION

Penitus enim tibi O Phoebe attributa est cantus.[1]

The tradition is a beauty which we preserve and not a set of fetters to bind us. This tradition did not begin in A.D. 1870, nor in 1776, nor in 1632, nor in 1564. It did not begin even with Chaucer.

The two great lyric traditions which most concern us are that of the Melic[2] poets and that of Provence. From the first arose practically all the poetry of the 'ancient world', from the second practically all that of the modern. Doubtless there existed before either of these traditions a Babylonian and a Hittite tradition whereof knowledge is for the most part lost. We know that men worshipped Mithra with an arrangement of pure vowel-sounds. We know that men made verses in Egypt and in China, we assume that they made them in Uruk. There is a Japanese metric which I do not yet understand, there is doubtless an agglutinative metric beyond my comprehension.

As it happens, the conditions of English and forces in the English tradition are traceable, for the most part, to the two traditions mentioned. It is not intelligent to ignore the fact that both in Greece and in Provence the poetry attained its highest rhythmic and metrical brilliance at times when the arts of verse and music were most closely knit together, when each thing done by the poet had some definite musical urge or necessity bound up within it. The Romans writing upon tablets did not match the cadences of those earlier makers who had composed to and for the Cÿthera and the Barbitos.[3]

As touching the parallel development of the twin arts in the modern world, it may be noted that the *canzon* of Provence became the *canzone* of Italy, and that when Dante and his contemporaries began to compose philosophic treatises in verse the *son* or accompaniment went maying on its own account, and in music became the sonata; and, from the date of the divorce, poetry declined until such time as Baif and the Pléïade[4] began to bring Greek and Latin and Italian renaissance fashions into France, and to experiment in music and 'quantity'.

The Italians of that century had renewed the art, they had written in Latin, and some little even in Greek, and had used the Hellenic meters. DuBellay translated Navgherius into French, and Spenser translated DuBellay's adaptations into English, and then as in Chaucer's time and times since then, *the English cribbed their technique from over the channel*. The Elizabethans 'made' to music, and they copied the experiments of Paris. Thus as always one wave of one of these traditions has caught and overflowed an earlier wave receding. The finest troubador had sung at the court of Coeur de Leon. Chaucer had brought in the 'making' of France and ended the Anglo-Saxon alliterative fashions. The *canzon* of Provence which had become the *canzone* and sonnet, had become *Minnesang;* it had become the ballade and it became many an 'Elizabethan' form. And at that age the next wave from Paris caught it, a wave part 'Romance' (in the linguistic sense) and part Latin. But Provence is itself Latin, in a way, for when the quantities of syllables had been lost through the barbarian invasions, rhyme had come in as courtly ornament. The first fragment of Provençal poetry is Latin with a Provençal refrain.

Dr Ker[5] has put an end to much babble about folk song by showing us *Summer is ycummen in* written beneath the Latin words of a very old canon.

II

A return to origins invigorates because it is a return to nature and reason. The man who returns to origins does so because he wishes to behave in the eternally sensible manner. That is to say, naturally, reasonably, intuitively. He does not wish to do the right thing in the wrong place, to 'hang an ox with trappings', as Dante puts it. He wishes not pedagogy but harmony, the fitting thing.

This is not the place for an extensive discussion of technical detail. Of the uses and abuses of rhyme I would say nothing, save that it is neither a necessity nor a taboo.

As to quantity, it is foolish to suppose that we are incapable of distinguishing a long vowel from a short one, or that we are mentally debarred from ascertaining how many consonants intervene between one vowel and the next.

As to the tradition of *vers libre*: Jannaris[6] in his study of the Melic poets comes to the conclusion that they composed to the feel of the thing, to the cadence, as have all good poets since. He is not inclined to believe that they were much influenced by discussions held in Alexandria some centuries after their deaths.

If the earnest upholder of conventional imbecility will turn at random to the works of Euripides, or in particular to such passages as *Hippolytus* 1268 *et Seq.*, or to *Alkestis* 266 *et seq.*, or idem 455 *et seq.*, or to *Phoenissae* 1030 *et circa,* or to almost any notable Greek chorus, it is vaguely possible that the light of *vers libre* might spread some faint aurora upon his cerebral tissues.

No one is so foolish as to suppose that a musician using 'four-four' time is compelled to use always four quarter notes in each bar, or in 'seven-eighths' time to use seven eighth notes uniformly in each bar. He may use one ½, one ¼ and one ⅛ rest, or any such combination as he may happen to choose or find fitting.

To apply this musical truism to verse is to employ *vers libre*.

To say that such and such combinations of sound and tempo are not proper, is as foolish as to say that a painter should not use red in the upper left hand corners of his pictures. The movement of poetry is limited only by the nature of syllables and of articulate sound, and by the laws of music, or melodic rhythm. Space forbids a complete treatise on melody at this point, and forbids equally a complete treatise on all the sorts of verse, alliterative, syllabic, accentual, and quantitative. And such treatises as the latter are for the most part useless, as no man can learn much of these things save by first-hand untrammeled, unprejudiced examination of the finest examples of all these sorts of verse, of the finest strophes and of the finest rhyme-schemes, and by a profound study of the art and history of music.

Neither is surface imitation of much avail, for imitation is, indeed, of use only in so far as it connotes a closer observation, or an attempt closely to study certain forces through their effects.

MR. HUEFFER AND THE
PROSE TRADITION
IN VERSE

In a country in love with amateurs, in a country where the incompetent have such beautiful manners, and personalities so fragile and charming, that one cannot bear to injure their feelings by the introduction of competent criticism, it is well that one man should have a vision of perfection and that he should be sick to the death and disconsolate because he cannot attain it.

Mr Yeats wrote years ago that the highest poetry is so precious that one should be willing to search many a dull tome to find and gather the fragments. As touching poetry this was, perhaps, no new feeling. Yet where nearly everyone else is still dominated by an eighteenth-century verbalism, Mr Hueffer* has had this instinct for prose. It is he who has insisted, in the face of a still Victorian press, upon the importance of good writing as opposed to the opalescent word, the rhetorical tradition. Stendhal had said, and Flaubert, de Maupassant and Turgenev had proved, that 'prose was the higher art'—at least their prose.

Of course it is impossible to talk about perfection without getting yourself very much disliked. It is even more difficult in a capital where everybody's Aunt Lucy or Uncle George has written

*Ford Madox Ford, the novelist. He changed his name from Hueffer to Ford at some time after the outbreak of the war of 1914–18.—Ed.

something or other, and where the victory of any standard save that of mediocrity would at once banish so many nice people from the temple of immortality. So it comes about that Mr Hueffer is the best critic in England, one might say the only critic of any importance. What he says to-day the press, the reviewers, who hate him and who disparage his books, will say in about nine years' time, or possibly sooner. Shelley, Yeats, Swinburne, with their 'unacknowledged legislators', with 'Nothing affects these people except our conversation', with 'The rest live under us'; Rémy de Gourmont, when he says that most men think only husks and shells of the thoughts that have been already lived over by others, have shown their very just appreciation of the system of echoes, of the general vacuity of public opinion. America is like England, America is very much what England would be with the two hundred most interesting people removed. One's life is the score of this two hundred with whom one happens to have made friends. I do not see that we need to say the rest live under them, but it is certain that what these people say comes to pass. They live in their mutual credence, and thus they live things over and fashion them before the rest of the world is aware. I dare say it is a Cassandra-like and useless faculty, at least from the world's point of view. Mr Hueffer has possessed the peculiar faculty of 'foresight', or of constructive criticism, in a pre-eminent degree. Real power will run any machine. Mr Hueffer said fifteen years ago that a certain unknown Bonar Law would lead the conservative party. Five years ago he said with equal impartiality that D. H. Lawrence would write notable prose, that Mr de la Mare could write verses, and that *Chance* would make Conrad popular.

Of course if you think things ten or fifteen or twenty years before anyone else thinks them you will be considered absurd and ridiculous. Mr Allen Upward,[1] thinking with great lucidity along very different lines, is still considered absurd. Some professor feels that if certain ideas gain ground he will have to re-write his lectures, some parson feels that if certain other ideas are accepted he will have to throw up his position. They search for the forecaster's weak points.

Mr Hueffer is still underestimated for another reason also: namely, that we have not yet learned that prose is as precious

and as much to be sought after as verse, even its shreds and
patches. So that, if one of the finest chapters in English is hidden in a claptrap novel, we cannot weigh the vision which made
it against the weariness or the confusion which dragged down
the rest of the work. Yet we would do this readily with a poem.
If a novel have a form as distinct as that of a sonnet, and if its
workmanship be as fine as that of some Pleiade rondel, we complain of the slightness of the motive. Yet we would not deny
praise to the rondel. So it remains for a prose craftsman like
Arnold Bennett to speak well of Mr Hueffer's prose, and for a
verse-craftsman like myself to speak well of his verses. And the
general public will have little or none of him because he does not
put on pontifical robes, because he does not take up the mega-
phone of some known and accepted pose, and because he makes
enemies among the stupid by his rather engaging frankness.

We may as well begin reviewing the *Collected Poems* with
the knowledge that Mr Hueffer is a keen critic and a skilled
writer of prose, and we may add that he is not wholly unsuc-
cessful as a composer, and that he has given us, in 'On Heaven',
the best poem yet written in the 'twentieth-century fashion'.

I drag in these apparently extraneous matters in order to focus attention on certain phases of significance, which might
otherwise escape the hurried reader in a volume where the actual achievement is uneven. Coleridge has spoken of 'the miracle that might be wrought simply by one man's feeling a thing
more clearly or more poignantly than anyone had felt it before'.
The last century showed us a fair example when Swinburne
awoke to the fact that poetry was an art, not merely a vehicle
for the propagation of doctrine. England and Germany are still
showing the effects of his perception. I cannot belittle my belief
that Mr Hueffer's realization that poetry should be written at
least as well as prose will have as wide a result. He himself will
tell you that it is 'all Christina Rossetti', and that 'it was not
Wordsworth', for Wordsworth was so busied about the ordinary word that he never found time to think about *le mot juste*.

As for Christina, Mr Hueffer is a better critic than I am, and I
would be the last to deny that a certain limpidity and precision

are the ultimate qualities of style; yet I cannot accept his opinion. Christina had these qualities, it is true—in places, but they are to be found also in Browning and even in Swinburne at rare moments. Christina very often sets my teeth on edge—and so for that matter does Mr Hueffer. But it is the function of criticism to find what a given work is, rather than what it is not. It is also the faculty of a capital or of high civilization to value a man for some rare ability, to make use of him and not hinder him or itself by asking of him faculties which he does not possess.

Mr Hueffer may have found certain properties of style first, for himself, in Christina, but others have found them elsewhere, notably in Arnaut Daniel and in Guido, and in Dante, where Christina herself would have found them. Still there is no denying that there is less of the *ore rotundo*[2] in Christina's work than in that of her contemporaries, and that there is also in Hueffer's writing a clear descent from such passages as:

'I listened to their honest chat:
    said one: 'To-morrow we shall be
Plod plod along the featureless sands
    And coasting miles and miles of sea.'
Said one: 'Before the turn of tide
    We will achieve the eyrie-seat.'
Said one: 'To-morrow shall be like
    To-day, but much more sweet.''

We find the qualities of what some people are calling 'the modern cadence' in this strophe, also in 'A Dirge', in 'Up Hill', in—

'Somewhere or other there must surely be
The face not seen, the voice not heard.'

and in—

'Sometimes I said: 'It is an empty name
    I long for; to a name why should I give

The peace of all the days I have to live?'—
  Yet gave it all the same.'

Mr Hueffer brings to his work a prose training such as
Christina never had, and it is absolutely the devil to try to quote
snippets from a man whose poems are gracious impressions,
leisurely, low-toned. One would quote 'The Starling', but one
would have to give the whole three pages of it. And one would
like to quote patches out of the curious medley, 'To All the
Dead'—save that the picturesque patches aren't the whole or
the feel of it; or Sussmund's capricious 'Address', a sort of 'Inferno' to the 'Heaven' which we are printing for the first time
in another part of this issue. But that also is too long, so I content myself with the opening of an earlier poem, 'Finchley
Road'.

'As we come up at Baker Street
Where tubes and trains and 'buses meet
There's a touch of fog and a touch of sleet;
And we go on up Hampstead way
Toward the closing in of day. . . .

You should be a queen or a duchess rather,
Reigning, instead of a warlike father,
In peaceful times o'er a tiny town,
Where all the roads wind up and down
From your little palace—a small, old place
Where every soul should know your face
And bless your coming.'

I quote again, from a still earlier poem where the quiet of his
manner is less marked:

'Being in Rome I wonder will you go
  Up to the hill. But I forget the name . . .
Aventine? Pincio? No: I do not know
  I was there yesterday and watched. You came.'

(*I give the opening only to 'place' the second portion of the poem.*)

'Though you're in Rome you will not go, my You,
Up to that Hill . . . but I forget the name.
Aventine? Pincio? No, I never knew . . .
I was there yesterday. You never came.

I have that Rome; and you, you have a Me,
You have a Rome, and I, I have my You;
My Rome is not your Rome: my You, not you.
          . . . . . For, if man knew woman
I should have plumbed your heart; if woman, man,
Your Me should be true I . . . If in your day—
You who have mingled with my soul in dreams,
You who have given my life an aim and purpose,
A heart, an imaged form—if in your dreams
You have imagined unfamiliar cities
And me among them, I shall never stand
Beneath your pillars or your poplar groves, . . .
Images, simulacra, towns of dreams
That never march upon each other's borders,
And bring no comfort to each other's hearts!'

I present this passage, not because it is an example of Mr Hueffer's no longer reminiscent style, but because, like much that appeared four years ago in 'Songs from London', or earlier still in 'From Inland', it hangs in my memory. And so little modern work does hang in one's memory, and these books created so little excitement when they appeared. One took them as a matter of course, and they're not a matter of course, and still less is the later work a matter of course. Oh well, you all remember the preface to the collected poems with its passage about the Shepherd's Bush exhibition, for it appeared first as a pair of essays in *Poetry,* so there is no need for me to speak further of Mr Hueffer's aims or of his prose, or of his power to render an impression.

There is in his work another phase that depends somewhat
upon his knowledge of instrumental music. Dante has defined
a poem* as a composition of words set to music, and the
intelligent critic will demand that either the composition of
words or the music shall possess a certain interest, or that
there be some aptitude in their jointure together. It is true that
since Dante's day—and indeed his day and Casella's³ saw a re-
beginning of it—'music and 'poetry' have drifted apart, and
we have had a third thing which is called 'word music'. I mean
we have poems which are read or even, in a fashion, intoned,
and are 'musical' in some sort of complete or inclusive sense
that makes it impossible or inadvisable to 'set them to music'.
I mean obviously such poems as the First Chorus of 'Atalanta'
or many of Mr Yeats' lyrics. The words have a music of their
own, and a second 'musician's' music is an impertinence or an
intrusion.

There still remains the song to sing: to be 'set to music', and
of this sort of poem Mr Hueffer has given us notable examples
in his rendering of Von der Vogelweide's 'Tandaradei' and, in
lighter measure, in his own 'The Three-Ten':

'When in the prime and May-day time dead lovers went a-
     walking,
How bright the grass in lads' eyes was, how easy poet's talking!
Here were green hills and daffodils, and copses to contain them:
Daisies for floors did front their doors agog for maids to chain
     them.
So when the ray of rising day did pierce the eastern heaven
Maids did arise to make the skies seem brighter far by seven.
Now here's a street where 'bus routes meet, and 'twixt the wheels
     and paving
Standeth a lout who doth hold out flowers not worth the having.
*But see, but see! The clock strikes three above the Kilburn Station,
Those maids, thank God, are 'neath the sod and all their genera-
     tion.*

*or at any rate a canzone.

What she shall wear who'll soon appear, it is not hood nor
  wimple,
But by the powers there are no flowers so stately or so simple.
And paper shops and full 'bus tops confront the sun so brightly,
That, come three-ten, no lovers then had hearts that beat so
  lightly
As ours or loved more truly,
Or found green shades or flowered glades to fit their loves more
  duly.
And see, and see! 'Tis ten past three above the Kilburn Station,
Those maids, thank God! are 'neath the sod and all their
  generation.'

Oh well, there are very few song writers in England, and it's
a simple old-fashioned song with a note of futurism in its very
lyric refrain; and I dare say you will pay as little attention to it
as I did five years ago. And if you sing it aloud, once over, to
yourself, I dare say you'll be just as incapable of getting it out of
your head, which is perhaps one test of a lyric.

It is not, however, for Mr Hueffer's gift of song-writing that
I have reviewed him at such length; this gift is rare but not
novel. I find him significant and revolutionary because of his insistence upon clarity and precision, upon the prose tradition; in
brief, upon efficient writing—even in verse.

VORTICISM

I had put the fundamental tenet of vorticism in a "Vortex" in the first *Blast* as follows:—

Every concept, every emotion presents itself to the vivid consciousness in some primary form. It belongs to the art of this form. If sound, to music; if formed words, to literature; the image, to poetry; form, to design; colour in position, to painting; form or design in three planes, to sculpture; movement, to the dance or to the rhythm of music or verses.

I defined the vortex as "the point of maximum energy," and said that the vorticist relied on the "primary pigment," and on that alone.

These statements seemed to convey very little to people unfamiliar with our mode of thought, so I tried to make myself clear, as follows:—

VORTICISM

"It is no more ridiculous that a person should receive or convey an emotion by means of an arrangement of shapes, or planes, or colours, than that they should receive or convey such emotion by an arrangement of musical notes."

I suppose this proposition is self-evident. Whistler said as much, some years ago, and Pater proclaimed that "All arts approach the conditions of music."

Whenever I say this I am greeted with a storm of "Yes, but" . . . s. "But why isn't this art futurism?" "Why isn't?" "Why don't?" and above all: "What, in Heaven's name, has it got to do with your Imagiste poetry?"

Let me explain at leisure, and in nice, orderly, old-fashioned prose.

We are all futurists to the extent of believing with Guillaume Apollinaire that "On ne peut pas porter *partout* avec soi le cadavre de son père." But "futurism," when it gets into art, is, for the most part, a descendant of impressionism. It is a sort of accelerated impressionism.

There is another artistic descent *viâ* Picasso and Kandinsky; *viâ* cubism and expressionism. One does not complain of neo-impressionism or of accelerated impressionism and "simultaneity," but one is not wholly satisfied by them. One has perhaps other needs.

It is very difficult to make generalities about three arts at once. I shall be, perhaps, more lucid if I give, briefly, the history of the vorticist art with which I am most intimately connected, that is to say, vorticist poetry. Vorticism has been announced as including such and such painting and sculpture and "Imagisme" in verse. I shall explain "Imagisme," and then proceed to show its inner relation to certain modern paintings and sculpture.

Imagisme, in so far as it has been known at all, has been known chiefly as a stylistic movement, as a movement of criticism rather than of creation. This is natural, for, despite all possible celerity of publication, the public is always, and of necessity, some years behind the artists' actual thought. Nearly anyone is ready to accept "Imagisme" as a department of poetry, just as one accepts "lyricism" as a department of poetry.

There is a sort of poetry where music, sheer melody, seems as if it were just bursting into speech.

There is another sort of poetry where painting or sculpture seems as if it were "just coming over into speech."

The first sort of poetry has long been called "lyric." One is accustomed to distinguish easily between "lyric" and "epic" and "didactic." One is capable of finding the "lyric" passages in a drama or in a long poem not otherwise "lyric." This division is in the grammars and school books, and one has been brought up to it.

The other sort of poetry is as old as the lyric and as honourable, but, until recently, no one had named it. Ibycus and Liu Ch'e[1] presented the "Image." Dante is a great poet by reason of this faculty, and Milton is a wind-bag because of his lack of it. The "image" is the furthest possible remove from rhetoric. Rhetoric is the art of dressing up some unimportant matter so as to fool the audience for the time being. So much for the general category. Even Aristotle distinguishes between rhetoric, "which is persuasion," and the analytical examination of truth. As a "critical" movement, the "Imagisme" of 1912 to '14 set out "to bring poetry up to the level of prose." No one is so quixotic as to believe that contemporary poetry holds any such position. . . . Stendhal formulated the need in his *De L'Amour*:—

"La poésie avec ses comparaisons obligées, sa mythologie que ne croit pas le poète, sa dignité de style à la Louis XIV et tout l'attirail de ses ornements appelés poétique, est bien au dessous de la prose dès qu'il s'agit de donner une idée claire et précise des mouvements de cœur, or dans ce genre on n'émeut que par la clarté."

Flaubert and De Maupassant lifted prose to the rank of a finer art, and one has no patience with contemporary poets who escape from all the difficulties of the infinitely difficult art of good prose by pouring themselves into loose verses.

The tenets of the Imagiste faith were published in March, 1913, as follows:—

I. Direct treatment of the "thing," whether subjective or objective.
II. To use absolutely no word that does not contribute to the presentation.
III. As regarding rhythm: to compose in sequence of the musical phrase, not in sequence of the metronome.

There followed a series of about forty cautions to beginners, which need not concern us here.

The arts have indeed "some sort of common bond, some inter-recognition." Yet certain emotions or subjects find their most appropriate expression in some one particular art. The work of art which is most "worth while" is the work which would need a hundred works of any other kind of art to explain it. A fine statue is the core of a hundred poems. A fine poem is a score of symphonies. There is music which would need a hundred paintings to express it. There is no synonym for the *Victory of Samothrace* or for Mr. Epstein's flenites.[2] There is no painting of Villon's *Frères Humains*. Such works are what we call works of the "first intensity."

A given subject or emotion belongs to that artist, or to that sort of artist who must know it most intimately and most intensely before he can render it adequately in his art. A painter must know much more about a sunset than a writer, if he is to put it on canvas. But when the poet speaks of "Dawn in russet mantle clad," he presents something which the painter cannot present.

I said in the preface to my *Guido Cavalcanti*[3] that I believed in an absolute rhythm. I believe that every emotion and every phase of emotion has some toneless phrase, some rhythm-phrase to express it.

(This belief leads to *vers libre* and to experiments in quantitative verse.)

To hold a like belief in a sort of permanent metaphor is, as I understand it, "symbolism" in its profounder sense. It is not necessarily a belief in a permanent world, but it is a belief in that direction.

Imagisme is not symbolism. The symbolists dealt in "association," that is, in a sort of allusion, almost of allegory. They degraded the symbol to the status of a word. They made it a form of metonomy. One can be grossly "symbolic," for example, by using the term "cross" to mean "trial." The symbolist's *symbols* have a fixed value, like numbers in arithmetic, like 1, 2, and 7. The imagiste's images have a variable significance, like the signs *a*, *b*, and *x* in algebra.

Moreover, one does not want to be called a symbolist, because symbolism has usually been associated with mushy technique.

On the other hand, Imagisme is not Impressionism, though one borrows, or could borrow, much from the impressionist method of presentation. But this is only negative definition. If I am to give a psychological or philosophical definition "from the inside," I can only do so autobiographically. The precise statement of such a matter must be based on one's own experience.

In the "search for oneself," in the search for "sincere self-expression," one gropes, one finds some seeming verity. One says "I am" this, that, or the other, and with the words scarcely uttered one ceases to be that thing.

I began this search for the real in a book called *Personae,* casting off, as it were, complete masks of the self in each poem. I continued in long series of translations, which were but more elaborate masks.

Secondly, I made poems like "The Return," which is an objective reality and has a complicated sort of significance, like Mr. Epstein's "Sun God," or Mr. Brzeska's "Boy with a Coney." Thirdly, I have written "Heather," which represents a state of consciousness, or "implies," or "implicates" it.

A Russian correspondent, after having called it a symbolist poem, and having been convinced that it was not symbolism, said slowly: "I see, you wish to give people new eyes, not to make them see some new particular thing."

These two latter sorts of poems are impersonal, and that fact brings us back to what I said about absolute metaphor. They are Imagisme, and in so far as they are Imagisme, they fall in with the new pictures and the new sculpture.

Whistler said somewhere in the *Gentle Art*: "The picture is interesting not because it is Trotty Veg, but because it is an arrangement in colour." The minute you have admitted that, you let in the jungle, you let in nature and truth and abundance and cubism and Kandinsky,[4] and the lot of us. Whistler and Kandinsky and some cubists were set to getting extraneous matter out of their art; they were ousting literary values. The Flaubertians talk a good deal about "constatation." "The 'nineties" saw a movement against rhetoric. I think all these things move together, though they do not, of course, move in step.

The painters realise that what matters is form and colour. Musicians long ago learned that programme music was not the ultimate music. Almost anyone can realize that to use a symbol *with an ascribed or intended meaning* is, usually, to produce very bad art. We all remember crowns, and crosses, and rainbows, and what not in atrociously mumbled colour.

The image is the poet's pigment.* The painter should use his colour because he sees it or feels it. I don't much care whether he is representative or non-representative. He should *depend*, of course, on the creative, not upon the mimetic or representational part in his work. It is the same in writing poems, the author must use his *image* because he sees it or feels it, *not* because he thinks he can use it to back up some creed or some system of ethics or economics.

An *image,* in our sense, is real because we know it directly. If it have an age-old traditional meaning this may serve as proof to the professional student of symbology that we have stood in the deathless light, or that we have walked in some particular arbour of his traditional paradiso, but that is not our affair. It is our affair to render the *image* as we have perceived or conceived it.

Browning's "Sordello" is one of the finest *masks* ever presented. Dante's "Paradiso" is the most wonderful *image*. By that I do not mean that it is a perseveringly imagistic performance. The permanent part is Imagisme, the rest, the discourses with the calendar of saints and the discussions about the nature of the moon, are philology. The form of sphere above sphere, the varying reaches of light, the minutiæ of pearls upon foreheads, all these are parts of the Image. The image is the poet's pigment; with that in mind you can go ahead and apply Kandinsky, you can transpose his chapter on the language of form and colour and apply it to the writing of verse. As I cannot rely on your having read Kandinsky's *Ueber das Geistige in der Kunst,* I must go on with my autobiography.

---

*The image has been defined as "that which presents an intellectual and emotional complex in an instant of time."

Three years ago in Paris I got out of a "metro" train at La Concorde, and saw suddenly a beautiful face, and then another and another, and then a beautiful child's face, and then another beautiful woman, and I tried all that day to find words for what this had meant to me, and I could not find any words that seemed to me worthy, or as lovely as that sudden emotion. And that evening, as I went home along the Rue Raynouard, I was still trying and I found, suddenly, the expression. I do not mean that I found words, but there came an equation . . . not in speech, but in little splotches of colour. It was just that—a "pattern," or hardly a pattern, if by "pattern" you mean something with a "repeat" in it. But it was a word, the beginning, for me, of a language in colour. I do not mean that I was unfamiliar with the kindergarten stories about colours being like tones in music. I think that sort of thing is nonsense. If you try to make notes permanently correspond with particular colours, it is like tying narrow meanings to symbols.

That evening, in the Rue Raynouard, I realized quite vividly that if I were a painter, or if I had, often, *that kind* of emotion, or even if I had the energy to get paints and brushes and keep at it, I might found a new school of painting, of "non-representative" painting, a painting that would speak only by arrangements in colour.

And so, when I came to read Kandinsky's chapter on the language of form and colour, I found little that was new to me. I only felt that some one else understood what I understood, and had written it out very clearly. It seems quite natural to me that an artist should have just as much pleasure in an arrangement of planes or in a pattern of figures, as in painting portraits of fine ladies, or in portraying the Mother of God as the symbolists bid us.

When I find people ridiculing the new arts, or making fun of the clumsy odd terms that we use in trying to talk of them amongst ourselves; when they laugh at our talking about the "ice-block quality" in Picasso, I think it is only because they do not know what thought is like, and that they are familiar only with argument and gibe and opinion. That is to say, they can only enjoy what they have been brought up to consider enjoyable, or what some essayist has talked about in mellifluous phrases. They think only "the shells of thought," as De Gourmont calls them; the thoughts that have been already thought out by others.

Any mind that is worth calling a mind must have needs beyond the existing categories of language, just as a painter must have pigments or shades more numerous than the existing names of the colours.

Perhaps this is enough to explain the words in my "Vortex"*:—

"Every concept, every emotion, presents itself to the vivid consciousness in some primary form. It belongs to the art of this form."

That is to say, my experience in Paris should have gone into paint. If instead of colour I had perceived sound or planes in relation, I should have expressed it in music or in sculpture. Colour was, in that instance, the "primary pigment"; I mean that it was the first adequate equation that came into consciousness. The Vorticist uses the "primary pigment." Vorticism is art before it has spread itself into flaccidity, into elaboration and secondary applications.

What I have said of one vorticist art can be transposed for another vorticist art. But let me go on then with my own branch of vorticism, about which I can probably speak with greater clarity. All poetic language is the language of exploration. Since the beginning of bad writing, writers have used images as ornaments. The point of Imagisme is that it does not use images *as ornaments*. The image is itself the speech. The image is the word beyond formulated language.

I once saw a small child go to an electric light switch and say, "Mamma, can I *open* the light?" She was using the age-old language of exploration, the language of art. It was a sort of metaphor, but she was not using it as ornamentation.

One is tired of ornamentations, they are all a trick, and any sharp person can learn them.

The Japanese have had the sense of exploration. They have understood the beauty of this sort of knowing. A Chinaman

*Appearing in the July number of *Blast*.

said long ago that if a man can't say what he has to say in twelve lines he had better keep quiet. The Japanese have evolved the still shorter form of the *hokku*.

> "The fallen blossom flies back to its branch:
>   A butterfly."

That is the substance of a very well-known *hokku*. Victor Plarr tells me that once, when he was walking over snow with a Japanese naval officer, they came to a place where a cat had crossed the path, and the officer said, "Stop, I am making a poem." Which poem was, roughly, as follows:—

> "The footsteps of the cat upon the snow:
>   (are like) plum-blossoms."

The words "are like" would not occur in the original, but I add them for clarity.

The "one image poem" is a form of super-position, that is to say, it is one idea set on top of another. I found it useful in getting out of the impasse in which I had been left by my metro emotion: I wrote a thirty-line poem, and destroyed it because it was what we call work "of second intensity." Six months later I made a poem half that length; a year later I made the following *hokku*-like sentence:—

> "The apparition of these faces in the crowd:
>   Petals, on a wet, black bough."

I dare say it is meaningless unless one has drifted into a certain vein of thought.* In a poem of this sort one is trying to record the precise instant when a thing outward and objective transforms itself, or darts into a thing inward and subjective.

---

*Mr. Flint and Mr. Rodker have made longer poems depending on a similar presentation of matter. So also have Richard Aldington, in his *In Via Sestina*, and "H. D." in her *Oread,* which latter poems express much stronger emotions than that in my lines here given. Mr. Hueffer gives an interesting account of a similar adventure of his own in his review of the Imagiste anthology.

This particular sort of consciousness has not been identified with impressionist art. I think it is worthy of attention.

The logical end of impressionist art is the cinematograph. The state of mind of the impressionist tends to become cinematographical. Or, to put it another way, the cinematograph does away with the need of a lot of impressionist art.

There are two opposed ways of thinking of a man: firstly, you may think of him as that toward which perception moves, as the toy of circumstance, as the plastic substance *receiving* impressions; secondly, you may think of him as directing a certain fluid force against circumstance, as *conceiving* instead of merely reflecting and observing. One does not claim that one way is better than the other, one notes a diversity of the temperament. The two camps always exist. In the 'eighties there were symbolists opposed to impressionists, now you have vorticism, which is, roughly speaking, expressionism, neo-cubism, and imagism gathered together in one camp and futurism in the other. Futurism is descended from impressionism. It is, in so far as it is an art movement, a kind of accelerated impressionism. It is a spreading, or surface art, as opposed to vorticism, which is intensive.

The vorticist has not this curious tic for destroying past glories. I have no doubt that Italy needed Mr. Marinetti, but he did not set on the egg that hatched me, and as I am wholly opposed to his æsthetic principles I see no reason why I, and various men who agree with me, should be expected to call ourselves futurists. We do not desire to evade comparison with the past. We prefer that the comparison be made by some intelligent person whose idea of "the tradition" is not limited by the conventional taste of four or five centuries and one continent.

Vorticism is an intensive art. I mean by this, that one is concerned with the relative intensity, or relative significance of different sorts of expression. One desires the most intense, for certain forms of expression *are* "more intense" than others. They are more dynamic. I do not mean they are more emphatic, or that they are yelled louder. I can explain my meaning best by mathematics.

There are four different intensities of mathematical expression known to the ordinarily intelligent undergraduate, namely: the arithmetical, the algebraic, the geometrical, and that of analytical geometry.

For instance, you can write

$$3 \times 3 + 4 \times 4 = 5 \times 5,$$
or differently, $3^2 + 4^2 = 5^2$.

That is merely conversation or "ordinary common sense." It is a simple statement of one fact, and does not implicate any other.

Secondly, it is true that

$$3^2 + 4^2 = 5^2, \quad 6^2 + 8^2 = 10^2, \quad 9^2 + 12^2 = 15^2, \quad 39^2 + 52^2 = 65^2.$$

These are all separate facts, one may wish to mention their underlying similarity; it is a bore to speak about each one in turn. One expresses their "algebraic relation" as $a^2 + b^2 = c^2$.

That is the language of philosophy. It MAKES NO PIC- TURE. This kind of statement applies to a lot of facts, but it does not grip hold of Heaven.

Thirdly, when one studies Euclid one finds that the relation of $a^2 + b^2 = c^2$ applies to the ratio between the squares on the two sides of a right-angled triangle and the square on the hy- potenuse. One still writes it $a^2 + b^2 = c^2$, but one has begun to talk about form. Another property or quality of life has crept into one's matter. Until then one had dealt only with numbers. But even this statement does not *create* form. The picture is given you in the proposition about the square on the hy- potenuse of the right-angled triangle being equal to the sum of the squares on the two other sides. Statements in plane or de- scriptive geometry are like talk about art. They are a criticism of the form. The form is not created by them.

Fourthly, we come to Descartian or "analytical geometry." Space is conceived as separated by two or by three axes (de- pending on whether one is treating form in one or more planes). One refers points to these axes by a series of co-ordinates. Given the idiom, one is able *actually to create.*

Thus, we learn that the equation $(x-a)^2 + (y-b)^2 = r^2$ governs the circle. It is the circle. It is not a particular circle, it is any circle and all circles. It is nothing that is not a circle. It is the circle free of space and time limits. It is the universal, existing in perfection, in freedom from space and time. Mathematics is dull ditchwater until one reaches analytics. But in analytics we come upon a new way of dealing with form. It is in this way that art handles life. The difference between art and analytical geometry is the difference of subject-matter only. Art is more interesting in proportion as life and the human consciousness are more complex and more interesting than forms and numbers.

This statement does not interfere in the least with "spontaneity" and "intuition," or with their function in art. I passed my last *exam,* in mathematics on sheer intuition. I saw where the line *had* to go, as clearly as I ever saw an image, or felt *caelestem intus vigorem.*

The statements of "analytics" are "lords" over fact. They are the thrones and dominations that rule over form and recurrence. And in like manner are great works of art lords over fact, over race-long recurrent moods, and over to-morrow.

Great works of art contain this fourth sort of equation. They cause form to come into being. By the "image" I mean such an equation; not an equation of mathematics, not something about *a, b,* and *c,* having something to do with form, but about *sea, cliffs, night,* having something to do with mood.

The image is not an idea. It is a radiant node or cluster; it is what I can, and must perforce, call a VORTEX, from which, and through which, and into which, ideas are constantly rushing. In decency one can only call it a VORTEX. And from this necessity came the name "vorticism." *Nomina sunt consequentia rerum,* and never was that statement of Aquinas more true than in the case of the vorticist movement.

It is as true for the painting and the sculpture as it is for the poetry. Mr. Wadsworth and Mr. Lewis[5] are not using words, they are using shape and colour. Mr. Brzeska and Mr. Epstein are using "planes in relation," they are dealing with a relation of planes different from the sort of relation of planes dealt with in geometry, hence what is called "the need of organic forms in sculpture."

I trust I have made clear what I mean by an "intensive art." The vorticist movement is not a movement of mystification, though I dare say many people "of good will" have been considerably bewildered.

The organization of forms is a much more energetic and creative action than the copying or imitating of light on a haystack.

There is undoubtedly a language of form and colour. It is not a symbolical or allegorical language depending on certain meanings having been ascribed, in books, to certain signs and colours.

Certain artists working in different media have managed to understand each other. They know the good and bad in each other's work, which they could not know unless there were a common speech.

As for the excellence of certain contemporary artists, all I can do is to stand up for my own beliefs. I believe that Mr. Wyndham Lewis is a very great master of design; that he has brought into our art new units of design and new manners of organisation. I think that his series "Timon" is a great work. I think he is the most articulate expression of my own decade. If you ask me what his "Timon" means, I can reply by asking you what the old play means. For me his designs are a creation on the same *motif*. That *motif* is the fury of intelligence baffled and shut in by circumjacent stupidity. It is an emotional *motif*. Mr. Lewis's painting is nearly always emotional.

Mr. Wadsworth's work gives me pleasure, sometimes like the pleasure I have received from Chinese and Japanese prints and painting; for example, I derive such pleasure from Mr. Wadsworth's "Khaki." Sometimes his work gives me a pleasure which I can only compare to the pleasure I have in music, in music as it was in Mozart's time. If an outsider wishes swiftly to understand this new work, he can do worse than approach it in the spirit wherein he approaches music.

"Lewis is Bach." No, it is incorrect to say that "Lewis is Bach," but our feeling is that certain works of Picasso and certain works of Lewis have in them something which is to painting what certain qualities of Bach are to music. Music was vorticist in the Bach-Mozart period, before it went off into romance and sentiment and description. A new vorticist music would come from a new computation of the mathematics of harmony, not from a mimetic representation of dead cats in a fog-horn, alias noise-tuners.

Mr. Epstein is too well known to need presentation in this article. Mr. Brzeska's sculpture is so generally recognized in all camps that one does not need to bring in a brief concerning it. Mr. Brzeska has defined sculptural feeling as "the appreciation of masses in relation," and sculptural ability as "the defining of these masses by planes." There comes a time when one is more deeply moved by that form of intelligence which can present "masses in relation" than by that combination of patience and trickery which can make marble chains with free links and spin out bronze until it copies the feathers on a general's hat. Mr. Etchells[6] still remains more or less of a mystery. He is on his travels, whence he has sent back a few excellent drawings. It cannot be made too clear that the work of the vorticists and the "feeling of inner need" existed before the general noise about vorticism. We worked separately, we found an underlying agreement, we decided to stand together.

NOTE

I am often asked whether there can be a long imagiste or vorticist poem. The Japanese, who evolved the hokku, evolved also the Noh plays. In the best "Noh" the whole play may consist of one image. I mean it is gathered about one image. Its unity consists in one image, enforced by movement and music. I see nothing against a long vorticist poem.

On the other hand, no artist can possibly get a vortex into every poem or picture he does. One would like to do so, but it is beyond one. Certain things seem to demand metrical expression, or expression in a rhythm more agitated than the rhythms acceptable to prose, and these subjects, though they do not contain a vortex, may have some interest, an interest as "criticism of life" or of art. It is natural to express these things, and a vorticist or imagiste writer may be justified in presenting a certain amount of work which is not vorticism or imagisme, just as he might be justified in printing a purely didactic prose article. Unfinished sketches and drawings have a similar interest; they are trials and attempts toward a vortex.

AFFIRMATIONS

AS FOR IMAGISME

The term 'Imagisme' has given rise to a certain amount of discussion. It has been taken by some to mean Hellenism; by others the word is used most carelessly, to designate any sort of poem in *vers libre*. Having omitted to copyright the word at its birth I cannot prevent its misuse. I can only say what I meant by the word when I made it. Moreover, I cannot guarantee that my thoughts about it will remain absolutely stationary. I spend the greater part of my time meditating the arts, and I should find this very dull if it were not possible for me occasionally to solve some corner of the mystery, or, at least to formulate more clearly my own thoughts as to the nature of some mystery or equation.

In the second article of this series[1] I pointed out that energy creates pattern. I gave examples. I would say further that emotional force gives the image. By this I do not mean that it gives an 'explanatory metaphor'; though it might be hard to draw an exact border line between the two. We have left false metaphor, ornamental metaphor to the rhetorician. That lies outside this discussion.

Intense emotion causes pattern to arise in the mind—if the mind is strong enough. Perhaps I should say, not pattern, but pattern-units, or units of design. (I do not say that intense emotion is the sole possible cause of such units. I say simply that they can result from it. They may also result from other sorts of

AFFIRMATIONS 293

energy.) I am using this term 'pattern-unit', because I want to get away from the confusion between 'pattern' and 'applied decoration'. By applied decoration I mean something like the 'wall of Troy pattern'. The invention was merely the first curley cue, or the first pair of them. The rest is repetition, is copying.

By pattern-unit or vorticist picture I mean the single jet. The difference between the pattern-unit and the picture is one of complexity. The pattern-unit is so simple that one can bear having it repeated several or many times. When it becomes so complex that repetition would be useless, then it is a picture, an 'arrangement of forms'.

Not only does emotion create the 'pattern-unit' and the 'arrangement of forms', it creates also the Image. The Image can be of two sorts. It can arise within the mind. It is then 'subjective'. External causes play upon the mind, perhaps; it so, they are drawn into the mind, fused, transmitted, and emerge in an Image unlike themselves. Secondly, the Image can be objective. Emotion seizing up some external scene or action carries it intact to the mind; and that vortex purges it of all save the essential or dominant or dramatic qualities, and it emerges like the external original.

In either case the Image is more than an idea. It is a vortex or cluster of fused ideas and is endowed with energy. If it does not fulfil these specifications, it is not what I mean by an Image. It may be a sketch, a vignette, a criticism, an epigram or anything else you like. It may be impressionism, it may even be very good prose. By 'direct treatment', one means simply that having got the Image one refrains from hanging it with festoons.

From the Image to Imagisme: Our second contention was that poetry to be good poetry should be at least as well written as good prose. This statement would seem almost too self-evident to need any defence whatsoever. Obviously, if a man has anything to say, the interest will depend on what he has to say, and not on a faculty for saying 'exiguous' when he means 'narrow', or for putting his words hindside before. Even if his thought be very slight it will not gain by being swathed in sham lace.

Thirdly, one believes that emotion is an organiser of form,

not merely of visible forms and colours, but also of audible forms. This basis of music is so familiar that it would seem to need no support. Poetry is a composition or an 'organisation' of words set to 'music'. By 'music' here we can scarcely mean much more than rhythm and timbre. The rhythm form is false unless it belong to the particular creative emotion or energy which it purports to represent. Obviously one does not discard 'regular metres' because they are a 'difficulty'.

Any ass can say:

'John Jones stood on the floor. He saw the ceiling' or decasyl-labicly,
    'John Jones who rang the bell at number eight.'

There is no form of platitude which cannot be turned into iambic pentameter without labour. It is not difficult, if one have learned to count up to ten, to begin a new line on each eleventh syllable or to whack each alternate syllable with an ictus.

Emotion also creates patterns of timbre. But one 'discards rhyme', not because one is incapable of rhyming neat, fleet, sweet, meet, treat, eat, feet, but because there are certain emotions or energies which are not to be represented by the over-familiar devices or patterns; just as there are certain 'arrangements of form' that cannot be worked into dados.

Granted, of course, that there is great freedom in pentameter and that there are a great number of regular and beautifully regular metres fit for a number of things, and quite capable of expressing a wide range of energies or emotions.

The discovery that bad *vers libre* can be quite as bad as any other sort of bad verse is by no means modern. Over eleven centuries ago Rihaku (Li Po) complained that imitators of Kut-sugen (Ch'u Yuan) couldn't get any underlying rhythm into their *vers libre,* that they got 'bubbles not waves'.

Yo ba geki tai ha Kai riu to mu giu.

'Yoyu and Shojo stirred up decayed (enervated) waves. Open current flows about in bubbles, does not move in wave lengths.' If a man has no emotional energy, no impulse, it is of course much easier to make something which looks like 'verse' by reason of having a given number of syllables, or even of accents, per line, than for him to invent a music or rhythm-structure. Hence the prevalence of 'regular' metric. Hence also bad *vers libre*. The only advantage of bad *vers libre* is that it is, possibly, more easy to see how bad it is . . . but even this advantage is doubtful.

By bad verse, whether 'regular' or 'free', I mean verse which pretends to some emotion which did not assist at its parturition. I mean also verse made by those who have not sufficient skill to make the words move in rhythm of the creative emotion. Where the voltage is so high that it fuses the machinery, one has merely the 'emotional man' not the artist. The best artist is the man whose machinery can stand the highest voltage. The better the machinery, the more precise, the stronger, the more exact will be the record of the voltage and of the various currents which have passed through it.

These are bad expressions if they lead you to think of the artist as wholly passive, as a mere receiver of impressions. The good artist is perhaps a good seismograph, but the difference between man and a machine is that man can in some degree 'start his machinery going'. He can, within limits, not only record but create. At least he can move as a force; he can produce 'order-giving vibrations'; by which one may mean merely, he can departmentalise such part of the life-force as flows through him.

To recapitulate, then, the vorticist position; or at least my position at the moment is this:

Energy, or emotion, expresses itself in form. Energy, whose primary manifestation is in pure form, i.e., form as distinct from likeness or association can only be expressed in painting or sculpture. Its expression can vary from a 'wall of Troy pattern' to Wyndham Lewis's 'Timon of Athens', or a Wadsworth woodblock. Energy expressing itself in pure sound, i.e., sound as distinct from articulate speech, can only be expressed in music. When an energy or emotion 'presents an image', this may find adequate expression in words. It is very probably a waste of energy to express it in any more tangible medium. The verbal expression of the image may be reinforced by a suitable or cognate rhythm-form and by timbre-form. By rhythm-form and

timbre-form I do not mean something which must of necessity
have a 'repeat' in it. It is certain that a too obvious 'repeat' may
be detrimental.

The test of invention lies in the primary figment, that is to say,
in that part of any art which is peculiarly of that art as distinct
from 'the other arts'. The vorticist maintains that the 'organising'
or creative-inventive faculty is the thing that matters; and that the
artist having this faculty is a being infinitely separate from the
other type of artist who merely goes on weaving arabesques out
of other men's 'units of form'.

Superficial capability needs no invention whatsoever, but a
great energy has, of necessity, its many attendant inventions.

CHINESE POETRY

It is because Chinese poetry has certain qualities of vivid presentation; and because certain Chinese poets have been content to set forth their matter without moralizing and without comment that one labours to make a translation, and that I personally am most thankful to the late Ernest Fenollosa for his work in sorting out and gathering many Chinese poems into a form and bulk wherein I can deal with them.

I do not think my views on poetry can be so revolutionary and indecent as some people try to make out, for some months ago I heard Selwyn Image[1] talking of Christmas Carols and praising, in them, the very qualities I and my friends are always insisting on. Selwyn Image belongs to an older and statelier generation and it is not their habit to attack traditional things which they dislike, and for that reason the rather irritating work of revising our poetical canon has been left for my contemporaries, who come in for a fair share of abuse.

I shall not, in this article, attempt any invidious comparisons between English and Chinese poetry. China has produced just as many bad poets as England, just as many dull and plodding moralizers, just as many flaccid and over-ornate versifiers.

By fairly general consent, their greatest poet is Rihaku or "Li Po," who flourished in the eighth century A.D. He was the head of the court office of poetry, and a great "compiler." But this last title must not mislead you. In China a "compiler" is a very different person from a commentator. A compiler does not merely gather together, his chief honour consists in weeding out, and even in revising.

Thus, a part of Rihaku's work consists of old themes rewritten, of a sort of summary of the poetry which had been before him, and this in itself might explain in part the great variety of his work. Nevertheless, when he comes to treat of things of his own time he is no less various and abundant. I confine myself to his work because I can find in it examples of the three qualities of Chinese poetry which I wish now to illustrate.

The first great distinction between Chinese taste and our own is that the Chinese *like* poetry that they have to think about, and even poetry that they have to puzzle over. This latter taste has occasionally broken out in Europe, notably in twelfth-century Provence and thirteenth-century Tuscany, but it has never held its own for very long.

The following four-line poem of Rihaku's has been prized for twelve centuries in China:

THE JEWEL-STAIRS GRIEVANCE[2]

The jewelled steps are already quite white with dew,
It is so late that the dew soaks my gauze stockings,
And I let down the crystal curtain
And watch the moon through the clear autumn.

I have never found any occidental who could "make much" of that poem at one reading. Yet upon careful examination we find that everything is there, not merely by "suggestion" but by a sort of mathematical process of reduction. Let us consider what circumstances would be needed to produce just the words of this poem. You can play Conan Doyle if you like.

First, "jewel-stairs," therefore the scene is in a palace.

Second, "gauze stockings," therefore a court lady is speaking, not a servant or common person who is in the palace by chance.

Third, "dew soaks," therefore the lady has been waiting, she has not just come.

Fourth, "clear autumn with moon showing," therefore the man who has not come cannot excuse himself on the grounds that the evening was unfit for the rendezvous.

Fifth, you ask how do we know she was waiting for a man? Well, the title calls the poem "grievance," and for that matter, how do we know what she was waiting for?

This sort of Chinese poem is probably not unfamiliar to the reader. Nearly every one who has written about Chinese has mentioned the existence of these short, obscure poems. In contrast to them, in most rigorous contrast, we find poems of the greatest vigour and clarity. We find a directness and realism such as we find only in early Saxon verse and in the Poema del Cid, and in Homer, or rather in what Homer would be if he wrote without epithet; for instance, the following war poem. The writer expects his hearers to know that Dai and Etsu are in the south, that En is a bleak north country, and that the "Wild Goose Gate" is in the far northeast, and the "Dragon Pen" is in the very opposite corner of the great empire, and probably that the Mongols are attacking the borders of China. Given these simple geographical facts the poem is very forthright in its manner.

> The Dai horse,[3] from the south, neighs against the north wind,
> The birds of Etsu have no love for En, in the north.
> Emotion is of habit.
> Yesterday we went out of the Wild Goose Gate,
> To-day from the Dragon Pen.
> Surprised. Desert Turmoil. Sea sun.
> Flying snow bewilders the barbarian heaven.
> Lice swarm like ants over our accoutrements,
> Our mind and spirit are on getting forward the feather-silk
>   banners.
> Hard fight gets no reward.
> Loyalty is difficult to explain.
> Who will be sorry for General Rishogu, the swift-moving,
> Whose white head is lost for this province.

There you have no mellifluous circumlocution, no sentimentalizing of men who have never seen a battlefield and who
wouldn't fight if they had to. You have war, campaigning as it
has always been, tragedy, hardship, no illusions. There are two
other fine war poems which are too long to quote here, one reputed to be by Bunno: a plodding of feet, soldiers living on
fern-shoots, generals with outworn horses; another by Rihaku,
supposedly spoken by a sentinel watching over a long-ruined
village. There are no walls, there are decaying bones, enduring
desolation.

(To be concluded)

CHINESE POETRY—II

There are two other qualities in Chinese poetry which are, I think, little suspected. First, Chinese poetry is full of fairies and fairy lore. Their lore is "quite Celtic." I found one tale in a Japanese play; two ghosts come to a priest to be married, or rather he makes a pilgrimage to their tomb and they meet him there. The tale was new to me, but I found that Mr. Yeats had come upon a similar story among the people of Aran. The desire to be taken away by the fairies, the idea of souls flying with the sea-birds, and many other things recently made familiar to us by the Celtic school, crop up in one's Chinese reading and are so familiar and so well known to us that they seem, often, not worth translating.

If the reader detests fairies and prefers human poetry, then that also can be found in Chinese. Perhaps the most interesting form of modern poetry is to be found in Browning's "Men and Women." This kind of poem, which reaches its climax in his unreadable "Sordello," and is most popular in such poems as "Pictor Ignotus," or the "Epistle of Karshish," or "Cleon," has had a curious history in the west. You may say it begins in Ovid's Heroides," which purport to be letters written between Helen and Paris or by Œnone and other distinguished persons of classical pseudo-history; or you may find an earlier example in Theocritus' Idyl of the woman spinning at her sombre and

magic wheel. From Ovid to Browning this sort of poem was
very much neglected. It is interesting to find, in eighth-century
China, a poem which might have been slipped into Browning's
work without causing any surprise save by its simplicity and its
naïve beauty.

THE RIVER-MERCHANT'S WIFE[4]

(A Letter)

While my hair was still cut straight across my forehead
I played about the front gate, pulling flowers.
You came by on bamboo-stilts, playing horse.
You walked about my seat, playing with blue plums.
And we went on living in the village of Cho-kan:
Two small people, without dislike or suspicion.

At fourteen I married you, My Lord,
*　　I never laughed, being bashful.*
Lowering my head, I looked at the wall.
Called to, a thousand times, I never looked back.
*　　At fifteen I stopped scowling,*
I desired my dust to be mingled with your dust
*　　Forever, and forever, and forever.*
Why should I climb the look-out?
*　　At sixteen you departed,*
You went into far Ku-to-yen, by the river of swirling eddies.
*　　And you were gone for five months.*

The monkeys make sorrowful noise overhead.
You dragged your feet, by the gate, when you were departing.
Now the moss is grown there; the different mosses,
Too deep to clear them away.
The leaves fall early this autumn, in wind.
The paired butterflies are already yellow with August,
Over the grass in the west garden.

They hurt me.
I grow older.
If you are coming down through the narrows of the river
  Kiang
Please let me know beforehand
And I will come out to meet you,
  As far as Cho-fu-sa.

I can add nothing, and it would be an impertinence for me to thrust in remarks about the gracious simplicity and completeness of the poem.

There is another sort of completeness in Chinese. Especially in their poems of nature and of scenery they seem to excel western writers, both when they speak of their sympathy with the emotions of nature and when they describe natural things.

For instance, when they speak of mountainous crags with the trees clinging head downward, or of a mountain pool where the flying birds are reflected, and

Lie as if on a screen,

as says Rihaku.

The scenes out of the marvellous Chinese painting rise again and again in his poems, but one cannot discuss a whole literature, or even all of one man's work in a single essay.

THE CHINESE WRITTEN CHARACTER AS A MEDIUM FOR POETRY

[*This essay was practically finished by the late Ernest Fenollosa; I have done little more than remove a few repetitions and shape a few sentences.*

We have here not a bare philological discussion, but a study of the fundamentals of all aesthetics. In his search through unknown art Fenollosa, coming upon unknown motives and principles unrecognised in the West, was already led into many modes of thought since fruitful in 'new' Western painting and poetry. He was a forerunner without knowing it and without being known as such.

He discerned principles of writing which he had scarcely time to put into practice. In Japan he restored, or greatly helped to restore, a respect for the native art. In America and Europe he cannot be looked upon as a mere searcher after exotics. His mind was constantly filled with parallels and comparisons between Eastern and Western art. To him the exotic was always a means of fructification. He looked to an American renaissance. The vitality of his outlook can be judged from the fact that although this essay was written some time before his death in 1908 I have not had to change the allusions to Western conditions. The later movements in art have corroborated his theories. E.P. 1918.]

This twentieth century not only turns a new page in the book of the world, but opens another and a startling chapter. Vistas of strange futures unfold for man, of world-embracing cultures half-weaned from Europe, of hitherto undreamed responsibilities for nations and races.

The Chinese problem alone is so vast that no nation can afford to ignore it. We in America, especially, must face it across the Pacific, and master it or it will master us. And the only way to master it is to strive with patient sympathy to understand the best, the most hopeful and the most human elements in it.

It is unfortunate that England and America have so long ignored or mistaken the deeper problems of Oriental culture. We have misconceived the Chinese for a materialistic people, for a debased and worn-out race. We have belittled the Japanese as a nation of copyists. We have stupidly assumed that Chinese history affords no glimpse of change in social evolution, no salient epoch of moral and spiritual crisis. We have denied the essential humanity of these peoples; and we have toyed with their ideals as if they were no better than comic songs in an 'opéra bouffe.'

The duty that faces us is not to batter down their forts or to exploit their markets, but to study and to come to sympathize with their humanity and their generous aspirations. Their type of cultivation has been high. Their harvest of recorded experience doubles our own. The Chinese have been idealists, and experimenters in the making of great principles; their history opens a world of lofty aim and achievement, parallel to that of the ancient Mediterranean peoples. We need their best ideals to supplement our own—ideals enshrined in their art, in their literature and in the tragedies of their lives.

We have already seen proof of the vitality and practical value of Oriental painting for ourselves and as a key to the Eastern soul. It may be worth while to approach their literature, the intensest part of it, their poetry, even in an imperfect manner.

I feel that I should perhaps apologize* for presuming to follow that series of brilliant scholars, Davis, Legge, St. Denys and Giles,[1] who have treated the subject of Chinese poetry with a wealth of erudition to which I can proffer no claim. It is not as

---

*[The apology was unnecessary, but Professor Fenollosa saw fit to make it, and I therefore transcribe his words. E.P.]

a professional linguist nor as a sinologue that I humbly put forward what I have to say. As an enthusiastic student of beauty in Oriental culture, having spent a large portion of my years in close relation with Orientals, I could not but breathe in something of the poetry incarnated in their lives.

I have been for the most part moved to my temerity by personal considerations. An unfortunate belief has spread both in England and in America that Chinese and Japanese poetry are hardly more than an amusement, trivial, childish, and not to be reckoned in the world's serious literary performance.[2] I have heard well-known sinologues state that, save for the purposes of professional linguistic scholarship, these branches of poetry are fields too barren to repay the toil necessary for their cultivation.

Now my own impression has been so radically and diametrically opposed to such a conclusion, that a sheer enthusiasm of generosity has driven me to wish to share with other Occidentals my newly discovered joy. Either I am pleasingly self-deceived in my positive delight, or else there must be some lack of aesthetic sympathy and of poetic feeling in the accepted methods of presenting the poetry of China. I submit my causes of joy.

Failure or success in presenting any alien poetry in English must depend largely upon poetic workmanship in the chosen medium. It was perhaps too much to expect that aged scholars who had spent their youth in gladiatorial combats with the refractory Chinese characters should succeed also as poets. Even Greek verse might have fared equally ill had its purveyors been perforce content with provincial standards of English rhyming. Sinologues should remember that the purpose of poetical translation is the poetry, not the verbal definitions in dictionaries.

One modest merit I may, perhaps, claim for my work: it represents for the first time a Japanese school of study in Chinese culture. Hitherto Europeans have been somewhat at the mercy of contemporary Chinese scholarship. Several centuries ago China lost much of her creative self, and of her insight into the causes of her own life; but her original spirit still lives, grows, interprets, transferred to Japan in all its original freshness. The Japanese today represent a stage of culture roughly corresponding to that of China under the Sung dynasty. I have been fortunate in studying for many years as a private pupil under Professor Kainan Mori, who is probably the greatest living authority on Chinese poetry. He has recently been called to a chair in the Imperial University of Tokio.

My subject is poetry, not language, yet the roots of poetry are in language. In the study of a language so alien in form to ours as is Chinese in its written character, it is necessary to inquire how these universal elements of form which constitute poetics can derive appropriate nutriment.

In what sense can verse, written in terms of visible hieroglyphics, be reckoned true poetry? It might seem that poetry, which like music is a *time art,* weaving its unities out of successive impressions of sound, could with difficulty assimilate a verbal medium consisting largely of semi-pictorial appeals to the eye.

Contrast, for example, Gray's line:[3]

The curfew tolls the knell of parting day

with the Chinese line:

| Moon | Rays | Like | Pure | Snow |

Unless the sound of the latter be given, what have they in common? It is not enough to adduce that each contains a certain body of prosaic meaning; for the question is, how can the Chinese line imply, *as form,* the very element that distinguishes poetry from prose?

On second glance, it is seen that the Chinese words, though visible, occur in just as necessary an order as the phonetic symbols of Gray. All that poetic form requires is a regular and flexible sequence, as plastic as thought itself. The characters may be seen and read, silently by the eye, one after the other:

Moon rays like pure snow.

Perhaps we do not always sufficiently consider that thought is successive, not through some accident or weakness of our subjective operations but because the operations of nature are successive. The transferences of force from agent to object, which constitute natural phenomena, occupy time. Therefore, a reproduction of them in imagination requires the same temporal order.*

Suppose that we look out of a window and watch a man. Suddenly he turns his head and actively fixes his attention upon something. We look ourselves and see that his vision has been focused upon a horse. We saw, first, the man before he acted; second, while he acted; third, the object toward which his action was directed. In speech we split up the rapid continuity of this action and of its picture into its three essential parts or joints in the right order, and say:

Man sees horse.

It is clear that these three joints, or words, are only three phonetic symbols, which stand for the three terms of a natural process. But we could quite as easily denote these three stages of our thought by symbols equally arbitrary, *which had no basis in sound;* for example, by three Chinese characters:

Man   **Sees**   **Horse**

If we all knew *what division* of this mental horse-picture each of these signs stood for, we could communicate continuous thought to one another as easily by drawing them as by speaking words. We habitually employ the visible language of gesture in much this same manner.

But Chinese notation is something much more than arbitrary

*[Style, that is to say, limpidity, as opposed to rhetoric. E.P.]

symbols. It is based upon a vivid shorthand picture of the operations of nature. In the algebraic figure and in the spoken word there is no natural connection between thing and sign: all depends upon sheer convention. But the Chinese method follows natural suggestion. First stands the man on his two legs. Second, his eye moves through space: a bold figure represented by running legs under an eye, a modified picture of an eye, a modified picture of running legs, but unforgettable once you have seen it. Third stands the horse on his four legs.

The thought-picture is not only called up by these signs as well as by words, but far more vividly and concretely. Legs belong to all three characters: they are *alive*. The group holds something of the quality of a continuous moving picture.

The untruth of a painting or a photograph is that, in spite of its concreteness, it drops the element of natural succession.

Contrast the Laocoön statue with Browning's lines:[4]

'*I sprang to the stirrup, and Joris, and he*

. . . .

And into the midnight we galloped abreast.'

One superiority of verbal poetry as an art rests in its getting back to the fundamental reality of *time*. Chinese poetry has the unique advantage of combining both elements. It speaks at once with the vividness of painting, and with the mobility of sounds. It is, in some sense, more objective than either, more dramatic. In reading Chinese we do not seem to be juggling mental counters, but to be watching *things* work out their own fate.

Leaving for a moment the form of the sentence, let us look more closely at this quality of vividness in the structure of detached Chinese words. The earlier forms of these characters were pictorial, and their hold upon the imagination is little shaken, even in later conventional modifications. It is not so well known, perhaps, that the great number of these ideographic roots carry in them a *verbal idea of action*. It might be thought that a picture is naturally the picture of a *thing*, and that therefore the root ideas of Chinese are what grammar calls nouns.

But examination shows that a large number of the primitive

Chinese characters, even the so-called radicals, are shorthand
pictures of actions or processes.

For example, the ideograph meaning 'to speak' is a mouth
with two words and a flame coming out of it. The sign meaning
'to grow up with difficulty' is grass with a twisted root (*vide*
Plates 2 and 4). But this concrete *verb* quality, both in nature and
in the Chinese signs, becomes far more striking and poetic when
we pass from such simple, original pictures to compounds. In
this process of compounding, two things added together do not
produce a third thing but suggest some fundamental relation between them. For example, the ideograph for a 'messmate' is a
man and a fire (*vide* Plate 2, col. 2).

A true noun, an isolated thing, does not exist in nature.
Things are only the terminal points, or rather the meeting points,
of actions, cross-sections cut through actions, snap-shots.
Neither can a pure verb an abstract motion, be possible in nature. The eye sees noun and verb as one: things in motion, motion in things, and so the Chinese conception tends to represent
them.*

The sun underlying the bursting forth of plants=spring.

The sun sign, tangled in the branches of the tree sign=east
(*vide* Plate 2).

'Rice-field' plus 'struggle'=male (*vide* Plate 2, col. 3).

'Boat' plus 'water'=boat-water, a ripple (*vide* Plate 2, col. 1).

Let us return to the form of the sentence and see what power
it adds to the verbal units from which it builds. I wonder how
many people have asked themselves why the sentence form exists at all, why it seems so universally necessary *in all languages?* Why *must* all possess it, and what is the normal type of
it? If it be so universal, it ought to correspond to some primary
law of nature.

I fancy the professional grammarians have given but a lame
response to this inquiry. Their definitions fall into two types:
one, that a sentence expresses a 'complete thought'; the other,
that in it we bring about a union of subject and predicate.

The former has the advantage of trying for some natural

---

*[Axe *striking* something; dog *attending* man=dogs him.] [*Vide* Plate 2, col. 3.]

objective standard, since it is evident that a thought can not be the test of its own completeness. But in nature there is *no* completeness. On the one hand, practical completeness may be expressed by a mere interjection, as 'Hi! there!', or 'Scat!', or even by shaking one's fist. No sentence is needed to make one's meaning more clear. On the other hand, no full sentence really completes a thought. The man who sees and the horse which is seen will not stand still. The man was planning a ride before he looked. The horse kicked when the man tried to catch him. The truth is that acts are successive, even continuous; one causes or passes into another. And though we may string ever so many clauses into a single compound sentence, motion leaks everywhere, like electricity from an exposed wire. All processes in nature are interrelated; and thus there could be no complete sentence (according to this definition) save one which it would take all time to pronounce.

In the second definition of the sentence, as 'uniting a subject and a predicate,' the grammarian falls back on pure subjectivity. *We* do it all; it is a little private juggling between our right and left hands. The subject is that about which *I* am going to talk; the predicate is that which *I* am going to say about it. The sentence according to this definition is not an attribute of nature but an accident of man as a conversational animal.

If it were really so, then there could be no possible test of the truth of a sentence. Falsehood would be as specious as verity. Speech would carry no conviction.

Of course this view of the grammarians springs from the discredited, or rather the useless, logic of the Middle Ages. According to this logic, thought deals with abstractions, concepts drawn out of things by a sifting process. These logicians never inquired how the 'qualities' which they pulled out of things came to be there. The truth of all their little checker-board juggling depended upon the natural order by which these powers or properties or qualities were folded in concrete things, yet they despised the 'thing' as a mere 'particular,' or pawn. It was as if Botany should reason from the leaf-patterns woven into our table-cloths. Valid scientific thought consists in following as closely as may be the actual and entangled lines of forces as they pulse through things. Thought deals with no bloodless concepts but watches *things move* under its microscope.

The sentence form was forced upon primitive men by nature itself. It was not we who made it; it was a reflection of the temporal order in causation. All truth has to be expressed in sentences because all truth is the *transference of power*. The type of sentence in nature is a flash of lightning. It passes between two terms, a cloud and the earth. No unit of natural process can be less than this. All natural processes are, in their units, as much as this. Light, heat, gravity, chemical affinity, human will, have this in common, that they redistribute force. Their unit of process can be represented as:

term	*transference*	*term*
from	*of*	*to*
which	*force*	*which*

If we regard this transference as the conscious or unconscious act of an agent we can translate the diagram into:

agent	*act*	*object*

In this the act is the very substance of the fact denoted. The agent and the object are only limiting terms.

It seems to me that the normal and typical sentence in English as well as in Chinese expresses just this unit of natural process. It consists of three necessary words: the first denoting the agent or subject from which the act starts, the second embodying the very stroke of the act, the third pointing to the object, the receiver of the impact. Thus:

Farmer	*pounds*	*rice*

The form of the Chinese transitive sentence, and of the English (omitting particles), exactly corresponds to this universal form of action in nature. This brings language close to *things*, and in its strong reliance upon verbs it erects all speech into a kind of dramatic poetry.

A different sentence order is frequent in inflected languages like Latin, German or Japanese. This is because they are inflected, i.e. they have little tags and word-endings, or labels, to show which is the agent, the object, etc. In uninflected languages, like English and Chinese, there is nothing but the order of the words to distinguish their functions. And this order would be no sufficient indication, were it not the *natural order*—that is, the order of cause and effect.

It is true that there are, in language, intransitive and passive forms, sentences built out of the verb 'to be,' and, finally, negative forms. To grammarians and logicians these have seemed more primitive than the transitive, or at least exceptions to the transitive. I had long suspected that these apparently exceptional forms had grown from the transitive or worn away from it by alteration, or modification. This view is confirmed by Chinese examples, wherein it is still possible to watch the transformation going on.

The intransitive form derives from the transitive by dropping a generalised, customary, reflexive or cognate object: 'He runs (a race).' 'The sky reddens (itself).' 'We breathe (air).' Thus we get weak and incomplete sentences which suspend the picture and lead us to think of some verbs as denoting states rather than acts. Outside grammar the word 'state' would hardly be recognised as scientific. Who can doubt that when we say 'The wall shines,' we mean that it actively reflects light to our eye?

The beauty of Chinese verbs is that they are all transitive or intransitive at pleasure. There is no such thing as a naturally intransitive verb. The passive form is evidently a correlative sentence, which turns about and makes the object into a subject. That the object is not in itself passive, but contributes some positive force of its own to the action, is in harmony both with scientific law and with ordinary experience. The English passive voice with 'is' seemed at first an obstacle to this hypothesis, but one suspected that the true form was a generalised transitive verb meaning something like 'receive,' which had degenerated into an auxiliary. It was a delight to find this the case in Chinese.

In nature there are no negations, no possible transfers of negative force. The presence of negative sentences in language

would seem to corroborate the logicians' view that assertion is
an arbitrary subjective act. We can assert a negation, though nature can not. But here again science comes to our aid against the
logician: all apparently negative or disruptive movements bring
into play other positive forces. It requires great effort to annihi-
late. Therefore we should suspect that, if we could follow back
the history of all negative particles, we should find that they
also are sprung from transitive verbs. It is too late to demonstrate such derivations in the Aryan languages, the clue has
been lost; but in Chinese we can still watch positive verbal con-
ceptions passing over into so-called negatives. Thus in Chinese
the sign meaning 'to be lost in the forest' relates to a state of
non-existence. English 'not'=the Sanskrit na, which may come
from the root na, to be lost, to perish.

Lastly comes the infinitive which substitutes for a specific
colored verb the universal copula 'is,' followed by a noun or an
adjective. We do not say a tree 'greens itself,' but 'the tree is
green'; not that monkeys bring forth live young,' but that 'the
monkey is a mammal.' This is an ultimate weakness of language. It has come from generalising all intransitive words into
one. As 'live,' 'see,' 'walk,' 'breathe,' are generalised into states
by dropping their objects, so these weak verbs are in turn reduced to the abstractest state of all, namely bare existence.

There is in reality no such verb as a pure copula, no such
original conception: our very word exist means 'to stand forth,'
to show oneself by a definite act. 'Is' comes from the Aryan root
as, to breathe. 'Be' is from bhu, to grow.

In Chinese the chief verb for 'is' not only means actively 'to
have,' but shows by its derivation that it expresses something
even more concrete, namely 'to snatch from the moon with the

hand.' 有 Here the baldest symbol of prosaic analysis is

transformed by magic into a splendid flash of concrete poetry.

I shall not have entered vainly into this long analysis of the sentence if I have succeeded in showing how poetical is the Chinese

form and how close to nature. In translating Chinese, verse especially, we must hold as closely as possible to the concrete force of the original, eschewing adjectives, nouns and intransitive forms wherever we can, and seeking instead strong and individual verbs.

Lastly we notice that the likeness of form between Chinese and English sentences renders translation from one to the other exceptionally easy. The genius of the two is much the same. Frequently it is possible by omitting English particles to make a literal word-for-word translation which will be not only intelligible in English, but even the strongest and most poetical English. Here, however, one must follow closely what is said, not merely what is abstractly meant.

Let us go back from the Chinese sentence to the individual written word. How are such words to be classified? Are some of them nouns by nature, some verbs and some adjectives? Are there pronouns and prepositions and conjunctions in Chinese as in good Christian languages?

One is led to suspect from an analysis of the Aryan languages that such differences are not natural, and that they have been unfortunately invented by grammarians to confuse the simple poetic outlook on life. All nations have written their strongest and most vivid literature before they invented a grammar. Moreover, all Aryan etymology points back to roots which are the equivalents of simple Sanskrit verbs, such as we find tabulated at the back of our Skeat.[5] Nature herself has no grammar.* Fancy picking up a man and telling him that he is a noun, a dead thing rather than a bundle of functions! A 'part of speech' is only *what it does*. Frequently our lines of cleavage fail, one part of speech acts for another. They *act for* one another because they were originally one and the same.

Few of us realise that in our own language these very differences once grew up in living articulation; that they still retain life.

---

*[Even Latin, living Latin, had not the network of rules they foist upon unfortunate school-children. These are borrowed sometimes from Greek grammarians, even as I have seen English grammars borrowing oblique cases from Latin grammars. Sometimes they sprang from the grammatising or categorising passion of pedants. Living Latin had only the feel of the cases: the ablative and dative emotion. E.P.]

It is only when the difficulty of placing some odd term arises, or when we are forced to translate into some very different language, that we attain for a moment the inner heat of thought, a heat which melts down the parts of speech to recast them at will.

One of the most interesting facts about the Chinese language is that in it we can see, not only the forms of sentences, but literally the parts of speech growing up, budding forth one from another. Like nature, the Chinese words are alive and plastic, because *thing* and *action* are not formally separated. The Chinese language naturally knows no grammar. It is only lately that foreigners, European and Japanese, have begun to torture this vital speech by forcing it to fit the bed of their definitions. We import into our reading of Chinese all the weakness of our own formalisms. This is especially sad in poetry, because the one necessity, even in our own poetry, is to keep words as flexible as possible, as full of the sap of nature.

Let us go further with our example. In English we call 'to shine' a *verb in the infinitive,* because it gives the abstract meaning of the verb without conditions. If we want a corresponding adjective we take a different word, 'bright.' If we need a noun we say 'luminosity,' which is abstract, being derived from an adjective. To get a tolerably concrete noun, we have to leave behind the verb and adjective roots, and light upon a thing arbitrarily cut off from its power of action, say 'the sun' or 'the moon.' Of course there is nothing in nature so cut off, and therefore this nounising is itself an abstraction. Even if we did have a common word underlying at once the verb 'shine,' the adjective 'bright' and the noun 'sun,' we should probably call it an 'infinitive of the infinitive.' According to our ideas, it should be something extremely abstract, too intangible for use.*

The Chinese have one word, *ming* or *mei.* Its ideograph is the sign of the sun together with the sign of the moon. It serves as verb, noun, adjective. Thus you write literally, 'the sun and moon of the cup' for 'the cup's brightness.' Placed as a verb,

---

*[A good writer would use 'shine' (i.e. to shine), 'shining', and 'the shine' or 'sheen', possibly thinking of the German *'schöne'* and *'Schönheit';* but this does not invalidate Professor Fenollosa's contention. E.P.]

you write 'the cup sun-and-moons,' actually 'cup sun-and-moon,' or in a weakened thought, 'is like sun,' i.e. shines. 'Sun-and-moon cup' is naturally a bright cup. There is no possible confusion of the real meaning, though a stupid scholar may spend a week trying to decide what 'part of speech' he should use in translating a very simple and direct thought from Chinese to English.

The fact is that almost every written Chinese word is properly just such an underlying word, and yet it is *not* abstract. It is not exclusive of parts of speech, but comprehensive; not something which is neither a noun, verb, nor adjective, but something which is all of them at once and at all times. Usage may incline the full meaning now a little more to one side, now to another, according to the point of view, but through all cases the poet is free to deal with it richly and concretely, as does nature.

In the derivation of nouns from verbs, the Chinese language is forestalled by the Aryan. Almost all the Sanskrit roots, which seem to underlie European languages, are primitive verbs, which express characteristic actions of visible nature. The verb must be the primary fact of nature, since motion and change are all that we can recognise in her. In the primitive transitive sentence, such as 'Farmer pounds rice,' the agent and the object are nouns only in so far as they limit a unit of action. 'Farmer' and 'rice' are mere hard terms which define the extremes of the pounding. But in themselves, apart from this sentence-function, they are naturally verbs. The farmer is one who tills the ground, and the rice is a plant which grows in a special way. This is indicated in the Chinese characters. And this probably exemplifies the ordinary derivation of nouns from verbs. In all languages, Chinese included, a noun is originally 'that which does something,' that which performs the verbal action. Thus the moon comes from the root *ma,* and means, 'the measurer.' The sun means that which begets.

The derivation of adjectives from the verb need hardly be exemplified. Even with us, today, we can still watch participles passing over into adjectives. In Japanese the adjective is frankly part of the inflection of the verb, a special mood, so that every verb is also an adjective. This brings us close to nature, because everywhere the quality is only a power of action regarded as having an abstract inherence. Green is only a certain rapidity of vibration, hardness a degree of tenseness in cohering. In Chinese the adjective always retains a substratum of verbal meaning. We should try to render this in translation, not be content with some bloodless adjectival abstraction plus 'is.'

Still more interesting are the Chinese 'prepositions'—they are often post-positions. Prepositions are so important, so pivotal in European speech only because we have weakly yielded up the force of our intransitive verbs. We have to add small supernumerary words to bring back the original power. We still say 'I see a horse,' but with the weak verb 'look' we have to add the directive particle 'at' before we can restore the natural transitiveness.*

Prepositions represent a few simple ways in which incomplete verbs complete themselves. Pointing toward nouns as a limit, they bring force to bear upon them. That is to say, they are naturally verbs, of generalised or condensed use. In Aryan languages it is often difficult to trace the verbal origins of simple prepositions. Only in *'off'* do we see a fragment of the thought 'to throw off.' In Chinese the preposition is frankly a verb, specially used in a generalised sense. These verbs are often used in their special verbal sense, and it greatly weakens an English translation if they are systematically rendered by colorless prepositions.

Thus in Chinese, by=to cause; to=to fall toward; in=to remain, to dwell; from=to follow; and so on.

Conjunctions are similarly derivative; they usually serve to mediate actions between verbs, and therefore they are necessarily themselves actions. Thus in Chinese, because=to use; and=to be included under one; another form of 'and'=to be parallel; or=to partake; if=to let one do, to permit. The same is true of a host of other particles, no longer traceable in the Aryan tongues.

---

*[This is a bad example: we can say 'I look a fool'. 'Look', transitive, now means resemble. The main contention is, however, correct. We tend to abandon specific words like *resemble* and substitute, for them, vague verbs with prepositional directors, or riders. E.P.]

Pronouns appear a thorn in our evolution theory, since they have been taken as unanalysable expressions of personality. In Chinese, even they yield up their striking secrets of verbal metaphor. They are a constant source of weakness if colorlessly translated. Take, for example, the five forms of 'I.' There is the sign of a 'spear in the hand'=a very emphatic I; five and a mouth=a weak and defensive I, holding off a crowd by speaking; to conceal=a selfish and private I; self (the cocoon sign) and a mouth=an egoistic I, one who takes pleasure in his own speaking; the self presented is used only when one is speaking to one's self.

I trust that this disgression concerning parts of speech may have justified itself. It proves, first, the enormous interest of the Chinese language in throwing light upon our forgotten mental processes, and thus furnishes a new chapter in the philosophy of language. Secondly, it is indispensable for understanding the poetical raw material which the Chinese language affords. Poetry differs from prose in the concrete colors of its diction. It is not enough for it to furnish a meaning to philosophers. It must appeal to emotions with the charm of direct impression, flashing through regions where the intellect can only grope.* Poetry must render what is said, not what is merely meant. Abstract meaning gives little vividness, and fullness of imagination gives all. Chinese poetry demands that we abandon our narrow grammatical categories, that we follow the original text with a wealth of concrete verbs.

But this is only the beginning of the matter. So far we have exhibited the Chinese characters and the Chinese sentence chiefly as vivid shorthand pictures of actions and processes in nature. These embody true poetry as far as they go. Such actions are *seen,* but Chinese would be a poor language, and Chinese poetry but a narrow art, could they not go on to represent also what is unseen. The best poetry deals not only with natural images but with lofty thoughts, spiritual suggestions and obscure relations. The greater part of natural truth is hidden in processes too minute for vision and in harmonies too large, in

*[Cf. principle of Primary apparition, 'Spirit of Romance'. E.P.]

vibrations, cohesions and in affinities. The Chinese compass these also, and with great power and beauty.

You will ask, how could the Chinese have built up a great intellectual fabric from mere picture writing? To the ordinary Western mind, which believes that thought is concerned with logical categories and which rather condemns the faculty of direct imagination, this feat seems quite impossible. Yet the Chinese language with its peculiar materials has passed over from the seen to the unseen by exactly the same process which all ancient races employed. This process is metaphor, the use of material images to suggest immaterial relations.*

The whole delicate substance of speech is built upon substrata of metaphor. Abstract terms, pressed by etymology, reveal their ancient roots still embedded in direct action. But the primitive metaphors do not spring from arbitrary *subjective* processes. They are possible only because they follow objective lines of relations in nature herself. Relations are more real and more important than the things which they relate. The forces which produce the branch-angles of an oak lay potent in the acorn. Similar lines of resistance, half-curbing the out-pressing vitalities, govern the branching of rivers and of nations. Thus a nerve, a wire, a roadway, and a clearing-house are only varying channels which communication forces for itself. This is more than analogy, it is identity of structure. Nature furnishes her own clues. Had the world not been full of homologies, sympathies, and identities, thought would have been starved and language chained to the obvious. There would have been no bridge whereby to cross from the minor truth of the seen to the major truth of the unseen. Not more than a few hundred roots out of our large vocabularies could have dealt directly with physical processes. These we can fairly well identify in primitive Sanskrit. They are, almost without exception, vivid verbs. The wealth of European speech grew, following slowly the intricate maze of nature's suggestions and affinities. Metaphor was piled upon metaphor in quasi-geological strata.

*[Compare Aristotle's *Poetics*: 'Swift perception of relations, hallmark of genius'. E.P.]

Metaphor, the revealer of nature, is the very substance of poetry. The known interprets the obscure, the universe is alive with myth. The beauty and freedom of the observed world furnish a model, and life is pregnant with art. It is a mistake to suppose, with some philosophers of aesthetics, that art and poetry aim to deal with the general and the abstract. This misconception has been foisted upon us by mediaeval logic. Art and poetry deal with the concrete of nature, not with rows of separate 'particulars,' for such rows do not exist. Poetry is finer than prose because it gives us more concrete truth in the same compass of words. Metaphor, its chief device, is at once the substance of nature and of language. Poetry only does consciously* what the primitive races did unconsciously. The chief work of literary men in dealing with language, and of poets especially, lies in feeling back along the ancient lines of advance.† He must do this so that he may keep his words enriched by all their subtle undertones of meaning. The original metaphors stand as a kind of luminous background, giving color and vitality, forcing them closer to the concreteness of natural processes. Shakespeare everywhere teems with examples. For these reasons poetry was the earliest of the world arts; poetry, language and the care of myth grew up together.

I have alleged all this because it enables me to show clearly why I believe that the Chinese written language has not only absorbed the poetic substance of nature and built with it a second work of metaphor, but has, through its very pictorial visibility, been able to retain its original creative poetry with far more vigor and vividness than any phonetic tongue. Let us first see how near it is to the heart of nature in its metaphors. We can watch it passing from the seen to the unseen, as we saw it passing from verb to pronoun. It retains the primitive sap, it is not

---

*[*Vide* also an article on 'Vorticism' in the *Fortnightly Review* for September 1914. 'The language of exploration' now in my 'Gaudier-Brzeska'. E.P.]
†[I would submit in all humility that this applies in the rendering of ancient texts. The poet, in dealing with his own time, must also see to it that language does not petrify on his hands. He must prepare for new advances along the lines of true metaphor, that is interpretative metaphor, or image, as diametrically opposed to untrue, or ornamental, metaphor. E.P.]

cut and dried like a walking-stick. We have been told that these people are cold, practical, mechanical, literal, and without a trace of imaginative genius. That is nonsense.

Our ancestors built the accumulations of metaphor into structures of language and into systems of thought. Languages today are thin and cold because we think less and less into them. We are forced, for the sake of quickness and sharpness, to file down each word to its narrowest edge of meaning. Nature would seem to have become less like a paradise and more and more like a factory. We are content to accept the vulgar misuse of the moment.

A late stage of decay is arrested and embalmed in the dictionary.

Only scholars and poets feel painfully back along the thread of our etymologies and piece together our diction, as best they may, from forgotten fragments. This anaemia of modern speech is only too well encouraged by the feeble cohesive force of our phonetic symbols. There is little or nothing in a phonetic word to exhibit the embryonic stages of its growth. It does not bear its metaphor on its face. We forget that personality once meant, not the soul, but the soul's mask. This is the sort of thing one can not possibly forget in using the Chinese symbols.

In this Chinese shows its advantage. Its etymology is constantly visible. It retains the creative impulse and process, visible and at work. After thousands of years the lines of metaphoric advance are still shown, and in many cases actually retained in the meaning. Thus a word, instead of growing gradually poorer and poorer as with us, becomes richer and still more rich from age to age, almost consciously luminous. Its uses in national philosophy and history, in biography and in poetry, throw about it a nimbus of meanings. These centre about the graphic symbol. The memory can hold them and use them. The very soil of Chinese life seems entangled in the roots of its speech. The manifold illustrations which crowd its annals of personal experience, the lines of tendency which converge upon a tragic climax, moral character as the very core of the principle—all these are flashed at once on the mind as reinforcing values with accumulation of meaning which a phonetic language can hardly hope to attain. Their ideographs are like blood-stained battle-flags to an old campaigner. With us, the poet is the only one for whom the accumulated treasures of the race-words are real and active. Poetic language is always vibrant with fold on fold of overtones and with natural affinities, but in Chinese the visibility of the metaphor tends to raise this quality to its intensest power.

I have mentioned the tyranny of mediaeval logic. According to this European logic thought is a kind of brickyard. It is baked into little hard units or concepts. These are piled in rows according to size and then labeled with words for future use. This use consists in picking out a few bricks, each by its convenient label, and sticking them together into a sort of wall called a sentence by the use either of white mortar for the positive copula 'is,' or of black mortar for the negative copula 'is not.' In this way we produce such admirable propositions as 'A ring-tailed baboon is not a constitutional assembly.'

Let us consider a row of cherry trees. From each of these in turn we proceed to take an 'abstract,' as the phrase is, a certain common lump of qualities which we may express together by the name cherry or cherry-ness. Next we place in a second table several such characteristic concepts: cherry, rose, sunset, iron-rust, flamingo. From these we abstract some further common quality, dilutation or mediocrity, and label it 'red' or 'redness.' It is evident that this process of abstraction may be carried on indefinitely and with all sorts of material. We may go on for ever building pyramids of attenuated concept until we reach the apex 'being.'

But we have done enough to illustrate the characteristic process. At the base of the pyramid lie *things,* but stunned, as it were. They can never know themselves for things until they pass up and down among the layers of the pyramids. The way of passing up and down the pyramid may be exemplified as follows: We take a concept of lower attenuation, such as 'cherry'; we see that it is contained under one higher, such as 'redness.' Then we are permitted to say in sentence form, 'Cherryness is contained under redness,' or for short, '(The) cherry is red.' If, on the other hand, we do not find our chosen subject under a given predicate we use the black copula and say, for example, '(The) cherry is not liquid.'

From this point we might go on to the theory of the syllogism, but we refrain. It is enough to note that the practised logician finds it convenient to store his mind with long lists of nouns and adjectives, for these are naturally the names of classes. Most text-books on language begin with such lists. The study of verbs is meagre, for in such a system there is only one real working verb, to wit, the quasi-verb 'is.' All other verbs can be transformed into participles and gerunds. For example, 'to run' practically becomes a case of 'running.' Instead of thinking directly, 'The man runs,' our logician makes two subjective equations, namely: The individual in question is contained under the class 'man'; and the class 'man' is contained under the class of 'running things.'

The sheer loss and weakness of this method are apparent and flagrant. Even in its own sphere it can not think half of what it wants to think. It has no way of bringing together any two concepts which do not happen to stand one under the other and in the same pyramid.

It is impossible to represent change in this system or any kind of growth.

This is probably why the conception of evolution came so late in Europe. *It could not make way until it was prepared to destroy the inveterate logic of classification.*

Far worse than this, such logic can not deal with any kind of interaction or with any multiplicity of function. According to it, the function of my muscles is as isolated from the function of my nerves, as from an earthquake in the moon. For it the poor neglected things at the bases of the pyramids are only so many particulars or pawns.

Science fought till she got at the things.

All her work has been done from the base of the pyramids, not from the apex. She has discovered how functions cohere in things. She expresses her results in grouped sentences which embody no nouns or adjectives but verbs of special character.

The true formula for thought is: The cherry tree is all that it does. Its correlated verbs compose it. At bottom these verbs are transitive. Such verbs may be almost infinite in number.

In diction and in grammatical form science is utterly opposed to logic. Primitive men who created language agreed with science and not with logic. Logic has abused the language which they left to her mercy.

Poetry agrees with science and not with logic.

The moment we use the copula, the moment we express subjective inclusions, poetry evaporates. The more concretely and vividly we express the interactions of things the better the poetry. We need in poetry thousands of active words, each doing its utmost to show forth the motive and vital forces. We can not exhibit the wealth of nature by mere summation, by the piling of sentences. Poetic thought works by suggestion, crowding maximum meaning into the single phrase pregnant, charged, and luminous from within.

In Chinese character each word accumulated this sort of energy in itself.

Should we pass formally to the study of Chinese poetry, we should warn ourselves against logicianised pitfalls. We should be ware of modern narrow utilitarian meanings ascribed to the words in commercial dictionaries. We should try to preserve the metaphoric overtones. We should be ware of English grammar, its hard parts of speech, and its lazy satisfaction with nouns and adjectives. We should seek and at least bear in mind the verbal undertone of each noun. We should avoid 'is' and bring in a wealth of neglected English verbs. Most of the existing translations violate all of these rules.

The development of the normal transitive sentence rests upon the fact that one action in nature promotes another; thus the agent and the object are secretly verbs. For example, our sentence, 'Reading promotes writing,' would be expressed in Chinese by three full verbs. Such a form is the equivalent of three expanded clauses and can be drawn out into adjectival, participial, infinitive, relative or conditional members. One of many possible examples is, 'If one reads it teaches him how to

write.' Another is, 'One who reads becomes one who writes.'
But in the first condensed form a Chinese would write, 'Read
promote write.' The dominance of the verb and its power to
obliterate all other parts of speech give us the model of terse
fine style.

I have seldom seen our rhetoricians dwell on the fact that the
great strength of our language lies in its splendid array of transitive verbs, drawn both from Anglo-Saxon and from Latin
sources. These give us the most individual characterisations of
force. Their power lies in their recognition of nature as a vast
storehouse of forces. We do not say in English that things seem,
or appear, or eventuate, or even that they are; but that they *do*.
Will is the foundation of our speech.* We catch the Demi-urge
in the act. I had to discover for myself why Shakespeare's English was so immeasurably superior to all others. I found that it
was his persistent, natural, and magnificent use of hundreds of
transitive verbs. Rarely will you find an 'is' in his sentences. 'Is'
weakly lends itself to the uses of our rhythm, in the unaccented
syllables; yet he sternly discards it. A study of Shakespeare's
verbs should underlie all exercises in style.

We find in poetical Chinese a wealth of transitive verbs, in
some way greater even than in the English of Shakespeare. This
springs from their power of combining several pictorial elements in a single character. We have in English no verb for
what two things, say the sun and moon, both do together. Pre-
fixes and affixes merely direct and qualify. In Chinese the verb
can be more minutely qualified. We find a hundred variants
clustering about a single idea. Thus 'to sail a boat for purposes
of pleasure' would be an entirely different verb from 'to sail for
purposes of commerce.' Dozens of Chinese verbs express various shades of grieving, yet in English translations they are usually reduced to one mediocrity. Many of them can be expressed
only by periphrasis, but what right has the translator to neglect
the overtones? There are subtle shadings. We should strain our
resources in English.

It is true that the pictorial clue of many Chinese ideographs

*[Compare Dante's definition of 'rectitudo' as the direction of the will.]

CHINESE CHARACTER AS A MEDIUM FOR POETRY

can not now be traced, and even Chinese lexicographers admit that combinations frequently contribute only a phonetic value. But I find it incredible that any such minute subdivision of the idea could have ever existed alone as abstract sound without the concrete character. It contradicts the law of evolution. Complex ideas arise only gradually, as the power of holding them together arises. The paucity of Chinese sound could not so hold them. Neither is it conceivable that the whole list was made at once, as commercial codes of cipher are compiled. Foreign words sometimes recalled Chinese ideograms associated with vaguely similar sound? Therefore we must believe that the phonetic theory is in large part unsound? The metaphor once existed in many cases where we can not now trace it. Many of our own etymologies have been lost. It is futile to take the ignorance of the Han dynasty for omniscience.* It is not true, as Legge said, that the original picture characters could never have gone far in building up abstract thought. This is a vital mistake. We have seen that our own languages have all sprung from a few hundred vivid phonetic verbs by figurative derivation. A fabric more vast could have been built up in Chinese by metaphorical composition. No attenuated idea exists which it might not have reached more vividly and more permanently than we could have been expected to reach with phonetic roots. Such a pictorial method, whether the

*[Professor Fenollosa is borne out by chance evidence. Gaudier-Brzeska sat in my room before he went off to war. He was able to read the Chinese radicals and many compound signs almost at pleasure. He was used to consider all life and nature in the terms of planes and of bounding lines. Nevertheless he had spent only a fortnight in the museum studying the Chinese characters. He was amazed at the stupidity of lexicographers who could not, for all their learning discern the pictorial values which were to him perfectly obvious and apparent. A few weeks later Edmond Dulac, who is of a totally different tradition, sat here, giving an impromptu panegyric on the elements of Chinese art, on the units of composition, drawn from the written characters. He did not use Professor Fenollosa's own words—he said 'bamboo' instead of 'rice'. He said the essence of the bamboo is in a certain way it grows; they have this in their sign for bamboo, all designs of bamboo proceed from it. Then he went on rather to disparage vorticism, on the grounds that it could not hope to do for the Occident, in one lifetime, what had required centuries of development in China. E.P.]

Chinese exemplified it or not, would be the ideal language of the world.

Still, is it not enough to show that Chinese poetry gets back near to the processes of nature by means of its vivid figure, its wealth of such figure? If we attempt to follow it in English we must use words highly charged, words whose vital suggestion shall interplay as nature interplays. Sentences must be like the mingling of the fringes of feathered banners, or as the colors of many flowers blended into the single sheen of a meadow.

The poet can never see too much or feel too much. His metaphors are only ways of getting rid of the dead white plaster of the copula. He resolves its indifference into a thousand tints of verb. His figures flood things with jets of various light, like the sudden up-blaze of fountains. The prehistoric poets who created language discovered the whole harmonious framework of nature, they sang out her processes in their hymns. And this diffused poetry which they created, Shakespeare has condensed into a more tangible substance. Thus in all poetry a word is like a sun, with its corona and chromosphere; words crowd upon words, and enwrap each other in their luminous envelopes until sentences become clear, continuous light-bands.

Now we are in condition to appreciate the full splendor of certain lines of Chinese verse. Poetry surpasses prose especially in that the poet selects for juxtaposition those words whose overtones blend into a delicate and lucid harmony. All arts follow the same law; refined harmony lies in the delicate balance of overtones. In music the whole possibility and theory of harmony are based on the overtones. In this sense poetry seems a more difficult art.

How shall we determine the metaphorical overtones of neighbouring words? We can avoid flagrant breaches like mixed metaphor. We can find the concord or harmonising at its intensest, as in Romeo's speech over the dead Juliet.

Here also the Chinese ideography has its advantage, in even a simple line; for example, 'The sun rises in the east.'

The overtones vibrate against the eye. The wealth of composition in characters makes possible a choice of words in which a single dominant overtone colors every plane of meaning. That is perhaps the most conspicuous quality of Chinese poetry. Let us examine our line.

Sun   Rises   (in the)   East

The sun, the shining, on one side, on the other the sign of the east, which is the sun entangled in the branches of a tree. And in the middle sign, the verb 'rise,' we have further homology; the sun is above the horizon, but beyond that the single upright line is like the growing trunk-line of the tree sign. This is but a beginning, but it points a way to the method, and to the method of intelligent reading.

JAMES JOYCE, AT LAST THE NOVEL APPEARS*

It is unlikely that I shall say anything new about Mr. Joyce's novel, *A Portrait of the Artist as a Young Man.* I have already stated that it is a book worth reading and that it is written in good prose. In using these terms I do not employ the looseness of the half-crown reviewer.

I am very glad that it is now possible for a few hundred people to read Mr. Joyce comfortably from a bound book, instead of from a much-handled file of EGOISTS or from a slippery bundle of type-script. After much difficulty THE EGOIST itself turns publisher and produces *A Portrait of the Artist* as a volume, for the hatred of ordinary English publishers for good prose is, like the hatred of the *Quarterly Review*[1] for good poetry, deep-rooted, traditional.

Since Landor's *Imaginary Conversations*[2] were bandied from pillar to post, I doubt if any manuscript has met with so much opposition, and no manuscript has been more worth supporting.

Landor is still an unpopular author. He is still a terror to fools. He is still concealed from the young (not for any alleged indecency, but simply because he did not acquiesce in certain popular follies). He, Landor, still plays an inconspicuous role in

A Portrait of the Artist as a Young Man, by James Joyce. THE EGOIST LTD. Ready now, price 6a.

university courses. The amount of light which he would shed on the undergraduate mind would make students inconvenient to the average run of professors. But Landor is permanent.

Members of the "Fly-Fishers" and "Royal Automobile" clubs, and of the "Isthmian," may not read him. They will not read Mr. Joyce. *E pur si muove.*[3] Despite the printers and publishers the British Government has recognized Mr. Joyce's literary merit. That is a definite gain for the party of intelligence. A number of qualified judges have acquiesced in my statement of two years ago, that Mr. Joyce was an excellent and important writer of prose.

The last few years have seen the gradual shaping of a party of intelligence, a party not bound by any central doctrine or theory. We cannot accurately define new writers by applying to them tag-names from old authors, but as there is no adequate means of conveying the general impression of their characteristics one may at times employ such terminology, carefully stating that the terms are nothing more than approximation.

With that qualification, I would say that James Joyce produces the nearest thing to Flaubertian prose that we have now in English, just as Wyndham Lewis has written a novel which is more like, and more fitly compared with, Dostoievsky than is the work of any of his contemporaries. In like manner Mr. T. S. Eliot comes nearer to filling the place of Jules La Forgue in our generation. (Doing the "nearest thing" need not imply an approach to a standard, from a position inferior.)

Two of these writers have met with all sorts of opposition. If Mr. Eliot probably has not yet encountered very much opposition, it is only because his work is not yet very widely known.

My own income was considerably docked because I dared to say that Gaudier-Brzeska was a good sculptor and that Wyndham Lewis was a great master of design. It has, however, reached an almost irreducible minimum, and I am, perhaps, fairly safe in reasserting Joyce's ability as a writer. It will cost me no more than a few violent attacks from several sheltered, and therefore courageous, anonymities. When you tell the Irish that they are slow in recognizing their own men of genius they reply with street riots and politics.

Now, despite the jobbing of bigots and of their sectarian publishing houses, and despite the "Fly-Fishers" and the types which they represent, and despite the unwillingness of the print-packers (a word derived from pork-packers) and the initial objections of the Dublin publishers and the later unwillingness of the English publishers, Mr. Joyce's novel appears in book form, and intelligent readers gathering few by few will read it, and it will remain a permanent part of English literature—written by an Irishman in Trieste and first published in New York City.[4] I doubt if a comparison of Mr. Joyce to other English writers or Irish writers would much help to define him. One can only say that he is rather unlike them. *The Portrait* is very different from *L'Education Sentimentale,* but it would be easier to compare it with that novel of Flaubert's than with anything else. Flaubert pointed out that if France had studied his work they might have been saved a good deal in 1870. If more people had read *The Portrait* and certain stories in Mr. Joyce's *Dubliners* there might have been less recent trouble in Ireland. A clear diagnosis is never without its value.

Apart from Mr. Joyce's realism—the school-life, the life in the University, the family dinner with the discussion of Parnell depicted in his novel—apart from, or of a piece with, all this is the style, the actual writing: hard, clear-cut, with no waste of words, no bundling up of useless phrases, no filling in with pages of slosh.

It is very important that there should be clear, unexaggerated, realistic literature. It is very important that there should be good prose. The hell of contemporary Europe is caused by the lack of representative government in Germany, *and* by the nonexistence of decent prose in the German language. Clear thought and sanity depend on clear prose. They cannot live apart. The former produces the latter. The latter conserves and transmits the former.

The mush of the German sentence, the straddling of the verb out to the end, are just as much a part of the befoozlement of Kultur and the consequent hell, as was the rhetoric of later Rome the seed and the symptom of the Roman Empire's decadence and extinction. A nation that cannot write clearly cannot be trusted to govern, nor yet to think.

Germany has had two decent prose-writers, Frederick the Great and Heine—the one taught by Voltaire, and the other saturated with French and with Paris. Only a nation accustomed to muzzy writing could have been led by the nose and bamboozled as the Germans have been by their controllers.

The terror of clarity is not confined to any one people. The obstructionist and the provincial are everywhere, and in them alone is the permanent danger to civilization. Clear, hard prose is the safeguard and should be valued as such. The mind accustomed to it will not be cheated or stampeded by national phrases and public emotionalities.

These facts are true, even for the detesters of literature. For those who love good writing there is no need of argument. In the present instance it is enough to say to those who will believe one that Mr. Joyce's book is now procurable.

PARIS LETTER

May, 1922

Ulysses

Πολλῶγ δ' ἀνθρῶπων ἴδεν ἄστε α, καὶ υόον ἔγνω. All men should "Unite to give praise to Ulysses"; those who will not, may content themselves with a place in the lower intellectual orders; I do not mean that they should all praise it from the same viewpoint; but all serious men of letters, whether they write out a critique or not, will certainly have to make one for their own use. To begin with matters lying outside dispute I should say that Joyce has taken up the art of writing where Flaubert left it. In Dubliners and The Portrait he had not exceeded the Trois Contes or L'Education; in Ulysses he has carried on a process begun in Bouvard et Pécuchet;[1] he has brought it to a degree of greater efficiency, of greater compactness; he has swallowed the Tentation de St. Antoine whole, it serves as comparison for a single episode in Ulysses. Ulysses has more form than any novel of Flaubert's. Cervantes had parodied his predecessors and might be taken as basis of comparison for another of Joyce's modes of concision, but where Cervantes satirized one manner of folly and one sort of highfalutin' expression, Joyce satirizes at least seventy, and includes a whole history of English prose, by implication.

Messrs Bouvard and Pécuchet are the basis of democracy; Bloom also is the basis of democracy; he is the man in the street, the next man, the public, not our public, but Mr. Wells' public; for Mr. Wells he is Hocking's public, he is *l'homme moyen sensuel;* he is also Shakespeare, Ulysses, The Wandering Jew, the Daily Mail reader, the man who believes what he sees in the papers, Everyman, and "the goat" . . . πολλὰ πάθεν . . . κατα θυμὸν.

Flaubert having recorded provincial customs in Bovary and city habits in L'Education, set out to complete his record of nineteenth century life by presenting all sorts of things that the average man of the period would have had in his head; Joyce has found a more expeditious method of summary and analysis. After Bouvard and his friend have retired to the country Flaubert's incompleted narrative drags; in Ulysses anything may occur at any moment; Bloom suffers *kata thumon;* "every fellow mousing round for his liver and his lights": he is *polumetis* and a receiver of all things.

Joyce's characters not only speak their own language, but they think their own language. Thus Master Dignam stood looking at the poster: "two puckers stripped to their pelts and putting up their props. . . .

"Gob that'd be a good pucking match to see, Myler Keogh, that's the chap sparring out to him with the green sash. Two bob entrance, soldiers half price. I could easy do a bunk on ma. When is it? May the twenty second. Sure, the blooming thing is all over."

But Father Conmee was wonderfully well indeed: "And her boys, were they getting on well at Belvedere? Was that so? Father Conmee was very glad to hear that. And Mr. Sheehy himself? Still in London. The House was still sitting, to be sure it was. Beautiful weather it was, delightful indeed. Yes, it was very probable that Father Bernard Vaughn would come again to preach. O, yes, a very great success. A wonderful man really."

Father Conmee later "reflected on the providence of the Creator who had made turf to be in bogs where men might dig it out and bring it to town and hamlet to make fires in the houses of poor people."

The dialects are not all local, on page 406 we hear that:

"Elijah is coming. Washed in the Blood of the Lamb. Come on, you winefizzling, ginsizzling, booseguzzling existences! Come on, you dog-gone, bullnecked, beetlebrowed, hogjowled, peanut-brained, weaseleyed fourflushers, false alarms and excess baggage! Come on, you triple extract of infamy! Alexander J. Christ Dowie, that's yanked to glory most half this planet from 'Frisco Beach to Vladivostok. The Deity ain't no nickel dime bumshow. I put it to you that he's on the square and a corking fine business proposition. He's the grandest thing yet, and don't you forget it. Shout salvation in King Jesus. You'll need to rise precious early, you sinner there, if you want to diddle Almighty God. . . . Not half. He's got a coughmixture with a punch in it for you, my friend, in his backpocket. Just you try it on."

This varigation of dialects allows Joyce to present his matter, his tones of mind, very rapidly; it is no more succinct than Flaubert's exhaustion of the relation of Emma and her mother-in-law; or of Père Rouault's character, as epitomized in his last letter to Emma; but it is more rapid than the record of "received ideas" in Bouvard et Pécuchet.

Ulysses is, presumably, as unrepeatable as Tristram Shandy; I mean you cannot duplicate it; you can't take it as a "model," as you could Bovary; but it does complete something begun in Bouvard; and it does add definitely to the international store of literary technique.

Stock novels, even excellent stock novels, seem infinitely long, and infinitely encumbered, after one has watched Joyce squeeze the last drop out of a situation, a science, a state of mind, in half a page, in a catechismic question and answer, in a tirade à la Rabelais.

Rabelais himself rests, he remains, he is too solid to be diminished by any pursuer; he was a rock against the follies of his age; against ecclesiastic theology, and more remarkably, against the blind idolatry of the classics just coming into fashion. He refused the lot, lock, stock, and barrel, with a greater heave than Joyce has yet exhibited; but I can think of no other prose author whose proportional status in pan-literature is not modified by the advent of Ulysses.

James (H.)[2] speaks with his own so beautiful voice, even sometimes when his creations should be using *their* own; Joyce speaks if not with the tongue of men and angels, at least with a many-tongued and multiple language, of small boys, street preachers, of genteel and ungenteel, of bowsers and undertakers, of Gertie McDowell and Mr. Deasey.

One reads Proust and thinks him very accomplished; one reads H. J. and knows that he is very accomplished; one begins Ulysses and thinks, perhaps rightly, that Joyce is less so; that he is at any rate less gracile; and one considers how excellently both James and Proust "convey their atmospheres"; yet the atmosphere of the Gerty-Nausika episode with its echoes of vesper service is certainly "conveyed," and conveyed with a certitude and efficiency that neither James nor Proust have excelled.

And on the home stretch, when our present author is feeling more or less relieved that the weight of the book is off his shoulders, we find if not gracile accomplishments, at any rate such acrobatics, such sheer whoops and hoop-las and trapeze turns of technique that it would seem rash to dogmatize concerning his limitations. The whole of him, on the other hand, lock, stock, and gunny-sacks is wholly outside H. J.'s compass and orbit, outside Proust's circuit and orbit.

If it be charged that he shows "that provincialism which must be forever dragging in allusions to some book or local custom," it must also be admitted that no author is more lucid or more explicit in presenting things in such a way that the imaginary Chinaman or denizen of the forty-first century could without works of reference gain a very good idea of the scene and habits portrayed.

Poynton with its spoils forms a less vivid image than Bloom's desired two story dwelling house and appurtenances. The recollections of In Old Madrid are not at any rate highbrow; the "low back car"[3] is I think local. But in the main, I doubt if the local allusions interfere with a *general* comprehension. Local details exist everywhere; one understands them *mutatis mutandis*, and any picture would be perhaps faulty without them. One must balance obscurity against brevity. Concision itself is an obscurity for the dullard.

In this super-novel our author has also poached on the epic, and has, for the first time since 1321, resurrected the infernal figures; his furies are not stage figures; he has, by simple reversal, caught back the furies, his flaggellant Castle ladies. Telemachus, Circe, the rest of the Odyssean company, the noisy cave of Aeolus gradually place themselves in the mind of the reader, rapidly or less rapidly according as he is familiar or unfamiliar with Homer. These correspondences are part of Joyce's mediaevalism and are chiefly his own affair, a scaffold, a means of construction, justified by the result, and justifiable by it only. The result is a triumph in form, in balance, a main schema, with continuous inweaving and arabesque.

The best criticism of any work, to my mind the only criticism of any work of art that is of any permanent or even moderately durable value, comes from the creative writer or artist who does the next job; and *not*, not ever from the young gentlemen who make generalities about the creator. Laforgue's Salomé is the real criticism of Salammbô; Joyce and perhaps Henry James are critics of Flaubert. To me, as poet, the Tentation is *jettatura*, it is the effect of Flaubert's time on Flaubert; I mean he was interested in certain questions now dead as mutton, because he lived in a certain period; fortunately he managed to bundle these matters into one or two books and keep them out of his work on contemporary subjects; I set it aside as one sets aside Dante's treatise De Aqua et Terra, as something which matters now only as archaeology. Joyce, working in the same medium as Flaubert, makes the intelligent criticism: "We might believe in it if Flaubert had first shown us St. Antoine in Alexandria looking at women and jewellers' windows."

Ulysses contains 732 double sized pages, that is to say it is about the size of four ordinary novels, and even a list of its various points of interest would probably exceed my alloted space; in the Cyclops episode we have a measuring of the difference between reality, and reality as represented in various lofty forms of expression; the satire on the various dead manners of language culminates in the execution scene, blood and sugar stewed into clichés and rhetoric; just what the public deserves, and just what the public gets every morning with its porridge, in the Daily Mail and in sentimento-rhetorical journalism; it is perhaps the most savage bit of satire we have had since Swift suggested a cure for famine in Ireland. Henry James complained of Baudelaire, "Le Mal, you do yourself too much honour ... our impatience is of the same order as ... if for the 'Flowers of Good' one should present us with a rhapsody on plum-cake and eau de cologne." Joyce has set out to do an inferno, and he has done an inferno.

He has presented Ireland under British domination a picture so veridic that a ninth rate coward like Shaw (Geo. B.) dare not even look it in the face. By extension he has presented the whole occident under the domination of capital. The details of the street map are local but Leopold Bloom (*né Virag*) is ubiquitous. His spouse Gea-Tellus the earth symbol is the soil from which the intelligence strives to leap, and to which it subsides *in saeculum saeculorum*. As Molly she is a coarse-grained bitch, not a whore, an adulteress, *il y en a*. Her ultimate meditations are uncensored (bow to psychoanalysis required at this point). The "censor" in the Freudian sense is removed, Molly's night-thoughts differing from those versified in Mr. Young's once ubiquitous poem[4] are unfolded, she says ultimately that her body is a flower; her last word is affirmative. The manners of the genteel society she inhabits have failed to get under her crust, she exists presumably in Patagonia as she exists in Jersey City or Camden.

And the book is banned in America, where every child of seven has ample opportunity to drink in the details of the Arbuckle case,[5] or two hundred other equodorous affairs from the 270,000,000 copies of the 300,000 daily papers which enlighten us. One returns to the Goncourt's question, "Ought the people to remain under a literary edict? Are there classes unworthy, misfortunes too low, dramas too ill set, catastrophies, horrors too devoid of nobility? Now that the novel is augmented, now that it is the great literary form ... the social inquest, for psychological research and analysis, demanding the studies and imposing on its creator the duties of science ... seeking the facts ... whether or no the novelist is to write with the accuracy, and thence with the freedom of the savant, the historian, the physician?"

Whether the only class in America that tries to think is to be hindered by a few cranks, who cannot, and dare not interfere with the leg shows on Broadway? Is any one, for the sake of two or three words which every small boy has seen written on the walls of a privy, going to wade through two hundred pages on consubstantiation or the biographic bearing of Hamlet? And ought an epoch-making report on the state of the human mind in the twentieth century (first of the new era) be falsified by the omission of these half dozen words, or by a pretended ignorance of extremely simple acts. Bloom's day is uncensored, very well. The foecal analysis, in the hospital around the corner, is uncensored. No one but a Presbyterian would contest the utility of the latter exactitude. *A great literary masterwork is made for minds quite as serious as those engaged in the science of medicine.* The anthropologist and sociologist have a right to equally accurate documents, to equally succinct reports and generalizations, which they seldom get, considering the complexity of the matter in hand, and the idiocy of current superstitions.

A Fabian milk report is of less use to a legislator than the knowledge contained in L'Education Sentimentale, or in Bovary. The legislator is supposed to manage human affairs, to arrange for comity of human agglomerations. *Le beau monde gouverne*—or did once—because it had access to condensed knowledge, the middle ages were ruled by those who could read, an aristocracy received Macchiavelli's treatise before the serfs. A very limited plutocracy now gets the news, of which a fraction (not likely to throw too much light upon proximate markets) is later printed in newspapers. Jefferson was perhaps the last American official to have any general sense of civilization. Molly Bloom judges Griffith derisively by "the sincerity of his trousers,"[6] and the Paris edition of the Tribune tells us that the tailors' congress has declared Pres. Harding to be our best dressed Chief Magistrate.

Be it far from me to depreciate the advantages of having a president who can meet on equal trouserial terms such sartorial paragons as Mr. Balfour and Lord (late Mr.) Lee of Fareham (and Checquers) but be it equidistant also from me to disparage the public utility of accurate language which can be attained only from literature, and which the succinct J. Caesar, or the lucid Macchiavelli, or the author of the Code Napoléon, or Thos. Jefferson, to cite a local example, would have in no ways despised. Of course it is too soon to know whether our present ruler[7] takes an interest in these matters; we know only that the late pseudo-intellectual Wilson did not, and that the late bombastic Teddy did not, and Taft, McKinley, Cleveland, did not, and that, as far back as memory serves us no American president has ever uttered one solitary word implying the slightest interest in, or consciousness of, the need for an intellectual or literary vitality in America. A sense of style could have saved America and Europe from Wilson; it would have been useful to our diplomats. The *mot juste* is of public utility. I can't help it. I am not offering this fact as a sop to aesthetes who want all authors to be fundamentally useless. We are governed by words, the laws are graven in words, and literature is the sole means of keeping these words living and accurate. The specimen of fungus given in my February letter shows what happens to language when it gets into the hands of illiterate specialists.

Ulysses furnishes matter for a symposium rather than for a single letter, essay, or review.

Explanatory Notes

POEMS

TO THE RAPHAELITE LATINISTS

First published in *Book News Monthly* in January 1908, while Pound was an instructor at Wabash College in Crawfordsville, Indiana, the poem illustrates Pound's early application of classical myth and allusion through artificial, slightly archaic language. Pound used the pseudonym "Weston Llewmys" for several of his earliest publications, including two prose statements on beauty in *A Quinzaine for This Yule* (London, 1908). In the first statement, introducing the volume, he declares that "beauty should never be presented explained," believing it is "Marvel and Wonder." The second, following his lyric "Fortunatus," celebrates the "current of strange happiness" similar to the winds Dante "beheld whirling the passion-pale shapes in the nether gloom."

CINO

Published in 1908, the title refers to a fictitious troubadour of fourteenth-century Provence, Cino Polnesi, but may be linked to the Italian poet, jurist, and friend of Dante's, Cino da Pistoia (1270–1337). Dante included him, with Arnaut Daniel and Bertran de Born, as preeminent love poets in *De Vulgari Eloquentia*. In *The Spirit of Romance* (1910), Pound credits Cino, along with Cavalcanti and Dante, with bringing the "Italian canzone form to perfection" (*SR*, 109).

Written in 1907 while at Wabash College, the poem appeared in Pound's first printed book, the self-published *A Lume Spento* (150 copies), which he had printed in Venice in July 1908. The subtitle refers to Cino's exile from Pistoia in 1307. In an October 1908 letter to William Carlos Williams, Pound characterizes the poem as "banal. He [Cino] might be anyone. Besides he is catalogued in his epitaph" (*SL*, 6). A possible source is Arthur Symon's "Wanderer's Song" (1899), which Pound had read and admired in America (see *LE*, 367). T. S. Eliot, in his earliest essay on Pound ("Ezra Pound, His Metric and Poetry"), cites "Cino" as one of the poems showing Browning's influence. Cino also appears in Browning's *Sordello*, which was an early influence on Pound (see *SR*, 132).

1. **Wind-runeing:** Pound's attempt at an Old English kenning.
2. **Luth:** Old French, "lute."
3. **Peste!:** Italian, "plague" or "pestilence."
4. **Sinistro:** Sinister or left-handed.
5. **'Pollo Phoibee:** Phoebus Apollo, designating the sun.
6. **aegis-day:** Shield day.
7. **boss:** Convex projection at the center of the shield.
8. **rast-way:** Path.

NA AUDIART

Written at Wabash College and published in *A Lume Spento* (1908). The poem was inspired by the fifth stanza of Bertran de Born's *"Dompna Pois de Me No'us Cal,"* which Pound would translate in 1914 (see *Personae*, 1990:107-8). *"Na Audiart"* is Provençal for "Lady Audiart." The title and epigram make up line 1 of stanza 5 of de Born's poem.

1. *Que be-m vols mal:* A slightly altered line from Bertran de Born's poem, which reads "Though thou wished me ill." The line reappears as an epigram at the end of the poem.
2. **Note:** Pound's headnote refers to the Provençal nobleman and poet Bertran de Born (c. 1140–1215). De Born ended his life in a monastery. Dante describes him in the *Inferno*.
3. **"Miels-de-Ben":** In French, rather than Provençal, it is *"Mieux que Bien,"* and means "better than good."
4. **gold:** In illuminated manuscript.
5. **lays:** A short lyric or narrative meant to be sung; Old French, *lai*.
6. **Aultaforte:** Provençal, "Autefort"; French, "Hautefort," the castle of Bertran de Born.
7. **limning:** Embellishing with a bright color or gold, often in illuminated manuscripts.
8. **wry'd:** Twisted.

VILLONAUD FOR THIS YULE

Written in 1907 and published in 1908 in *A Lume Spento,* the poem has its source in François Villon (1431–1463?). A criminal who frequented the demimonde, Villon was sentenced to hang in 1463, but was, instead, banished for ten years. Villon appears in *SR,* chapter VIII; for Pound, he was the example of both the end of medieval writing and the beginning of modern. Pound admired his directness of speech. Dante's vision is real because he saw it, but Villon's "verse is real, because he lived it," writes Pound (*SR,* 178).

Villon's life and testament became the focus of Pound's 1920–21 opera written in Paris, *Le Testament.* A reference to Villon appears in *Mauberley* at 1. 18 of "E. P. Ode." The sources for "Villonaud for This Yule" are two poems by Villon, *"Ballade des dames du Temps Jadis"* and *"Ballade de la Belle Heaumière,"* translations of which appear in Pound's anthology, *Confucius to cummings.* The parentheses in "Villonaud for This Yule" refer to events surrounding the Nativity but may evoke Villon's mockery of religion, an element Pound noted in Villon's work in *SR,* 168.

1. **gueredon:** Old French, "reward" or "requital."
2. **foison:** Old French, "plentiful" or "powerful."
3. **feat:** Old French, "fitting," "apt."

HISTRION

From *A Quinzane for This Yule* (1908), subtitled "Being selected from a Venetian sketch-book—'San Trovaso,'" published by Pound in London in 1908. The poem first appeared in the *Evening Standard & St. James Gazette,* October 25, 1908. A footnote of Pound's in the typescript reads, "I do not teach—I awake" (*CEP,* 299).

1. **the Florentine:** Dante Alighieri (1265–1321), admired by Pound. See chapter VII, "Dante," *SR.*

IN DURANCE

Written in 1907 but not published until *Personae* (1909), the work is a personal poem disclosing, in a more conversational manner, the desires of the speaker. The poetic decorum of Pound's earlier poems is here relaxed.

REVOLT

From *Personae* (1909). The subtitle, "Against the Crepuscular Spirit in Modern Poetry," suggests an attack against the derivative language of the Pre-Raphaelites and the Decadents, which the poem upholds. "Crepuscular" means pertaining to twilight; dim or obscure.

SESTINA: ALTAFORTE

In "How I Began" (1913), Pound outlines the composition of the poem published in Ford Madox Ford's *English Review* II in June 1909, Pound's first appearance in an English magazine. Comprised of seven stanzas with an epigraph, it is based on a war song by the twelfth-century troubadour Bertran de Born. Pound provides a translation of the song in *SR*, 47–48. The vignettes that make up de Born's poem are each introduced with the phrase *"e platz mi,"* "it pleases me." Pound echoes this repetitive structure, but through the form of the sestina, a form that rotates a set of six six-line stanzas and a three-line envoi, linked by an intricate pattern of repeated line endings. It is the most elaborate of the medieval French fixed forms using only six end words, normally unrhymed. According to Pound, it was invented by Arnaut Daniel (*SR*, 26); Sir Philip Sidney introduced it into English in his *Arcadia* (1590). The sestina offered Pound what he describes in his article "How I Began" as "the curious involution and recurrence" of form. He wrote the first strophe of "Sestina: Altaforte" and then "went to the British Museum to make sure of the right order of the permutations . . . I did the rest of the poem at a sitting."

Pound's first reading of the poem in public, at the Poets' Club at the Tour Eiffel restaurant in Soho on April 22, 1909, was as memorable as it was voluble. Spoons jumped on the table and a screen had to be placed around the gathering so as not to disturb other diners. He also "opened fire" with the poem for his friend, the sculptor Gaudier-Brzeska, commenting that "I think it was the 'Altaforte' that convinced him that I would do to be sculpted" (*GB*, 43).

1. **Loquitur:** Latin, "he speaks."
2. *En:* Provençal, "Sir" or "Lord."
3. **Dante:** Dante placed Bertran in the Ninth Circle of Hell in *The Inferno* as a "Sower of Discord" for setting Prince Henry against his brother Richard and their father Henry II. Pound translated this passage from Dante in *SR*, 45.

4. **Eccovi!:** Italian, "Here you are."
5. **jongleur:** The troubadour's singer, Papiols.
6. **destriers:** War horses trained to rear up before the enemy.

PIERE VIDAL OLD

Appearing first in *Exultations* (1909), the poem is based on the life of the Provençal troubadour Piere Vidal (1175-1215), who supposedly sang better than any man in the world (*LE*, 95). Pound also translated Vidal's "Song of Breath," *SR*, 49. "Piere Vidal Old" is a persona, not a translation; however, it is based on an incident in Vidal's life (which Pound records in his epigraph) that he located in an early Provençal biography of the poet. The story is apocryphal.

1. **guerdon:** "Reward" (see "Villonaud," note 1).

BALLAD OF THE GOODLY FERE

From *Exultations* (1909), the poem appears to have been written in April 1909, according to a letter to Pound's father, and appeared in both book form and in *The English Review* in October 1909. In "How I Began," Pound describes how he wrote the poem one afternoon at the British Museum reading room, provoked by "a certain sort of irreverence that was new to me." He also realized that it was the first poem he had written that "everyone could understand." Yeats would celebrate it in a speech in 1914 as a work of permanent value, although Eliot excluded it from Pound's *Selected Poems* (1928) "because it has a much greater popularity than it deserves" (*SP.*, 21).

1. **Simon Zelotes:** The apostle.

"BLANDULA, TENULLA, VAGULA"

First published in *Canzoni* (1911), the title refers to the dying words of the emperor Hadrian, suggesting the wandering, tenuous soul. Pound includes his own adaptation of the first line of the Latin—*"Animula vagula blandula"*—at the end of his obituary on Rémy de Gourmont (*SP,* 393) and will repeat the *"vagula, tenulla"* phrase in Canto CV of *The Cantos*.

1. **Sirmio:** Latin name for Sirmione, a promontory on the southern shore of Lago di Garda, in northern Italy, where Catullus had a

villa. Sirmione was favored by Pound, who first visited in March 1910. He returned many times and met Joyce for the first time there in 1920.

2. **triune:** Three in one.
3. **Riva:** A town to the north of Lago di Garda.

UND DRANG

Pound's first long poem appeared in *Canzoni* (1911); it is also his first to employ sequence as a formal device, a technique that he will extend in *Homage to Sextus Propertius* and *Hugh Selwyn Mauberley*. The work anticipates in its structure and subject Pound's later efforts to define the role of the poet and the place of poetry in the modern world. Pound never republished the first six sections of the poem after their appearance in the American edition of *Lustra* (1917), only the last six (sections seven through twelve), although without section numbers to indicate that they were part of a sequence (see *Personae*, 47–52). In the poem, the ironic, casual, and urbane confront visionary affirmation undercut by world-weary despair through the juxtaposition of moods and the shadow of detachment.

1. **Binyon:** Laurence Binyon (1869–1943), writer, art expert, poet, translator of Dante, and keeper of prints and drawings at the British Museum. In 1908, he published *Paintings in the Far East* in four volumes. In the 1930s he became a friend of Pound's, who was then translating *The Divine Comedy*. It was Binyon who advised Yeats that "slowness is beauty" (Canto LXXXVII). Binyon variously appears in *The Cantos*.
2. **Aengus:** Pound borrows the figure of the wanderer from Yeats's "Song of the Wandering Aengus," in *The Wind Among the Reeds*.
3. **"Far buon tempo e trionfare":** "To have fine weather and triumph."
   "I have . . . mind": Swinburne, "The Triumph of Time," l. 49.
4. **Oisin:** Pound alludes to Yeats's "The Wanderings of Oisin" (1889) and the idea that man is independent of time and space.
5. **beryl:** A hard mineral occurring in green, bluish green, yellow, pink, or white hexagonal prisms.
6. **chrysoprase:** An apple green translucent quartz valued as a gem.
7. **Benacus:** Lago di Garda in northern Italy, where Pound spent the spring of 1910 working on his translations of Cavalcanti. Via its association with Catullus and the Renaissance Latin poet Pound most admired, Marc Antony Flaminius, Lago di Garda was a sacred

space for Pound. It became a recurrent setting in *The Cantos,* especially the Pisan sequence, and was where Pound first met Joyce.

8. **HORAE BEATAE INSCRIPTIO:** Inscription for an "Hour of Happiness."

9. **Sir Roger de Coverley:** Imaginary country gentleman created by the eighteenth-century English prose writer Joseph Addison.

10. **sic crescit gloria mundi:** "Thus the glory of the world increases," an ironic adaptation of the Latin motto *"Sic transit gloria mundis"* ("So the glory of the world fades").

11. **aegrum vulgus:** Diseased rabble.

12. **cari laresque, penates:** Dear family and household gods.

REDONDILLAS, OR SOMETHING OF THAT SORT

Originally to be set in page proof for *Canzoni* (1911) as "Locksley Hall, forty years further," this poem of 114 lines mirrors Tennyson's "Locksley Hall, Sixty Years After." In it, Pound imitates the meter and material of Tennyson with acknowledgment to Byron and Whitman. A *redondilla* is a Spanish verse form, an octo-syllabic quatrain with a rhyme scheme of *abba.* Pound found the poem, his first attempt at creating poetry out of history while offering his own opinions of the world, too serious when he reviewed page proof of *Canzoni* and, after attempting to rewrite it, withdrew it. The volume without the poem appeared in July 1911. Pound gave the poem to a friend and it was acquired by the Ransom Humanities Research Center at the University of Texas at Austin in 1958.

The poem first appeared in 1967 in *Poetry Australia* (XV) and then in a separate edition of 110 copies signed by Pound and printed by Robert Grabhorn and Andrew Hoyem. This edition contains Pound's "Notes on the Proper Names in the Redondillas." The title echoes a passage in *The Spirit of Romance* where, after Pound quotes and translates four lines from Lope de Vega, he writes, "those lines are at the beginning of some careless redondillas, presenting the thoughts he takes with him journeying" (*SR,* 208). Below is Pound's "Notes on the Proper Names in the Redondillas":

Yeats (W. B.), specialist in the renaissances.

   T. Roosevelt (Theodore), president of one of the American republics early in the twentieth century. Not to be confused with Theodoric, *Gothorum imperator.*

   Plarr (V.G.), of the Rhymers' Club.

Vance, an American Painter, chief works: "Christ appearing on the Waters" (Salon, Paris '03) and the new bar-room in San Diego.

Whiteside, an American landscape painter.

Bergson, French postpragmatical philosopher.

Klimt of Vienna and Zwintscher of Leipzig. Two too modern painters.

Spinoza, the particular passages I had in mind run as follows: "The more perfection a thing possesses the more it acts, and the less it suffers, and conversely the more it acts, the more perfect it is."—*On the power of the intellect or human liberty,* Proposition, xi. "When the mind contemplates itself and its power of acting, it rejoices, and it rejoices in proportion to the distinctness with which it imagines itself and its power of action."—*Origin and nature of the affects,* xiii.

And another passage for which I cannot at the moment give the exact references, where he defines "the intellectual love of anything" as "the understanding of its perfections."

1. **Garda:** Lago di Garda in northern Italy, where Pound visited often and the location of Catullus's villa.
2. **Desenzano:** A town on Lago di Garda.
3. **"*Mi Platz*":** "It pleases me," an allusion to one of Bertran de Born's war songs.
4. **Plarr:** Victor Plarr (1863–1929), Librarian of the Royal College of Surgeons, London, and author of an 1896 collection of poems, *In the Dorian Mood*.
5. **Nietzsche:** Friedrich Nietzsche (1844–1900), German philosopher trained as a classical philologist, author of *The Birth of Tragedy, Beyond Good and Evil, The Genealogy of Morals, Thus Spake Zarathustra,* and other works.
6. **risorgimenti:** Revival or renaissance.
7. **Paul Verlaine:** French poet (1844–1896) who appears at the end of Canto LXXIV.
8. **rôti de dindon:** Roast turkey.
9. **Tamlin:** *Tam Lin,* a Scottish fairy ballad.
10. **Arma . . . ab oris:** Parallel to the opening line of Virgil's *Aeneid*.
11. **Nascitur ordo:** "Order is born."
12. **Ehrlich:** Paul Ehrlich (1854–1915), German bacteriologist who

won the Nobel Prize for physiology/medicine in 1908 for his work on immunology.

13. **Fracastori ... "De Morbo":** Possibly "De Morbo Gallico," a study of syphilis.

14. *Admiror, sum ergo:* "I admire, therefore I am."

15. **Schopenhauer:** Arthur Schopenhauer (1788–1860), German philosopher who emphasized pessimism.

16. **Lucretius:** C. 95–55 B.C.E. Roman poet and Epicurean philosopher.

17. **tornata:** A return, although in Provençal it is similar to an envoi.

18. **saeculum in parvo:** "Century in miniature."

19. **Steibelt:** Daniel Steibelt (1765–1823), German composer and pianist.

TO WHISTLER, AMERICAN

The poem first appeared in *Poetry* (October 1912), and was reprinted in the 1949 edition of *Personae: The Collected Poems of Ezra Pound.* The occasion for writing the poem was an exhibition of Whistler's paintings at the Tate Gallery in September 1912. Pound early admired Whistler, who in his move to Europe anticipated Pound's own expatriate act. To Harriet Monroe at *Poetry,* Pound wrote that he counted Whistler as "our only great artist" and that his "informal salute," his poem, might not be out of place at "the threshold of what I hope is an endeavor to carry into our American poetry the same sort of life and intensity which he [Whistler] infused into modern painting" (*SL,* 10). In his critique of America, *Patria Mia* (1912; reprint, Chicago: R. Seymour, 1950), Pound cites Whistler with Henry James as the only two great artists from the United States (47). He elaborates his comments on Whistler on pp. 50–51, 64 of the work.

PORTRAIT D'UNE FEMME

Pound sent the poem to the *North American Review* in January 1912, where it was rejected on the grounds that he had used the letter *r* three times in the first line and that it was difficult to pronounce. Pound understood this reasoning as proof of the compliance of American editors to fixed formulas of literary success (see *Patria Mia*). It appeared in *Smart Set* for November 1913, reprinted from *Ripostes* (1912). Eliot has a poem with a similar title, "Portrait of a Lady," in *Prufrock and Other Observations* (1917).

1. **Sargasso Sea:** This sea lies between the Azores, the Canaries, and the Cape Verde Islands in the North Atlantic.

N.Y.

First published in *Ripostes* (London, 1912) and reprinted in *Smart Set* the following year, the poem marks Pound's disappointment upon his return to America in June 1910 and time spent unproductively in New York. He departed for Europe in February 1911. The version of the poem that appears in *Umbra* (London: Mathews, 1920) includes the note "Madison Ave. 1910."

THE SEAFARER

Published in the *New Age* (November 30, 1911), as the opening example in a series of twelve articles entitled "I Gather the Limbs of Osiris," the poem is Pound's rendering, rather than translation of the well-known Anglo-Saxon poem. Reprinted in *Ripostes* (1912). Pound freely treated the original text, omitting the fourth, moralizing section of the extant poem and excluding the Christian references in the text of the poem he does present. He freely renders "englum" as "English" rather than "angels." The poem, some argued, had been "edited" by Pound into a kind of hedonism by excluding the Christian and the moral. Asked in 1912 how much of the poem was his and how much was the original, he replied, "As nearly literal, I think, as any translation can be" (*SP*, 39).

Pound saw a connection between the theme of "The Seafarer" and the outsider, the wanderer, and the "Exile's Letter" by Li Po, which would appear in his next volume, *Cathay* (1915). Indeed, he believed that there was no eighth-century poem equal to "Exile's Letter" except "The Seafarer," which displays "the West on a par with the Orient" (*ABC*, 51). Some felt, however, that Pound was ignorant of Anglo-Saxon and mistranslated a great deal of the original. But Pound follows a homophonic system of translation, one that re-creates the Anglo-Saxon reading tradition through a kind of "phonetic simulacrum" (Michael Alexander, *Earliest English Poems*, 117).

THE RETURN

Meaning expressed by form is part of the intent of "The Return," which first appeared in *The English Review* of June 1912, reprinted in

Ripostes (1912) a few months later. The poem is the equivalent of the Vorticist technique of sculpture represented by Gaudier-Brzeska and Jacob Epstein: planes in relation to each other. Gaudier-Brzeska described this as the arrangement of his emotions "SOLELY FROM THE ARRANGEMENT OF SURFACES. I shall present my emotions by the ARRANGEMENT OF MY SURFACES, THE PLANES AND LINES BY WHICH THEY ARE DEFINED" (*GB,* 28). Impressed, Yeats remarked that the poem seemed as if Pound "were translating at sight from an unknown Greek masterpiece" (*Oxford Book of Modern Verse, 1892–1935* [1935]). He also valued its use of rhythm, remarking that in its free verse structure, it was "the most beautiful poem that has been written in the free form, one of the few in which I find real organic rhythm" (Stock, 191). Pound included the poem in his 1914 anthology, *Des Imagistes.*

FRATRES MINORES

From *BLAST* (vol. 1, June 20, 1914), with the first two and last lines canceled in ink in most copies. The poem indicts the limpidity and failure of nerve among English poets to confront directly the harsh reality of the war and suffering.

THE COMPLETE POETICAL WORKS OF T. E. HULME

Originally appearing at the end of *Ripostes* (1912), these five poems with a "Prefatory Note" satirize the poetic output of the philosopher and aesthetician T. E. Hulme (1883–1917), who helped to organize the Poets' Club, then broke away to form a counter group in 1909, which Pound joined that April. Hulme met Henri Bergson in 1907 and became an important supporter, translating and publishing his *Introduction to Metaphysics* a few years later. Hulme's call for a "visual, concrete" language made an impression on the young Pound. Canto XVI from Pound's *Cantos* refers to Hulme's experiences in World War I.

SALUTATION THE THIRD

An aggressive satire unfavorably attacking reviewers from the *Times* of London, which appeared in *BLAST* (vol. 1, June 20, 1914).

SONG OF THE BOWMEN OF SHU

Appearing first in *Cathay* (1915), a set of poems drawn from Pound's work with the notebooks of Ernest Fenollosa (1853–1908), American scholar of the Far East. In London, in 1913, Fenollosa's widow presented Pound with sixteen notebooks and other manuscripts belonging to her husband. The notebooks contained the Chinese characters for the original poems, followed by Japanese pronunciations and rough translations. Pound chose Japanese names for the Chinese poets. The 1915 edition of *Cathay* contained eleven poems, including Pound's translation of "The Seafarer," to show the similarity of T'ang Dynasty and Anglo-Saxon views of exile. When the volume appeared as a section of *Lustra*, Pound added five more poems and dropped "The Seafarer," which appeared elsewhere in the collection.

1. **fern-shoots:** Gaudier-Brzeska, who sent this poem and two others while at the Front, wrote to Pound that "the poems depict our situation in a wonderful way. We do not yet eat the young nor old fernshoots but we cannot be over-victualled where we stand" (*GB*, 58).
2. **Ken-nin:** Chinese, *Hsien-yün* (the Huns).
3. **sorrow:** Gaudier-Brzeska wrote to John Cournos in December 1914, "when you have turned to a warrior you become hardened to many evils . . . like the Chinese bowmen in Ezra's poem we had rather at fern shoots than go back now" (in Kenner, 203).
4. **Bunno:** Wen-Wang, that is, King Wen of the Chou Dynasty. Supposedly, Wen, the commander in chief of the western provinces dispatched against the Huns, composed the poem in the persona of a common soldier to show his sympathy.

THE RIVER SONG

A translation of two separate poems by Li Po. Likely confused by the pagination in Fenollosa's notebook, Pound conflated the two poems into one. The translation of the title in Chinese is actually "Chanting on the river."

1. **shato-wood:** Chinese, *Sha-t'ang*, spice wood.
2. **Sennin:** Described by Pound as "the Chinese spirits of nature or of the air" (*SL*, 180).
3. **Kutsu:** Chinese, Chū Yüan.
4. **King So:** Chinese, King Ch'u.

5. **Han:** The Han River, which flows from northeast-central China into the Yangtze at Hankow.
6. **And I have moped:** Here Pound dissolves the title of a second poem by Li Po into the continuous text of a single poem. This was Pound's infamous mistake in *Cathay,* possibly traced to his confusing a blank, left-hand page in the Fenollosa notebook with the absence of comment rather than the beginning of a new poem.
7. **"Kwan, Kuan":** Onomatopoetic bird call.
8. **Ko:** Chinese capital Hao, capital of the kings Wen and Wu of the Chou Dynasty.
9. **Jo-run:** The Shang-lin Park, famous for its court life.

THE RIVER-MERCHANT'S WIFE: A LETTER

First published in *Cathay* (1915), the poem in Chinese translates as "The Song of Ch'ang-kan." In a 1918 essay, "Chinese Poetry—II," Pound suggests that this eighth-century poem could easily "have slipped into Browning's work without causing any surprise save by its simplicity and its naive beauty." George Steiner in *After Babel* praises the closeness of Pound's version to Li Po's original, communicating "precisely the nuance of ceremonious innocence" (358).

1. **Ku-to-yen:** An islet called Yen-yū-tui; original allusion is to a song on the dangers of sailing by the Yen Yū rocks in the Chū-t'ang River.
2. **Kiang:** *Chiang,* but generally the word for river itself.
3. **Cho-fu-Sa:** A beach several hundred miles upriver from Nanking.

EXILE'S LETTER

First published in *Poetry* in March 1915 with a note that partly read "from the Chinese of Rihaku (Li Po), usually considered the greatest poet of China: written by him while in exile about 760 a.d." The Chinese title translates as "Remembering our Excursion in the Past: A Letter sent to Commissary Yen of Ch'ao County." Pound favored this poem, reprinting it in *Cathay* (see *SL,* 64). In *Umbra* (1920), Pound cited "Exile's Letter" with "The Seafarer" and "Homage to Sextus Propertius" as his major works. In the first edition of *Cathay,* "Exile's Letter" immediately preceded "The Seafarer" to emphasize their contemporaneity.

TENZONE

This poem first appeared in *Poetry* in April 1913, in a series titled "Contemporania," which also included "The Garden," "Dance Figure," "Pax Saturni," "A Pact," and the first version of "In a Station of the Metro." It was reprinted in *Lustra* (1916).

1. **Tenzone:** Italian for debate or dialogue.
2. **centaur:** Mythological beast with the head, body, and arms of a man and the body and legs of a horse. In "The Serious Artist" (1913), Pound wrote that "poetry is a centaur. The thinking word arranging, clarifying faculty must move and leap with the energizing sentiment, musical faculties. It is precisely the difficulty of this amphibious existence that keeps down the census record of good poets" (*LE*, 52).

THE GARDEN

Part of the "Contemporania" series in *Poetry*, April 1913, reprinted in *Lustra* (1916). Richard Aldington parodied the poem; the first line was in turn reused by Pound in "1915: February." Aldington begins, "Like an armful of greasy engineer's-cotton/Flung by a typhoon against a broken crate of ducks' eggs/She stands by the rail of the Old Bailey dock" (*Egoist*, January 15, 1914).

1. *En robe de parade:* From the opening of Albert Samain's *Au Jardin de l'Infante* (1893): "*Mon ame est un infante en robe de parade.*"

1915: FEBRUARY

Written in 1915 during the war, the poem appeared for the first time in 2003 in Pound, *Poems and Translations,* edited by Richard Sieburth (2003), 1176–77. Offsetting the realistic depiction of war is myth, as the narrator places both the "smeared" engineer and the artist on the margin as "outlaws."

1. **Grettir:** "Grettis Saga," an Icelandic outlaw saga from about 1320 about Grettir the Strong, who kills a man at fourteen and is banished for three years to Norway where he does good deeds. On his return, he battles the ghost of Glam the Shepherd, who ravages the countryside terrorizing people. But Grettir is again outlawed for accidentally causing a fire that kills the son of a chieftain. He is himself killed by bounty hunters and the ghosts of those he has earlier murdered.

2. **Skarpheddin:** Variously Skarphedinn or Skarp-Hedin, the oldest son of Njáil in "Njáls Saga" (also known as "The Story of Burnt Njál"), an epic Icelandic prose narrative from about 1289. The poem tells of a multigenerational feud in Iceland about A.D. 950 to 1015. At its core is the tragedy of the farmer and sage Njál, who with his family is burned alive in his home by a confederacy of enemies. Graphic violence and magic accompany the tragedy.

3. **Grendel:** The demon fiend who haunts the countryside in *Beowulf,* at one point snatching thirty men from Herot, the mead hall of Hrothgar, the king of Danes. Beowulf arrives with fellow Geats to help, and engages Grendel in a bloody battle in which he wrenches away Grendel's arm, proudly hanging it from the rafter of Herot. Grendel's mother comes to seek revenge and Beowulf battles her underwater.

4. *dies irae:* Latin, "day of wrath;" opening words of the first verse of a medieval Latin hymn sung at Requiem masses.

COMMISSION

Published first in the "Contemporania" series in *Poetry,* April 1913, reprinted in *Lustra,* first edition (1916), but omitted from the trade edition published the following month because the publisher, Elkin Mathews, objected. The indebtedness and echo of Whitman is apparent.

A PACT

Another work from the "Contemporania" series in *Poetry,* April 1913; reprinted in *Lustra* (1916). In the first published version of the poem, Pound had "truce" for "pact" in line 1.

1. **Walt Whitman:** Whitman (1819–1892), American bardic poet, author of *Leaves of Grass.* See Pound's essay, "What I Feel about Walt Whitman" (1909), where, after criticizing the poet, he writes, "The vital part of my message, taken from the sap and fibre of America, is the same as his." Pound also refers to Whitman as his "spiritual father." In *Patria Mia,* Pound wrote that Whitman "was not an artist but a reflex, the first honest reflex, in an age of papier-maché letters" (24).

FURTHER INSTRUCTIONS

Originally printed in *Poetry,* November 1913; reprinted in *Lustra* 1916.

1. **Santa Maria Novella:** A Dominican convent in Florence.

A SONG OF THE DEGREES

Originally sections III–V in a series of seven poems published in *Poetry,* November 1913, under the title of "Xenia," Latin for "a gift to friends." Derived from a collection of mottoes with the same title by Martial, the Roman poet; reprinted in *Lustra* (1916). Aldington parodied Pound's poem, beginning, "Rest me with mushrooms, / For I think the steak is evil."

1. **A Song of the Degrees:** Psalms 120–34 are subtitled "A Song of Degrees."

ITÉ

Published first in *Poetry* III (November 1913); reprinted in *Lustra* (1916).

1. **Ité:** Latin for "go."
2. **Sophoclean light:** Pound told Harriet Monroe, editor of *Poetry,* in January 1915, that he wished for "a bit more Sophoclean severity" to counteract the current preference for "looseness, lack of rhythmical construction and intensity" (*SL,* 50).

LIU CH'E

First published in Pound's Imagist anthology, *Des Imagistes* (1914) and reprinted in *Lustra* (1916), the poem may have derived from H. A. Giles, *A History of Chinese Literature* (1901). Giles begins his version with

The sound of rustling silk is stilled,
With the dust the marble courtyard filled,
No footfalls echo on the floor[.]

1. **Liu Ch'e:** Also Wu-ti (157–87 B.C.E.), author of the original. In 140 B.C.E., he became the sixth emperor of the Han Dynasty.

THE COMING OF WAR: ACTÆON

Published in *Poetry*, March 1915; reprinted in *Lustra* (1916). In book III of the *Metamorphosis*, Ovid tells how Actæon was changed into a stag by the goddess Artemis (Diana) and torn to pieces by his own hounds because he had seen her bathing. Pound also incorporates the story in Canto IV and mentions Actæon in Canto LX.

1. **Lethe:** River over which dead souls pass to Hades. Also the river of forgetfulness.
2. **greaves!:** Armor to cover the shins.

IN A STATION OF THE METRO

There are two versions of the poem, which differ in spacing and punctuation. The first version appeared in *Poetry*, April 1913, as part of the "Contemporania" series. The second version appears in *Lustra* (1916). Pound provides an account of the composition of the poem in "How I Began" (1913) and in his essay "Vorticism," reprinted in *Gaudier-Brzeska* (1916). He writes, in part, that "in a poem of this sort one is trying to record the precise instant when a thing outward and objective transforms itself, or darts into a thing inward and subjective" (*GB*, 89). On the importance of the spacing of the rhythmic units in the early printings of the poem—in *Poetry* and the *New Freewoman* (August 1913)—see *SL*, 17. The poem first appeared in its revised form in *Lustra* (1916). Aldington's parody of the work reads:

> The apparition   of these poems   in a crowd:
> White faces   in a black   dead faint.
> (*Egoist*, January 15, 1914).

THE ENCOUNTER

Originally poem IX of "Zena," in *Smart Set* for December 1913; reprinted in *Lustra* (1916).

L'ART, 1910

Originally in *BLAST* (I, June 1914); reprinted in *Lustra* (1916).

ANCIENT MUSIC

First published in *BLAST* (II, July 1915); reprinted in the first American edition of *Lustra* (1917). The reference is to the essayist and scholar William P. Ker (1855–1923), who, according to Pound, "put an end to much babble about folk song by showing us *Summer is ycummen in* [is] written beneath the Latin words of the first known example of a canon" (*Poetry,* January 1914).

PROVINCIA DESERTA

Published originally in *Poetry* (V, March 1915) and reprinted in *Lustra* (1916); the title refers to C. M. Doughty's *Travels in Arabia Deserta* (1888). The place-names in the poem are sites Pound visited during his walking tour through southern France in the summer of 1912. Rochecouart, Chalais, Montagnac, and Hautefort are all associated with Bertran de Born. Mareuil was the home of the troubadour Arnaut de Mareuil; Ribyrac, the home of Arnaut Daniel. Chalus is where Richard Coeur de Lion was killed. Excideuil was the birthplace of the troubadour Giraut de Borneil.

VILLANELLE: THE PSYCHOLOGICAL HOUR

Appeared first in *Poetry* (VII, December 1915); reprinted in *Lustra* (1916). A villanelle is a sixteenth-century French form composed of an uneven number (usually five) of tercets rhyming *aba,* with the final quatrain rhyming *abaa*. The first and third lines of the opening tercet are repeated alternately as the third lines of the succeeding tercets and together as the final couplet of the quatrain. The form was originally used for pastoral songs. The best-known villanelle in English is Dylan Thomas's "Do Not Go Gentle into That Good Night" (1952).

NEAR PERIGORD

Published in *Poetry* in December 1915 and then *Lustra* (1916). Pound's notes to the poem accompany its appearance in *Poetry,* along with a translation of Bertran de Born's "Dompna puois de mi no'us cal," a work that long intrigued Pound. Pound glosses this poem in his epigraph to "Na Audiart" and in *The Spirit of Romance*. The poem by Bertran sees the poet seeking consolation for being rejected by his lady Maente of Montaignace, by constructing an ideal Lady composed of the qualities of the outstanding women of Provence. In his *Poetry* note,

Pound wrote that of the "possibility of a political intrigue behind the apparent love poem we have no evidence save that offered by my own observation of the geography of Perigord and Limoges" (*Poetry*, December 1915, 145-46). Perigord is the Provençal town of Périgueux, the center of the counts of Périgord.

In the poem Pound imagines that Bertran de Born, enemy of the Count of Périgord and his brother-in-law Tairiran, who holds the castle of Montaignac, addresses a song (the "Dompna puois") to Maent, chatelaine of Montaignac. In this song, Bertran says he will make a "borrowed lady" from the finest qualities of all the region's women. A series of question then fashions Pound's poem, such as whether or not Bertran was in love with Maent. Answers remain open as Pound imagines a discussion between Arnaut Daniel and Richard Coeur de Lion, followed by a love scene on the banks of the Auvézère river, which runs near Bertran's castle. What is the nature of Bertran's intrigues? That remains unanswered in Pound's work, which explores the link between love and politics, showing how Bertran used poetry to subvert the power of his enemies through praise of the women he admired.

1. *A Perigord . . . ab malh:* The opening lines of a poem by Bertran de Born, which Pound translates in *The Spirit of Romance* as "At Perigord near to the wall, / Aye, within a mace throw of it" (*SR*, 45).

2. **Cino:** Pound's adopted persona in the poem may be suggested by Cino da Pistoia (cf. "Cino"), grouped by Dante with Bertran de Born and other poets in *De Vulgari Eloquentia*, book II.

3. **Uc St. Circ:** Uc de Saint Circ, a Provençal troubadour and possibly biographer of Bertran de Born. Pound cites him in *The Spirit of Romance* (*SR*, 41).

4. **En:** "Lord" or "Sir" in Provençal.

5. **canzone:** Bertran's "Dompna Soissenbuda" ("Borrowed Lady"), which Pound proceeds to summarize.

6. **Maent:** The Lady Maent of Montaignac, whom Bertran addresses in his poem.

7. **Montfort:** The Lady Elis (or Alice) of Monfort, sister of Maent.

8. **Bel Miral:** "Fair Mirror," an unidentified lady.

9. **Tairiran:** Maent's husband, Guillem Talairan.

10. **Altafort:** Bertran de Born's castle. In French, "Hautefort."

11. **Dante:** Dante set Bertran with the "Sowers of Discord" in the Ninth Circle of Hell for causing Prince Henry to rebel against his brother Richard Coeur de Lion and their father, King Henry II (*Inferno*, XXVIII).

12. **"counterpass"**: Dante's "contrapasso" (*Inferno*, XXVIII, 1.142), glossed by Pound as "the laws of eternal justice" (*SR*, 127). Bertran's punishment, a severed head, is matched to his supposed crime.

13. **Foix**: In the foothills of the Pyrenees, at the junction of the rivers Arget and Ariège.

14. ***"Et albirar ab lor bordon"***: Pound translates this as "And sing not all they have in mind" in a song translated from "the sardonic Count of Foix" (*LE*, 100–101).

15. **heaumes**: Helmets or crests.

16. **Aubeterre**: East of Hautefort.

17. **Ventadour**: Ventadorn northeast of Hautefort, the home of Lady Maria Maent's sister.

18. ***trobar clus* with Daniel**: Intricate verse form concealing hermetic meaning of Provençal poetry used often by Arnaut Daniel.

19. **dies**: Richard was hit by an arrow in the shoulder while attacking Châlus and died of the wound on April 6, 1199.

20. ***life's counterpart***: From Dante's *Inferno*, XXVIII, ll. 118–23, 139–42.

21. ***Ed eran***: Pound translates these lines from Dante as "and they we two in one and one in two" in *The Spirit of Romance* (*SR*, 45).

22. **Auvezere**: River near Hautefort.

23. **day's eyes**: Daisies.

24. **émail**: Enamel.

L'HOMME MOYEN SENSUEL

First appeared in the *Little Review* (IV, September 1917); reprinted in *Pavannes and Divisions* (1918). The title, "The Average Sensual Man," originated with Matthew Arnold in his essay "George Sand," in *Mixed Essays* (1879).

1. **"I hate a dumpy woman"**: Byron, *Don Juan* I, lxi.

2. **infant tick . . . *Atlantic***: Ellery Sedgwick (1872–1960), editor of *The Atlantic* from 1908 to 1938.

3. **Comstock's self**: Antony Comstock (1844–1915), founder of the Society for the Suppression of Vice.

4. **A novelist, a publisher and a preacher**: In 1913, President Wilson appointed novelist Thomas Nelson Page and publisher Walter Hinges Page as ambassadors to Italy and Great Britain. The preacher was Henry Van Dyke, a Presbyterian minister and popular author, appointed minister to the Netherlands and Luxembourg from 1913 to 1917.

5. **Mabie ... Woodberry:** Magazine editors and critics Hamilton Mabie, Lyman Abbott, and George Woodberry.

6. **Hiram Maxim:** Pound may be conflating Sir Hiram Maxim, inventor of the machine gun, or his son, the inventor of the silencer, with the critic Hudson Maxim, author of *The Science of Poetry and the Philosophy of Language* (1910).

7. **pantosocracy:** "Equal rule of all," and the name of the unrealized utopian community planned on the Susquehanna River in Pennsylvania. Originated by Robert Southey and S. T. Coleridge.

8. **Dr. Parkhurst:** Reformer and Presbyterian minister, Charles Henry Parkhurst, president of the Society for the Prevention of Crime in New York.

9. **"Prolific Noyes":** Alfred Noyes (1880–1958), who by 1915 had published more than sixteen volumes of poetry.

10. **Gilder ... *De mortuis verum*":** Richard W. Gilder (1844–1909), poet and editor of *The Century* from 1881 until his death. *De mortuis verum*: "the dead speak truthfully."

11. **"Message to Garcia":** A popular inspirational essay of 1899 by Elbert Hubbert recounting the heroism of an American lieutenant during the Spanish-American War.
    Mosher: Thomas Bird Mosher (1852–1933), publisher and editor of the *Bibelot*, known for publishing pirated books. He refused to publish Pound's *A Lume Spento*.

12. **De Gourmont:** Rémy de Gourmont (1858–1915), French author admired by Pound and one of the founders of the *Mercure de France*. In the *New Age* for July 26, 1917, Pound quoted Gourmont on the decline of contemporary language: "Fifty grunts and as many representative signs will serve all needful communication." In his essay on Gourmont, Pound writes that he was "an artist of the nude. He was an intelligence almost more than an artist," concerned only with "the permanent human elements." Gourmont, he adds, "arouses the sense of the imagination, preparing the mind for receptiveness" (*LE*, 340, 345). Pound's translation of Gourmont's "*Physique de l'amour; essai sur l'instinct sexuel*" (1903) appeared as "*The Natural Philosophy of Love*" in 1922.

13. **Rodyheaver's:** Homer Rodeheaver (1880–1955), evangelist. Beginning in 1913, he made several recordings of revival hymns and temperance songs.

HOMAGE TO SEXTUS PROPERTIUS

First appeared as "Poems from Propertius Series" in *Poetry* (XIII, March 1919) and subsequently in six parts in *The New Age* (June–August 1919). Published in book form in *Quia Pauper Amavi* (1919). Its first separate printing was in 1934. Pound referred to the poem as a "major persona," or mask, praising and criticizing the first-century Roman poet Propertius, employing irony, mockery, and humor, which Pound defined as *logopœia*, "the dance of the intellect among words," emphasizing the "ironical play" of language. *Logopœia*, he added "does not translate; though the attitude of mind it expresses may pass through a paraphrase" (*LE*, 25). What he seeks in his translation is "the original author's state of mind" (*LE*, 25).

Homage to Sextus Propertius is alternately satiric and political, drawing parallels between's Pound's critique of Britain in 1917 and Propertius's critique of the Roman Empire. In uncovering and emphasizing the irony in Propertius, Pound frees him from Victorian obfuscation and sentimentalizing. But when four sections of the poem appeared in *Poetry* in March 1919, it aroused the anger of the classicist W. G. Hale, who attacked its numerous errors, declaring Pound ignorant of Latin. Pound replied that he had not done a translation of Propertius but attempted to restore vitality to the poet's work (see *SL*, 149, 229–30). The translation is "creative" and closer to an adaptation. Eliot, in the introduction to Ezra Pound, *Selected Poems* (1928), called it "a paraphrase, or still more truly . . . a *persona*" (SPo, 19).

Pound explained that he used the term "homage" as Debussy did in *"Homage à Rameau,"* a piece of music recalling the manner of Rameau. In 1922, Hardy told Pound that the poem would be clearer retitled as "Propertius Soliloquizes." Later editions added "1917" after the title. Pound based his work on a series of poems from the extant four books of the Roman elegist Sextus Aurelius Propertius (born c. 500 B.C.E.).

1. **Callimachus . . . Philetas:** Callimachus (c. 305–240 B.C.E.) was a Greek elegiac poet from Cyrene, also a grammarian and cataloguer at the Alexandrian Library. He was best known for his poem "Dremas" and various epigrams and love lyrics. Philetas (c. 330–275 B.C.E.) was a Greek poet and grammarian from the island of Cos in the Sporados; his work became a source for Latin love poetry.

2. **We have kept:** The Latin original reads *"Exactus termi pumic versus eat,"* translated literally as "Let the verse glide, polished by the sharp pumice stone."

3. **Simois:** A tributary of the Scamander River, which rises against Achilles in *The Iliad* in book XXI.

4. **Hector:** Son of Priam, king of Troy, and Trojan commander. Killed by Achilles in battle, tied to a chariot by his heels and dragged through the dust (*Iliad,* book XXII).

5. **Polydmantus . . . Deiphoibos:** Polydamas, son of Panthoos, was a Trojan officer and adviser to Hector. Helenus and Deiphoibos were sons of Priam and Hecuba. After the death of Paris in the Trojan War, Helenus pursued Helen, who rejected him in favor of Deiphoibos.

6. **Paris:** Son of Priam. His abduction of Helen, wife of King Menelaus of Sparta, brother of Agamemnon, was the cause of the Trojan War.

7. **Ilion . . . Troad:** The Roman Ilium (Greek, "Ilion," i.e., Troy) was the capital of the district called Troad (Greek, "Troias").

8. **Oetian gods:** Mount Oeta in central Greece was the legendary site of the death of Hercules as a mortal.

9. **Phoebus in Lycia:** Phoebus (Greek, "bright") was a name for Apollo, the god of light, whose cult in Greece probably originated in Lycia, an ancient coastal district of southwest Asia Minor.

10. **devirginated young ladies:** The original Latin, *"Gaudeat in solito tacta puella sono"* ("Let my girl be touched by the sound of a familiar music and rejoice in it"), contradicts Pound's rendering. W. G. Hale found Pound's reading of *"tacta puella"* ("peculiarly unpleasant") without basis in the Latin. Pound apparently read *"tacta"* as the opposite of *"intacta"* ("untouched," "virgin"). This is perhaps the most controversial line in the poem, although recent critics like Hugh Kenner in *The Pound Era* and J. P. Sullivan in *Ezra Pound and Sextus Propertius* support the ambiguous reading of Pound.

11. **Cithaeron shook up the rocks:** In legend, Amphio enchanted the stones from Mount Cithaeron to form the walls of Thebes, the capital of Boeotia.

12. **Polyphemus?:** The cyclops blinded by Odysseus (*Odyssey,* book IX).

13. **Taenarian columns:** Columns made of black marble from Taenarus, Sparta.

14. **Marcian vintage:** Water from the Marcian aqueduct that fed the grottoes, pools, and fountains of wealthy Romans.

15. **Numa Pompilius:** The second king of Rome.

16. **Jove in East Elis:** The sacred precinct at Olympia in Elis (modern Ilia) contained a colossal statue of Zeus (i.e., Jove).

17. **Helicon:** A mountain range in central Greece and the celebrated home of the Muses.

18. **Bellerophon's horse:** Bellerophon slew the Chimaera with the help of the winged horse Pegasus.

19. **father Ennius:** Quintus Ennius (239–169 B.C.E.) was considered to be the father of Latin poetry on the basis of *Annales,* his epic poem on the history of Rome.

20. **Curian brothers . . . Horatian javelin:** The three Curian brothers from Alba Longa fought the three Horatian brothers from Rome. They killed two of the Horace brothers, then were themselves killed by the third, who then set up their javelins at the corner of the basilica in the center of Rome to celebrate the victory.

21. **Q. H. Flaccus:** The Latin poet Horace (Quintus Horatius Flaccus).

22. **battle at Cannae:** Ancient city of Apulia and site of the Roman defeat by Hannibal.

23. **Silenus . . . Tegaean Pan:** Silenus, a satyr in Greek mythology known for his drunkenness, prophetic song, and lechery; Tegaean Pan is the Arcadian and Greek fertility god. Tegea was a town in Arcadia.

24. **Cytherean mother:** Aphrodite, from her association with the Ionian island of Cythera; her chariot was pulled by doves.

25. **Gorgon's lake:** A lake of blood flowing from Medusa's neck when Perseus killed her.

26. **thyrsos:** The thyrsus was the wand, bound with vines or ivy, carried by Dionysus and his followers during orgiastic rites.

27. **Calliope:** Muse of epic poetry, who speaks as if offended by Propertius's desertion.

28. **Suevi:** Germanic forces who crossed the Rhine in 29 B.C.E. but were defeated by the Roman general Gaius Carinas.

29. **Cypris:** Aphrodite, commonly thought to have risen from the sea near Paphos in Cyprus, where she was worshipped as a goddess of fertility.

30. **Lygdamus:** Propertius's slave, who had an affair with Propertius's mistress, Cynthia. Hence the irony of the phrase "constant young lady."

31. **orfevrerie:** An ornament worked in gold.

32. **Pierides!:** The Muses, whose reputed home before Helicon was Pieria on the northern slopes of Mount Olympus.

33. **Ossa . . . Pelion:** Allusion is to the attempt of the twin giants Otus and Ephiates to climb up to heaven by piling Mount Ossa on Olympus and Mount Pelion on Mount Ossa.

34. **Caesarial *ore rotundos*:** "With round mouth." Bombast in the official, public style.

35. **Phrygian fathers:** Asiatic style of the royal family of Troy.

36. **Acheron:** One of the five rivers of Hades.

37. **Marius and Jugurtha together:** Caius Marius (157–86 B.C.E.), seven times consul, captured and put to death Jugurtha, the ruler of Numidia, in 104 B.C.E.

38. **the Cytherean:** Aphrodite, who with Persephone was a rival for the love of Adonis (see note 24).

39. **Endymion:** A handsome shepherd on Mount Latmos loved by the moon goddess Diana, who descended to embrace him every night while he slept.

40. **Juno's Pelasgian temples:** Juno (Greek, Hera) was the female equivalent of Jupiter and the goddess of women. In legend, she was brought up by Temenus, son of Pelasgus in Arcadia. "Pelasgian" denotes all pre-Grecian peoples in the Mediterranean.

41. **Pallas:** Pallas Athene was the patron goddess of Athens and Greek cities in general.

42. **Io . . . Callisto:** Io was turned into a heifer by Zeus and persecuted by the jealous Hera. Ino was the second wife of the king of Themes, Athamus. Driven insane by Hera, she jumped into the sea and was transformed into the sea goddess Leucothea. Andromeda was offered to a sea serpent because her mother, Cassiopeia, had offended the Nereids (sea maidens) by boasting of her beauty. Perseus was the slayer of Medusa, who changed the monster into stone and married Andromeda. Callisto was the mother by Zeus of Arcas, the legendary ancestor of the Arcadians. Hera changed Callisto into a bear, who was almost killed by Arcas when hunting. Zeus intervened and changed Callisto and Arcas into the constellations Ursa Major and Ursa Minor.

43. **Semele:** Consumed by Zeus's lightning in the conception of Dionysus.

44. **beauties of Maeonia:** The beautiful women in Homer whose reputed birthplace was in Maeonia, ancient name of Lydia in Asia Minor.

45. **rhombs:** Noisy rhombus wheel of part IV of the poem.

46. **Avernus:** A lake in Campania, near Naples. The name is used to refer to the underworld, partly because Aeneas descended to the underworld in a nearby cavern.

47. **Persephone and Dis:** Persephone was carried off by Pluto while picking flowers in the meadows of Enna, Sicily. She ruled as queen of the dead for half the year. "Dis" is the Roman corruption of the Greek, "Pluto," also called Hades.

48. **Iope . . . Campania:** Iope is Cassiopeia, wife of Ethiopian king

Cepheas and mother of Andromeda. Propertius may have used the name for metrical reasons. Tyro: the lover of Poseidon, visited by him in the form of the river Enipeus. Pasiphae, the daughter of the sun, wife of Minos and mother of the Minotaur. Achaia, a name given to separate territories in the north and along the southern shore of Greece. Troad, the district of Troy. Campania is a fertile and wealthy district south of the Roman Latium.

49. **Sidonian night cap:** A nightcap from Sidon, Phoenicia, known for its distinctive purple dye.

50. **feathery sandals of Perseus:** Hermes lent Perseus wings for his feet as an aid in obtaining the Gorgon's head.

51. **Cytherean:** Another name for Aphrodite, caught by her husband, Hephaestus, in an act of adultery with Ares (Mars). Hephaestus entangled her and Mars in a net and exposed them to the ridicule of the gods. On their release, however, Aphrodite renewed her virginity in the sea (see notes 24 and 38).

52. **Ida:** Pound personifies Mount Ida, where Paris was brought up and fell in love with the nymph Oenone.

53. **Hyrcanian:** Hyrcania, a region south of the Caspian Sea.
    Eos: Goddess of the dawn.

54. **Via Sacra:** Principal street in Rome that ran past the Temple of Vesta; also the street of prostitutes.

55. **Colchis:** The destination of Jason and the Argonauts. Jason returned with Medea, the king's daughter, but abandoned her for Glauce.

56. **Lynceus:** An Argonaut, but here a fictitious name for a minor poet.

57. **Achelöus . . . Antimachus:** Achelöus was a river god who fought Hercules for the hand of Deianira twice, the second time in the form of a bull; Adrastus was the king of the Argos and leader of the Seven against Thebes. Achenor is the name given to Pheltes, son of the king of Nemea who saw his death as an ill-omen. Propertius has Archemorus, "forerunner of death." Aeschylus, founder of Greek tragedy, whose works include *Seven Against Thebes*. Antimachus: Greek writer and poet author of the fifth-century epic *Thebaïs*.

58. **Actian marshes:** Actium was the site of Octavian's defeat of Anthony and Cleopatra (31 B.C.E.), which marked the end of the Roman Republic and the beginning of the Empire.

59. **Ilian . . . Lavinian beaches:** Ilian is Trojan, hence Roman. Aeneas, hero of the *Aeneid*, is described as founding a Trojan settlement in Latium, which was the origin of Rome. Lavinia is Latium. Lavinia is also the daughter of the king of Latium courted by Aeneas.

60. **Thyrsis and Daphnis:** Figures in book VII of Virgil's *Ecologues*. Thyrsis is defeated in a singing match presided over by Daphnis.

61. **Tityrus:** A sheperd in Virgil's *Ecologues* sometimes identified as Virgil himself.

62. **Hamadryads:** Tree nymphs.

63. **Ascraeus:** Ascra in Boeotia was home of Hesiod, the author of *Works and Days,* a realistic picture of rustic life.

64. **Varro . . . Leucadia:** Varro is the Latin poet Publius Terentius Varro. His love poems to Leucadia are lost.

65. **Calvus . . . Quintilia:** Calvus, orator and poet, whose love poems to his wife or mistress, Quintilia, are lost.

66. **Gallus . . . Lycoris:** Cornelius Gallus was a friend to Virgil and first prefect of Egypt who wrote four books of love poems, since lost, to the actress Cytheris, called Lycoris in the poems.

HUGH SELWYN MAUBERLEY

Mauberley was first published in an edition of two hundred copies by the Egoist Press (London) in June 1919, without Pound's name. Or, rather, it had simply the initials "E. P." after the title and no other indication of an author. This was the first appearance of the poem in print. No American edition of the poem as a separate publication appeared, although *The Dial* published the first six sections of part I in September 1920 and a slightly revised form of the entire poem appeared in *Poems 1918–1921* (1921). The *Dial* edition omitted the "E. P." that precedes the title of the first poem, "E. P. Ode Pour L'Election de Son Sepulchre." The omission was repeated in the poem's first American appearance, *Poems 1918–21.* Not until *Selected Poems* in 1949 were the initials returned.

Pound said that Mauberley was a popularization of *Propertius,* the two poems sharing a disdain for conventional but limited literary models. Mauberley, however, is more disillusioned and disenfranchised than Propertius and disturbed by the world around him. In *Personae* (1926), Pound also added this note: "The sequence is so distinctly a farewell to London that the reader who chooses to regard this as an exclusively American edition may as well omit it and turn at once to ["Homage to Sextus Propertius"]." In that edition, the subtitle reads "(Contacts and Life)," which Pound declared was "the actual order of the subject matter."

1. *"Vocat . . . umbram":* "The heat calls us into the shade."
2. **E. P. Ode Pour L'Election de Son Sepulchre:** "Ode for the Selection of His Tomb," an adaptation of the title of an ode by Pierre de Ronsard.
3. **Capaneus:** One of the seven warriors dispatched from Argos to attack Thebes. Boasting that not even a thunderbolt from Zeus could prevent him from scaling the city, Capaneus was struck down by lightning. He appears in Dante's *Inferno,* XIV, emblem of defiance.
4. **Ἴδμεν . . . Τροίη:** *Odyssey,* book XII, from the sirens' song: "For we know all the toils that are in wide Troy."
5. *L'an . . . eage:* "In the thirtieth year of his life," adapted from the opening of François Villon's *Le Testatment.*
6. **Attic grace:** A pure classical style associated with Attica, a region forming the southeast part of central Greece. Superseding the Attic dialect was a single, common Greek dialect under the Athenian Empire.
7. **barbitos:** Seven-stringed instrument resembling the lyre.
8. **Samothrace:** A Greek island, home of the Winged Victory and renowned for its worship of Dionysus. Saint Paul visited the island.
9. **τὸ καλόν:** "The beautiful."
10. **Pisistratus:** A beneficent Athenian tyrant (605–527 B.C.E.) who encouraged the Dionysian rites, especially in their dramatic form.
11. **τίν . . . θεὸν:** "What man, what hero, what God," adapted from Pindar's *Olympian Ode* II.1: "What god, what hero, what man shall we loudly praise?"
12. **pro domo:** For the home.
13. **pro patria . . . "et decor":** Excised from Horace: *"Dulce et decorum est pro patria mori"*—"It is sweet and fitting to die for one's country."
14. **usury:** The practice of lending money at an exorbitant or illegal rate of interest. This is the first poem by Pound to use the word, which would become a key term in his later work, especially *The Cantos.* Its use coincides with his meeting and studying the Social Credit theories of Major C. H. Douglas, whose *Economic Democracy* Pound reviewed in April 1920 for the *Athenaeum* and the *Little Review.*
15. **Yeux Glauques:** Glaucous eyes, a phrase used by Théophile Gautier in his *Mademoiselle de Maupin ("L'oeil glauque")* to evoke the dull grayish green or grayish blue gaze common in Pre-Raphaelite portraits of women.

16. **"Kings' Treasures":** "Of Kings Treasures" was the opening chapter in John Ruskin's *Sesame and Lilies* (1865).

17. **Cophetua:** Elizabeth Siddall modeled for Burne-Jones's *Cophetua and the Beggar-Maid* (1884).

18. **maquero:** Pimp. In context, it may refer to Dante Gabriel Rossetti's infidelities with Fanny Cornforth and perhaps Jane Morris, two of his models and lovers.

19. **"Siena mi fe': Disfecemi Maremma":** "Siena made me; Maremma undid me." Dante, *Purgatorio,* V.

20. **Monsieur Verog:** Victor Plarr (1863–1929), a member of the Rhymers' Club, author of *In the Dorian Mood* (1896) and librarian of the Royal College of Surgeons. Plarr was born near Strasbourg and came to England after the Franco-Prussian War. Pound mentions him at the end of "Siena Mi Fe'."

21. **Gallifet:** Gaston Gallifet, a French general in the Franco-Prussian War who led a cavalry charge at Sedan.

22. **Dowson:** Ernest Dowson (1867–1900), a poet Pound admired for epitomizing a decade (1900–1910). Pound cited Dowson's poem "Cynara" as an early influence on his work (*LE,* 367).
    Rhymers' Club: Group founded in the early 1890s by Yeats, Ernest Rhys, and T. W. Rolleston. Members included Dowson, Lionel Johnson, Victor Plarr, and Arthur Symons. Pound praised them to Floyd Dell, celebrating their work in "knocking bombast & rhetoric & Victorian syrup out of our verse" (in Ruthven, 136).

23. **Headlam:** Reverend Stewart D. Headlam (1847–1924), who resigned his curacy in 1878 after a lecture at a workingman's club on dancing and the theater.
    Image: Selwyn Image (1849–1930), artist and poet; member of the Rhymers' Club and Slade Professor of Fine Arts at Oxford. With Headlam, he founded the Church and Stage Guild. Coedited the *Hobby Horse,* a periodical that connected the nineties poets with the Pre-Raphaelites. Pound met Image in 1909 and numbered him with Olivia and Dorothy Shakespear as one of the most valuable figures he had so far met in London.

24. **Terpsichore:** Greek muse of the dance.

25. **Brennbaum:** German, "burnt tree," suggesting "burning bush."

26. **Horeb:** Where Moses made water flow from a rock.
    Sinai: The mountain where Moses saw the burning bush and was given the Ten Commandments.

27. **Mr. Nixon:** Pound said Nixon was "a fictitious name for a real person," that person most likely the prolific journalist, editor, and

novelist Arnold Bennett (1867-1931), whom Pound probably met through Ford Madox Ford.

28. **a friend of Blougram's:** Gigadibs, the literary man in Browning's poem "Bishop Blougram's Apology," in which the bishop substitutes material for spiritual pleasures.

29. **"Conservatrix of Milésien":** The salacious *Milesian Tales* did not survive antiquity. Pound adopts the phrase from Rémy de Gourmont's short story "Stratagèmes" (1894), which Pound later glossed as "Woman, the conservator, the inheritor of past gestures" in a postscript to his translation of Gourmont's *Natural Philosophy of Love* (1922).

30. **Pierian roses:** An allusion to a line from Sappho: "for you have no claim to the Pierian roses," addressed to a young girl. Pieria in Greece was a reputed home of the Muses.

31. **Lawes:** Henry Lawes (1596-1662) set to music "Goe lovely Rose" and other poems by Edmund Waller.

32. **"Vacuos ... morsus":** Epigraph adapted from Ovid, *Metamorphosis*, VII: "his empty mouth snaps at the air."

33. **Jacquemart:** Jules Jacquemart (1837-1880), a Parisian watercolorist and etcher who engraved the frontispiece of Gautier's *Émaux et Camées* (1881).

34. **Messalina:** Unfaithful wife of the Roman emperor Claudius, murdered at twenty-four. Her head appeared on coins struck early in Claudius's reign.

35. **Pier Francesca:** Piero della Francesa (1420-1492), Italian painter well known for his geometrical compositions and as a colorist.
Pisanello: Antonio Pisano (1397?-1455), Veronese painter and medalist. Pound included the reproduction of a letter seal by Pisanello as the frontispiece of his *Guide to Kulchur* (1938). Pound refers to him again in Cantos XXVI and LXXIV.
Achaia: The name originally of the two territories to the north and south of ancient Greece, but later taken to mean the entire country.

36. The passage, attributed to a pseudonymous Persian (most likely Pound), reads, "What do they know of love, and what can they understand? If they cannot understand poetry, if they have no feeling for music, what can they understand of this passion, in comparison with which the rose is coarse and the perfume of violets a clap of thunder?"

37. **diabolus in the scale:** Medieval music theorists called the augmented fourth the "devil in music."

38. **ANAN-GKE:** Necessity.

39. **NUKTOS AGALMA:** "Jewel of the Night." From the Greek pastoral poet Bion's address to the Evening Star.

40. **TO AGATHON:** The good.

41. **irides:** Plural of "iris," referring to both the flower and the membrane of the eye. Iris was also the messenger of the gods, whose sign to men was the rainbow.

42. **diastasis:** Separation or dilation.

43. **anæsthesis:** Loss of feeling or sensation.

44. **Cytheræan:** Aphrodite, who is said to have landed on the island of Cythera after her birth from the sea.

45. *apathein:* Greek, "impassivity" or "indifference," as of the gods to men.

46. **susurrus:** A whispering or rustling sound.

47. **Moluccas:** Spice-producing Moluccan Islands in the Malay Archipelago.

48. **Simoon:** Hot, dry sand-wind that sweeps across the African and Asian deserts in the spring and summer.

49. **Coracle:** Small boat used in ancient Britain made by covering a wicker frame with hide or leather.

50. **Luini:** Bernardino Luini (c. 1480–1532), Lombard painter known for religious frescoes and secular paintings.

51. **Anadyomene:** "Foam-born," the epithet of Aphrodite.

52. **Reinach:** Salomon Reinach (1858–1932), French art historian and archaeologist. His *Apollo* (1904) is a study of ancient sculpture.

THE CANTOS (1917–1922)

THREE CANTOS OF A POEM OF SOME LENGTH
CANTO I

First published in *Poetry* in June 1917 as "Three Cantos. I"; reprinted in *Quia Pauper Amavi* (London: Egoist Press, 1919) but later modified. The version appearing here is from *Poetry*. In February 1917, Pound sent "Three Cantos" to Alice Corbin Henderson, associate editor of *Poetry* then living in Sante Fe, New Mexico. She forwarded them to Harriet Monroe with a covering letter that reads in part: "really hate to let them go. I really like them tremendously. . . . Of course they are erudite—but there is life—and a poet's life—in it & through it all—considerable vision and depth—and beauty of style. You need to read it several times—at least I did." Monroe's reply, dated March 19, 1917, begins, "I read two or three pages of Ezra's Cantos and then took sick—no doubt that was the cause. Since then I haven't had brains enough to tackle it." A month later (she had loaned them to Robert Frost), she finished them, although she was not pleased: "erudition in seventeen languages," she complained. But they began to appear over the next three months, beginning in June 1917. For the Corbin/Monroe exchange, see *Letters of Ezra Pound to Alice Corbin Henderson,* ed. Ira B. Nadel (Austin: University of Texas Press, 1993), 193-95.

1. *Sordello:* Robert Browning's long narrative poem (1840) based on events in the life of the Mantua-born Provençal troubadour Sordello (1180?-1255), who, at the court of Count Ricciardo di San Bonifazzio, fell in love with the count's wife and abducted her at the request of her brothers. He was forced to flee with her to Provence, where he later performed military and diplomatic service for Charles I of Anjou, Naples, and Sicily. His reward was five castles, which he returned. He appears in Dante's *Purgatorio* as a too zealous patriot. Browning's *Sordello* is dramatized history with the narrator a character who confronts the struggles between the Guelphs and Ghibellines in thirteenth-century Florence.

2. **intaglio method:** A form of engraving or printing in which ink is forced into incised lines on a plate, the surface is wiped clean, dampened paper is placed on top, and the paper and plate are then run through a press. An impression from the design yields an image in relief. From the Italian *intagliare,* to cut or incise.

3. **Beaucaire's:** A city in southern France visited by Pound during his 1912 walking tour.

4. **Altaforte:** The castle of Bertran de Born.

5. **Alcazar:** A Spanish fortress or palace.

6. **Cardinal . . . Dante:** Peire Cardinal, troubadour poet (fl. 1210-1230); Pound wrote in *The Spirit of Romance* that "in so far as Dante is a critic of morals Cardinal must be held as his [Dante's] forerunner."

7. **Arnaut:** Arnaut Daniel, the twelfth-century Provençal poet favored by Pound, and the subject of a lecture in *The Spirit of Romance.* Daniel supposedly invented the sestina. See *SR,* 22-38 and Pound's essay "Arnaut Daniel," in *LE,* 109-48.

8. **font:** Fount. At the end of Book the Second of *Sordello,* the troubadour, despairing of his vocation, throws his crown of laurels into a fount at Mantua.

9. **Can Grande:** C. G. della Scala (1291-1329), lord of Verona and greatest member of the Ghibelline family that ruled Verona from

1277 to 1387. He was a friend and protector of Dante's and appears in Pound's Canto LXXVIII.

10. *Lo soleils plovil:* "The sun rains," from the final line of Arnaut Daniel's *"Lancan son passat li giure."*

11. **Darts ...** *"Lydiae":* Catullus compares his own lake, Lago di Garda, to the Lydian waters surrounding Sappho's island of Lesbos.

12. *lemures:* "Specters of the night."

13. **Glaukopos:** Epithet for the goddess Athena, traditionally translated as "blue-eyed," "gray-eyed," or "glare-eyed." Alan Upward in *The New Word* (1910), a work known to Pound, explains it as evoking the blinking, glinting light of an owl's eye or olive leaf.

14. *apricus:* "Drenched with sunlight."

15. **Asolo:** Setting for Browning's "Pippa Passes," and later the writer's residence.

16. **Dogana's curb:** At the edge of the chief Venetian customs house on the Grand Canal.

17. **Florian's:** Famous café on the south side of the Piazza San Marco, Venice. Cited later in Canto LXXVI.

18. **pre-Daun Chaucer:** The *Book of Daun Burnel the Ass* by Nigel Wircker (c. 1130-1200).

19. *hagoromo:* Japanese; title of a classical, one-act Noh play. The *hagoromo* is a "feather mantle" or magical cloak of a *Tennin* or nymph who leaves it hanging on a bough where it is found by a priest. The *hagoromo* is cited in Cantos LXXIV, LXXIX, and LXXX.

20. **Uc St. Circ:** Attributed author of commentary to several of Bertran de Born's poems (see "Near Perigord," note 3).

21. **Puvis:** Pierre Puvis de Chavannes (1824-1898), French muralist. His work is in the Sorbonne and Panthéon in Paris.

22. **Panisks:** Small woodland Pans, half human and half goat.

23. **Maenads:** Frenzied female spirits who participate in the forest rites of Dionysus.

24. **Ficinus:** Marsilio Ficino (1433-1499), under the patronage of Cosimo de' Medici, translated many Greek classics into Latin, including Plato's dialogues and the writings of Plotinus.

25. **Shang:** A Chinese dynasty.

26. **Kwannon:** Japanese goddess of mercy, who can also appear as the armed goddess of war. Spelled "Kuanon" in later editions.

27. **Guido:** Guido Cavalcanti (c. 1250-1300), Tuscan poet and friend of Dante favored by Pound. See "Cavalcanti," *LE,* 149-200, and Pound's poem "To Guido Cavalcanti," as well as his translation "Sonnets and Ballate of Guido Cavalcanti," in Pound, *Poems and Translations,* ed. Richard Sieburth (2003), 183-227.

28. **Or San Michele:** The loggia of Or San Michele in Florence contained a painted Madonna that in 1292 supposedly began to perform miracles.
29. **leapt:** Refers to Cavalcanti supposedly eluding an attack by Betto and his company by overleaping one of the high marble tombs in the cemetery of the Church of Santa Reparata.
30. **phantastikon:** In March 1913, Pound told Harriet Monroe that the term was "what Imagination really meant before the term was debased—presumable by the Miltonists, tho' probably before them. It has to do with the seeing of visions."
31. **Simonetta ... Aufidus:** Simonetta was the wife of Giuliano de' Medici, supposed model for Botticelli's Venus.
    Aufidus: Stream identified with the male zephyr in Botticelli's painting.
32. **Mantegna:** Italian painter Andrea Mantegna (1431–1506).
33. **Casella:** Musician who set Dante's poem to music.

CANTO II

Published in *Poetry* (X, July 1917) as "Three Cantos. II"; reprinted in *Quia Pauper Amavi* (London: Egoist Press, 1919).

1. **Leave Casella:** In *Purgatorio* II.2, Cato admonishes Dante for lingering with Casella, reminding Dante that he must move forward up the mountains.
2. **Mantuan palace:** Palace of the Gonzaga family.
3. **Joios, Tolosan:** Minor troubadours whose poetry Pound discovered in the *"Chansonnier du Roi"* in the Bibliothèque Nationale in 1912.
4. **"Y a ... em plor":** "And at the first flower I found, I burst into tears."
5. **Chalus:** Where Richard Coeur de Lion was killed.
6. **Dolmetsch:** Arnold Dolmetsch (1858–1940), French musician and instrument maker.
7. **"Yin-yo ... weeping":** Pound's arrangement of "Song of the Lute" by T'ang poet Po Chi, based on Fenollosa notebooks.
8. **"Rêveuse ... " plonge:** "Dreamer, so that I plunge," the first line of Mallarmé's *"Autre Eventail."*
9. **flamma dimanat:** "A flame steels down through my limbs," Catullus, LI.
10. **Viscountess of Pena:** Her adventures with Elis of Montfort are told in a *razos* of Uc de Saint Circ.

11. *bos trobaire:* "A good finder of song."

12. **Gourdon:** Pound visited the town of Gourdon in southern France in June 1912.

13. **My cid . . . Burgos:** Commander or Lord Cid, title given by the Moors to Ruy Diaz (1040?–1099), hero of the Spanish epic *El Cid*. Burgos, where Diaz lived and is buried, is the capital of Burgos Province in Old Castile. Pound visited the city on his University of Pennsylvania fellowship, and published the article "Burgos, a Dream City of Old Castile" in *Book News Monthly* (XXV, October 1906), 91–94.

14. *"Afe Minaya!":* Alférez (or Commander) Alvar Fáñez, Christian warrior in *El Cid*.

15. *Muy velida:* "Very beautiful."

16. *"Y dar . . . hierros":* "And the arms and the weapons gave new light."

17. **Kumasaka's ghost:** Reference to Noh play *Kumasaka* Pound included in part II of *"Noh" or Accomplishment* (1916).

18. **Toro,** *las almenas:* Toro is the Spanish city under siege by King Sancho and his advisers El Cid and Conde Ancures, outlined by Lope de Vega in his play *Las Almenas de Toro,* summarized by Pound in "The Quality of Lope de Vega," in *The Spirit of Romance.*

19. *"Mal fuego s'enciende!":* "An ill flame be kindled in her!"

20. *"Que . . . Rainha.":* "Who, after she was dead, was crowned queen."

21. **Camoens:** Luis Vaz de Camões (1524?–1580), Portuguese poet, author of the epic poem *Os Lusiadas.* See chapter X, "Camoens" in *The Spirit of Romance,* where Pound states, "Camoens writes resplendent bombast and at times it is poetry" (*SR*, 216).

22. **Houtmans . . . Renaissance:** In jail for debt at Lisbon, Cornelis Houtman "planned the Dutch East India Company. When Portugal fell, Holland seized the Oriental trade and soon after Roemer Visscher was holding a salon . . . connected [with] the names of Rembrandt, Spinoza [and] Vondel." Pound, *SR*, 221.

23. **Gaby wears Braganza:** The Braganza house ruled Portugal from 1640 to 1910. "Gaby" refers to Gaby Desbys, stage name of Marie-Elsie-Gabrielle Caire (1880–1920), French dancer and actress famous for her risqué performances and jewelry. For a time she was the mistress of King Manuel II of Portugal.

24. **a man:** Fred Vance, American painter whose chief work was *Christ appearing on the Waters* (Salon, Paris, 1903), mentioned in "Redondillas, or Something of That Sort."

CANTO III

Published in *Poetry* (X, August 1917) as "Three Cantos. III"; reprinted in *Quia Pauper Amavi* (London: Egoist Press, 1919).

1. **John Heydon:** Seventeenth-century English astrologer and alchemist
2. **"Omniformis ... est":** "Every intellect is capable of assuming every shape," from *De Occasionibus,* chapter 13, by the Greek scholar and Neoplatonist Porphyry.
3. **Psellus:** Byzantine philosopher, politician, writer, and Neoplatonist who lived from 1018 to 1105.
4. **Ficino:** Marsilio Ficino (1433–1499), under the patronage of Cosimo de' Medici, translated many Greek classics into Latin, among them Plato's dialogues and the work of Plotinus. Pound refers to him as translating "a Greek that was in spirit anything but 'classic,'" in *Gaudier-Brzeska.*
5. **Valla:** Fifteenth-century Italian humanist and Greek scholar, author of a defense of classical Latin, *Elegantiae linguae latinae.* His patron was Pope Nicholas V, founder of the Vatican Library.
6. **Sir Blancatz:** Blacatz, thirteenth-century poet whose death is lamented by Sordello.
7. **"Nec bonus ... bonus":** "Neither a good Christian nor a good Ciceronian."
8. **Corpore laniato:** "His body torn to pieces."
9. **Villari:** Italian historian Pasquale Villari (1827–1917).
10. **Andreas Divus:** Sixteenth-century translator of a Latin version of Homer's *Odyssey* (1538); Pound picked up the translation in Paris. The work would form part of the revised Canto I of *The Cantos.* For an account of Pound's reading discovery, see *LE*, 259–67.
11. **"Down to the ships":** Pound's version of Divus, which, with the lines that follow, would form the opening of the revised Canto I.
12. **ell-square pitkin:** "Little pit." A Poundian neologism.
13. **ingle:** Chimney corner, from the Scottish *inglenook.*
14. **Venerandam ... est:** "Worthy of veneration, golden-crowned and beautiful whose dominion is the walled cities of all sea-set Cyprus." From G. Dartona's Latin version of the second hymn to Aphrodite bound into Pound's copy of Andreas Divus.
15. **orichalci:** "Of copper."
16. **Argicida:** Slayer of Greeks, reference to Aphrodite's favoring the Trojans, especially Aeneas, over the Greeks.

THE FOURTH CANTO

First appeared in a private edition of forty copies in October 1919 as *The Fourth Canto* and then publicly in June 1920 under the same title in the *Dial* (LXVIII, June 1920) and then in *Poems 1918-1921* (New York: Boni and Liveright, 1921).

1. **ANAXIFORMINGES:** From "*Anaxiphormigges hymnoi,*" "Hymns that are lords of the lyre," the beginning of Pindar's "Olympian Ode II," emphasizing the power of poetry and recorded words.
   Aurunculeia!: Bride praised in Catullus's *Epithalamium*, LXI.

2. **Cadmus of Golden Prows:** Eponymous hero and founder of Thebes.

3. **Ityn, Ityn!:** Son of Procne and Tereus, king of Thrace. Procne killed her son Itys to cook and feed him to Tereus after she had discovered that he had raped Philomela, her sister, and cut out her tongue so that she could not tell anyone what happened. To escape the wrath of Tereus, Procne and Philomela turned into a swallow and a nightingale.

4. *Cabestan:* Guillems de Cabestanh, an ascetic troubadour who in Celtic legend became the lover of Lady Seremonda, wife of Ramon, lord of the castle of Rossillon, whom he served. Raymon killed Cabestanh and served his cooked heart to Seremonda.

5. **Rhodez:** Earlier spelling of Rodez, a small town with a cathedral on a plateau overlooking the river Aveyron. Pound visited the town in July 1912.

6. **Actaeon:** The hunter who accidentally came upon the naked Diana while she was bathing. She changed him into a stag, in which form he was pursued and killed by his own companions and dogs.

7. **Vidal:** Troubadour poet Peire Vidal of Tolosa. He dressed in wolfskins to court his lady, Loba of Penautier. "Loba" means shewolf. Like Actaeon, in pursuit of his love, Vidal became the prey of his own hounds. Pound translates the legend from the Provençal in *SR*, 178.

8. **Pegusa:** A lake (see Ovid, *Metamorphosis*, V).
   Gargaphia: Pool where Artemis annually renewed her virginity.
   Salmacis: Spring near Halikarnassos belonging to the water nymph Salmacis (see Ovid, *Metamorphosis* IV).

9. *e lo soleils plovil:* "Thus the light rains," from Pound's version of Arnaut Daniel's "*on soleills plovil.*"

10. **Ply over ply:** A recurrent simile in Pound's poetry and prose, found in Browning's *Sordello* V, 161-172, and in a number of Chinese poets Pound translated. The phrase also echoes Mallarmé's

"pli selon pli" in *"Rémemoration d'amis belges"* and *"Autre Éventail,"* where it describes the unfolding and folding of a fan.

11. **Takasago:** Japanese Noh play named after a legendary pine tree growing on the shore of Takasago Bay in southern Honshu. Like Fenollosa, Pound understood the play as a parallel to Greek drama.

12. **Ise:** Bay famous for its pine grove at Ano, mentioned near the end of the Japanese Noh play *Tamura*.

13. **Hymenaeus! . . . Hymenaee!:** "Hymen, hail! Hymen, hail Hymen!" from Catullus, LXI. Hymen is the god of marriage, whose color is saffron.

14. **Aurunculeia:** A bride praised in Catullus, *Epithalamium,* LXI.

15. **So-Gioku:** Japanese form of the name of fourth-century Chinese poet Sung Yü.

16. **Ecbatan:** City of Ecbatana on the Iranian plateau in northern Media, founded according to Herodotus by Deioces as the capital of the Median Empire. Meticulously mapped out to correspond in every detail with the plan of the universe, the city was an archetype of the perfectibility of human order, uniting nature and civilization.

17. **Danae:** Daughter of Acrisius, king of Argus, imprisoned at the top of a bronze tower by her father because an oracle said his daughter's son would kill him. There, she was visited by Zeus in a shower of golden light that poured into her lap. As a result, Danae bore him a son, Perseus, who did indeed accidentally kill his grandfather.

18. **Père Henri Jacques:** According to Pound, "a French priest (as a matter of fact he is a Jesuit)" (*SL,* 180).

19. **sennin on Rokku:** *Sennin* is the Japanese word for Chinese *hsien,* a genie or genies; literal Chinese translation of *sennin* means hermit or philosopher who has attained immortality by resisting desire. Rokku is a wrongly transcribed Japanese translation of a Chinese place-name, either a mountain or an island, according to Pound (*SL,* 180).

20. **Polhonac:** Viscount Heraclius III of Polhonac, a twelfth-century nobleman, persuaded by Guillaume St. Leidier to sing to his wife a seduction song written by and for the troubadour poet. The husband did not know he was assisting in the seduction of his wife.

21. **Gyges:** Bodyguard of King Candaules who killed the king and married the queen at her bequest.

22. **Garonne:** River in Provence recalled from Pound's 1919 walking tour.

23. **"Salve regina":** "Hail! . . . hail Queen!"

24. **Adige:** Italian river that rises in the Alps and flows into the Adriatic.
25. **Stefano:** Stefano de Verona, fifteenth-century painter of the *Madonna in hortulo.*

THE FIFTH CANTO

Published as "The Fifth Canto" as part of "Three Cantos," *Dial* (LXXI. 2, August 1921). Reprinted in *Poems 1918–1921* (New York: Boni and Liveright, 1921).

1. **Ecbatan:** See Fourth Canto, note 16.
2. **Iamblichus:** Fourth-century Greek Neoplatonic philosopher of light, which denoted oneness for him, the principle from which the plurality of things derives.
3. **"ciocco":** Log. The ancient game of striking a burning log and counting the sparks that fly up was used in fortune-telling.
4. **"Et omniformis":** "And omniform" from *"Omnis intellectus est omniformis":* ("Every intellect is capable of assuming every shape," the caption to item 10 in Ficino's *Opera Omnia II.* In Canto III, Pound implies that he came across the quotation in John Heydon's *Holy Guide.*
5. **"Da nuces!":** "Give nuts!" Distributing nuts in the street to celebrate a marriage was a Roman custom.
6. **Atthis:** Atthis betrayed her lover, Sappho.
7. **Mauleon:** Thirteenth-century professional soldier and poet, patron of Poicebot and other troubadours.
8. **Poicebot:** Gausbetz de Puegsibot (F. Poicebot), a monk who became a troubadour, roaming for sexual adventure. He discovers his wife similarly drifting when she offers herself to him in a brothel, equaling his own betrayal.
9. *romerya:* Provençal, *romeria,* "pilgrimage" or, figuratively, "roaming."
10. *Lei fassar . . . del:* Provençal wrongly transcribed for *se laisset ad el* ("yielded herself to him").
11. **Pieire de Maensac:** Two brothers, Peire and Austors, toss a coin as to who will win the castle and who will become a troubadour. The story illustrates the theme of possessiveness versus the unencumbered life.
12. *dreitz hom:* Upstanding fellow or "right man."
13. **John Borgia:** Giovanni Borgia, son of Pope Alexander VI and Vanozza Catanei, and younger brother of Cesare and Lucrezia

Borgia. He was murdered on June 14, 1497, in Rome, his body thrown into the Tiber.

14. **Varchi:** Benedetto Varchi, sixteenth-century Italian classical scholar and historian who wrote a history of Florence in which he criticizes the ruling Medici family.

15. **"SIGA MAL AUTHIS DEUTERON!":** "Silence once more a second time," lines from Aeschylus's *Agamemnon* mixed together.

16. *"Se pia? / O impia?":* "Whether noble / Or Ignoble." Varchi, III.

17. **Lorenzaccio:** Abusive name for Lorenzo de Medici used by his contemporaries and frequently by the historian Varchi.

18. **O si credesse:** "Or himself believed."

19. *Caina attende:* "Caina is waiting." Words addressed to Dante in *Inferno,* V, by Francesca da Rimini to transmit to her husband, Gianciotto Malatesta, who murdered her and her lover, his own brother Paolo.

20. **SIGA, SIGA!:** "Silence, silence."

21. **Schiavoni . . . Borgia:** Giorgio of the Slavonians, member of a colony of Dalmatian refugees that Pope Sixtus IV allowed to settle in Rome, saw the body of Giovanni Borgia, duke of Gandia, thrown into the Tiber on June 14, 1497.

22. **Barabello:** Society poet Baraballo of Gaeta, given a white elephant by Leo X, which balked at crossing a bridge when he attempted triumphantly to ride into Rome.

23. **Mozarello . . . ending:** Giovanni Mozzarello was a young Mantuan poet and scholar appointed governor of the fort of Mondaino near Rimini; resentful residents pushed him down a well with his mule. A month later both were found drowned.

24. **Sanazarro:** Late-fifteenth-century poet of Naples.

25. **Al poco . . . d'ombra:** "In the small hours with the darkness describing a huge circle" (Dante, *Rime* 1).

26. **Navighero:** Early-sixteenth-century Venetian poet who wrote in Latin and Italian. Praised by his peers for poetry in the school of Martial, he became so indignant at the remarks that he burned all his work.

27. **"O empia . . . deliberazione":** "Whether noble or ignoble, certainly a resolute and terrible decision." Varchi, III.

28. *Ma si morisse!:* "But if he were killed." Words of Lorenzo as reported by Varchi.

THE SIXTH CANTO

The first two-thirds were published as "The Sixth Canto" as part of "Three Cantos," in the *Dial* (LXXI. 2, August 1921). Reprinted as "The Sixth Canto" in *Poems 1918–1921* (New York: Boni and Liveright, 1921). Pound revised the Canto for its publication in 1925, considerably cutting sections but recalling passages in Canto LXXVI and other *Pisan Cantos*.

1. **Guillaume:** William IX, seventh count of Poitou. He participated in the First Crusade with a large retinue of women.
2. **Louis, French King:** Louis VII of France married Eleanor of Aquitaine on July 25, 1137, in Bordeaux.
3. **"E quand lo reis . . . faschée":** "And when King Louis heard it he was much riled."
4. **Gisors:** Commanding fortress on the river Epte in Normandy.
5. **Vexis:** Territory along the border of Normandy and France, long in dispute.
6. *Si tuit . . . Del mon:* "If all griefs and the laments and the pain of men." Pound would reuse the phrase in Canto LXXX.
7. **Alix:** Daughter of Louis and Eleanor, but Pound's source is in error since Alix could not have married her half brother Richard, son of Henry and Eleanor. It was Adelaide who was betrothed to Richard. Pound quoted from a text in which the scribe wrongly recorded the name of Alix instead of Adelaide.
8. **Frederic . . . Malek Kamel:** Frederick II in 1229 successfully negotiated with Malek-el-Kamel, thirteenth-century sultan of Cairo and nephew of Saladin, for the restoration and access to Christian sites in the Holy Land for the clergy. Crusader forces in the Holy Land influenced the decision of Malek to agree to the accord.
9. **Henry and Saladin:** Henry refers to the Holy Roman emperor Henry VI, who reigned from 1191 to 1197. In 1193, he was given the captured king Richard I of England, Richard Coeur de Lion, by Leopold V of Austria, with whom he quarreled on the Third Crusade. Saladin: Muslim warrior who lived from 1138 to 1193, great opponent of the Crusades and self-proclaimed sultan of Egypt, who defeated the Christian Crusaders at the battle of Hatten (near Tiberius) in 1187 and, after a three-month siege, captured Jerusalem.
10. **Tancred:** Likely Tancred of Lecce, who illegally assumed the crown of Sicily (1190–1194); his death favored the success of Henry VI's second expedition in 1194.

11. **Need *not* wed Alix:** Richard refused to marry his betrothed, Adelaide, who was made pregnant by her guardian, Henry II. At the same time, the French king demanded the return of either the princess or the fortress of Gisors. Estranged from his father, Richard sided with Philip II, the French king, who realized the necessity of dissolving the engagement between Richard and Adelaide. The marriage contract was annulled at Messina in 1191. Pound incorrectly states the date as 1190.

12. **Correze, Malemort:** Ruins of Malemort Castle, which Pound and his wife, Dorothy, visited after passing the marsh of the river Corrèze on their walking tour of Provence in July 1919. In the late twelfth century, it became the residence of Lady Audiart (Na Audiart) of Malemort, subject of a poem by Bertran de Born, translated by Pound in *Personae*.

13. **Domna jauzionda:** "Radiant lady," from a line in a poem by Bernart de Ventadour to Eleanor on her return to Provence after her separation from Louis VII.

14. **"Is shut by Eblis in":** Magarida of Torena married Eblis III of Ventadour in 1148; he shut her up in a dungeon out of jealousy and repudiated her in 1150 to marry Alice of Montpellier.

THE SEVENTH CANTO

Published as "The Seventh Canto" as part of "Three Cantos," in the *Dial* (LXXI. 2, August 1921). Reprinted as "The Seventh Canto" in *Poems 1918-1921* (New York: Boni and Liveright, 1921).

1. **"Man destroying and city-destroying,"** a repetition of the traditional puns on the name of Helen of Troy that Pound extends to Eleanor. The line suggests the origin of literature inspired by Helen's beauty, namely *The Iliad* and *The Odyssey*.

2. **"Si pulvis nullus":** "If no dust." This follows from the line just above, "Marble narrow for seats," which refers to Ovid, who in *Ars amatoria* advises the reader to follow a shapely girl into the theater and sit near her, where they will be forced, because of the seats, to squeeze together. Ovid goes on to say that if a speck of dust should "fall onto your lady's lap, flick it off with your fingers; if there be no speck of dust, well flick it off anyway" (*Ars amatoria*, I).

3. **e li mestiers ecoutes:** "And harken to the crafts" or "to the mysteries."

4. **y cavals armatz:** "And horses in armor," a quotation from a line by Bertran de Born.

5. **"ciocco":** "Log," alluding to Dante's image of the souls rising like sparks from the Fifth Circle to the Sixth in *Inferno* to mark the move from a medieval chronicle to the "imaginative vision" of Dante underscored by Pound in *The Spirit of Romance* (157).

6. **Un peu moisi ... baromètre:** "A little musty ... the floor being below garden level ... Against the wainscot ... a wicker armchair ... an old piano ... and under the barometer." From Flaubert's *Un Coeur Simple.*

7. *con gli occhi onesti e tardi ... Grave incessu:* "With eyes honest and slow," from Dante, *Purgatorio*, VI, referring to Sordello; "solemn movement," from *Inferno*, IV, referring to Homer, Horace, and Ovid as they approach Dante and Virgil in the poem.

8. **Ione, dead the long year:** Cf. Pound's poem "Ione, Dead the Long Year" in *Personae*, a lyrical elegy to the French-born dancer Jeanne Heyse, who used the professional name Ione de Forest. She committed suicide in Chelsea on August 2, 1912. She reappears in "Dance Figure," also in *Personae.*

9. **Liu Ch'e's lintel:** Reference to a Chinese poem by the emperor Liu Ch'e in which the emperor's dead mistress transforms into a dead leaf clinging to a threshold; Pound elevates her to the lintel.

10. **Elysée:** Hôtel de l'Elysée in Paris, where Pound had stayed and would await the arrival of Joyce in July 1920.

11. **Erard:** Famous French manufacturer of pianos. The following description is that of Frizt-René Vanderpyl's Paris apartment. Vanderpyl was an avant-garde Dutch novelist and poet Pound knew in Paris, and appears in Canto LXXIV.

12. **Smaragdos, chrysolitos; De Gama:** Emeralds, topazes from Propertius, *Elegies* II; Vasco da Gama, late-fifteenth-century Portuguese navigator and explorer who discovered the sea route to India via Africa.

13. **Le vieux commode en acajou:** "The old mahogany chest." The French should properly read "*La vieille commode.*"

14. **Ἑλέναυς, ἕλανδρος, ἑλέπτολις:** "ship-destroying and city-destroying."

15. **e quel remir:** "And that I may gaze upon her," from Arnaut Daniel's poem "*Doutz brais e critz,*" about his love for the wife of Guillem de Bouvila.

16. **Nicea:** Reference to the dancer Ione de Forest with parallels to the graceful statue of Nike of Samothrace at the Louvre. See note 8 above.

17. **"Toc":** Sham or ugly; French *patois.*

18. **O voi che ... barca:** "Oh you in the dinghy astern there," Pound's translation from Dante *Paradiso*, II, where Dante addresses the reader, who has been following the course of his "big ship," his epic.

19. **Sicheus:** Murdered husband of Dido, queen of Carthage, visited by Aeneas, who becomes her lover but leaves to sail for Italy. In her grief at this second loss, Dido commits suicide (*Aeneid*, I).

20. **Lorenzaccio:** Name of abuse for Lorenzo de' Medici, used by his contemporaries and often used by the historian Varchi. Appears earlier in Canto V. The allusion is to *Inferno*, III, and the spirits of those "who were never alive" and whose "blind life is so abject that they / are envious of every other fate" (Dante, *Inferno*, III: 64, 47-48).

21. **Ma si morisse!:** "But if he were killed!" Words of Lorenzo as reported by Varchi. Pound, however, has substituted *ma* ("but") for *o* ("or").

22. **E biondo:** "He is blond," *Inferno*, XII. Reference to the blond head of Obizzo d'Este, one of the most vengeful tyrants of thirteenth-century Italy.

EIGHTH CANTO

Published as "Eighth Canto," in the *Dial* (LXXII. 5, May 1922), the poem was revised in 1923 and reprinted with revisions as Canto II in *A Draft of XVI Cantos* (Paris: Three Mountains Press, 1925).

1. **Sichaeus:** See Canto VII, note 19.

2. **triremes:** Ancient galley having three banks of oars.

3. **Tyro:** Daughter of Salmoneus, who fell in love with the divine river Enipeus. Poseidon ("Neptunus") took on the river's form and raped her, protected by a dark wave.

4. **Lir:** Old Celtic sea god. Pound regarded seals as Lir's daughters. In ancient mythology, the seal is the animal most closely linked with Proteus. Reference in the next line is to Picasso's seal-like eyes.

5. **Eleanor, ἐλέναυς and ἐλέπτολις:** "ship-destroying and city-destroying." Eleanor is Helen of Troy, archetypal femme fatale.

6. **Schoeney's daughters:** Schoeneus was father of Atalanta, who, like Helen, caused many deaths through her beauty. Pound misremembers Arthur Golding's spelling; Schoenyes is his translation of Ovid.

7. **Scios; Naxos:** Scios is ancient Chios or modern Scio, an Aegean island; Naxos is the largest island of the Cyclades in the Aegean and a center of Dionysian worship.

8. **young boy:** Allusion to the young god Bacchus, originally a Cretan god of wine, fertility, and ecstasy, whose cult rose to challenge Apollo.

9. **King Pentheus:** Grandson of Cadmus. Refusing to worship Dionysus, he was torn to pieces by Dionysus's followers, the Maenads.

10. **Acoetes:** Pilot of the ship taking Dionysus to Naxos. He alone of the crew believed in the god and was spared. He emerges as one of the key early figures of *The Cantos,* along with Odysseus.

11. **Lyaeus:** Name means "deliverer from care"; applied to Dionysus as the god of wine.

12. **Olibanum:** Frankincense. Romans believed Bacchus responsible for the use of incense in ritual.

13. **Lycabs:** Crew member of Odysseus's, as is Medon, mentioned a few lines later.

14. **dory:** A kind of fish.

15. **Tiresias:** Theban seer. In Euripides's *Bacchae,* he appears with Cadmus on the way up the mountains to join a group of women in an orgy and to worship the god of wine and fertility.

16. **Cadmus:** Son of Phoenician king Agenor. His sister was Europa, carried off by Zeus, who abducted her in the form of a bull. Sent by his father to find her, Cadmus wandered as far as the oracle at Delphi, where he was given directions that led to the finding of Thebes.

17. **Ileuthyeria fair Dafne:** A conflation of Eileithyia, the goddess of childbirth, with the Greek, *Eleutheria* ("freedom"), a marine organism of the genus of bisexual jellyfish. Dafne is the daughter of Peneus, a river god. In flight from Apollo, Dafne was transformed into a laurel tree, which Pound altered to coral.

18. **So-shu:** Corruption of the Japanese name for Chinese Han Dynasty poet Ssu-ma Hsiang-ju.

19. **Hesperus:** Evening star sacred to Aphrodite. Pound associated Hesperus with nuptial hymns of Sappho and Catullus.

20. **Proteus:** Sea god with the power of metamorphosis and knowledge of the past and the future. In Aristophanes's *The Frogs,* Dionysus and his servant descend into Hades to search for a good poet but are greeted by the thunderous sound of frogs, which they try to drown out.

PROSE

WHAT I FEEL ABOUT WALT WHITMAN

Written in 1909 and in manuscript at the Beinecke Library, Yale University; transcribed from the manuscript and first published in *American Literature* (XXVII, 1, March 1955, 56–61). Reprinted in *Selected Prose 1909–1965*, ed. Cookson. Pound's ambivalent relationship with Whitman is expressed in this essay, in which Pound struggles between his distaste for the expansive self of Whitman and the recognition that Whitman "*is* America." Pound's 1913 poem, "A Pact," reprinted in *Lustra*, confirms his treaty with Whitman, which this early essay grudgingly acknowledges. As Pound wrote to his father in 1913, "Whitman is a hard nutt [but] *Leaves of Grass* is the book" (*SL*, 21).

1. **Carmen-Hovey period:** Bliss Carmen (1861–1929), Canadian poet who moved to New York and was an editor-writer for the *Independent* and the *Atlantic Monthly*, and edited, in ten volumes, *The World's Best Poetry*; Richard Hovey (1864–1900), American poet and philosopher best known for the long *Launcelot and Guenevere: A Poem in Dramas* (1891ff.). With Bliss Carmen, he wrote three series of books under the title *Songs from Vagaondia* (1893, 1896, 1900) that expressed male comradeship and an early American bohemianism.
2. *Patriam quam odi et amo:* Fatherland, partly hateful and loving.
3. **Marcel Schwob:** Schwob (1867–1905), French Symbolist writer best known for the *Double Heart* (1891) and *Imaginary Lives* (1896), a work admired by Borges.

THE WISDOM OF POETRY

First published in *The Forum* (New York, XLVII, 4, April 1912, 497–501); reprinted in Cookson, *SP*, 329–32. *The Forum* (1910–1916) was a monthly New York magazine devoted to literary, political, and intellectual issues published by Mitchell Kennerly, in which several poems by Pound appeared in 1910 and 1911. He referred to "The Wisdom of Poetry" as a "vitriolic essay" in a letter to Margaret Cravens. See *Ezra Pound and Margaret Cravens: A Tragic Friendship, 1910–1912*, ed. Omar Pound and Robert Spoo (Durham, NC: Duke University Press, 1988, 55). Pound in this essay challenges a scientific approach to art with an understanding of poetry as liberating the "world's consciousness," while identifying the many uses of poetry.

1. **Beardsley:** Aubrey Beardsley (1872–1898), English erotic illustrator favoring an Art Nouveau style influenced by Japanese art, who provided drawings for Oscar Wilde's *Salome*. Beardsley was known for his stylized, elongated figures of a sensuous character.
2. **jongleur:** Singers of others' songs in Provençal tradition. In Pound's "Near Perigord," Bertran de Born addresses his jongleur Papiol, his singer-deputy, to convey a song for him to another.
3. **Plarr:** Possibly the poet and librarian of King's College, London, Victor Plarr (1863–1929), who would become librarian of the Royal College of Surgeons and edit the eight-volume biographical dictionary of the fellows, which would include various mathematicians. He was a member of the Rhymers' Club and Pound often attended to hear Plarr's anecdotes of such Decadents as Lionel Johnson and Ernest Dowson.

PSYCHOLOGY AND TROUBADOURS

The essay first appeared in *Quest* (IV, October 1912, 37–53) and was reprinted as chapter V of *The Spirit of Romance* in editions published in 1932 and after. In it, Pound elaborates his ideas of the poet and the role of art in culture, divided into two schools: those who understand poetry as song and those who perceive it as ritual. In his discussion, he draws on his usual panoply of authors, including Horace, Catullus, Dante, Arnaut Daniel, and Peire Vidal. Science and religion, in competition with poetry, also figure importantly in the discussion, as do romance and sexuality. The essay was commissioned by G. R. S. Mead, one of Yeats's occult-minded friends. Pound wrote the essay in 1911 and delivered it as a lecture to the Quest Society. The major source of its ideas was the Rosicrucian book *Le Secret des Troubadours*, which Pound reviewed in September 1906 in *Book News Monthly*. Essentially, Pound argues that the *canzoni* of the troubadours were not vague love songs but allusions to a specific "love code" or "love cult" originating in the Eleusinian mysteries of ancient Greece.

1. **divagation:** A wandering or straying from the subject. To divagate is to wander.
2. **"trobar clus":** Troubadours of Provence who wrote or sang hermetic compositions, works that had hidden meanings.
3. **Arnaut:** Arnaut Daniel, thirteenth-century Provençal poet, who flourished from 1180 to 1200; favored by Pound and the subject of a lecture in *The Spirit of Romance*. He supposedly invented the

sestina, a poem of six six-line stanzas and a three-line envoi linked by an intricate pattern of repeated line endings. Praised by Dante, Arnaut appears in the *Purgatorio* section of *The Divine Comedy*. Petrarch called him the Grand Master of Love.

4. **Herrick or Decker:** Robert Herrick (1591–1674), Cavalier poet and admirer of Ben Jonson best known for his poems "Delight in Disorder" and "To the Virgins to Make Much of Time." Herrick published *Hesperides,* his collection of twelve hundred poems, in 1648. Thomas Decker (or Dekker), Elizabethan playwright (c. 1570–1632), best known for *The Spanish Moor's Tragedy* and *The Gentle Craft.*

5. **Guinicelli:** Guido Guinicelli (c. 1230–1276), Italian poet who wrote of love as inner spirituality or nobility without courtly connotations. Stylistically, he was a precursor to Cavalcanti and Dante, who called him their literary father.

6. **Trecento:** Italian term meaning the 300s, referring to the fourteenth century, the 1300s, the age of Dante, Petrarch, and Boccaccio.

7. **Remy de Gourmont:** Rémy de Gourmont, French essayist, novelist, poet, playwright, and philosopher who lived from 1858 to 1915. Involved with the Symbolist movement, he also cofounded the important French magazine the *Mercure de France.* Pound edited an issue of *The Little Review* in 1919 devoted to Gourmont and translated Gourmont's *The Natural Philosophy of Love* (1903) in 1922, in which Gourmont argued that aesthetic emotion prepares man for the reception of erotic emotion. "Art is the accomplice of love," he believed. *Le Latin Mystique* (1892) was Gourmont's first book of criticism; it focused on medieval hymnology.

8. **"prose di romanzi":** "Prose romances."

9. **"passada folor":** "Folly of the past." A contrite Arnaut admits his folly of the past to Virgil and Dante at line 143 of Canto XXVI of *Purgatorio.*

IMAGISME

This important statement about Imagism first appeared in *Poetry* (I, March 1913, 198–200). F. S. Flint is listed as author but Pound drafted the essay, which Flint partly rewrote. The essay is done as an interview with an Imagiste who sounds much like Pound. The assertive if not dogmatic speaker is also at times comic. Pound will repeat several of these maxims in "A Few Don'ts by an Imagiste" in the same issue, immediately following on pp. 200–206. For an account, see H.

Carpenter, *A Serious Character, The Life of Ezra Pound* (1988), 196–97.

HOW I BEGAN

First published in 1913 in *T. P.'s Weekly* (London: XXI, 552, June 6, 1913, 707), the article includes accounts of Elkin Mathews's acceptance of *Personae* and the composition of the "Ballad of the Goodly Fere," "Sestina: Altaforte," and "In a Station of the Metro."

1. **T. Truxton Hare:** A four-time all-American football player at the University of Pennsylvania from 1897 to 1900, T. Truxton Hare (1878–1956) could play almost any position—and did play guard, punter and dropkicker, and sometimes running back. He was team captain for his final two seasons and in his last game ran thirty-five yards for a touchdown against Harvard, dragging five opponents across the goal line. He won the silver medal in the hammer throw at the 1900 Olympics.
2. **"Goodly Fare":** This is Pound's "Ballad of the Goodly Fere," which first appeared in Ford Madox Hueffer's (later Ford) *English Review,* (III, October 1909, 382–84); that same month it appeared in the *Literary Digest* (New York): XXXIX, October 30, 1909, 730–31. The following year it appeared in the alumni issue of the *Hamilton* [College] *Literary Magazine.*

TROUBADOURS — THEIR SORTS AND CONDITIONS

This lengthy essay, which first appeared in the *Quarterly Review* (CCXIX, 437, October 1913, 426–40), reprinted in *Literary Essays of Ezra Pound,* ed. T. S. Eliot, and as "Appendix 1" in Pound, *A Walking Tour in Southern France,* ed. Richard Sieburth (1992, 87–98), is Pound's defense of the troubadours as crucial figures in the evolution of love poetry and modern verse forms. He further states that their lives were not so different from our own. Money was missed and boredom was everywhere. After beginning with a tapestry of Provençal writers, he complains of their contemporary neglect, many readers unaware that "the poetic art of Provence paved the way for the poetic art of Tuscany," notably Dante. Rather than use established collections as his sources, Pound preferred to study manuscripts at the Bibliothèque Nationale in Paris, where he worked in May 1912. Indeed, much of the essay grows out of Pound's walking tour of southern France in the summer of 1912, guided by *The Troubadours at Home,* by Justin H.

Smith, a two-volume travel book published in 1899, and the 1907 edition of Baedeker's *Southern France*. The trip included a climb through the Pyrenees to Arles and Nîmes.

1. **a man may walk:** Pound began his important walking trip on May 27, 1912, taking the train to Poitiers, traveling on that night to Angoulême. The final leg of the trip took him through the Auvergne, ending at Clermont on July 19, 1912. See Pound, *A Walking Tour of Southern France*, ed. R. Sieburth (1992).

2. **Miquel de la Tour:** Also known as Miquel de la Tor, late-thirteenth-century biographer of the troubadour Peire Cardinal. There is some dispute over Pound's reference because Pound read a manuscript in the Bibliothèque Nationale that said la Tour wrote it, not realizing it was a partial copy made a few years later than the original.

3. **Sordello:** Browning's *Sordello*, which Pound first read in 1904, became an influential work that he reread in 1915 as he began to think of *The Cantos*. To his father, he wrote "it is probably the greatest poem in English," and it provided a model for his new long poem, which was "all about everything" (in Carpenter, 287). Sordello is a medieval Provençal poet mentioned in the *Purgatorio;* Browning's long and complex poem is a narrative experiment where the narrator accompanies the subject. Pound considers imitating this device in the first of his "Three Cantos" (1917), opening with "Hang it all, there can be but one *Sordello!*" suggesting that he may want to imitate Browning's style. The revised opening to *The Cantos* drops the Sordello reference and style (see Carpenter, 288–90).

4. **Andreas Divus Justinopolitanus:** Pound purchased Divus's medieval Latin translation of *The Odyssey* at a Parisian bookstall; the volume became one of the key works for Pound's *Cantos*. He translated the opening lines in Canto III (1917) and then restructured the work to make them the new opening of the entire work.

THE SERIOUS ARTIST

The essay appeared in *New Freewoman* (I, October–November 1913) in three parts: parts I and II were published in October 1913 (161–63); part III was published in November 1913 (194–95; reprinted in *Literary Essays*, ed. Eliot, 41–57). This is Pound's early defense of writing poetry as an art, not an indulgence, and outlines his essential poetics: good writing reflects control, and poetry should possess the clarity that we see in prose. Clarity and intensity are its best features: "no interjections. No words flying off to nothing . . . objectivity and again objectivity," as he wrote Harriet Monroe in 1915 (*SL*, 48–50). Furthermore, the serious artist "is scientific in that he presents the image of his desire," as Pound writes in the essay where he also argues that "the touchstone of an art is its precision" in its search for "passionate simplicity."

1. **Sydney Webbs:** Sydney Webb (1859–1947) was an early Socialist and, with his wife Beatrice Webb and George Bernard Shaw, a member of the Fabian Society. He favored fact over imagination and criticized the role of the arts in society. He cofounded the London School of Economics.
2. **Aucassin:** Hero of the thirteenth-century French *fabliau, Aucassin and Nicolette,* a mixture of prose and poetry telling of thwarted love, war, loss, and recovery.
3. **the Victory of Samothrace and the Taj of Agra:** The Winged Victory, a winged female statue over eight feet in height, was found in 1863 in pieces on the island of Samothrace. It was reassembled at the Louvre in Paris, where it now stands. The Taj of Agra is the Taj Mahal in Agra, India, completed in 1648 and built over twenty-two years with approximately twenty thousand workers. Taj Mahal means "Crown Palace."
4. **ægrum vulgus:** "Diseased public."
5. **Parnassiads:** Pound refers to the Parnassians, a group of French nineteenth-century poets so-called because of their journal *Parnasse contemporain* (1866–1876). Théophile Gautier was an important influence on these writers, who included Leconte de Lisle, Sully Prudhomme, and Verlaine.

A RETROSPECT

This work combines a series of early essays and notes under this title gathered in *Pavannes and Divisions* (1918). "A Few Don'ts by an Imagiste," *Poetry* I.6, March 1913, 200–206. Reprinted as "A Retrospect" in *Pavannes and Divisions* (New York: Alfred A. Knopf, 1918) and in *Literary Essays,* ed. T. S. Eliot (London: Faber and Faber, 1954, 3–14). These essays didactically articulate Pound's ideas on Imagism and precise poetry, including his maxim: "Go in fear of abstractions."

1. **Mr. Flint:** Pound refers to F. S. Flint (1885–1960), a poet and critic who met Pound in 1909 and was a member of T. E. Hulme's Thursday-night poetry group, the Poets' Club, which met at the Tour Eiffel restaurant in Soho. Flint would review Pound's *canzoni* in the first issue of the *Poetry Review* (I [January 1912]: 28–29), complaining that much of his inspiration seemed "bookish."

2. **Harold Monro's magazine:** Harold Monro (1879–1932) owned the Poetry Bookshop in London and edited the *Poetry Review*, which published Flint's article "Contemporary French Poetry" in number VII (August 1912, 355–414). Pound, who gives the wrong year, refers to Flint's lengthy survey that opens with "The Generation of 1900" and ends with "F. T. Marinetti and *Le Futurisme*." In the first several pages, Flint describes Symbolism as a reaction against the flamboyance of the Romantics, the impassive descriptiveness of the Parnassians, and disgust with the "slice of life" of the naturalists. The essence of Symbolism is its intuitiveness, he argues.

3. **Duhamel's notes:** Georges Duhamel (1884–1966) and Charles Vildrac (1882–1971) published their seventy-one-page book, *Notes sur la technique poétique*, in 1910.

4. *Man and Superman:* George Bernard Shaw's play was published in 1903 and first performed in 1905, but without scene 2 of act 3. Subtitled *A Comedy and a Philosophy*, the work incorporates Nietzsche's idea of the superman in the conflict between man as a spiritual creator and woman as a guardian of the biological continuity of the human race. The third act is a dream episode entitled "Don Juan in Hell," based on the Don Juan legend, especially as it appears in Mozart's *Don Giovanni*.

5. **Metastasio:** Pietro Metastasio (1698–1782), eighteenth-century Italian poet, librettist, and composer who began his education as a goldsmith, then turned to law before becoming known as a composer of musical melodramas, ballets, cantatas, and *canzonette*. His musical drama *Attilio Regolo* is generally considered to be his masterpiece.

6. **S. S. McClure:** Samuel Sidney McClure (1857–1949) was an Irish-born American editor and publisher and the founder of America's first successful literary syndicate that would buy an author's article and then resell the rights to papers and magazines across America. In 1894, he and a partner began *McClure's Magazine*, which in four years had a circulation of 400,000 and soon began to publish muckraking articles by Lincoln Steffens and Ida

Tarbell. By 1912, McClure lost control of his company. Willa Cather ghostwrote his autobiography.

7. **Amyclas:** Mythical figure and king of Sparta, son of Lacedaemon; Amyclas marries Diomede and becomes the father of Argalus, Cynortas, and Hyacinthus.

8. **Catullus' parlour floor:** Catullus's villa was at Sirmione at Lago di Garda, the largest of northern Italian lakes and one of Pound's favorite spots in Italy, where he preferred to stay at the Hotel Eden. He went there first in 1910 to complete *The Spirit of Romance.* He would meet Joyce for the first time there in 1920 and would refer to the locale several times in *The Cantos.*

9. **The Provost of Oriel:** C. L. Shadwell—the provost of Oriel College in Oxford, at the time Pound's essay appeared. Charles Lancelot Shadwell (1849–1919) published a literal verse translation of *Purgatory* in two volumes between 1892 and 1899 containing, in volume 1, an introduction by Walter Pater. His second translation of *The Paradise of Dante Alighieri* appeared in 1915.

10. **John Yeats:** The painter John B. Yeats (1839–1922), father of W. B. Yeats, trained as a lawyer but chose to become a portrait painter. After his wife died, in 1900, he decided to move to New York in 1907 with his daughter Lily; he died there in 1922. Pound first met him in 1910 during a visit to New York. Later, at Yeats's boardinghouse, he met the lawyer John Quinn, who would eventually become Pound's patron, for the first time.

11. **battistrada:** Italian for trailblazer.

THE TRADITION

The essay appeared first in *Poetry III. 4* (January 1914) 137-41; it was reprinted in *Literary Essays,* ed. Eliot 91-3.

1. **Penitus enim tibi O Phoebe attributa est cantus:** Corrected to *"attribut*us *est cantus"* because *"attributa,"* feminine singular or neuter plural, has no corresponding noun, the phrase means "Because, O Phoebus, song has been entirely attributed to you."

2. **Melic:** Greek, *melos*—"song"; of or pertaining to verse intended to be sung, especially Greek lyric verse of the seventh to fifth centuries B.C.E.

3. **Cÿthera and the Barbitos:** The *cythera* (or *cithara*) is an ancient stringed instrument resembling a harp; the *barbitos* is a stringed instrument of the lyre family, also of the classical period.

4. **Baif and the Pléïade:** Jean Antoine de Baïf (1532–1589) was a French poet of the Pléïade group who wrote sonnets, didactic and satiric poetry, and plays. The Pléïade was a group of seven French poets circa 1533 who modeled themselves after the original Pléïade group of seven poets from Alexandria around 280 B.C.E. The French group, who encouraged the writing of literature in French rather than Latin to enrich their language and literature, included de Ronsard, Joachim du Bellay, Belleau, and Baïf.

5. **Dr Ker:** W. P. Ker (1855–1923), Scottish-born professor of literature at University College in London, author of *Epic and Romance* (1891), *Dante, Guido Guinicelli and Arnaut Daniel* (1909), and other works dealing with the French *chansons de geste,* the epic, and Scandinavian literature.

6. **Jannaris:** A. N. Jannaris (1852–1909), from Crete, was a distinguished scholar who held what was likely the first appointment at a British university in modern Greek when he became lecturer in Greek at Saint Andrew's University in Scotland in 1896. In 1895, he published a *Concise Dictionary of English and Modern Greek Language* and, in 1897, *An Historical Greek Grammar.*

MR. HUEFFER AND THE PROSE TRADITION IN VERSE

Appearing in *Poetry* IV.3 (June 1914, 111–20), under this title, the essay was reprinted as "The Prose Tradition in Verse" in *Literary Essays,* ed. T. S. Eliot, 371–77. This review of Hueffer's *Collected Poems* outlines Pound's admiration for Hueffer's (later Ford's) critical foresight and precise poetry, which he hopes achieves the clarity of prose. "Poetry" Hueffer asserts and Pound praises, "should be written at least as well as prose."

1. **Allen Upward:** Upward (1863–1926) was an English lawyer and traveler interested in folklore and anthropology, especially that of Nigeria. Pound reviewed his book *The Divine Mystery* (1907) in the *New Freewoman* of November 15, 1913. Upward's sequence of poems, "Scented Leaves—from a Chinese Jar," appeared in *Poetry* (1913), secured by Pound, who visited Upward that year. In turn, Upward introduced Pound to Chinese literature and culture, ostensibly through H. A. Giles's *History of Chinese Literature* (1901). At about the same time, Pound met Mrs. Ernest Fenollosa, who would soon present him with her husband's papers, encouraging Pound's work on *Cathay* (1915) and then on "The Chinese Written Character" (1919).

2. *ore rotundo:* Round or full sound.
3. **Casella:** Alfredo Casella (1883–1947), Italian composer, pianist, and conductor who became professor of piano at the Liceo of Santa Cecilia, Rome, in 1915 and introduced the music of Ravel and Stravinsky to Italy.

VORTICISM

This essay by Pound, first published in the *Fortnightly Review* (XCVI [N.S.], 573, September 1, 1914, [461]–471), was reprinted as chapter XI of *Gaudier-Brzeska* (1916). In it he identifies the characteristics of Vorticism as he traces the origin of the movement via a history of Vorticist art and poetry. For other statements on Vorticism, see *Ezra Pound and the Visual Arts,* ed. Harriet Zinnes (New York: New Directions, 1980), 150–57.

1. **Ibycus and Liu Ch'e:** Ibycus was a Greek lyric poet and contemporary of Anacreon, who flourished in the sixth century B.C.E. He wrote seven books of lyrics, many of them erotic, and in the Aeolian melic style. Liu Ch'e, also known as the emperor Wu-Ti of the Han Dynasty, was born in 156 B.C.E. and died c. 87 B.C.E. A patron of the arts, he also instituted the study of Confucius as a state religion; the *I Ching* or *Book of Changes* was completed during his reign. Pound's poem entitled "Liu Ch'e," in the Chinese style, appeared in *Des Imagistes* (1914) and was reprinted in *Lustra* (1916–17).
2. **Mr. Epstein's flenites:** Jacob Epstein (1880–1959), American-born British sculptor admired by Pound. After studies with Rodin in Paris in 1902, Epstein moved to London in 1905, where he worked in a bold, harsh style, a bronze portrait sculptor and creator of large figures. His expressionistic figure titled *Rock-Drill,* composed of harsh planes, would become the title and image of Pound's late volume of *The Cantos* entitled *Section: Rock-Drill* (1955). "Flenites" appears to be Pound's term for the sculpture of intersecting planes and edges Epstein favored. Pound wrote on Epstein in "Affirmations," published in *The New Age* (January 21, 1915, 311–12); enlarged and reprinted in *GB,* 95–102. In "Art Notes," from 1919, Pound referred to Epstein as "the devastator" (*EP and the Visual Arts,* 104).
3. *Guido Cavalcanti:* In Pound's introduction to *The Sonnets and Ballate of Guido Cavalcanti* (1912), he writes, "I believe in an ultimate and absolute rhythm as I believe in an absolute symbol or metaphor" (xxi).

4. **Kandinsky:** Wassily Kandinsky (1866–1944) was an early abstract painter born in Moscow. His *Concerning the Spiritual in Art* appeared in English in 1914; Pound refers to it in this essay. He also considered Kandinsky a forerunner of Vorticism.

5. **Mr. Wadsworth and Mr. Lewis:** Edward Wadsworth (1889–1949) was an English artist whose illustrations and translations from Kandinsky's *Uber das Geistige in der Kunst (Concernng the Spiritual in Art)* appeared in *BLAST*, no. 1. Wadsworth also participated in the June 1915 Vorticist Exhibition. Wyndham Lewis (1882–1957) was an English painter, novelist, and satirist who met Pound in 1909. He edited *BLAST* and wrote *Tarr* (1918), a novel about expatriate Paris before World War I that Pound favored. His series of illustrations, *Timon,* were challenging, warlike Cubist forms that appeared in *BLAST* and were admired by Pound.

6. **Mr. Etchells:** Frederick Etchells (1886–1973), English artist who contributed illustrations to *BLAST,* nos. 1 and 2, and participated in the June 1915 Vorticist Exhibition.

AFFIRMATIONS . . . AS FOR IMAGISME

Number four in a series of eight weekly articles under the heading "Affirmations" appearing in the *New Age* in 1915. Pound, in this segment, published in *New Age* (XVI, January 28, 1915, 349–50, reprinted in *Selected Prose 1909–1965,* ed. William Cookson [London: Faber and Faber, 1978], 344–47), defines Imagism and its link to Vorticism. He reiterates his claim that for poetry to be "good poetry [it] should be at least as well written as good prose," while developing a theory of image creation and expression.

1. The second article in the series dealt with Vorticism alone.

CHINESE POETRY

This two-part essay published in 1918 in *To-day* ("Chinese Poetry. I," *To-day,* III.14, April 1918, 54–57; "Chinese Poetry. II," *To-day,* III.15, May 1918, 93–95) reflects Pound's new grasp of Chinese poetry and its importance for writers. Following the publication of *Cathay* in 1915, Pound thought himself something of an expert in Chinese and in this essay he makes the case for the excellence of Chinese writing by concentrating on the work of Li Po, a poet of the eighth century. Pound structures his response on the qualities of Chinese poetry he favors: the Chinese appreciation of complexity, the clarity of their verse (poetry without sentimentality), the presence of mythology, the "gracious simplicity" of the best writing and finally the completeness of Chinese writing in their nature poetry. He also acknowledges the importance of the work of Ernest Fenollosa, which introduced him to this literature.

1. **Selwyn Image:** Pound met Image (1849–1930) through Elkin Mathews, his London publisher. Appropriately, Image was a painter (mostly of stained glass), an illustrator, and a poet from the 1890s set. He was also a member of the Rhymers' Club. He published and collected various Christmas carols, many of them contributed to the first edition of the *English Carol Book* (1913). Hugh Selwyn Mauberley's middle name, from Pound's 1920 poem of the same name, might possibly derive from Selwyn Image.

2. **"The Jewel-Stairs Grievance":** This is Pound's version taken from *Cathay* (1915), where it appears on page 13, the title alternately printed as "The Jewel Stairs' Grievance."

3. *The Dai horse:* Pound's version of this poem, entitled "South-Folk in Cold Country," appears on page 31 as the final poem of *Cathay* (1915).

4. **"The River-Merchant's Wife":** Although there are variations in the stanza breaks and punctuation, this is Pound's version from *Cathay* (1915), where it appears on pages 11–12.

THE CHINESE WRITTEN CHARACTER AS A MEDIUM FOR POETRY

Published first in four installments in *The Little Review* (VI, September–December 1919, reprinted in *Instigations,* 1920), the poem's first separate publication was in 1936, with the subtitle "An Ars Poetica," published by Stanley Nott in London as part of the "Ideogramic Series Edited by Ezra Pound." This edition included a foreword by Pound, a brief "Terminal Note," and an appendix titled "With Some Notes [on Chinese Written Characters] by a Very Ignorant Man."

This lengthy work, written by the American Orientalist Ernest Fenollosa (1853–1908) and "amended" by Pound, although the words "Edited with notes by" appear just before Pound's name, is an influential statement of Poundian aesthetics. At the opening of *'Noh' or Accomplishment* (1917), Pound writes that the "life of Ernest Fenollosa was the romance par excellence of modern scholarship. He went to Japan as a professor of economics. He ended as Imperial Commissioner of Arts." In an introductory note to "The Chinese

Written Character," Pound explains that he has done "little more than remove a few repetitions and shape a few sentences," but his editorial hand, marked by precise statements and clear sentences, seems everywhere.

In a letter to John Quinn of January 10, 1917, Pound wrote that Fenollosa "anticipated a good deal of what has happened in art (painting and poetry) during the last ten years and his essay is basic for all aesthetics, but I doubt it that will cut much ice" (*Selected Letters of EP to Quinn,* ed. Materer, 93). Yet, Pound found in Fenollosa an articulation of his own poetics, especially the idea that "poetic thought" crowds "maximum meaning into the single phrase." The attitude of Fenollosa toward the art of the ideogram and Chinese poetry confirmed and extended many of Pound's ideas concerning Imagism and the value of the ideogram, which *Cathay* (1915) demonstrated and which *The Cantos* would incorporate.

1. **Davis, Legge, St. Denys and Giles:** Fenollosa/Pound refers here to four early historian-scholars of Chinese literature: Sir John Francis Davis, governor of Hong Kong in the 1840s and author of such titles as *The Chinese, A General Description of the Empire* (1836), and *The Poetry of the Chinese* (1870); James Legge, who in the 1850s translated into English Confucian and Taoist texts and became the first professor of Chinese at Oxford, as well as publishing the seven-volume *Chinese Classics* (2nd ed. rev., 1893–95); Marquis d'Hervey-Saint Denys, who published a valuable anthology of T'ang poetry in 1852 as well as other volumes; and Herbert Giles, a British consular official in China from 1867 to 1892 and later professor of Chinese at Cambridge. In 1892, he completed the first exhaustive Chinese-English dictionary but is perhaps best known for the Wade-Giles system of Romanizing Mandarin. Among his many books is the *History of Chinese Literature* (1901).

2. **serious literary performance:** Pound responded strongly to a similar view concerning the inadequate reception and understanding of poetry in England and America in "The Serious Artist." See the essay reprinted above.

3. **Gray's line:** Fenollosa/Pound refers to the first line of Thomas Gray's (1716–1771) "Elegy Written in a Country Churchyard" (1751).

4. **Laocoön statue . . . Browning's lines:** Pound refers to *Laocoön and His Sons,* the statue in the Vatican from the first century, discovered in 1506 in Rome. It depicts the Trojan priest Laocoön struggling with sea monsters sent by the gods who favored the Greeks.

Laocoön tried to warn the Trojans not to bring in the wooden horse, but to little avail. The two lines of poetry are from the opening stanza of Robert Browning's (1812–1889) "How They Brought the Good News from Ghent to Aix," *Dramatic Romances and Lyrics* (1845).

5. **Skeat:** W. W. Skeat (1835–1912), philologist and professor of Anglo-Saxon at Cambridge from 1878 to 1912. Pound likely refers to Skeat's *A Primer of English Etymology* (1892). Ten years earlier, Skeat published *A Concise Etymological Dictionary of English* (1882).

JAMES JOYCE, AT LAST THE NOVEL APPEARS

Pound's praiseworthy review of *A Portrait of the Artist as A Young Man*, to celebrate publication of the first English edition (London: Egoist Press, 1917), appeared in the *Egoist* IV (February 1917) 21–22, the very month the volume became available. The edition used American sheets because English printers (seven in all) would not accept responsibility for printing it; under British law, printers, as well as publishers, could be prosecuted for printing immoral work. In his remarks, Pound states that clear thinking depends on clear prose and declares a link between good writing and good government: "a nation that cannot write clearly cannot be trusted to govern, nor yet to think."

1. *Quarterly Review:* Edited by the conservative G. W. Prothero, the *Quarterly Review* resisted new movements and authors. When *BLAST* first appeared, Prothero wrote to Pound saying that he would never publish anything by a contributor to that magazine, although he had previously published Pound's "Troubadours—Their Sorts and Conditions" (*QR*, CCXIX, October 1913, 426–40) and in 1914 would publish "The Classical Drama of Japan" (*QR*, CCI, October 1914, 450–77), which Pound edited from Fenollosa's manuscript.

2. **Landor's** *Imaginary Conversations*: Walter Savage Landor (1775–1864) was a poet, classicist, and essayist best known for the informal style of his popular *Imaginary Conversations*, which began to appear in 1824–1829, with a later set in 1853. The conversations—more gentle debates—took place between various historical and literary figures and were known for their successful evocation of personality and often pithy statements, such as "we talk on principle but we act on interest." They also contained sentiments Pound would recognize, such as "North America may one day be very rich

and powerful; she cannot be otherwise: but she will never gratify the imagination as Europe does" ("William Penn and Lord Peterborough"). Additionally, Pound admired Landor's critical attitude and his often argumentative nature, which, because of various legal issues, caused him to live in Europe at two different periods of his life (1814–1835; 1858–1864). Landor died in Florence and is buried there.

At Stone Cottage, in the winter of 1915–1916, Pound and Yeats, taking turns, read Landor's nine-volume *Imaginary Conversations* out loud. Landor, however, had great difficulty at first finding a publisher for his work. Pound published a note on Landor in the *Future* (II, November 1917, 10–12) and began to imitate his style in a set of "Imaginary Letters" (some of them written by Wyndham Lewis), which began to appear in the *Little Review* (IV, September 1917, 20–22). These would continue to November 1918. Dickens caricatured Landor as Boythorn in *Bleak House* (1853); the novelist Ian Sinclair more recently titled his 2001 mystery *Landor's Tower; Or, the Imaginary Conversations* and drew on Landor's character.

3. *E pur si muove:* Italian, "but one also moves" or changes.

4. **New York City:** B. W. Huebsch of New York published the first edition of *A Portrait of the Artist as a Young Man* on December 29, 1916. Harriet Shaw Weaver's Egoist Press purchased 750 sets of sheets for the English publication of the novel, which appeared on February 12, 1917.

PARIS LETTER, MAY 1922, *ULYSSES*

Pound's celebration of *Ulysses,* part of his "Paris Letter" series, appeared in the American journal the *Dial* (LXXII, June 1922, [623]–639), edited by Scofield Thayer. The purpose of the review was to introduce American readers to a banned but revolutionary book, which Pound calls a "super-novel." Representative quotes illustrate the power of the prose. Other contributors to the June 1922 issue include Picasso, D. H. Lawrence, Hart Crane, George Santayana, and Yeats.

1. **Bouvard et Pécuchet:** Flaubert's unfinished comic novel of 1881, favored by Pound, who expanded the ideas on Flaubert and Joyce he expressed in "Paris Letter, *Ulysses*" in "Joyce et Pécuchet" in *Mercure de France* (CLVI, June 1, 1922, 307–20), written in French. On November 22, 1918, Pound wrote Joyce that he had just reread

Bouvard et Pécuchet and that "Bloom certainly does all Flaubert set out to do and does it in one tenth the space" (*EP to JJ*, ed. Read [New York: New Directions, 1967], 145.)

2. **James (H.):** Henry James (1843–1916), American novelist; Pound met him in London in February 1912, introduced to him by Ford Madox Hueffer (later Ford).

3. **Poynton . . . In Old Madrid . . . "low back car":** Reference is to Henry James's novel *The Spoils of Poynton* (1897), which deals with the possession and loss of antiques and treasures of the great Poynton home. "In Old Madrid" refers to a song in the "Sirens" episode of *Ulysses* by Henry Trotere; it is also a 1911 film of the same name, directed by Thomas H. Ince. Joyce uses the phrase "Low back car" in the "Eumaeus" section of *Ulysses*; it refers to a poem of the same name, one version by Samuel Love, another by John McCormick. See *Ulysses*, ed. H. W. Gabler (New York: Vintage Books, 1986), 11.733 and 16.1886, for the two citations. Numbers refer to the episodes and lines.

4. **Mr. Young's once ubiquitous poem:** Edward Young (1683–1765), English poet and author of *The Complaint, or Night Thoughts on Life, Death and Immortality* (1742–1745). This ten-thousand-line blank verse poem remained popular throughout the eighteenth century. William Blake illustrated a deluxe edition of the work in 1797. Joyce quotes a line from the poem in the "Ithaca" section of *Ulysses* at 17.644.

5. **the Arbuckle case:** Roscoe Conkling Arbuckle (1887–1933), known as "Fatty" Arbuckle, was an American silent-film comedian. In September 1921, Arbuckle and two friends drove to San Francisco and held a party in the Saint Francis Hotel. One of the invited women, Virginia Rappe, became seriously ill and died three days later of peritonitis. The district attorney, however, pursued charges against Arbuckle for raping or attempting to rape the woman. A doctor who conducted the autopsy on Rappe found no evidence that violence played any part in her death. A trial nevertheless proceeded, but although Arbuckle was acquitted (the jury took three minutes to decide "Not guilty"), his career in the movies ended. The sensational event made national and international headlines.

6. **Griffith . . . "the sincerity of his trousers":** Arthur Griffith (1872–1922), Irish patriot instrumental in the final achievement of Ireland's independence in 1921–1922. He was briefly the first president of the Irish Free State. In 1899, he founded the Celtic Literary Society and the *United Irishman* newspaper. He also organized the Sinn Fein ("We Ourselves") movement, which agitated for Irish

independence and promoted separatist policies c. 1905–1906, and founded a newspaper of that name in 1906. The phrase was also understood to mean "Stand Together."

Molly Bloom uses the phrase "sincerity of his trousers" at 18.1231 of the "Penelope" section of *Ulysses* in reference to Arthur Griffith.

7. **our present ruler:** The Republican Warren G. Harding (1865–1923), twenty-ninth president of the United States, from 1921 to 1923, referred to in the previous paragraph of the essay as "our best dressed Chief Magistrate." A Democrat, William G. McAdoo, once referred to Harding's speeches as "an army of pompous phrases moving across the landscape in search of an idea."

Index of Titles and First Lines

FOR THE BEST IN PAPERBACKS, LOOK FOR THE

In every corner of the world, on every subject under the sun, Penguin represents quality and variety—the very best in publishing today.

For complete information about books available from Penguin—including Penguin Classics, Penguin Compass, and Puffins—and how to order them, write to us at the appropriate address below. Please note that for copyright reasons the selection of books varies from country to country.

In the United States: Please write to *Penguin Group (USA), P.O. Box 12289 Dept. B, Newark, New Jersey 07101-5289* or call 1-800-788-6262.

In the United Kingdom: Please write to *Dept. EP, Penguin Books Ltd, Bath Road, Harmondsworth, West Drayton, Middlesex UB7 0DA.*

In Canada: Please write to *Penguin Books Canada Ltd, 10 Alcorn Avenue, Suite 300, Toronto, Ontario M4V 3B2.*

In Australia: Please write to *Penguin Books Australia Ltd, P.O. Box 257, Ringwood, Victoria 3134.*

In New Zealand: Please write to *Penguin Books (NZ) Ltd, Private Bag 102902, North Shore Mail Centre, Auckland 10.*

In India: Please write to *Penguin Books India Pvt Ltd, 11 Panchsheel Shopping Centre, Panchsheel Park, New Delhi 110 017.*

In the Netherlands: Please write to *Penguin Books Netherlands bv, Postbus 3507, NL-1001 AH Amsterdam.*

In Germany: Please write to *Penguin Books Deutschland GmbH, Metzlerstrasse 26, 60594 Frankfurt am Main.*

In Spain: Please write to *Penguin Books S. A., Bravo Murillo 19, 1° B, 28015 Madrid.*

In Italy: Please write to *Penguin Italia s.r.l., Via Benedetto Croce 2, 20094 Corsico, Milano.*

In France: Please write to *Penguin France, Le Carré Wilson, 62 rue Benjamin Baillaud, 31500 Toulouse.*

In Japan: Please write to *Penguin Books Japan Ltd, Kaneko Building, 2-3-25 Koraku, Bunkyo-Ku, Tokyo 112.*

In South Africa: Please write to *Penguin Books South Africa (Pty) Ltd, Private Bag X14, Parkview, 2122 Johannesburg.*